Perilous Star

PERILOUS STAR

Kingdom Books LLC books may be purchased for educational, business, or sale promotional use. For information, please e-mail info@kingdombookspublishing.com with the subject Special Markets.

ISBN: **978-1-7357104-5-7** (Paperback)

ISBN: **978-1-7357104-4-0** (Ebook)

Cover Designed by Maja Kapunovic

For the creatives—
Never give up on your passion
Never devalue your worth
Your ideas are worth sharing
Your ideas are worth fighting for

BOOK ONE OF THE WESTERN ZODIAC

TRILOGY

Perilous Star

Alyssa Markins

KINGDOM BOOKS
PUBLISHING

Kingdom Books LLC
www.kingdombookspublishing.com

CHAPTER 1

Nearly 10,000 people evacuated from their homes this morning as more than a dozen wildfires continue to burn across the coast of Southern California. While weather experts say the fires are primarily being fueled by dry conditions and rising temperatures, others report that they've seen people, who are quickly becoming known as 'elementals,' stoking the infernos with their unnatural abilities and, in some cases, starting them. We have reporter Eliza Keller live at one of the evacuation points. Eliza, good morning."

The television's depressing drone drifted into the kitchen. Kaeli's gaze hardened as she focused on chopping vegetables, hoping the thud of the knife could shut out the sound.

"Turn that damn thing off," Trent grumbled from the other room. Kaeli sighed and rolled her eyes as her grip tightened around the knife. She closed her eyes and inhaled deeply before slamming the sharp utensil down on the counter.

"Lazy ass," she muttered under her breath so that her brother wouldn't hear. Of course it would be too inconvenient for him to get out of the chair and turn the TV off himself. She took a couple seconds to steady her breathing. For her mother's sake, she was trying her best to be hospitable during Trent's visit, but her brother never made it easy.

"I said turn that damn thing off!" Trent hollered. Kaeli ground her teeth as a warmth flushed through her body. She'd been relieved when Trent moved out as soon as he'd turned eighteen. It had been eight years since Trent had lived with her and her mother, three since she'd graduated highschool. Those eight years would have been nearly perfect if Kaeli hadn't needed to forgo higher education to help pay the bills, and if her mother didn't have it in her head that somehow they could be a normal family. She insisted that Trent visit at least every couple of months. The visits never ended well. Kaeli let out a strained breath and turned the heat on the stove. She would try to keep this visit as civil as possible. For her mom.

Kaeli frowned as she entered the living room and shot a pointed glance toward her brother sprawled out on the recliner chair. His eyes were closed. His arms laid crossed against his chest. That chair had been her dad's favorite before he'd died. Kaeli and her mother rarely ever sat in it, but her mother refused to get rid of it. Trent sat in it every time he came to visit.

Kaeli's jaw clenched as she spotted the remote on the coffee table situated about a foot away from the chair. She glared at the TV as she picked it up and viciously pressed the power button, silencing the newscaster. If she could just keep it together until the weekend was over, she wouldn't have to deal with this asshole for at least another month. She tossed the remote back onto the coffee table, making sure it landed with sufficient clatter.

"Anything else, your highness?" she growled. Trent cracked an eye open in a feeble attempt at eye contact.

"Food almost ready?" he grunted. His eye closed again. Kaeli opened her mouth to retort, but she spotted her mother walking down the short hallway to enter the living room. Her mouth instantly shut and a painful sorrow twisted in her gut. Her mom had never been the same since her dad's death. This woman was a shell of the vivacious mother Kaeli remembered from her early childhood. Her mom's golden blonde hair was up in a ragged bun and looked like it hadn't been washed in a couple of days. Her green eyes darted between Trent and Kaeli as she made her way toward the couch. Kaeli had been told by family friends that she looked just like her mother at her age, but watching the anxious, timid woman walk through the room, Kaeli didn't want to bear any resemblance to her.

"Is everything okay?" her mother asked in a breathy voice. Trent rolled his head to the side to look at her. Surprisingly, he had mustered up the energy to open both eyes.

"Yeah, Kaeli was just getting food." He tilted his head to look at Kaeli. His eyes narrowed and a cruel smile touched the corners of his mouth. "Chop, chop."

Kaeli bit her lip but didn't respond. Instead, she turned on her heel and stormed back to the kitchen. With a silent fury, she ramped up the stove heat to the highest setting and dumped the vegetables into it. Droplets of hot oil popped and crackled around her hands, but she didn't care. The heat coursed through her body again. She wanted to punch Trent in his stupid face but knew she couldn't. The last time a fight between her and Trent had escalated beyond words, it didn't end well. For either of them.

Kaeli shook her head as she focused her attention back on the food. She couldn't let a fight like that happen again. Not with her mom around.

She turned off the stove and began portioning the food on three separate plates.

"Kaeli! Seriously, what's taking you so long?" Trent yelled from the other room. Kaeli inhaled slowly as she picked one of the plates up off the counter. Her blood boiled as she entered the room. Her knuckles went white from gripping the edges of the plate. She approached her brother from behind the recliner. Ignoring all sense of reason, she raised the plate over him, released her grip, and let the plate fall into his lap. The meal completely disassembled, splattering rice and hot vegetables slathered in teriyaki sauce all over him.

Her mother jumped. Trent yelped. A stream of profanities escaped his mouth as he bolted up out of the recliner and turned to face Kaeli. Her heart hammered in her chest as she glared at him, wanting nothing more than to punch him square in the jaw. Murder danced in his eyes. She knew she should be scared, but right now, she felt as angry as he looked. Trying to keep her face impassive, she backed away from the recliner, putting as much distance between herself and her brother as she could in anticipation for the fight that would come next.

"You shouldn't have done that," he growled. Hate simmered in his eyes. They may have been related by blood, but the man standing in front of her was not her brother. He was a monster. She knew he could hurt her and *would* if she didn't play her cards right. Unfortunately, she wasn't in the mood for making rational decisions.

"I would do it again in a heartbeat," she hissed.

"Trent, Kaeli, please!" Her mom ran to Kaeli's side and latched onto her arm. "Just apologize." She glanced at Trent. "If she apologizes will that be enough?"

Trent cocked his head to the side, keeping his gaze trained on Kaeli. He smirked. Knowing she would never do that, he said, "*If* she apologizes."

Kaeli shook her mom off her arms and stepped to the side. She needed her mother to get out of the way so she wouldn't get hurt.

"I'm sick of you and your attitude. You can't bully me into doing everything for you!"

Her brother didn't spare any more words. With an agility that contradicted his size, he launched himself over the recliner. Before Kaeli could run to the next room, he had her pinned against the wall. A big hand wrapped around her throat, not enough to choke her, but just enough to cut off her blood supply. Their mother screamed and started sobbing uncontrollably. Kaeli clawed at Trent's hand, trying to pry away his fingers.

"Just because you're an adult doesn't mean you can mouth off to me like that." He raised his free hand, and Kaeli knew she was going to get hit if she didn't do something quick. Adrenaline rushed through her veins. Her pulse pounded in her ears. Her entire body felt like it was on fire. A bright light blinded her vision, and Trent howled. The pressure from her throat immediately disappeared. Kaeli blinked rapidly, regaining her sight just in time to see Trent fall to the floor, clutching his arm. He stared at her hands, a mix of anger and fear flickering in his eyes.

"What the hell are you?"

Kaeli looked at her hands. Her breath hitched. Tiny flames danced around her fingertips. She balled them up into fists and when she uncurled her grip, the flames were gone. Without a second glance at Trent or her mother, Kaeli ran back to the kitchen, swiped her wallet off the table, and darted out the door.

* * *

She kept running until her lungs burned. Letting out a heavy breath, she slowed her pace to a walk. She should have gone far enough to deter Trent from following her. Her brother talked big in person, but if he had to put in the extra effort, he rarely ever did. Plus, their mother would be screaming bloody murder, so he would most likely stay to calm things down and keep her from calling the police.

She let out a sigh. Trent and Kaeli had never been the best of friends as siblings growing up, but ever since her father had died in a car accident when she was eight, tension between them had only increased. That car crash still impacted her and her family in ways she didn't think she'd ever understand. Her mother had become increasingly emotionally unstable but refused to see a therapist. And Trent... Trent expressed his grief in other— mostly violent—ways toward Kaeli. Kaeli had lost count of the number of times their fights ended with him yelling: *If you weren't alive, none of this would have happened!*

Kaeli's lips pressed together as the words echoed through her mind. She kicked a stray piece of gravel on the pavement. There were times when she believed those words, even though she knew they weren't true. She let out a shaky breath as she mentally reviewed the newspaper article she had memorized since her father's death. Head-on collision. Fuel leakage. Engine combustion. Everything went up in flames. It couldn't have been her fault. The news would have said something about a young elemental wreaking havoc on society.

Kaeli held her hands out in front of her and stared at them as she walked. Flames. Fire. She could almost feel the heat of the blaze on her fingertips as clenched her hands before loosening them. Wildfires now burned up and down the West Coast. Why did it have to follow her everywhere?

She balled up her fists and stuffed them into her pockets, her thoughts snapping back to her present-day issues. There was no way she'd just... lit Trent on fire. Of course, she'd heard of the people they were now calling "elementals," but for *her* to actually *create* fire... She shook her head. It had to be her overly stressed brain playing tricks on her. She must've done something else that would have caused Trent to let go so quickly.

Kaeli stopped at an intersection and pressed the crosswalk button. Without realizing it, she'd walked the usual route to her favorite cafe, Bookish Coffee. It was exactly where she needed to be right now. Over the last couple of years, Bookish Coffee had become her safe haven whenever she needed to get away from her frazzled mother or, in instances like this, when Trent came to visit.

As Kaeli entered the coffee shop, she let out a quiet breath. A small smile crept onto her face as the heavenly aroma of espresso bled into her senses. She exhaled, releasing the tension that roiled up in her body. She was home.

Bookish Coffee was a two-story, industrial-style, library-themed cafe. On the bottom floor were booths tucked in alcoves designed to fit no more than two or three people. Each alcove was surrounded by a different genre of literature and came with a plethora of squishy pillows. The top floor was more suited for groups of people who wanted to socialize. It consisted of an open floor plan with plush couches situated around long wooden coffee tables. Tall bookcases outlined the perimeter of the whole upper space. Kaeli rarely ever went up to the second floor, especially on days like this when she just needed time to regroup alone. She walked up to the front counter bar to order. The barista at the register flashed her a huge grin.

"Glad to see you're back, Kaeli!"

"Uhhh," Kaeli said as she tilted her head slightly. "Glad to see you too..." her eyes flitted toward the barista's name tag, "Luis." Her gaze lowered as she cleared her throat. All of the workers seemed to know her name here, but she could never match their names to their faces. Luis's eyes sparkled as his smile grew even wider.

"So, what can I have the pleasure of getting you today?"

"I'll get a mocha with oat milk." Kaeli couldn't help but smile back. Everyone was always so nice here.

"Alright." Luis wrote her name on a cup and tapped on a few register buttons. "That'll be four dollars and fifty cents."

"Excuse me," a voice sounded from over her shoulder just as Kaeli was opening her wallet. She paused and turned around. An elderly couple stood behind her. The woman held out a ten-dollar bill. "Let us pay for your drink. You look like such a lovely young lady."

"Oh! Um, thank you, but—"

"We insist." The old man nodded his head.

"Thank... you... You're both so sweet." Kaeli smiled as she hesitantly took the money from the woman

The woman just smiled at her. Kaeli tried to mask the confusion on her face as she turned and gave the money to Luis. Stuff like this seemed to happen to her a lot in public. She didn't understand why. Kaeli tried to return the extra change to the couple, but they insisted she keep it. Reluctantly, Kaeli tucked the money away into her wallet, and settled into the most reclusive booth she could find.

She scanned the rows of books surrounding her, lighting up when she spotted one of her favorite titles. She plucked it off the shelf and ran her hand over the smooth, worn cover. She'd read this book countless times in this same alcove. *Mythos of the Stars.* It was an anthology of the mythological stories behind the constellations. Kaeli cracked open the cover and flipped to a random page, letting fate decide what she would read today. The dull buzz of coffee shop chatter faded to the back of her mind as she became absorbed in the story of how princess Andromeda was sacrificed to a nefarious sea monster, but was saved by the great hero Perseus.

"Here's your mocha, Kaeli." Luis's voice jolted Kaeli back to reality. She slowly raised her eyes up from the page as she registered his words.

"Sorry, I must have missed it when you called my name."

"Oh no, not at all." Luis leaned up against the side of the alcove and smiled. "I just thought I would bring it to you personally. Is there anything else I can get for you?" Without breaking eye contact, Kaeli wrapped her hand around the coffee, pulled it in close, and shook her head as she tried to get a read on the barista. Luis could have just been trying to go the extra mile, but she was getting the sense that perhaps he had ulterior motives. She retreated further into the booth, putting more space between herself and him.

"Thanks, but I'm good."

"You really like that book, don't you?" Luis nodded to the open book on the table. Kaeli repressed a sigh. She highly disliked small talk. She just wanted to get back to reading.

"Yeah... how did you know?"

"I see you read it almost every time you come here." Luis sounded a little too excited. Kaeli internally cringed. She was not appreciating this level of attention. Not knowing what to say in response, she remained quiet. They held eye contact for a torturous five seconds before Luis spoke up again.

"You can have the book if you want. Normally, if a customer wants to keep a book, we charge full price, but this one is on the house."

"Thank... you?" Kaeli didn't know how to respond.

"LUIS!" the manager at the counter barked. "We have customers. Get back on register." The smile on Luis's face fell. He made to walk back to the register but stopped mid-stride to look back at Kaeli.

"Seriously, the book is yours if you want," he winked. Kaeli pursed her lips, eyebrows knitting together as she leaned her head back against the cushioned backing of her seat and she watched Luis walk away. She was grateful for the free mocha and the free book, but she really needed some peace and quiet to herself right now.

Kaeli picked up her mocha and watched the crowd from her secluded space. Very few people were alone. Most had smiles on their faces and chatted quietly amongst their groups, oblivious to the world around them. As she took a sip from her drink, Kaeli noticed a man and a woman entering the cafe. An eerie silence cut through the buzzing chatter. Some people shifted to get a better look at the newcomers. Kaeli couldn't understand why, but her attention was inexplicably drawn to the strangers. It was almost the same sensation she had while reading books. All other sensory information faded to the background of her mind as if she were in a void, like she and these two people were the only ones that existed.

They were both attractive. The man was tall, well-built, but not overly muscular. He had tousled strawberry blonde hair and the most piercing green eyes Kaeli had ever seen. The woman next to him was also tall and had a lean, athletic figure. Her face was angular and her sharp grey eyes seemed to probe at the people in the cafe. Long, red-brown hair fell below her shoulder in frizzy curls.

The man made eye contact with Kaeli and as much as she tried to pull away, she couldn't. His gaze was like a tractor beam. He smiled and broke the connection before walking toward the counter with his female companion. With their backs now facing her, Kaeli looked away. The sounds of conversation and clinking glasses escalated again. Kaeli looked down at the table, keeping her eyes trained on her mocha. She reached for her book again and flipped through the pages, opening to the story of the Leo constellation. She was just getting into the battle where Hercules approached the Nemean Lion when she noticed the two strangers in her peripheral vision. They sat in the alcove directly across from her.

Kaeli shifted in her seat and cast a sidelong glance in their direction while still pretending to read. Her gaze flickered back to the book as she made eye contact with the handsome man. They stared at her without even trying to be discrete. The woman had her chin propped up on a fist and smirked. Who were these people? Why were they so freakishly interested in her? She tried to ignore their gazes for as long as she could, but eventually the awkwardness of the whole situation became too much. Kaeli cleared her throat and squared off her shoulders to face them directly.

"I'm sorry. Do I know you from somewhere?"

The man's face split into the most charming grin Kaeli had ever seen. His emerald eyes seemed to glitter like an actual gem, and Kaeli fought the temptation to drown in them. The woman sitting next to him rolled her eyes. Looking at them now, Kaeli *knew* she'd never met, or even seen, these people ever in her entire life. She definitely would have remembered their sense of presence—enticing but dangerous. A knot formed in her stomach. She shouldn't have said anything.

"No, I don't think so." The man stood up and sauntered over to Kaeli's table. He looked over her as he extended a hand. Kaeli tilted her head and gnawed at the inside of her lip. She could shut this interaction down and just leave, but something about this guy was just too… alluring. She took his hand, accepting the gesture. The man had a firm handshake. "My name is Leonardo."

"Leonardo…" Kaeli raised her eyebrows and smirked, "like the ninja turtle or the painter?"

The woman, still sitting at the table, let out a hysterical laugh that caused her to snort. The sound drew more than a couple of stares. Kaeli's smirk grew to a genuine smile.

"Well, um, yes. Both, I guess." Leonardo cleared his throat and shot a vicious look at the woman before refocusing his attention back to Kaeli.

"My name's Kaeli," Kaeli responded. "If we haven't met before, why do you keep staring at me?"

"Well, she gets right to the point," the woman said. The knot returned to Kaeli's stomach and she mentally kicked herself for telling them her real name. Despite the confidence she was trying to portray, she had no idea who these people were and their blatant interest was unnerving. She reached for the book on the table and closed it.

"Kaeli…" the man said her name as if he were tasting it. "That's a pretty name."

"Yes, I'm quite fond of it. " Kaeli swiped her book off the table and downed the rest of her mocha. Such a shame. She really did prefer to savor her espresso. She sighed as she set the empty mug on the table. "Well, it was nice meeting you, Leonardo, but I have places I need to be." She tilted her head to the woman. "And I never learned your name, but it was nice seeing you too."

"Maybe we'll see each other again sometime." Leonardo's smile seemed hopeful. Kaeli paused to consider him. He really was attractive. His whole being radiated with an intoxicating dazzle. She shook her head to clear her mind. His presence was too disarming. She needed to get out before she made a stupid decision.

"Probably not," she said flatly. She pushed her way out of the alcove past Leonardo and headed toward the exit.

"Enjoy the book!" Luis called after her from the register as Kaeli rushed toward the door. She took half a second to turn and nod in appreciation before leaving. When she reached the crosswalk, she turned to look through the window paneling of Bookish Coffee. Leonardo and his friend stood there, still staring at her with a piercing gaze. She quickly turned around and shivered. The crosswalk signaled that it was now safe for pedestrians to walk. Kaeli ran without looking back.

Alyssa Markins

CHAPTER 2

L eo stood next to his booth, keeping his eyes trained on Kaeli as she rushed across the street. He tilted his head to the side and wrinkled his nose. He hadn't intended to come off so strong. It'd been a while since he'd last been on Earth. He may have forgotten how to act naturally around humans, but when he had first seen Kaeli through the window at the cafe, he knew he needed to meet her in person. Aries jabbed him in the ribs.

"You realize you could have just said 'Leo,' right? Out of all of us, you're the only one who has a passable human name," she snorted. "So what did you think of her? Is she the right one?"

Leo cracked his neck as he considered the question. To be honest, he wasn't sure. He and Aries had left the Celestial Realm to come to Earth with the express mission of finding human recruits who could be trained to eventually take their place as zodiac signs. All of the zodiacs could identify which humans were compatible with their sign just by looking at them. It was almost like their sign hovered above the head of anyone who was born in their sun cycle. In order to tell if a human could *actually* become a zodiac, however, they needed to exhibit elemental skill sets and that needed to be demonstrated. Unfortunately, Leo and Aries were among the last of the zodiacs to find their new recruits and time was running out.

"I don't entirely know, but she's definitely giving off the right energy. It would be great if she can actually use fire." He paused. Kaeli disappeared from view. He tore his gaze away from the window and sat down with Aries, folding his hands under his chin. "What about you? Any luck finding your new recruit yet?"

"Nope. Still looking." Aries leaned back in her seat and crossed her arms over her chest. "I found a couple of could-be potential candidates, but none of them really have the right fight. I could crush them all instantly."

"You're not going to find any equals here, Aries. Most humans don't know all they are capable of, even without the ability to become a zodiac. You can't expect one of them to be prepared at your level, especially when you've been at this for what... over a thousand years now? I stopped keeping track."

"You may have low expectations for your future successor, but a future aries needs to have the ability to destroy armies."

"That doesn't mean you can expect a modern-day human to have the strength of a thousand men. They need to be taught. Spartans don't exist anymore."

"Have you *tried* teaching an aries? You leos are tame by comparison. And that's saying something." She rolled her eyes, cutting Leo off before he could respond and sighed as she scanned the room. "Don't worry. I know the deadline is coming soon. I'll have found someone by then."

"You better." Leo leaned back in his seat. The world was falling apart piece by piece. They were losing control of the elements and Earth was suffering the consequences. They needed extra help.

"I like her," Aries said, interrupting his thoughts. "I know you said you need to see her again to determine if she can use fire, but she felt right to me. I'd like to think I'm adept at identifying fire wielders. Even if she's not an aries, she's clearly got plenty of fire in her. And I know you saw her unconsciously using your leo charm ability on the coffee guy." She jerked her head toward Luis.

"We'll see," Leo smiled. "I'm not going to let her disappear on me, that's for sure."

A shout from outside the cafe interrupted their conversation. Leo and Aries whipped their heads toward the noise. On the other side of the large window stood a well-built young man with curly brown hair surrounded by a group of three rather nasty-looking individuals. Leo turned to Aries. Her grey eyes glowed with an inner brightness.

"He's one of mine." A wide grin broke out on her face. Leo chuckled.

"You want to go check it out?"

"Yes!" Aries shot up from the table, almost knocking it over, and narrowly avoided bowling over a couple enjoying their coffee as she rushed out the door. Leo dipped his head and mouthed an apology at them as he rushed to follow after her.

"I told you, I'll have it by tomorrow. Just lay off me, man," the young man shouted at the group that slowly closed in on him. Leo and Aries glanced at each other as they approached. The grin on Aries's face grew wider.

"You were supposed to have it today, Lukka." The biggest of the group shoved him and Lukka stumbled back a couple of feet. Regaining his balance, Lukka brushed off his shirt where the big guy had touched him, as if he needed to remove some filth. He raised an eyebrow, a dangerous glint flashing through his deep set eyes.

"You *don't* want to do that again." His voice carried a dark edge to it.

"Do what?" He shoved Lukka again.

Lukka stared at the guy straight in the eyes as a wide grin slowly spread across his face. He turned on his heel and sprinted off in the opposite direction.

"Get him!" the big guy yelled as the group started to take off. Aries slapped Leo's shoulder.

"We're following him," she said before running after the boys. Leo rubbed the spot where Aries had hit him. That was going to hurt later. He sighed before rushing after her.

They ran a couple of miles until they reached a shipping yard just off the coast. Aries sprinted ahead, not wanting to miss any of the action. Leo slowed to a walk, covering his nose and mouth with a hand as he tried not to gag. The smell of rotting fish and the skunky musk of marijuana assaulted his already enhanced senses. Cawing seagulls circled above, screaming at each other for their next meal. The whole lot was a maze of dull-colored shipping containers. A slight breeze blowing in sea spray tossed Leo's hair in front of his face. He shook it out of his eyes. He'd lost visuals on Lukka and the assailants, but he could hear angry shouts not too far off in the distance. He continued to walk in the general direction and came across Aries standing close to one of the shipping units, peeking her head around the corner. Her frizzy hair fell over her shoulder. Leo cleared his throat as he approached her. Aries turned, her hair flipping as she did so.

"Took you long enough, slow poke," she chuckled. Leo smirked.

"I figured you could track the kid on your own, so I decided to take my sweet time. Speaking of which," he nodded to the corner of the shipping container, "is he on the other side of that?" Aries nodded and motioned for Leo to join her. The gang had Lukka cornered against one of the containers, but he didn't seem worried in the least. As his back hit the iron wall, a lazy smile crossed his lips and he smoothed his curly hair away from his face. He squared off his shoulder and widened his stance as the thugs closed in around him.

"I'll give you guys one last chance to back off before— oof." Lukka's neck snapped to the side as the biggest guy's fist connected with his jaw. He laughed as Lukka spat out a glob of blood. Clearing his throat, Lukka straightened himself back to an upright standing position. A dangerous glint gleamed in his eyes. He smiled again, blood dripping over his teeth and down his chiseled jawline.

"Don't say I didn't warn you." He clenched both of his hands into fists and they ignited into balls of flame. Aries started flailing without tearing her eyes away from the unfolding fight. Leo took a step back to avoid getting hit again.

"He's the one, he's the one, he's the one!" she squealed. The two smaller guys started backing away, but the big one just stared at Lukka with pure hatred in his eyes.

"Should we interfere?" Leo asked. "This seems like it could get out of hand real fast."

"Yes! I'd love to show those punks what a real fight with the actual Aries looks like!"

"I didn't mean you should join them." Leo's hand shot out as he grabbed Aries at the nape of her shirt collar, pulling her back to prevent her from stepping into the fight. She shot him a vulgar gesture and let out a heavy sigh.

"Fine. We'll wait to see how this plays out. I guess it wouldn't hurt to see how he handles himself."

Lukka lunged toward the biggest guy and, dodging an oncoming punch, sank a flaming fist into his gut. The guy grunted, doubling over. The fire caught on his shirt. He screamed as he threw himself to the ground and rolled around like a madman. Lukka chuckled and turned to face the others.

"Anyone else have problems with my payment plan?"

Their eyes widened as they scampered away, stumbling over each other. Lukka glanced at the guy on the ground and smirked. He'd managed to extinguish the flames but didn't look like he was in any hurry to get up and continue fighting. Lukka unclenched his fists and the fire engulfing his hands disappeared. He bent down, grabbed the guy by his shirt, and pulled him closer so that their noses were almost touching.

"I suggest you go back to your employer and tell them my debts have already been paid off."

The guy's eyes widened as Lukka pulled him to his feet and shoved him off in the direction of his friends. He flashed one more terrified look at Lukka before running away.

Aries stepped out from behind the shipping container, slowly clapping her hands. Lukka jerked his head in their direction. Leo let out a long exhale, muttering under his breath as he followed Aries. This was not how he would go about enlisting his recruit.

"That was impressive," Aries chuckled as she neared Lukka. He crouched slightly, moving away from the oncoming couple. Leo scrunched his nose. He could smell the acidic, vinergary scent of unease wafting off him.

"Who are you?" Lukka growled. Aries cracked a smile in what Leo knew was an attempt to look friendly and non-threatening, but in reality, it just made her look creepy. Her resting bitch face was much more approachable than her smile.

"Name's Aries." She extended a hand. Lukka arched an eyebrow as he looked from Aries's hand, to her face, then back to her hand. Aries sighed.

"Okay, fine. I'll get straight to the point. Me and my colleague, Leo here," she jerked a thumb toward Leo, "we saw what you can do. I want you to come with me."

Lukka huffed a laugh. "Sorry, lady. Not interested." He turned his back to leave.

"Wait!" Aries held out a hand and a fire ball went soaring past Lukka's head. He froze before slowly turning to face the two zodiacs.

"You're... elementals?" He paused. "I've never met other—"

"Well, now you've met two, and I can guarantee you we're way more experienced at handling fire." She cleared her throat. "So, as I was saying, my friend and I would really appreciate it if you came with us."

"Is that a threat?" Lukka narrowed his eyes, sizzles of heat emanating from his shoulders and arms. Leo moved so he stood right over Aries's shoulder.

"Aries, careful. If he decides to use his fire, there's no telling what kind of damage he could do. This kid clearly doesn't have full control over his abilities yet."

"Whatever he throws, we can handle it," Aries snorted.

"I'm not worried about us! I'm worried about the environment. If he starts unintentionally destroying stuff, how is the earthen media going to explain that?"

"What the hell are you freaks?" Lukka interrupted. Aries tilted her head back and rolled her eyes at Leo.

"Great. Now you've scared him."

Leo opened his mouth to retort, but before he could, an unnatural sliver of shadow zigzagged across the concrete and disappeared into the large shadow of the shipping container. He snapped his mouth shut and his eyes widened. Aries slowly turned to Leo.

"We need to get Lukka out of here now."

"What are you guys talking about? What's going—"

A sharp crack and a flash of purple lightning interrupted Lukka. The unnatural sliver of darkness had solidified into a snake completely made of shadow that was big enough to swallow three people in one go. Purple electricity crackled where its eyes should have been. Leo's eyes widened as he rushed to pull Lukka away from the monstrous shadow snake.

"Not here," he muttered. Lukka's jaw dropped, and his eyes looked like they might pop out of their sockets. Leo tightened his grip to make sure Lukka wouldn't collapse. The kid might have been an aries, but this was too much for any human to take in without warning. Aries faltered back a couple of steps from the creature, but without losing her fighting stance.

"What are you doing here?" she growled. Her hand twitched and small flames appeared at her fingertips. The snake flashed a hideous smile that almost split its face in half.

"I would be careful with the fire if I were you," it hissed.

"It's right," Leo said to Aries. "Lukka could get hurt, and the last thing we need is a stray ember starting another wildfire on the West Coast."

He considered the snake. It was daylight. These things needed darkness to survive. Odds were if it tried to lunge too far away from the shadows of the container, it would dissipate. "I doubt it could do much damage to us in its current state, anyway."

"You ssshouldn't underessstimate me, lion." The snake lunged forward, fully opening its maw to reveal two nasty, pointed fangs that matched the color of its eyes.

Aries dodged left. Leo pulled Lukka to the right just as the snake's face crashed into the ground. It melted into the concrete and disappeared from sight. Leo looked at Lukka. All of the color drained from his face.

"What the *fuck* are you people?"

"We can explain later," Leo replied as he scanned the surroundings, trying to sense where the snake would reappear next.

"Okay, so," Aries took in a deep breath, "the snake isn't tangible, but it can still use its fangs. That's just fucking great."

The snake burst from the ground behind them and lunged to sink its fangs into Aries. Leo ditched Lukka by the shipping container and tackled Aries. The two tumbled away just in time. Aries shoved Leo off of her and scowled.

"I could've handled that."

The snake coiled and lowered its head to be level with the two of them. "My massster is getting ssstronger. Sssoon Ophiuchusss will be free."

"Are you sure we can't use fire?" Aries shot Leo a glare.

"I wouldn't recommend it." Leo let out a sigh through pursed lips. They both inched away from the snake that stared them down, calculating their movements.

"But this is Southern California! Fires happen all the time. Nobody would notice."

"People's lives get destroyed in those fires, Aries!"

"And if we don't play this right, ours will be!"

The snake lurched forward again. Aries's hands erupted into flames, but before she could do anything, the ground started to shake. The snake froze as a gaping hole appeared in the ground. As it fell into the abyss, the end of its tail whipped outward, smacking Lukka. He crumpled on the ground. A hissing screech echoed off the walls of the chasm as the snake disappeared into the darkness. The hole closed back up. Leo and Aries stood up, stunned.

A pointed cough sounded from behind them. Leo and Aries turned to see a tall man in black dress pants and a white button up shirt with the sleeves rolled up to his elbows. He wore dark shades that concealed his eyes. His hair was snow white and slicked back so that not a single hair poked out of place.

"You're welcome," the newcomer smirked. Aries's lips curled to a snarl.

"Capricorn. What are you doing here?" Leo asked.

"Libra asked me to trail the two of you in case you decided to do something reckless while looking for your recruits. Speaking of which," he nodded to where Lukka lay unconscious on the ground, "you might want to take care of that one. I'll see the two of you later. I'd get out of here quickly if I were you. That snake isn't going to stay buried forever." He turned his back and started walking away. A green light engulfed him and he vanished. The ground rumbled in his wake.

"He's right." Leo flashed a glance toward Aries as he readjusted his footing to avoid falling. "The kid's seen too much. We either need to take him back with us or—"

"Oh, we're taking him." Aries smiled at the unconscious Lukka with a wolfish grin. "He's exactly what I've been looking for." She approached Lukka and hoisted him up over her shoulders. Lukka moaned. Leo walked over to Aries and placed a hand on her arm. Both of their eyes glowed and they disappeared in a blaze of fiery orange light.

Alyssa Markins

CHAPTER 3

Lukka's vision slowly faded back in, but his head spun in circles. He took his time inhaling steady breaths until he felt like he could open his eyes without throwing up. His eyes fluttered open, and a wave of vertigo hit him so hard that he barely caught himself on his hands and knees before smashing his face into... His eyes widened as he scrambled to push himself to a sitting position.

He most definitely was no longer in the shipyard. It didn't even look like he was on Earth. His breath caught in his throat. He was in the middle of a circular stone platform... that looked like it was suspended in the void of outer space. At one end of the platform, a bridge made of pure rainbow connected to a larger land mass off in the distance. A hand wrapped around his arm and hauled him up to his feet. He looked up to see Aries. She had an amused grin plastered to her face. Lukka wanted to be furious, but at the moment, couldn't physically manage it.

"You'll be fine in a minute, kid. It takes a while to get used to teleporting, but you'll get the hang of it."

Lukka opened his mouth to respond… but nothing came out. *Teleporting?* He found himself leaning into Aries's grip for support as his mind desperately tried to untangle what in the hell was going on.

Off in the distance, he could see a beautiful—but livid—female approaching them from the bridge. She was tall, and blonde hair curled down in soft spirals past her square jawline. As she walked up to them, her soft hazel eyes carried a hard stare. Leo looked at Aries and smirked. He slung an arm over her shoulders.

"Someone's in trouble," he teased. Aries pursed her lips together and shot Leo a deadly side eye.

"Shut up." She squared off her shoulders and let out a heavy sigh as she got ready to face the woman.

"What are you thinking, dragging a human here totally unannounced?" The woman's sharp words cut through the remaining space as she walked the final steps across the bridge. "This is going to have serious repercussions. The earthen media will freak out *again,* and their law enforcement will only get more steeped in these missing person cases, not to mention the psychological trauma this poor boy is going to experience being teleported into the Celestial Realm without proper preparation. Dammit, Aries, we've talked about this."

"I didn't have a choice!" The vicious bite in Aries's voice caused the woman to wince. Lukka backed up a step toward Leo.

"Who is this lady?" he whispered. Leo chuckled.

"That's Libra. She and Aries tend to clash, but don't worry. Normally, their spats don't cause any damage."

"Libra. Aries…" Lukka looked up to consider the tall redhead standing next to him. *Leo.* And they'd referred to that stranger in the shipping yard as Capricorn. The women continued to yell at each other, but Lukka let their words fade to the background as he looked around at the kaleidoscope galaxy surrounding them. His brain would never trip this hard without help. He looked at Leo again and, squinting his eyes, poked the man in the arm. Leo furrowed his brows together as he did a double take at Lukka. Lukka looked at his finger. Leo definitely *felt* like a real person.

"Okay, look." Aries's booming voice snapped Lukka out of the daze. "Lukka saw and was *attacked* by one of the shadow snakes and he saw Capricorn split the fucking earth in two. Even if I didn't need a new recruit, we would've had to bring him back here anyway to keep him safe from the snake and give him a memory wipe."

"Um, excuse me." A hot anger boiled in Lukka's gut as he shoved his way past Leo to interrupt the conversation. "What do you mean, 'memory wipe?' None of this is my fault. You freaks decided to… to…" His voice trailed off. He didn't really have the words to explain anything he'd just seen, or what exactly had happened between the two seconds it took to get from Earth to wherever this place was. Libra crossed her arms over her chest and shifted her weight as she looked him up and down. She cocked her head to the side and slid her gaze toward Aries.

"Well, he certainly seems like a good recruit for you. Rash and doesn't think before he speaks."

"Listen, sweet cheeks," Lukka snapped. "I don't know what you mean by 'recruit,' but there's no way I'm joining whatever creepy zodiac cult you guys are part of." His nostrils flared. Libra's smirk grew wider as he pinned her with a glare. She returned her focus to Aries.

"On second thought, I'm glad you brought him. Seeing him get knocked down a couple pegs in training will be fun." She sighed, "But please, Aries, if this *ever* happens again, try to cover your trail better. You have no idea how his family will react to his disappearance or how this will affect his social circle."

"Or how his little gang buddies are going to feel when they don't get paid," Leo interjected. Aries and Libra shot him a glare. Leo stuffed his hands into his pockets and shrugged. "Just saying. The kid didn't look like he was too well off when we found him, anyway."

"Can someone tell me what the *hell* is going on here?! Who are you people? Why does it look like we're in outer space? How did I even get here? And why the hell do you keep calling me kid? I barely look younger than you." The anger in Lukka's gut grew hotter. The fire ached to burst from his hands.

The three self-proclaimed zodiacs cast uncertain glances amongst each other before refocusing on Lukka. Leo stepped forward, making direct eye contact. The fire in his gut settled slightly as a gentle warmth swept over him. The anger ebbed into something else… like an ease he knew he shouldn't feel but felt anyway.

"You've been chosen by this one." Leo jerked a thumb in Aries's direction. Aries grinned and gave Lukka two thumbs up. Leo smiled. "And trust me… even though we may not look it, we're all *much* older than you."

"Chosen for what?" The bite left Lukka's voice, but he still needed questions to be answered. This was all a lot to take in. Leo turned to look at Aries again. As soon as he broke eye contact, the rage flooded back into Lukka. Red spots speckled his vision as the gentle warmth transformed into scalding heat.

"Chosen for what?! " He couldn't control it anymore. The fire exploded out of him, consuming his entire body. To his surprise, none of the so-called zodiacs even flinched. Aries approached him and placed one hand on each of his shoulders. Like a vacuum, she sucked out all of his heat. The flames died down.

"This is going to take a bit of time to explain." She looked deep into his eyes, as if she could see right into his soul. It was the first time she sounded sincere in the few minutes Lukka had known her. His anger dissipated. His muscles went slack and calm nothingness embraced him. There was a familiarity in her eyes, as if the two of them were the same. Aries smiled her first non-terrifying smile.

"I'll answer all your questions, but not here. There's a better place for this. Will you stick with me long enough to at least clear all this up?"

Lukka paused. It sounded awkward, hearing her ask a question. He got the impression that wasn't something she normally did. Though the anger had faded, he couldn't help but feel like he'd been backed into a corner… one his fire couldn't get him out of. What other choice did he have? These people had brought him here. He had no idea where he was or how he would even go about getting home. Not to mention these people apparently had the ability to do memory wipes… somehow.

"I guess," he mumbled.

"Excellent." Aries's eyes glowed with excitement. "Then come with me and we'll get this all sorted out." She started walking toward the bridge and motioned for him to follow. Taking a deep breath, Lukka trailed after her.

Leo absentmindedly stroked his chin as he watched Aries and Lukka walk across the bridge. He had no doubt this human would do well in the Celestial Realm. If Lukka already had this much control of his fire, there was no telling what he would be capable of once properly trained as a zodiac. Aries would have fun training him. Now all he had to do was go back and find Kaeli. He turned to Libra.

"Well, it's been lovely touching base with you, but I need to go back to Earth," he smiled. "And since I know how much you hate being taken off guard, just know that when I come back, it *might* be with a human girl."

"Just stay out of trouble while you're down there and avoid the shadow snakes. And don't create any public displays of fire. And, if you could, take care of Lukka's legal situation. The last thing we need is attention being drawn to how people are disappearing without a trace."

"On it," Leo winked. Before Libra could add any more caveats, he disappeared in a blaze of red light.

He reappeared in the middle of a park. He turned his head back and forth to make sure no one had seen him materialize out of thin air. Thankfully, he had teleported to an empty grove of willow trees. He could hear the faint noise of children laughing and screaming on a playground a short distance away.

This was one of the inconvenient parts of teleporting between the Celestial Realm and Earth. While on Earth or in the Celestial Realm, he could choose exactly where he wanted to go as long as he could envision the location in his mind. He could also envision a person's face and teleport to their location. Between realms, however, he could only arrive in a generalized area. This had led to some awkward encounters in the past. Thankfully, today was not one of those days.

Leo stretched his arms and cracked his neck. First things first, he needed to get out of this park and take care of Lukka's legal trail. With one more glance around the grove to make sure no one was watching, he closed his eyes and envisioned a dark room with a single desk, a swivel chair, and a ridiculous amount of high-tech holographic computer screens. When he opened his eyes, he stood in that exact room.

This room was one of many neutral zones that existed between the Celestial Realm and Earth. They were physically located on Earth but inaccessible to humans without the help of a zodiac or Celestial Spirit. The Western Zodiacs had them dispersed throughout their jurisdictions in the North American and European continents.

Once it became clear that governments were going to digitize everything, the zodiacs created this particular room to store important information on the humans that fell under their earthen jurisdiction. These supernatural computers compiled everything from legal documents to social media profiles. Essentially, all Leo had to do to make Lukka legally and digitally disappear was hit the delete button. Then there would only be the pesky matter of dealing with the memories of his social circle. But Scorpio was normally the one who handled that sort of thing, being naturally gifted in the ways of mind manipulation.

Leo slid into the swivel chair. The holographic screens suspended in mid-air blinked to life in front of him, casting an eerie, pale blue glow, making him squint until his eyes adjusted to the light. He typed in Lukka's first name and narrowed down the geographic locations until a picture of his face popped up on the main screen. Leo tapped the image and a long page of text scrolled in front of him. He let out a long, low whistle as he scanned the files.

Lukka Valentino Moreci, as was his full name, apparently had quite the past. His family had died when he was ten in what authorities had documented as an accidental house fire. Leo cringed. Freak "accidents" happened to a lot of elementals at a young age, and after seeing how well Lukka could control his fire now, there was no doubt that his powers had manifested at an early age.

After his family's death, Lukka spent the remainder of his childhood hopping from different dysfunctional foster care families and juvenile hall. The habitual law breaking continued after he turned 18, but nothing serious enough to lock him up for more than a year at a time.

"Something tells me once your files get deleted, you won't have many people looking for you," Leo muttered. He tapped a couple keys, and just like that, Lukka was wiped from technical existence. One by one, the monitors displaying Lukka's birth certificate, criminal records, and social security went black. Everything and anything tracing back to him disappeared. Leo smiled as he rose up from the chair. Mission accomplished. Hopefully Libra would be appeased. Now he just had to find Kaeli. He would take care of her files after he found out if she was actually capable of being his recruit.

He leaned back in the chair, stretching his arms back and clasping his hands behind his head. He wanted to go about this the right way. Kaeli seemed skeptical of him during their first meeting. If he showed up now, he risked scaring her off. It would probably be best to silently trail her for a little while and see if her fire came out naturally. He closed his eyes and envisioned Kaeli's face.

CHAPTER 4

A few days later, Kaeli stood at the bus stop waiting for the 663 to pick her up from work. She shifted her weight and glanced at the time on her phone for what must've been the hundredth time as she waited for the bus to arrive. It was late. Not surprising given the horrendous amount of traffic that always hit around this hour, but that didn't make it any less annoying. She looked up from her phone and saw the outline of the awaited vehicle in the distance.

"Finally," she sighed, shoving her phone into her pocket and fishing her bus card out from her wallet. She pressed the button on the nearby pole to tell the bus to stop. It pulled up and the doors opened with a *whoosh.* Kaeli hoisted herself up the steep steps and scanned her card before putting it back in her wallet and surveying the seats for an unoccupied space. She froze in her tracks as she made eye contact with a familiar face staring back at her with an enticing smile. Leonardo from the coffee shop.

"You gonna sit down?" the bus driver grumbled.

"Yeah… sorry." Kaeli cleared her throat as she tore her gaze away from the attractive redhead. She let out a heavy exhale as she regained her mental composure and made her way to a window seat as far away from him as possible.

As the bus continued on its course, Kaeli actively avoided looking in Leonardo's direction, even as his gaze bored into the back of her neck— the heaviness of the stare made her hair stand on end. In an attempt to distract herself, she dug into her bag and pulled out *Mythos of the Stars.* Flipping it open to a random page, she started to read.

Scorpius, known as Scorpio in the Western Zodiac, is one of the brightest constellations to light the night sky…

Kaeli's mind wandered off into the two separate legends of Scorpius. In one legend, Artemis, goddess of the hunt, sent a scorpion to kill Orion, son of the sea god Poseidon, after he tried to sexually take advantage of her. In the other legend, Gaia had sent the scorpion to kill Orion after he made a boastful proclamation that he could destroy any creature on Earth. Regardless of the legend, Orion sounded like a total douchebag. Kaeli became so wrapped up in the book that she didn't notice the gentle, abnormal sway of the bus. It wasn't until the frantic murmurs of her fellow passengers disturbed her reading bubble that she realized something was wrong.

"Ladies and gentlemen, we are experiencing an earthquake," the bus driver's voice cut through the emerging panic. "Remain calm and hold onto the nearest bar or strap near you. If there are none within reach, get down low and hold on to the nearest seat until I can bring the bus to a complete stop."

Kaeli snapped the book shut, shoved it into her bag and, crouching low to the ground, gripped the metal fixtures holding the seat down in front of her. She tried to keep her limbs from shaking. Her heart started beating so fast it felt like it might pound out of her chest. She squeezed her eyes shut and tried to push away the mental images of a capsizing bus. Envisioning the worst wasn't going to help anything.

The abnormal sway built into a violent rock that threatened to tip the bus. Kaeli's knuckles turned white as she struggled to keep hold of the metal railing. Her arms felt like they would rip out of their sockets. She heard a scream and opened her eyes just in time to see a female passenger fly across the center aisle. A hand shot out and grabbed the woman just before her head slammed against an arm rest. Kaeli watched, wide-eyed and frozen, as Leonardo reeled in the woman and talked her down from hysterics in soft tones.

How the hell was he so calm? And strong enough to stop a flying woman with one hand? He made eye contact with her briefly and offered a grim smile before refocusing his attention on the woman he'd just saved, making sure she had a firm grip on the seat next to him. The aggressive tremors continued for what seemed like an eternity, but eventually began to subside. Somehow, the bus managed to stay upright.

After the ground remained still for several minutes, the bus driver's voice sounded over the loudspeaker.

"Ladies and gentlemen, please remain calm and exit the bus in an orderly fashion through the nearest emergency exit," his voice crackled. "Watch your step as you exit the vehicle."

Completely ignoring the driver's orders, the passengers made a mad dash to any opening within sight. Kaeli pressed herself as far away from the center aisle as she could to avoid the mob scrambling to get off the bus. She glanced across the aisle. Apparently, Leonardo had the same idea. He pressed against the opposite side of the bus, allowing everyone to push past him. The driver tried yelling over the panicked commotion, but his voice got lost in the sea of frenzied wails. Eventually, everyone had exited the bus except for

Leonardo and Kaeli. Their eyes locked. He grinned that ridiculously charming smile.

"After you, m'lady." He motioned for her to go ahead of him. Kaeli tilted her head to the side as she considered him. He had manners at least. Maybe she didn't need to be so suspicious of him. She figured there was at least a 50/50 chance he could be a perfectly nice, well-meaning bystander who just happened to be on the same bus. She pushed her way past the narrow seats and into the aisle. She was at the entryway, making her way down the steps when an aftershock tremor jolted the bus and a sense of momentary weightlessness warped her balance as she flew forward toward the upturned, cracked asphalt. A strong grip intercepted her fall and pulled her back. She grunted as she slammed against a firm body. Her eyes widened as she looked up to see Leonardo wrapped around her. She let out a shaky exhale in an attempt to steady her breath. Her gaze darted to the ground where she'd almost faceplanted. That would not have been a pretty sight. Leonardo held onto her for another minute until the ground stabilized before helping her exit the bus.

Kaeli's breath caught in her throat as she looked around at the wreckage. The world was in shambles. Apparently, the driver had been able to guide the bus into a rather large, mostly empty parking lot. The asphalt was uplifted and cracked in certain areas and various cars were strewn about in awkward angles. Many of the surrounding buildings had partially collapsed. Sidewalk benches were overturned and tree branches littered the landscape. Everywhere she turned, Kaeli saw destruction. People gradually ventured out into the street. Screams and cries pierced the air. A dull ache pulsed through her body. She folded her arms into her stomach and flinched. She looked down and saw the bruises already forming on her skin. Those were only going to get worse. She always bruised so easily. Leonardo cleared his throat, drawing Kaeli's attention away from the rapid bruising.

"Are you okay?" His voice had a soothing tone and his eyebrows were pulled down in a thoughtful stare.

"Yeah, I..." Kaeli took a moment to steady her voice. "I think so." She gingerly brushed the discolorations on her skin and tilted her head as she considered Leonardo. There didn't seem to be a single mark on his body. It wasn't like he'd fallen into a pit of shattered glass or anything, but there was no way he should have escaped the earthquake completely unscathed. She shook her head to clear her mind, but everything felt fuzzy. This guy just saved her from suffering a major head injury and all she could think about was how he felt... off.

"Thanks for... for... saving my face," she said, more quietly than she intended. She hoped she could control the rising heat threatening to creep across her cheeks. Leonardo smirked, and all semblance of control was lost. Her cheeks flamed.

"Well, I couldn't just let you get hurt," he glanced at her. His gaze lingered over the bruising on her arms. "Although I'm sorry I couldn't do more."

"It's okay. I'll be fine." Kaeli rubbed her neck in what she hoped looked like a nonchalant gesture while her toes curled nervously from within her shoes. She looked over Leonardo. The more she stared, the more perfect he seemed to appear. His skin seemed to literally glow. How could he not even have a single scratch? What was this guy? "You, um... You seem to be okay. You didn't get hurt... at all?"

Leonardo chuckled. "I tend to be lucky that way."

"Luck." Kaeli pursed her lips together. This guy was definitely more than just lucky. The sound of a wailing baby interrupted her thoughts, and she whirled around to see a mother trying to comfort her child. *Mom!* A wave of adrenaline pulsed through her veins. Her hands trembled and balled them into tight fists, rubbing her thumbs over her knuckles. She turned back to Leonardo.

"I need to get home to make sure my family is okay. My neighborhood is within walking distance from here. Thanks again…" her voice trailed off as she turned to walk away, but Leonardo put a gentle hand on her shoulder.

"Do you mind if I come with you? There's a lot of damage around here. I want to make sure you're safe."

Kaeli blinked. Her mind went blank. Leonardo's emerald eyes twinkled, and she felt herself being drawn to his presence. If she was honest with herself, she wanted an excuse to be near him. And he had protected her. Plus, it would be useful to have an extra set of hands around if she needed to navigate any rubble.

"Okay."

"Great." Leonardo grinned as he flourished his hand. "Lead the way."

Kaeli's heart sank as they continued the trek to her house. Destruction was everywhere, and it only got worse the further they walked. Asphalt was cracked; concrete, upturned. Some houses had only suffered minimal structural damage while others were completely collapsed. Her throat constricted as she tried to push out images of her mother being crushed in their apartment complex. Right now, she just had to get home. Then she could deal with whatever came next.

"Watch out!" Leonardo's voice cut through her thoughts. A streetlight creaked nearby. She turned to see it toppling toward her. Leonardo tackled her out of the way. Kaeli's eyes widened. Every muscle in her body stiffened as the streetlight smashed through the concrete where she'd stood just seconds ago. A couple of dogs started barking across the street. Leonardo moved in front of her, obstructing her view of the toppled light.

"I can only imagine how worried you must be right now," he said, placing both of his hands on her shoulders, "but you need to stay aware. It's not safe out here right now."

Kaeli bit her lip and nodded her head tersely. She needed to pull it together.

"My place is just up the street and around that corner." She pointed up the block. Leonardo winced, and Kaeli understood why. The damage only continued to get worse. She pressed a hand into her stomach, trying to keep the rising nausea at bay. *Don't jump to conclusions,* she told herself. *Wait until you actually get there, and then figure out how to react.* She stepped ahead of Leonardo and kept walking, keeping an eye out for any more collapsing structures.

As they approached the complex, a lump in Kaeli's throat dropped to the pit of her stomach. Her heart started racing, and she subconsciously reached for Leonardo's arm to steady herself. He made no move to pull away.

"That's where you live?" Leonardo pointed straight ahead, and Kaeli found herself vaguely nodding. Her unit was destroyed— the middle portion completely caved in. Some of the outer structure was still intact, but most of it had collapsed. Kaeli's mind went blank. There was nothing she could say or do. Her home was gone.

"Do you know if any of your family was inside?" Leonardo asked. Kaeli tried to mentally latch onto the soft tones of his voice as if they could anchor her to reality.

"I... I don't know." Her voice caught in her throat. She inhaled, closed her eyes, and let out a shaky breath. "My... my brother wouldn't be there, but my mom..." Her voice trailed off. Logically, she knew there was no way her mother would have left the house. An image of her mother's limp body crushed beneath the ruins rushed through Kaeli's imagination. Her heart raced again as heat coursed through her veins. She'd already lost one parent. She *couldn't* lose another. Her heart beat faster and faster until the sound of it thrashed in her ears, blocking out all other noise. She rushed toward the rubble in a delusional frenzy and frantically clawed through bits of fractured stone and wood. Broken glass cut her hands, but she didn't care. Didn't even feel the pain. She *had* to find her mom.

Trickles of blood dripped through her fingers. Somewhere in the back of consciousness, she could hear Leonardo yelling at her, but she pushed his voice to the back of her mind along with all other sensory information. She couldn't stop looking. She had to make sure her mom was alive. A scream wrenched from her throat as she tore through the debris.

"Kaeli!" Leonardo grabbed her shoulders and pulled her away from the ruins. Kaeli kicked and squirmed against him, but he remained solidly in place. "Kaeli, you can't go digging through all of that. The rest of this structure is incredibly unstable."

"Let me go!" Kaeli tried to kick, but her adrenaline surge died down. A deep exhaustion seeped into her bones. She wilted in Leonardo's arms as tears sprang to her eyes. "Mom..." she sniffled and rubbed her eyes to stop the tears.

"I'm… sorry…" Leonardo let go of Kaeli, and she sank to her knees, staring at the destruction before her. She wrapped her arms around herself and swayed back and forth. This couldn't be happening. This wasn't real.

As she stared at the rubble, a slight flicker caught her eye. She couldn't quite make it out, but she was certain she'd just seen a shadow move in the midst of all the ruin. For a brief moment, hope fluttered through her only to be quickly offset by a looming apprehension that made the hairs on her arm stand straight up. Something was off. The shadow had moved too fast and didn't sift any of the rubble. Kaeli blinked her eyes rapidly as she pushed herself up off the ground. She took a half step forward.

"Mom?" her voice cracked.

"Kaeli… if you mom was in there… there's no way…"

Kaeli let Leonardo's voice fade to the background as she squinted, trying to peer through the fallen wooden beams and concrete.

"I… saw something." She could sense the tension rolling off Leonardo, but she had to know if there was even a sliver of a chance her mother could be alive. She took another couple of steps forward. *There!* The shadows shifted again. Something was definitely moving underneath all of the wood, brick, and drywall.

"Kaeli, wait." Leonardo put a firm hand on her shoulder, stopping her from nearing the fallen units. She turned to face him and about to open her mouth in protest, but as she did, something erupted from the ruin. She shrieked and jumped closer to Leonardo. The flicker of shadow didn't belong to her mother. It didn't belong to anything human at all. It was a snake. A larger-than-life snake that looked like it was made up of shadows, had blazing, electric purple eyes, and a jaw that could easily swallow a human whole. The snake uncoiled from the wreckage, standing like a cobra waiting to attack, looming over them. Leonardo maneuvered Kaeli behind him.

"Not here too," he muttered. Kaeli clenched her jaw as her muscles trembled. The snake opened its huge maw. Kaeli winced and latched onto Leonardo's arm. He seemed way too calm as he faced the snake head-on, but it was a stability she needed in the face of this monstrosity.

"Sssoo, Leo, we meet again," the snake hissed. Kaeli's eyes widened. This monster could talk? And it knew Leonardo on a first name basis? His muscles tensed, and she looked up into his eyes. A dangerous fury danced behind his gaze. However he knew this snake monster, clearly they weren't on friendly terms.

"Why are you here?" he growled. The snake let out a sizzling sound as if it tried to laugh. The noise grated against her ears, and she cringed as she attempted to calm her shaking limbs.

"Sssame asss you," the snake hissed. "Massster needsss recruitsss too."

"What is going on here?" Kaeli couldn't help the squeak that escaped her throat. As soon as she uttered the words, she clamped a hand over her mouth. The snake diverted all of its attention to her. She shouldn't have said anything. Her body quivered violently as her knees buckled, but she maintained eye contact. Something in her gut told her fear would only feed this monster. Leonardo wrapped an arm around her waist, helping her to stay upright.

"Sssooo, ssshe'sss the one you're after." The snake slithered closer toward them. Leonardo once again positioned Kaeli so that he was standing in front of her. Kaeli didn't break eye contact with the monster. "Massster will like her."

"Kaeli, you need to run," Leonardo spoke in low tones.

"But what about you?" Kaeli whispered back. She saw the corner of his mouth twitch upward in a ruthless grin.

"I can fight it off."

"I wouldn't be sssooo sssure, lion," the snake hissed. Its electric eyes crackled and before Kaeli could mentally register what was going on, the snake lunged toward Leonardo, jaws wide open.

"NO!" she screamed as she pushed Leonardo to the side. All of her panic, fear, and anger coiled and exploded out of her. She reached out a hand toward the snake and fire erupted from her open palm, burning on sheer adrenaline. The snake screeched as the shadows burned away in the light of the blaze. Kaeli closed her hand into a fist. The fire immediately extinguished. Eyes wide in disbelief, she looked at her hand before making shaky eye contact with Leonardo.

"What... what just... happened..." her voice cracked. A high-pitched ringing sound pulsed through her head. Specks of black dotted her vision. The world spun. She widened her stance in an attempt to keep her footing. Leonardo took both of her hands into his.

"I can explain all of this to you, but we need to get out of here," he stared deeply into her eyes. A comforting warmth washed through her. "I know a safe place, but I'll only take you there if you want to come. Do you trust me?" Kaeli swallowed, and barely mustered the strength to nod her head yes. She had no choice. Her family was gone. Her home was gone. And apparently monsters with a penchant for eating people existed. Any semblance of life as she'd known it was destroyed the moment she incinerated that snake. A bitter smile crept onto Leonardo's lips.

"Okay, good." He pulled her into his chest, wrapped one arm around her waist, and placed his free hand at the top of her back. "Brace yourself," he whispered. Before Kaeli could even inhale, they disappeared into thin air.

Alyssa Markins

CHAPTER 5

Kaeli fell to the ground, her lungs wheezing for air as she violently coughed. She tried to brace herself for impact, but her arms wouldn't move. Her body totally froze in shock. Just as she was about to faceplant on the floor, Leonardo scooped her up and kept her standing. A tingling sensation started in her fingertips and gradually spread through her entire body. She flexed her fingers, opening and closing them into a fist, relieved her body had decided to listen to her again. Leonardo patted her on the back as she struggled to settle her breathing.

"You'll feel better in a moment. It takes a little bit of time to adjust to teleporting, especially when going between realms, but you'll be okay," he said. Kaeli hunched over, placing her hands on her knees as she gulped in air.

"What… the hell… was that?" Her mind raced with everything that had just happened. The snake. The fire. *Teleporting?* None of this made any sense. Her chest tightened as she looked around and realized that wherever she was, it definitely wasn't Earth. As she looked out into the seemingly infinite expanse, all she could see was what looked like outer space. The pictures she'd seen of distant galaxies in past science classes were painting the sky, easily visible for the eye to see. Her mouth went dry, and her stomach tightened as she turned in a slow circle, trying to comprehend how any of this was possible. Her gaze dropped to the ground as she shook her head.

"I'm going crazy. This can't be real. This *can't be real,"* she locked eyes with Leonardo, who offered her a weak smile. He leaned in and lightly touched her forearm.

"You're not going crazy," he said quietly, as if she were a skittish animal that would run off. "It's real."

"How…" Kaeli kept her eyes trained on Leonardo. She took in a couple of steady breaths. "We were attacked by a… a talking shadow snake. And you magically teleported us. And now I'm in the middle of outer space still able to breathe oxygen." She shook her head. "I shot fire from my hands." She held her open palms in front of her face and stared at them. That had felt real. She could remember the warmth, the tingling sensation of anger and fear. "I'm dreaming. I know I'm dreaming. I *have* to be dreaming."

"Kaeli," Leonardo took both of her hands in his and let out a long sigh. Kaeli's lip quivered as she looked at him with wide eyes. A warm glow surrounded his being, and his touch on her skin seemed comforting, as if everything would be okay as long as he held on to her. "I know this is all really strange for you. This is normal. Humans don't typically come here."

That last sentence broke the trance. Kaeli pulled her hands away and took a couple of steps back. The glow surrounding Leonardo faded.

"Humans… what do you mean humans?" her voice cracked. Leonardo smacked his forehead with an open palm.

"Think before you speak, Leo!" He let out a sigh, cleared his throat, and went to take a step toward Kaeli. When she backed up, he leaned away and held up his hands in surrender. "Everything will start making sense soon. I promise. I just need you to trust me."

"Trust you?" Kaeli almost laughed. Her mind was on the verge of hysterics. A familiar tingling sensation built in the tips of her fingers. "Why should I trust you?"

"If it weren't for me, you would be dead." Leonardo lifted his chin and tilted his head as he cautiously lowered his hands. His tone sounded like a soothing balm to Kaeli's ears, but she couldn't bring herself to accept that her situation was anything other than dangerous. Her eyes darted back and forth. She tried to avoid looking out at the vast expanse of galaxy surrounding her. It just made her head spin worse. Leo took one careful step toward her. This time she didn't back away from him. "Eventually, you would have gone back to your house. That snake creature would have regenerated and would've been right there waiting for you. One of two things after that would have happened. It would've either killed you, or you would've exploded into fire again and destroyed not only yourself, but everyone around you because you have no idea how to control it. I brought you here because I knew you would be safe. I know none of this makes sense, but you *can* trust me."

The conflict raged inside Kaeli. She wanted to trust this man, but her mind could not accept the current situation. She was about to open her mouth to respond, but cut herself off short when a billow of pale purple smoke appeared nearby. A woman emerged from the plume and walked toward them.

"Not now, Libra," Leonardo muttered. Kaeli tilted her head as she looked up at him. She absentmindedly tugged at the ends of her shirt as she watched the stranger approach.

"You took her from Earth without erasing her records, Leo!" the woman yelled. "I expect this kind of recklessness from Aries, but you're supposed to have things more under control!"

"Hold up," Kaeli interrupted. She shook her head and blinked her eyes rapidly as she exhaled a deep breath. *"Libra, Aries, Leo?!"* She turned and glared at the man who had called himself Leonardo. It was starting to not sound like a coincidence that the snake had called him Leo. The hair at the nape of her neck stood on end as the tingling sensation crawled up her arms. "What does she mean you took me without erasing my records? Who the *hell* are you people? Some kind of... of zodiac cult?" Small sparks of flame jumped from her fingertips. Kaeli yelped in surprise and closed her hands into fists. The sparks disappeared. Libra raised an eyebrow.

"I see you didn't brief her on anything before bringing her to the Celestial Realm." Her voice oozed with disapproval.

"I didn't have a choice." Leo held his hands up. He flashed Kaeli an apologetic glance before turning back to Libra. "The snake that attacked Aries and me at the shipyard came back, but this time it was specifically waiting for her." He nudged his head in Kaeli's direction. "I made a snap decision. If I hadn't, the creature would have killed her. I'll get her records settled as soon as I get a chance. When they're gone, there won't be a physical trail left to her anyway."

"How can you even say that? She's a total mental mess right now. You didn't even prepare her at all..."

Kaeli looked around. Libra, Aries, Leo... what in the hell was going on here? They stood in the center of an ancient looking stone rune at the junction of two dirt paths that branched out to the right and left. The right path led to elaborate gardens filled with towering flower trees and shrubs in a variety of colors, while the left led to a series of craggy mountains capped with snow. Ahead of her arched a translucent bridge swirling with the colors of the rainbow. It connected to a circular platform that floated high above what looked to be a city constructed almost entirely out of glass, gold, and colored crystals.

She walked toward the bridge in sheer awe, her heart racing and eyes widening in wonder. As she approached the entrance to the bridge, she looked down. A sudden sway of nausea caused her to hold out both arms for balance. The ground they stood on floated completely mid-air. She took a couple of steps back and dropped to her knees. Her brain needed another moment to reorient itself.

"What is this place?" she whispered. She stared across the bridge. A slight wind caressed her hair against her cheek, drawing her gaze to the platform on the other side. She thought she saw a faint silhouette of a man sitting at the center. She pushed herself back up to a standing position and brushed her hair away from her face, tucking it behind her ear. As she stood, the figure seemed to shift with her. An overwhelming fascination washed over her. Her hand brushed slowly through the length of her hair as her gaze locked onto the stranger. She took a step forward. The intrigue pulsed through her, calling her to cross to the other side. Without giving a second thought about the man who had brought her here, or the woman he currently argued with, Kaeli crossed the bridge.

She forced her gaze to stay on the platform ahead. The rainbow bridge was wide and sturdy despite the illusion created by the swirling colors, but Kaeli couldn't entirely dismiss the sense of vertigo that threatened her sense of balance. As she approached the platform, she could see the outside of it was rimmed with all of the signs from the Western Zodiac. The man stood at the center, still as stone, facing away from her. Kaeli's pulse thrummed. As she neared the end of the bridge, she could make out a few more details.

His long, dark hair was pulled back into a short, low ponytail. He wore fitted black pants that tucked into a pair of sturdy combat boots, and a fitted blazer jacket that rolled up just above his elbows to reveal the corded muscle in his forearms. As Kaeli approached, he turned around and regarded her with calculating, brooding eyes. Her gaze was immediately drawn to the scorpion tattoo that peeked out from the top of his slightly unbuttoned, wine red shirt. She raised her eyes to meet his and stopped dead in her tracks. Her muscles tensed, and she turned her head just slightly to keep the bridge within her peripheral vision. The man smiled, revealing a pointy-toothed grin. Kaeli bit her lip but tried to keep any other signs of her racing pulse under control. This man was extremely attractive… unnaturally so… but he exuded a dangerous energy Kaeli didn't trust. He sauntered toward her. Kaeli lifted her chin a little as he approached, attempting to portray a confidence she did not feel.

"Well, look what the cat dragged in…" He was standing in front of her now, hand extended. Kaeli's already tense muscles froze completely. The man's piercing sapphire stare held her rooted to her spot on the platform. She swallowed. His grin grew wider. "What's your name, gorgeous?"

"Kaeli," she said through gritted teeth as she did her best to maintain eye contact. She tentatively reached out her hand to take his. "Who are you?"

"It's a pleasure to you, Kaeli." Without breaking the stare, the man raised Kaeli's hand to his lips and brushed it with a soft kiss. Kaeli couldn't stop the rush of heat rising to her cheeks. His voice was deep and alluring, and if it didn't sound so powerful, Kaeli thought she could fall asleep to it.

"I'm Scorpio." A shiver ran down Kaeli's spine. Leo, Aries, Libra, and now Scorpio. This Celestial Realm seemed to become more real with every new discovery.

"*Kaeli!*"

The sound of her name snapped her out of the trance. Scorpio broke eye contact with her, and the enticing smile he'd had just moments before slipped from his face. He released Kaeli's hand and tugged down the cuffs of his blazer as he flicked a cursory glance toward the direction of the voice. Kaeli turned to see Leo running across the bridge. Leo reached her, grabbed her by the shoulders, and spun her to face him.

"Don't *ever* wander off like that again! This place can be dangerous if you don't know where you're going." He raised his eyes to Scorpio and scowled.

"What are you, my guardian?" Kaeli shook free from his grip and took a step back. "Sorry, I didn't realize I was supposed to stay with the guy who teleported me into some alternate... realm."

"You should keep a better eye on your recruit, Leo," Scorpio sneered. "She's a fire sign. You didn't honestly expect her to sit still and patiently wait for someone to explain this crazy situation to her?"

"Recruit?" Kaeli spun to face Scorpio. "What do you mean I'm his recruit?"

"Oh, he hasn't told you?" Scorpio kept his gaze trained on Leo as a slow smile crept onto his face. He cocked his head and looked down at Kaeli. "Well, I suppose someone has some explaining to do."

Leo pushed his way past Kaeli. His eyes glowed a fiery red.

"Leave her alone," he spat. He turned to face Kaeli. "You need to listen to me." His expression was so severe that Kaeli felt compelled to do as he said. "Do *not* mess with this guy. He might seem charming, but he's more dangerous than he looks."

Scorpio chuckled.

"While I appreciate the compliment, I'm afraid I'll have to exit this intriguing conversation. There are more important things that need my attention." He ambled past the two of them, pausing at the base of the bridge to look back at Kaeli. "Take what this guy says with a grain of salt. He can be a little dramatic." He winked before crossing the bridge.

"He's insufferable," Leo muttered. Kaeli stared after Scorpio with wide eyes until he disappeared from view. She slowly turned and really considered Leo for the first time. There was something different about him here in this... Celestial Realm. He gave off a type of golden glow and all the features that had made him so attractively noticeable in the coffee shop were somehow sharpened.

"Why is he so dangerous?" Kaeli asked.

"There's... a lot... going on in the Celestial Realm and on Earth." Leo ran a hand through his hair and let out a heavy sigh. "The world is kind of at a crossroads. Most of it wouldn't make sense to you right now."

Kaeli tilted her head, chewing the words, and this world, over in her mind.

"And you're... actually Leo." She let out a long exhale. She couldn't believe she was even entertaining this idea.

"Yup," he grinned. It was so disarmingly charming that Kaeli found herself wanting to believe all of this was really happening, but none of it aligned with her perception of reality. She couldn't force herself to believe just because she wanted something to be true.

"And that... was Scorpio," she continued to speak slowly, more to herself than to Leo. She allowed her gaze to flicker toward his eyes. The fiery red was gone, and they'd returned to their brilliant emerald coloring. "You mentioned the name Aries, and that blonde-haired woman was Libra…"

Kaeli looked down to the ground and repeated the names. Regardless of whether or not these people were the actual zodiac signs, they obviously thought they were. She made direct eye contact with Leo. "So where am I exactly, and what am I doing here? Why did Scorpio call me your recruit?"

"I know you're skeptical about all this," Leo said. "That's normal. The Celestial Realm is different, and there's a reason why most mortals never get to see it, or even know that it, or we for that matter, actually exist." He pulled his lips into a tight thin line and tugged on his chin as if he thought about how to phrase what he needed to say next: "This, the Celestial Realm." He gestured to the galaxy sky above and the sparkling city below. "This is where all of the members of the zodiac reside. Not just the Western Zodiac either. Lunar, Native American, Gaelic, Mayan, you name a culture, and their zodiac is living within a specific district in the Celestial Realm. Some hold more power or responsibility than others depending on the size of the culture, or cultures, affiliated with us, but we never totally disappear. We've all been charged with guarding not only the Celestial Spirits that live in our territories, but also the cultures associated with us. Each zodiac has been entrusted with certain responsibilities, but lately, well, for about the last fifty years or so, things have been getting out of hand. Our strength isn't what it used to be, and we need to train new mortals to help us keep things in balance."

Kaeli's mind spun as she started fidgeting with the hem of her shirt.

"So, what, I'm like… some type of chosen mortal?" Kaeli's thoughts raced back to the book that Luis had given her. According to mythology, the constellations were nearly all formed by mortals who had done extraordinary things. That didn't describe her at all. She was just a normal girl with a crappy history. Her thoughts flashed back to the argument she'd had with Trent and the snake who had attacked her. A line from the news story that had been playing on the TV the last time she saw Trent flashed through her mind. *Others report that they've seen people, who are quickly becoming known as "elementals," stoking the infernos with their unnatural abilities and in some cases, starting them.* Maybe she wasn't as normal as she thought.

"You could say that," Leo smiled. "You were born under my sign and have the ability to control fire. That's one of the reasons I wanted to bring you here, and why Scorpio called you my recruit." He clapped both of his hands together into a prayer position and brought them to his lips. "I need your help, Kaeli." She shifted her weight as she exhaled a long breath. Her mind raced and a slight headache pounded at her temples.

"I know all of this is overwhelming," Leo continued. "The Celestial Realm really wasn't meant for mortals, so everything will take a while to get used to. For now, how about I take you to House Ignis. It's a kind of refuge for the signs in our element. You'll probably feel more at ease there, and I'll be able to tell you more information. Sound good?"

Kaeli steadied her breathing. She still didn't know what to think. This was either a classic "heroine gets thrust into destiny" situation, or it was the strangest dream she'd ever had. If it was the latter, she really didn't have anything to fear. If it was the former, well, how could she outrun destiny?

"Sounds good," she agreed. A huge grin broke out over Leo's face.

"Excellent. Follow me then. It's this way."

Trent lumbered through the blocks of wreckage as he made his way toward his mother's apartment. After the fight he'd had with Kaeli, he didn't have the slightest intention to return to his family anytime soon, but after the earthquake, he felt like he should at least go back to check on his mother. He had first contacted the closest shelters, but they were unable to provide him with any useful information. Paramedic crews littered the walkways, strategically moving debris and occasionally pulling out a victim. There weren't many pedestrians wandering around, but it had been about a day since the earthquake. Most likely the survivors had regrouped at the local relief centers. His eyes darted around the neighborhood, and a growing sense of dread formed in the pit of his stomach.

When he approached the apartment complex, time seemed to stop. If anyone had still been inside during the earthquake, there was no way they could have survived. He froze, every muscle encased in ice. The structure had completely toppled. Chunks of concrete jutted out from piles of wooden beams. A gaping hole cleared the center of the ruins. Maybe one of the paramedic crews had found his mother and rescued her.

"Sir?" A voice sounded from behind him, but Trent refused to acknowledge it. He still couldn't get his muscles to move. "Sir, unless you are a certified medical professional, I'm going to have to ask you to leave."

"Did you find anyone here?" Trent swallowed as his heart pounded against his chest. He clenched his fists till his knuckles turned white. His mom had to be okay. She had to be. The paramedic frowned. His forehead wrinkled

"Are you an occupant at this address?"

"My mom and sister are! Now tell me. *Did you find anyone?"*

"We've found a few bodies." The paramedic cleared his throat. Trent's eyes widened as a fresh wave of ice overtook his senses. He didn't respond to the paramedic. Didn't think he could. The paramedic took a step forward and placed a hand on Trent's shoulder.

"I'm very sorry for your loss, sir," he sighed, "but I'm afraid you're still going to need to exit the disaster zone. It's not safe for you here."

"I'm. Not. Leaving." Trent growled through gritted teeth.

"Then I will be forced to call security so they can escort you away." the paramedic reached for his handheld radio, flickered his gaze toward Trent, then pressed the comm button. The radio barely let out a *blip* before something erupted from the ruins of the building. An ominous shadow loomed over him. Trent slowly turned to face it. His jaw dropped. Standing before him was a larger than life snake made entirely out of shadows and purple lightning. The paramedic dropped his radio and screamed.

"Ssshut up," the snake hissed. The snake shot out at the paramedic—and devoured him whole. The sound of Trent's heartbeat thrashed in his ears. His eyes bulged. Every muscle in his body tensed. The snake turned its attention toward him.

"Sssooo. You're related to the girl."

In an instant, the snake slithered right up to Trent's face.

"Massster will be so pleasssed to sssee you."

Before he could even utter a word, the snake reared its head back and plunged into Trent's chest. A tingling sensation overtook his skin and every muscle that felt like ice now burned with fire. He wanted to open his mouth. To scream. But some force kept him from doing so.

Let'sss goooo.

The voice of the snake echoed in his mind. As if on cue, Trent robotically turned around and walked away from the devastating wreckage that had killed his last surviving parent.

CHAPTER 6

K aeli followed Leo across the bridge back to where they first materialized into the Celestial Realm. She failed to notice before, but on the ground was a series of runes that formed a circle. Leo led her to the center, took her hand, smiled, and muttered some words under his breath. Before she had a chance to process what was happening, the world swirled around her. Her stomach rose to the top of her throat, and just as she thought she might puke, everything righted itself again. Leo held on to her shoulders as she swayed back and forth.

"A little warning before teleporting would be appreciated." Her nose scrunched and a scowl crossed her face.

"Sorry," Leo chuckled. "We use these teleportation portals as our main form of transportation here in the Celestial Realm. I promise after you do it a couple of times, your body adjusts. You'll learn how to use them yourself soon enough."

"I'm not sure I want to." Kaeli shrugged herself away from Leo. Admittedly, the side effects hadn't been as debilitating as the first time. She could already stand upright.

It still looked like they were in the middle of outer space, but they stood on a floating platform covered in runes and grass. Surrounding the platform were four smaller floating islands forming a diamond shape. Each had a singular, unique house at the center. An intricate weave of suspended bridges connected everything together.

The house to their left had a modern, multi-level square structure. What really stood out about it, however, was the opaque glass that constructed every wall and the multiple waterfalls cascading off the edges.

The house to the right was a tall tower made of white-washed stone. The tower incorporated various archways and came to a point at the very top. Green vines and other types of foliage spiraled upwards and curled around the tower.

To the left of the platform was an adobe style home made out of pale colored clay. Various domed parts of the roof peeked out over dense foliage. Colorful mosaic tiles peppered the sloping edges.

The house to the north was circular, shaped like a coliseum. Billowing arches ran the diameter of the building, and each column contained a blazing torch. A series of gargoyles rested on top of spires running along the top of the building. Kaeli turned to look at Leo, her mouth slightly agape. Leo smiled.

"This one is ours." His chest puffed out slightly. "You're going to like it even more on the inside."

They crossed the bridge and approached the building, entering through one of the many archways. Kaeli looked around with wide eyes as she traced the stone columns. It was exactly what she imagined Rome must have looked like in its glory days… with modern updates. As they passed through a particularly large archway, she looked up. Her breath caught in her throat. Concave domes constructed the entire ceiling. At the downward peak of each dome hung a prism lantern, each with a tiny flame on the inside that sent out a kaleidoscope of rainbows.

"This is beautiful," she murmured.

"Yes, it is," Leo chuckled. "It's nice to see someone appreciate it for the first time. After living here for over a millennium, some things start to lose their luster." He cleared his throat and said, "If you want to enter the house, you can pass through any of the archways. There are three entrances. You can just keep walking in a circle until you find one." He walked up to a stone door that had an engraving of a lion with a flame behind it. "Each entrance is inspired by one of us, but you can go through any door you please. They'll just take you to different parts of the house. Only fire signs and fire spirits are allowed in here. You also won't be able to go inside any of the other houses, but that doesn't really matter because this one is the best." He casually held his hand in front of the door, flames flickered between his fingers. He pushed, and the door opened with a grating screech. Kaeli cocked her head to the side.

"Fire spirits?"

"LEO, YOU'RE BACK!" a high-pitched voice squealed, and a dash of red light smacked into Leo, causing him to stumble back a couple of steps. Kaeli yelped as she jumped back.

"Zodiac signs aren't the only inhabitants of the Celestial Realm," Leo grunted. The flash of light dimmed a little and a humanoid shape started to take form. A girl embraced Leo in what looked like a really painful bear hug. Leo cleared his throat and tried to pry the girl off of him. She was having none of it. "Kaeli, this is Liani. Liani is a fire spirit who works as the weapons keeper here at House Ignis. Liani, Kaeli is my new zodiac recruit."

"OH MY GOSH. How rude of me! Hi!" Liani shoved Leo away from her and dashed up to Kaeli, her hand extended. Leo stumbled back a couple of steps. "My name is Liani." A wide grin nearly split her face in two.

"I just said that." Leo smoothed out his now wrinkled clothes. Kaeli knit her eyebrows together as she took Liani's hand.

"Nice to meet you?" Kaeli didn't mean for the words to sound like a question, but she couldn't help the tinge of inflection. Liani was unlike anyone, or anything, she'd ever seen. Although she was humanoid in form, she definitely was not human. Her skin was a vibrant, almost translucent red. Even though she had a firm grip, her fingers seemed to wisp off at the tips. Almost like they faded into smoke. She had playful, sparkling hazel eyes, and wild, curly dark brown hair that floated behind her. She wore gladiator sandals and a pleated tunic that looked like it was straight out of a history textbook. Liani released the handshake and pulled Kaeli into a hug.

"If Leo ever gives ya any trouble, let me know." She pushed away from Kaeli, holding her out at arm's length. "Like he said, I'm the weapons keeper," she said as her voice dropped a notch. "I can show you where to get all the stabby things." She winked. Leo crossed his arms and frowned.

"You know I can hear you right?" he sighed and shook his head. "If you don't mind, Liani, I was giving Kaeli the tour of the place."

"Oh, yes, of course! I didn't mean to interrupt your important, official, zodiac business." She flashed a sassy smile while doing a slight curtsy. "I think I have some more devices designed for torture that need polishing anyway." She turned to Kaeli. "Don't worry! We'll get more chances to talk later!" And with those parting words, Liani skipped down the hallway. Kaeli stared after her with wide eyes. Leo chuckled.

"Liani tends to have that sort of effect on people." He patted Kaeli on the shoulder. "Don't worry, she starts to grow on you after a while. Here, let's go this way!" He swooped his hands toward a corridor to the right of them. "This hallway takes us to where you'll be staying."

The interior of the building would have been dark if it weren't for the excessive number of torches lining the entirety of the walls and lanterns dangling from the ceiling. She tilted her head and stared at the flickering lights, thinking it odd that the fire didn't seem to emit any heat. She stepped closer to one of the torches and waved her hand in front of it. The little flame followed her gesture.

"Why aren't they hot?" She turned away from the torch and jogged a couple of feet to catch up to Leo.

"Magic!" Leo spread his fingers wide and wiggled them in front of his face.

"You've got to be kidding me."

"Well, it's not entirely inaccurate." Leo dropped his hands and cleared his throat. "Most humans would consider it to be magic. Really, it's just how life is here in the Celestial Realm. Fire is our element, so fire can't hurt us. It actually helps us recharge and gain strength which is one of the reasons why it's everywhere in our house. Any of the other signs, or Celestial Spirits from different elements would be a lot more uncomfortable in here." He stopped in front of a large, charcoal black door with an intricate silver handle. "Trainees stay in here." He gripped the handle and turned to look at Kaeli. "This is the only door like this on the first floor, so it should be easy enough to find, but if you ever get lost, just ask one of the spirits and they'll help you find it." He pushed the door open and Kaeli took in a sharp breath when she saw the interior.

It was enormous. At the far end of the room was a fireplace with a flame that blazed taller than her. Much like the torches, however, it didn't give off any heat. The marble hearth was rimmed in gold, reflecting the light of the fire into the rest of the room. Above the fireplace was a large flat screen television. Kaeli's eyebrows squished together and she turned to look back at Leo.

"A TV?" she tilted her head.

"It's good for keeping tabs on what's happening on Earth," Leo grinned. "Difficult to sift through all the biased reporting, but most of the time you can get some accurate idea of current events. Or at least people's perception of them."

Positioned in front of the fireplace were three large, plush red couches situated in a U-shape with a solid gold table in the center. Kaeli's eyes widened as she slowly turned, taking in the whole room. Three doors lined the walls— one with a ram, one with an archer, and one with a lion. When she saw the back wall, her jaw went entirely slack and her shoulders dropped. Everything else faded from her mind as she stared at the spectacle before her. It was floor to ceiling books, enough to fill a small library. Two ladders on either side of the door led to a balcony about three quarters up the ginormous bookshelf. Overstuffed cushions were scattered near the railing.

"Ah, yes, the books." Leo stepped in behind her. "Every trainee room in each house has one of these collections. It contains the history of the Western Celestial Spirits and Zodiacs up to the present day. Don't worry. We don't expect you to read all of them." He clapped his hands and rubbed them together. "This is the common room where you'll be staying with the other two recruits. The door with the lion on it leads to your private quarters."

"I need a minute." Kaeli staggered over to one of the red couches and plopped down onto it. The cushy material pulled her into a big hug. She closed her eyes, letting out a much-needed sigh. This was luxury beyond what she could even imagine, and it was her house. Her head spun. Too much was happening too fast. She cracked one eye open as the cushions shifted. Leo sat down next to her.

"You remind me of when I saw this room for the first time." He propped his feet up on the gold table, slung his arm around the back of the couch, and gazed off in the distance at nothing in particular. Kaeli shifted to an upright seated position.

"It's unreal," she murmured.

"It starts to feel more normal after a while," Leo smiled. "Come on. You'll have plenty of time to rest on this couch later. I want to introduce you to the other fire signs. Sagittarius is out right now, but Aries should be here with her recruit."

Kaeli let out a heavy sigh.

"Okay." She struggled to push herself up off the couch. "Show me what other craziness is going on here."

As they walked through the intricately constructed passages of the house, Leo pointed out all of the rooms that could be of any importance to Kaeli: the kitchen and dining room, the study halls, the gardens, the indoor training rooms. All of the rooms had at least three things in common. They were all decorated with red and gold themes. They all had an abundance of torches and fireplaces, and they were all more luxurious than anything Kaeli could have ever imagined living in on Earth. On the tour, Kaeli met many more fire spirits working in the house, but none were as enthusiastic about seeing Leo as Liani had been. Aries and her recruit, however, were more difficult to track down. After thoroughly checking the rooms, Leo led the way outside to the innermost part of the coliseum.

Kaeli was once again speechless as they exited the indoors and came upon the vast arena nestled at the heart of House Ignis. She had seen some of the strength and conditioning rooms inside of the house, but nothing compared to the training field in front of her. The entire courtyard was filled with military and gladiator grade obstacle courses. Kaeli's eyes widened as she let out a long, low whistle.

"Hmmmm," Leo's arms crossed over his chest as she scanned the arena. "Still no sign of Aries. Oh! But there's someone who would know where she is. Pyronius!" Leo's voice projected out into a roar. Kaeli cringed, covering her ears with her hands, but it was too late. Everything was ringing already. Leo glanced at her and flashed an apologetic smile.

"Sorry. That won't bug you much longer."

"Again, warnings would be nice." She crinkled up her nose.

A figure approached them from one of the arched tunnels. The ringing faded from her ears, and her shoulders tensed as the monster of a spirit came closer. He was *huge,* easily exceeding seven feet in height. His skin was a dark red; his eyes, an earthy brown. He wore black jogger pants and an iron plated leather vest that accentuated his thick muscles and wide chest. When he reached them, he stood in front of Leo, legs spread wide, and crossed his beastly arms over his chest. An involuntary tremble twitched in her hands. Breathing suddenly became a little more difficult. This fire spirit was unlike any she had seen in the house.

"What?" Pyronius growled in a low, throaty voice. Leo didn't even blink twice.

"Have you seen Aries around?" His voice was completely conversational, as if he didn't recognize that this being could probably slap him away like a housefly. "I'm trying to find her and Lukka to introduce them to my recruit, Kaeli." He smacked his forehead. "How rude of me! I didn't even introduce her to you. Pyronius, Kaeli. Kaeli, this is Pyronius. He is a retired former general of the armies in the Celestial Realm. Now he works here as the arena keeper and makes sure we all stay in top fighting condition."

Kaeli had to crane her neck to look up at him.

"Hi," she squeaked. *Get it together, Kaeli! He's going to think you're weak.* The former general regarded her with an arched eyebrow.

"She's rather small."

"Yes, yes, yes." Leo waved. "Now that formalities are out of the way, have you seen Aries and Lukka?" Pyronius opened his mouth and Kaeli covered her ears in anticipation for what would happen next.

"Lukka, get your ass over here!"

Kaeli could have sworn the ground shook just a little. In the distance on the other side of the arena, she saw a figure standing at the top of the zipline course. He turned in their direction and waved before pushing off the zipline platform and coasting to the ground. Pyronius turned to Leo as Lukka jogged over to them.

"Aries is meeting with the other zodiacs at the platform." Pyronius fixed Leo with a hard stare. "As you should be."

"Crap! I forgot," Leo sighed.

"'Sup guys?" Lukka approached the group. He wore workout gear. A thin sheen of sweat glistened on his tan skin, and Kaeli couldn't help but notice the burn scars covering his arms. Shaggy brown curls stuck to his forehead. A big, infectious smile grew on his face as his gaze fell on Kaeli. "Who's the new girl?"

"New girl?" Leo raised an eyebrow. "You've only been here for about three days."

"Still longer than her." Lukka winked and extended a hand. "Name's Lukka, as you probably heard. What's yours?"

"Kaeli." She took his hand in a firm grip and couldn't help but smile back. His dark eyes glittered with magnetic energy.

"Well, glad to see the two of you getting along," Leo cut in as he patted both of them on the back, pushing them slightly closer together. "Pyronius was so kind as to remind me that I have an important meeting to attend, so I'm going to let the two of you get to know each other a little better. Have fun! Don't leave the house." He faced Pyronius and stared at him with a dead set expression. "Make sure they don't leave the house."

Pyronius grunted in response.

"Okay, great!" Leo clapped them both on the back one more time before turning to leave. Kaeli and Lukka watched him disappear in silence. It was only when he was out of sight that they realized they still held hands. They let go simultaneously and took a couple of steps back from each other. Pyronius let out a heavy sigh.

"Former general reduced to babysitter," his deep voice rumbled. He turned to face Lukka and Kaeli, fixing them with a hard stare. "I have better things to do than watch the two of you form new bonds of friendship, but I swear to you, if you leave this house, you will *regret* it. Are we clear?"

"Yes, sir," Lukka and Kaeli said at the same time. The response was almost involuntary, a natural reflex in the presence of this warrior.

"Good," Pyronius huffed, but the slightest hint of a smile formed at the corner of his mouth. He turned his back and stalked back to the underground tunnels. Kaeli let out a breath when she was sure he was out of hearing distance. Maybe one day she would feel more comfortable around him, but she didn't expect that day to come anytime soon.

"This is awesome!" Lukka's words crashed through her thoughts. Kaeli shook her head as she peeled her gaze away from Pyronius to look at Lukka. He grinned. "We have the whole place to ourselves! Well, mostly. There's the spirits, but I've found they mostly leave you alone unless you talk to them first."

"You probably didn't meet Liani then," Kaeli snorted. Lukka cocked his head to the side.

"Can't say that I have." He stuck his hands in his pockets, and his shoulders relaxed as his gaze settled in on Kaeli. "So, how did you end up in the Celestial Realm? You're the first human I've seen since I got here."

The smile on Kaeli's face fell as she thought back to the earthquake. A heaviness settled into her chest and an icy chill shot through her bones. She wrapped her arms around herself and her lower lip quivered as her imagination replayed images of the terrifying snake. And her mom... if she had somehow survived the collapse of the building... there's no way that snake would have let her live. A light touch fell on her shoulder. She blinked her eyes rapidly, bringing herself back into the present moment. Lukka stood close to her, eyebrows knitted together in concern.

"Whatever happened, I'm sorry. I should have realized that could've been a loaded question. You don't have to talk about it. I normally don't make a habit of talking about my past either."

Kaeli nodded her head, reassuring herself that everything would be okay, that she could keep it together, as she let out a shaky exhale.

"Where are you from?" she asked in an attempt to sound like she could actually be a friendly person. Lukka removed his hand from her shoulder and offered a small smile.

"California. LA area. What about you?"

"Me too!" Kaeli's hands fell to her sides. Her eyebrows shot up. "Wait… Leo said you'd only been here for about three days. Three days ago was around the first time I saw him and… there was a woman with him."

Lukka tilted his head back, his eyes squinting a little.

"Did she happen to have wild red brown hair and a ridiculous self-possessed air about her?"

"I mean, I don't know about ridiculous, but she seemed pretty confident…"

"That was definitely Aries," Lukka nodded with finality. "That's crazy! They probably found me the same day they met you!" He shoved his hands in his pockets and looked around the arena. "So, Leo and Pyronius just dumped us here with nothing to do… We should explore the house!"

"Leo just finished showing me the house while we were looking for you and Aries." Kaeli narrowed her eyes, not sure what Lukka was trying to get at.

"Yeah, but he showed you what *he* wanted you to see, not the stuff that's actually interesting." The roguish smile returned to his face. "There's this weird room I found earlier. Follow me, I'll show it to you!" Before Kaeli could even agree to his proposition, he trotted off toward the tunnels leading to the house. Not wanting to be left alone amidst the training equipment and obstacle courses, Kaeli followed. She had to admit, even though Lukka seemed a little enthusiastic, his energy was definitely contagious.

CHAPTER 7

L ukka led the way through the tunnels, but as they neared the stairs that
would take them back to the upper levels, he veered off to a small stone
archway hiding in the shadows. Without the residual light from the torches
illuminating the main stairway, Kaeli would never have seen it.

"You must've been really bored if you resorted to looking for secret
passageways for entertainment." Kaeli hesitated at the entrance. Her eyes
followed the curve of the smooth stone arch. A soft breeze wafted toward
her, blowing her hair slightly away from her face. The darkness in the tunnel
swallowed his figure. Kaeli jogged a couple of steps to catch up.

"I didn't start doing this for fun," Lukka's voice echoed off the
walls. The hairs on Kaeli's arms stood on end as the air became increasingly
drafty. Kaeli tucked her face into her elbow in an attempt to block out the
heavy smell of must. Lukka lifted up a hand and flicked his wrist. A small
ball of fire danced in his palm, illuminating his face just enough for Kaeli to
see his cocky smile.

"I heard some spooky voice coming from these tunnels," he said. Kaeli struggled to keep up with his brisk pace. "Aries didn't show me anything down here, but no one said I couldn't check it out."

"Because the first thing you should do when you hear spooky voices is go running after them." Kaeli rolled her eyes. Lukka chuckled.

"They were annoying me. I wanted to make them shut up." He shrugged as if this was a completely normal, everyday experience. He came to a sudden halt, and Kaeli almost smacked into his back. Lukka tilted his head, listening for something. "I think this is it." He lowered his voice.

Kaeli shifted from side to side as she looked around for anything that would mark this location as something other than a dark tunnel. A chill shot down her spine as she realized she just followed a relative stranger, who apparently heard voices, into an isolated area. She slowly started to back away from Lukka as he touched the wall with his non-burning hand. She was just about to turn and run when his enthusiastic voice stopped her.

"Found it!" Lukka pressed against a stone in the wall.

Kaeli's eyes widened as a large section of solid stone paneling screeched. It groaned as it disappeared, revealing a hallway that stretched out into infinity. Shadows swirled through the air, and a blast of wind blew her hair away from her face, forcing her to squint. Lukka stepped through the newly formed entrance with no hesitation whatsoever.

"I know it looks freaky, but trust me, it's worth it."

Even though Kaeli could still see Lukka's silhouette, his voice echoed as if in a distant canyon. Against her better judgement, she placed one foot into the hallway. Something about the shadows called to her, like a tug in the back of her mind beckoning her to the beyond.

As she crossed through the entrance, the shadows embraced her and shot a clammy tremor through her bones. Her pulse raced as her vision turned to black. She was caught in a void with no sense of direction.

"Give it a minute!" Lukka sounded like he was nearby. She latched onto those words as an anchor and forced herself to pace her breathing. As her heart rate steadied, her eyes adjusted to the darkness. Lukka's body took shape. He'd been standing right in front of her this whole time.

"What is this place?" her voice, though steady, was barely louder than a whisper. Lukka's white teeth shone against the darkness as he chuckled.

"Just keep waiting. I swear it gets better."

Kaeli didn't have to wait for long before she understood what Lukka was talking about. The heavy shadows shifted around her. The mysterious, pitch black hallway gradually melted into a dark navy blue. She reached out to touch where the wall should have been, but her hand swiped through empty air. Silver pinpoints dotted the navy void, and, as she continued to stare, she saw they formed constellations. Kaeli felt like she stood in the middle of the night sky. All of the panic she felt moments ago morphed into disbelief. Her head spun as she tried to reorient her sense of direction, but it was no use. The stars grew brighter and some semblance of a floor started to take shape. Kaeli sank to her knees to keep herself from falling. Streaks of purple and blue haze wafted through the mass of navy. Her jaw slackened.

"Wow."

"Right?!" Lukka stood with his legs spread wide and fists propped on his hips, looking like a conqueror surveying his new land. "But this isn't even the really cool part. Look over there." He moved next to Kaeli and pointed off into the distance. Kaeli pushed herself to her feet. Her eyes widened. She walked past Lukka and blinked a couple times to clear her vision. The hallway expanded into a circular dead end. At the very center of the circle was a double door made out of the same smooth, black stone as the hallway walls, draped in rusted iron chains. A snake was carved into the stone where the two doors met, and the longer Kaeli stared at it, the more it looked like it actually slithered between the doors. Or maybe it was trying to break free from the chains. Her breath caught for a flicker of a second. For a brief moment, she swore the snake's eyes flashed with a purple light. She whirled around to face Lukka.

"We need to get out of here." She tried to keep her heart from racing, but her voice betrayed her with a tremor. Images of the snake erupting from the ruins of her house flashed through her mind. She let out a shaky breath. "Whatever those voices were... I don't want any part of it."

"Maybe you're right." Lukka's cocky grin fell from his face, and Kaeli wondered what sort of experience he'd been through to wipe that seemingly permanent smile from his lips, and why it happened so suddenly. His eyes darted between Kaeli and the door as he shifted uncomfortably.

"I'm definitely right." She stared Lukka straight in the eyes and grabbed his wrist. "We're leaving." She walked briskly back the way they had come, Lukka following not far behind. Just as they reached the entrance that would lead them out of the dark hallway, however, a soft murmur drifted toward them.

Open the dooor. Set me freeee.

Barely louder than a whisper, it made every hair on Kaeli's body prickle in fear. She and Lukka froze in their tracks. Kaeli side-eyed Lukka.

"Please tell me I'm not the only one who heard that?" her voice wavered, and she tried to gulp down the nervousness riding up her throat. Lukka's hand twitched.

"No, you're not. But I kind of wish you were."

Open the door, the voice hissed.

"Okay, we need to leave now." She tugged at Lukka's wrist again, but his feet remained rooted to the floor. She turned to face him and her mouth dropped open as Lukka slowly turned toward the door.

"What the hell are you doing?! We need to get out of here!" she whispered through gritted teeth. She tried to tug Lukka to the exit, but he was an immovable rock. "Why. Won't. You. Move?" she grunted.

She turned to see what could have possibly rendered Lukka immobile. That was a mistake. The chains on the door began to rattle as loud thumps boomed through the air, as if someone pounded on the other side.

LET ME OUT.

Kaeli knew then why Lukka wouldn't move. Her own feet were firmly planted on the ground, refusing her internal commands to turn in the opposite direction and run for her life. Her stomach flipped in somersaults as she had no choice but to stare at the door. Purple lightning illuminated the snake's eyes. She wanted to cry out in frustration, but even her voice refused to obey her.

Come to me.

The voice was softer now, almost enticing, and to her dismay, Kaeli's body heeded the command. Lukka's did too. Step by step, they approached the door. The light from the snake's eyes grew brighter as the same purple light started to glow between the crack in the middle of the two doors. Every muscle in Kaeli's body trembled. The sound of her heartbeat thrashed in her ears. She inwardly pleaded for her legs to stop walking, but still she advanced forward, step by agonizing step. She and Lukka were within inches of the door now.

Just a little closer.

The whisper almost seemed to caress her cheek. Kaeli shuddered. As the traces of the whisper dissipated, a wave of dark shadow blasted from the door, knocking Lukka flat on his back. Kaeli regained control over her arms and threw her hands up to protect her face, her fists instinctually igniting in a fiery blaze. The shadow settled over her and, swirling around her body, intertwined with the flames dancing around her hands. Kaeli's brief moment of control slipped away as the shadow tugged her closer toward the door. The tips of her fingers only grazed the surface of the smooth, cold stone when the shadow pulsed, sending a searing pain shooting toward the base of her neck. Kaeli shrieked as her body twitched in response, unable to pull away.

"What the *hell* is going on!" A sharp female voice snapped through the darkness. A wave of dizziness washed over Kaeli. The shadow froze and then flew back through the cracks of the door, as if it had never existed. Kaeli choked out a breath, her throat raw with pain. Her fire extinguished and the invisible grip on her muscles disappeared. Lukka groaned as he slowly pushed himself to his feet. Together, they watched wide-eyed and stunned as the door faded away into nothing, leaving them standing alone in the middle of the starry void. Lukka glanced at Kaeli.

"That was Aries. We need to get out of here ASAP."

Kaeli nodded in agreement, and they sprinted out the way they came.

As soon as they stepped foot out of the secret panel wall, they ran straight into Leo and the woman who'd been with him at the coffee shop.

"Dammit," Lukka whispered.

"What the hell were you two doing?" Aries's eyes narrowed into a death glare as her lips pursed into a tight thin line. When neither Kaeli nor Lukka offered up an immediate answer, Aries fixed her dagger gaze solely on Lukka. Kaeli let out the tiniest sigh of relief. "I'm only going to ask this one more time. What. Were. You. Doing?"

Lukka took in a deep breath before answering. His expression hardened. He looked like he was about to step onto a battlefield.

"I was showing Kaeli around the house. I found a secret tunnel here." He pointed to the entrance they were now standing just outside of. He looked over his shoulder, back to where the door had been. His eyebrows knitted together as his hand fell limp by his side. "There was a door in there with... snakes. But it disappeared."

Aries eyes widened. Leo pushed past her to get a look inside of the room.

"What did the door look like?" he asked.

"Kind of ancient with a bunch of chains, and snakes that seemed to... move." Kaeli's voice cracked as she whispered out the answer. "There were shadows that were trying to... get us to open the door. But they ran away as soon as we heard Aries."

Leo paused and slowly turned to look at Aries. The two shared a look before Aries rounded on Lukka again.

"What did I tell you about roaming around this place?" she asked through gritted teeth. Lukka visibly suppressed a sarcastic huff.

"That it's unpredictable, and some things are dangerous, and I really shouldn't go to areas you haven't shown me yet." He crossed his arms and titled his head to the side. Kaeli got the feeling Aries and Lukka had been over this conversation before.

"Then *why* would you go looking for mysterious secret rooms?!" Aries's hands and arms began to sizzle with heat. An uneasy knot formed in the pit of Kaeli's stomach, and she took a step back from Lukka. Leo had said that fire couldn't hurt them here, but the look on Aries's face suggested otherwise.

"Well, what do you expect me to do?" Lukka's eyes narrowed, and he clenched his hands into tight fists. Kaeli raised her eyebrows, her gaze darting between Lukka and Aries. A heated argument was definitely not the way she would have chosen for this conversation to go. "I'm either in my room, or you make me stay in the arena most of the time with that Pyronius dude for training! Training gets boring! I'm not going to stay out in the courses all day while you're off doing... whatever it is you do!"

Aries was about to open her mouth to retort, but Leo coughed. Loudly. She spun to face him.

"What?!"

"Calm down. You're overreacting."

"How can you say that?! You sensed that dark presence just the same as I did. They could have seriously gotten hurt! Kaeli just got here. Lukka's only been for a couple of days, and already Ophiu—"

Leo coughed again. Aries glared at him but didn't say anything else. She closed her eyes and took a couple of deep breaths before her sizzle faded. When she opened her eyes, she still looked pissed, but not like she was about to murder someone.

"You can bet we'll be talking about this later." Her words were in response to Leo, but directed at Lukka. She paused, peering into the room before shaking her head. "Let's get the two of you back to the main part of the house."

When they wove their way back to the main arena, Pyronius stood nonchalantly, leaning against the base of the staircase. His arms crossed over his massive chest.

"There you are," his deep voice rumbled through the tunnel. "Sagittarius finally arrived with his recruit. They're waiting for you at the northern entrance." Before anyone could respond, the hulking spirit pushed off of the pillar and stalked away. Leo let out a sigh as he fixed Lukka and Kaeli with a concerned gaze.

"Are the two of you okay?"

"More or less," Lukka said. Kaeli nodded. She didn't feel okay, but she would gladly welcome any distraction that would get her out of this hallway.

"Good." Leo flashed a small smile. "On our way out, Liani told us Sagittarius found his recruit. We decided to introduce you guys before our meeting. It's time for you two to meet your third teammate."

✱ ✱ ✱

Leo and Aries led the way into what turned out to be a long and painfully silent walk. Lukka attempted to make small talk, but Aries shot him a look so sharp, Kaeli could practically feel the daggers. Neither of them had said anything since, leaving Kaeli to mull over the recent events. The farther away they walked from the mysterious tunnel, the more her muscles relaxed and her breath evened out, but her mind wouldn't stop replaying the moment the shadow forced her to use her fire, or the electric purple eyes of the snake.

A shudder ran through her shoulders as the memory of the snake's eyes burned into her skull. She felt like it was watching her, studying her movement. A small pain itched at the back of her neck when she suddenly smacked into Leo. All thoughts of the snake disappeared as he turned around and offered a reassuring grin. She rubbed her nose to soothe the ache.

"Welcome to the northern entrance!" He spread his arms as if he revealed something majestic. Really, this door looked almost identical to the one he'd first taken her through, except that a centaur shooting an arrow off into the sky was engraved into the stone instead of a lion. His smile fell a little. "Are you sure you're okay?"

Kaeli opened her mouth to answer, but she was interrupted by the doors creaking open. Two figures stood at the entrance, but the light made them look like nothing more than silhouettes. It wasn't until the doors shut that Kaeli could make out the details. The taller one, whom she guessed was Sagittarius, was bigger in build than Leo and had dark, tanned skin. His black hair was pulled back and fell just below his shoulders. If he took off his shirt and sat on a horse, he would be the quintessential image of a romance cover novel. The guy standing next to him was taller than average, but not too muscular. His thick, dirty blonde hair was styled into an edgy faux hawk with a design stenciled into the left side of his shaved head. He wore a partially button downed v-neck shirt with an unzipped high collar jacket.

"Hey, guys!" he said before anyone could introduce him. "Name's Joseph." He extended a hand.

"Lukka," Lukka nodded as he stepped forward and firmly took Joseph's hand. Kaeli noticed both of them tighten their grip more than was necessary. She rolled her eyes.

"I'm Kaeli," she said, giving a little wave with her hand, but not stepping into the handshake war. Neither of the boys seemed like they wanted to let go first.

"Nice to meet you, Kaeli," Joseph smiled. Kaeli smiled back. Lukka glared at Joseph and yanked his hand away. Sagittarius stepped past Joseph, tilting his head in greeting.

"As you've probably figured by now, I'm Sagittarius." His voice was deep and smooth like velvet. "It's an honor to meet two humans so willing to sacrifice their lives for the sake of the world."

"Wait… *what?*" Lukka spun to face Aries. "What does he mean '*sacrifice our lives?*'"

Kaeli cast a sidelong glance at Leo, who seemed to be actively avoiding eye contact with her. "I thought the whole point of you bringing me here was because I 'wouldn't be safe' on earth."

Sagittarius looked between Aries and Leo, his face scrunched in a stern expression. "The two of you didn't fully brief your recruits before bringing them here?"

Leo and Aries fidgeted in an almost nervous manner. The reaction looked unnatural.

"There was, uh, an… emergency situation that came up. Couldn't really just leave them on Earth without some disastrous repercussions." Aries let out a little cough. Sagittarius raised a skeptical eyebrow and crossed his arms.

"Still, you should have at least warned them of the dangers before dragging them here completely clueless."

"Again… *what dangers?*" Lukka flashed Aries a murderous stare. "I get why you brought me here initially, but I've been here for three fucking days, and you didn't think it was a good idea to bring any of this up?!"

Seconds went by without a reply before Sagittarius sighed and shook his head.

"Cowards. Spineless cowards. Unable to even own up to your own wrongdoings," he muttered. He cleared his throat and focused his attention on Lukka and Kaeli. "Since your mentors have failed to properly inform you of what's to come, I suppose the task falls on my shoulders," he sighed. "As you've witnessed on Earth, things are an absolute wreck. Unexplained fires, earthquakes, hurricanes. We are the ones charged with keeping all of that in balance. Our job has become increasingly difficult as of late due to the…

emergence... of an old enemy. It's disrupting the natural order of things." He glanced at Leo and Aries before returning his focus back to Lukka and Kaeli.

"There is a good chance all of us will not make it through the coming battle. We need to ensure the universe will not fall apart should that happen."

Kaeli turned to Leo. Familiar warmth tingled in her gut but suppressed the rising flame that itched to be set free. "I mean, I know my odds weren't looking good on Earth, but this doesn't exactly sound any safer. When were you going to tell me all of this?"

"I was... hoping it would just sort of come up naturally... before tonight when we have our official orientation feast." Leo cleared his throat and tugged at his shirt sleeves.

Kaeli pursed her lips and could almost swear she blew steam out of her nose. She looked at Lukka who faced Joseph, still standing serenely near the entrance with his hands tucked into his pant pockets.

"So, Sagittarius told you all this, and you still agreed?" The murderous fire in his eyes had dissipated to a slight ember.

"Yeah," Joseph shrugged his shoulders. "I mean, it's dangerous, but the consequences if we don't succeed are worse. There aren't a lot of mortals that have everything needed to become a zodiac. We do. Not to mention we're doing this to help save the world." A small smirk played onto the corner of his lips. "This is pretty much our chance to be superheroes."

"Superheroes..." Lukka's voice was so soft, Kaeli wasn't sure if anyone was supposed to hear it. "Lukka... Defender of the World. Yeah, that has a nice ring to it. Alright!" His voice returned to its overbearing volume. "I'm in!"

"Not like you really had a choice, kid," Aries coughed. Sagittarius flashed her a condescending stare. She countered with a terrifying grin. Kaeli crossed her arms and ground her teeth together as she glared at Leo. The urge to burst into flame had died down but heat still flushed through her body. Leo's arms hung limp at his sides as he peered at Kaeli.

"I'm sorry," his voice cracked just slightly. "That snake would really have come back to kill you, and I needed a recruit… I didn't know what else to do."

Kaeli opened her mouth to retort, but instead let out a tense sigh. She shook her head as she turned away from Leo. She just needed a minute to process. An image of her mother flashed through her mind. Tightness gripped her heart, but she stuffed down the rising grief. She couldn't deal with this now. At the apartment, she had incinerated a huge snake creature. If her being an elemental wasn't enough to worry about, the fact that a giant shadow snake would have been following her was more than enough to ensure that nowhere she went would actually be safe. She supposed Leo really hadn't had much of a choice.

"I guess what's done is done." She let out a heavy exhale and let her arms fall to her sides unhooked her arms. "What was that about an orientation feast?"

Leo's expression instantly brightened. "Joseph was the last recruit we needed to bring to the Celestial Realm. Now that you're all here, we planned to have a feast tonight so everyone can meet each other. Official training will start tomorrow."

"Official training?" Lukka whirled on Aries again. "So these last three days you've been having me train for no reason?"

Aries shrugged. "Never too early to get a head start." She grinned and slapped her recruit on the back. "But I'll give you the rest of the day off.

Let's get the three of you to your rooms so you can relax for a bit and get ready. This thing is fancy." She walked past Lukka and strutted down the hall.

Lukka narrowed his eyes and sidled up next to Kaeli as they followed the zodiacs down the hall. "I don't know if I trust this. She hasn't told me to relax since I got here."

"I guess we'll find out soon enough," Kaeli said.

CHAPTER 8

After leaving the recruits safely in their rooms to get ready for the upcoming feast, Leo, Aries, and Sagittarius left House Ignis and walked toward the portal circle that would take them to the zodiac meeting platform. Leo refused to look at Sagittarius as the three walked on in silence. The look of betrayal on Kaeli's face kept running through his mind. He hadn't meant for any of these events to play out the way they had, but really, he didn't know what he could have done differently. After she had incinerated the snake, there would have been no safe place for Kaeli on Earth. She didn't have any idea how to control this fire and would have been considered a menace to society just like all the other elementals, especially since her abilities fully awoke during a natural disaster. Bringing her to the Celestial Realm was the best thing he could have done for her given the circumstances… and coincidently the most convenient thing that could have happened. But still. He couldn't shake the nagging guilt that itched at his soul every time he remembered the look in her eyes.

"I can't believe you failed to inform your recruits about any of this before bringing them to the Celestial Realm," Sagittarius said with a slight growl in his voice. Leo let out a small sigh. They had almost made it to the portal without having this conversation.

"It's not like it was our fault," Aries spat. "We didn't have a choice. The snakes attacked both of them on Earth. And then Lukka found that stars-damned door, and Kaeli..." Her voice cut off as they reached the circle. Leo flashed her a silencing glare as they stepped into it. Sagittarius muttered their location. When they reappeared at the base of the bridge leading to the platform, Sagittarius spun to face them.

"You mean to say that Ophiuchus has already gained enough power to send the snakes to Earth?"

"It would appear so." Leo ran a hand through his hair and scratched the back of his neck. "Not at full strength, but enough to do damage. But that's why we're having this meeting. To figure out what we can do about it."

"And Lukka found the entrance to the door?" Sagittarius asked.

Aries bit her lip and nodded. "The strongholds around Ophiuchus' prison in the Dream Realm have weakened to the point where they can physically influence the Celestial Realm." She turned to Leo. "Kaeli and Lukka could have *died*. We'll need to stay extra vigilant about this."

The three walked across the rest of the rainbow bridge in silence. About half of the zodiacs were already on the platform, each standing on their symbol around the perimeter of the circle. Leo broke away from the trio to take his place in between Cancer and Virgo. As he approached, Virgo held out a hand. Leo grasped it and the two clapped each other on the back.

"Haven't seen you around in a while," Virgo said. Compared to the other zodiacs, Virgo was small, although compared to regular humans, he would be around average height and build. He was, however, meticulously put together, from his perfectly ironed button-down shirt and pleated pants, to the subtle wave in his dark hair.

"Been a little busy on Earth lately." Leo grinned as he turned to Cancer and ducked his head in greeting. Cancer nodded back. Leo tried not to make direct eye contact with the burly zodiac. They got along pretty well, considering they were elemental opposites, but Cancer's large sea-foam green eyes really unnerved him— not that he would ever admit that to anyone. The color was just too pastel in contrast to his vibrant orange hair and beard to be considered natural by any standards. The guy was super nice, but he just looked… off.

Leo cleared his throat and moved to stand on his symbol. In the distance, he could see Taurus and Pisces making their way over the bridge. Taurus was tall, slender, and had a straight blonde bob that bounced around her face as she walked. Pisces was much shorter and had pin straight, jet black hair that fell to her lower back. Although the two looked like polar opposites standing next to each other, they spent a lot of time together.

"Figures Taurus would be the last one here," Virgo muttered as she shook her head. Taurus and Pisces walked to their symbols on the platform.

"Alright, everyone, listen up! We've got some serious shit to talk about." Aries's voice cut through the idle chatter. Everyone fell silent. A few of the zodiacs shot her an unappreciative glare.

"Right," Leo spoke up. "We all know the elements on Earth have been getting a little… unruly, as of late, and that Ophiuchus is getting stronger."

"Allegedly," Scorpio said. His arms were crossed over his chest.

"It's not allegedly anymore," Aries said. "We've got proof now. Leo and I both had to fight one of those snakes while we were picking up my recruit. Capricorn was there too."

All of the attention shifted to Capricorn who stood stoically in his spot. It was impossible to read his expression.

"It's true." His voice was heavy, but conveyed neither boredom nor urgency.

"I had a second encounter with a snake on Earth as well," Leo said. "Right before I brought Kaeli here. It mentioned something about needing to gather recruits for Ophiuchus. If Ophiuchus is strong enough to send the snakes to Earth on a regular basis, we're going to have a lot more to worry about than just the elements going haywire."

"So, what are we going to do about it?" Virgo asked. "We obviously can't allow this to continue happening."

"We may need to start interacting more directly with Earth," Libra said. "For instance, maybe someone," her eyes darted toward Aries, "could be in California, putting out wildfires instead of playing with *her* or his recruit here." Aries opened her mouth to retort, but Sagittarius interrupted.

"While I was retrieving Joseph, I was able to subdue one of the major fires. Unfortunately, I was unable to extinguish the entire inferno because such a feat would arouse suspicion, but it is manageable now, and the human firefighters should be able to handle remaining embers." He looked pointedly at Libra. Aries stuck out her tongue. Libra's lip curled back in distaste.

"So we all agree we need to be more directly involved in handling the events on Earth," Virgo said. "That still leaves us to decide what we're going to do about the snakes and Ophiuchus gaining power."

"I'm afraid we have more bad news regarding Ophiuchus," Leo cleared his throat. Every eye shot toward him. Leo inhaled deeply and kept his voice steady as he said, "The strongholds around the prison in the Dream Realm have weakened considerably. Ophiuchus can now physically influence the Celestial Realm. Lukka was exploring House Ignis, and apparently there were voices leading him and Kaeli to one of the hidden passage portals that go to the library catacombs... where the door to the Dream Realm is located."

"You mean Ophiuchus is now strong enough to directly send messages from the Dream Realm prison?" Capricorn arched an eyebrow.

"How were you careless enough to let them just 'stumble' into the catacombs?!" Libra lashed out. "Lukka's only been here for a couple of days. Kaeli has only been here for a couple of hours! Did it not occur to you that maybe they need a little more supervision before pursuing all the ins and outs of the Celestial Realm on their own?"

"I told Pyronius to watch them." Leo narrowed his eyes.

"Reeeelax." Aries rolled her eyes and propped a fist on her hip. "We got there in time before anything really bad happened. I mean—did they look brainwashed? Sure. Could they have potentially died? Absolutely. But at the end of the day, they're okay, and now we know how strong Ophiuchus is getting. We'll definitely be keeping a closer eye on them from now on."

"I hope so," Scorpio sneered. "It would've been tragic if they had died and you needed to start your recruit process all over again."

"Give it a rest," Leo bit back. "We know what we're doing. Your personal jabs aren't going to help the situation."

"Personal jabs?" Scorpio raised his eyebrows in mock concern. "We're talking about the fate of the world here, and you think I'm trying to make personal jabs at your house? Typical lion. Making this all about you."

"Okay, that's enough," Libra interjected. "It sounds like, at this moment, there's nothing more we can do about Ophiuchus until we get more information. For now, we need to continue monitoring the situation on Earth, train our recruits to the best of our ability, and have the Celestial Guard look into securing potential breach points from the Dream Realm. Are we in agreement?" There were a few nodding heads and murmurs of consensus. "Good," Libra sighed. "Then this meeting is officially adjourned."

Leo locked eyes with Scorpio as the rest of the zodiacs left the platform. Fire burned inside of him as Scorpio let out half a chuckle and sauntered across the platform in his direction. Leo crossed his arms over his chest and cocked his head back ever so slightly.

"What do you want?"

"Just wanted to see how Kaeli is really doing. Coming to the Celestial Realm for the first time is enough shock as it is. Experiencing *that* within the first few hours of arrival." The tiniest hint of a grin crossed his face as he shook his head. "I can't imagine."

Leo allowed a small flicker of fire to flash through his eyes.

"I don't know what your game is here," he growled in a low voice, "but I don't trust you. Some of the signs haven't been around for as long as we have, but I still remember those first few months after we locked Ophiuchus away. How the scorpio before you ended up *dying...*" He let his voice trail off at the insinuation. The smile on Scorpio's face fell to a scowl as something dark flashed through his eyes.

"You should keep a better eye on your recruit," his lip curled back, "She seems nice. Wouldn't want anything terrible to happen to her." He turned before Leo had a chance to retort. Leo bit his lip as Scorpio stalked away. He clenched his hands into tight fists as he reined in the urge to tackle the insufferable scorpion off the platform. A light touch on his shoulder snapped him back to reality as he turned to see Aries standing next to him.

"We should get back to the house. The spirits will be coming to set this up for the feast soon." She turned her head to look at Scorpio. "Don't let that asshole get in your head. You're better than that." She looked back up to Leo a wicked grin forming on her face. "But if it would make you feel better, I could catch him off guard sometime and cut off his—"

"No need!" Leo interjected, but he couldn't stop the small chuckle that bubbled up. "Whatever he's up to, we can deal with it."

"If you say so," Aries shrugged, "but if you want me to execute plan A, say the word." She winked and then walked away. Leo shook his head, but the smile remained on his face as he followed after her.

✶✶✶

Trent couldn't scream. Couldn't even blink as the terrifying snake that had taken over his body forced him to walk—more like glide—to some secluded ruins and then just... whooshed... into this dark void filled with nothing but mountains and shadows and barren trees. *Wrong. Wrong. Wrong.* The words pounded through his head. His muscles shrieked at him to fight, to run, to do *anything* besides advance into the shadows, but he couldn't stop as he continued to drift through the darkness.

A sharp chill raised the hair on his arms as he entered a mountain pass. The craggy rocks reached toward the sky, making him feel like he was stuck in a fishbowl. The air smelled stale, and stuck in the back of his throat, making him feel like he needed to throw up. As he moved through the pass, a green fog settled in, faint at first, but soon it became so thick Trent couldn't see more than a foot ahead. His blood thrashed through his veins, every instinct begging him to get the hell away from wherever this was.

Patienccce, the snake's voice hissed in his mind. *We're almost home.*

Trent's eyes tried to widen as a black stone castle cut through the sickly fog. Jagged peaks likely helped blend the castle into the mountain from above, but up close, it was an ominous, gothic horror show. Trent internally cringed as the snake led him right to the front door, forced his hand to grasp the handle, and opened it.

As he walked through the entrance, each footstep echoed across the black marble floor. The entryway was barren save for a roaring fireplace that burned with a blue flame to his right, and a broad staircase that led into an unknown darkness in front of him.

Now we wait. The snake's words bounced through his skull. Trent stood, rooted in place, wishing more than anything that he could turn tail and run. A clicking sound echoed from the top of the staircase as the shadows started to shift. Trent's muscles trembled and a fresh wave of nausea washed over him. The noise stopped and time stood still.

"I wasn't expecting any visitors today." It was a woman's voice. Low, silky, and feminine, it seemed at odds with the harsh features of the castle. Trent's nausea subsided. The women chuckled. "Come, Egkhelus, let the poor boy go. He looks absolutely petrified."

Trent stumbled backwards as a force rushed through him. He clutched his stomach as he gasped for breath, his lungs suddenly desperate to breathe their own air. He blinked as he watched the shadow snake slither toward the mysterious woman, and his mouth fell open as he realized a brood of shadowy snakes surrounded her.

"I apologize about Egkhelus," the woman spoke again. "He's not one for manners... although I suppose most snakes really aren't. But back to the situation at hand: Why are you here? What brings you to the Dream Realm?"

"I... I don't want to be here." Trent choked out the words. His legs trembled, and he fell to his knees as a pain gripped his lungs. "I just want to go... home..."

"Oh, don't be silly," the woman laughed. "There must be some reason why you wanted to come, or else Egkhelus wouldn't have been able to bring you here. Now let's see...." The snakes shifted as the woman stepped forward. Trent forgot the pain in his chest as the most beautiful woman he'd ever laid eyes on sauntered down the staircase, the snakes following after her. Elegant purple robes billowed behind her as she walked, and her dark brown hair cascaded down in waves. Her vibrant purple eyes assessed him with amusement as if he was a new toy. She approached him and took his face in her hands. Her touch was cold and smooth. Trent closed his eyes, wanting to lean into the feeling. She tilted his chin upwards.

"What haunts you so that you would go seeking out my lair?" she whispered. He opened his eyes. And screamed. A burning fire torched through every organ in his body, and dark spidery fingers moved through his brain, picking through his memories. He saw the ruins of his house. He saw his mother sick in bed. He saw his father, burning in the car accident, and then he saw Kaeli. His lips curled back into a snarl. It didn't matter that she stood there crying and confused in his memory of the car accident that killed his father. What mattered was the fire dancing in her hands. The fire that destroyed the car. *Her* fire that had ruined his life.

The woman's laughter echoed through his ears and reverberated until it was all he could hear. The spidery fingers retracted, the fire subsided, and

Trent found himself on all fours, gasping for air once again. He looked up at the woman. Every muscle in his body trembled with fear... and rage.

"What did you do," he spat. The woman smiled at him. Not a mocking smile, but one filled with kindness and sympathy.

"I found out why you came to me." She smoothed his hair back. He flinched at her touch. "Your sister... You want revenge. But you're afraid of her fire. Afraid that she is too powerful for you. That's why you've spent your life trying to beat her down." The woman knelt so she was eye level with Trent and took both of his hands into hers. "I can make you strong. That's why you are here. But I can only give you this strength if you willingly agree to own it. The power I can give you is not an easy one to bear." Trent squeezed his eyes shut and tried to steady his breathing. Tried to think of anything besides Kaeli standing over their dead father, or Kaeli destroying their childhood home, or anything besides Kaeli at all. But he couldn't. Red spots flecked his vision, and he knew, more than anything else in the world, he wanted her to pay for what she had done to him.

"Make me strong," he growled.

"I was hoping you'd say that." The woman smiled as she helped Trent stand to his feet. "My name is Elethia by the way." She took his hand and led him up the staircase into the shadows.

CHAPTER 9

K aeli sighed in pure bliss as she stepped out of the steamy shower. She wrapped the softest towel to ever grace her skin around her torso, and tendrils of evaporating water curled around her feet. The bathroom and walk-in closet in her new living space were by far the most luxurious she'd ever seen. She felt like she was walking through a model bathroom from a luxury home magazine as she crossed over the cool tile floor and into the closet. She let the towel fall carelessly around her ankles as she perused the selection of clothes. There were way too many, mostly in shades of red, orange, and gold, with a few blue accent pieces.

"What am I supposed to wear?"

As if to answer the question, the closet came alive. Racks of hanging clothes started spinning, sorting through the different outfits. Kaeli took a couple of steps back, debating whether or not she should run in a panic, or see what the closet had in store. Just as she had nearly exited the closet, it presented two outfits for her. The first was a red, floor length dress with a slit on the left side that came up mid-thigh and spaghetti straps with a sweetheart neckline. It was paired with a belt made out of gold rings, a thin gold necklace, and strappy gold high heels. The second outfit was a deep orange high-waisted skirt and crop top combo. The skirt was also floor length, but it had a slit on each side. The top was cut straight across the neckline, and the sleeves were designed so they only covered the sides of the shoulder. A turquoise choker with a gold lion pendant hanging from it and gold heels with interlacing turquoise straps paired with the outfit.

"I guess this is a formal event," Kaeli said to herself. She looked between the two outfits, unsure of which one to pick. Finally, she decided on the second. The first was a classic, but she didn't feel like cosplaying as Jessica Rabbit at the moment. She dried her hair and worked to put it in a long, stylized braid that fell just below the middle of her back. Wispy layers fell in front of her face, lightly framing her chin. She slipped into the outfit and raised her eyebrows as she caught a glimpse of herself in the ornately decorated floor length mirror. It fit perfectly, hugging and flowing with her curves in all the right places.

"I could get used to having a magic closet."

A pounding on the door snapped her out of her staring.

"Hey, slowpoke, you almost done in there? Aries said we need to go soon!" It was Lukka. Kaeli sighed as she turned away from the mirror. She wasn't ready for the pampering session to be finished.

"Coming!" she yelled. Kaeli smoothed out her skirt as she took one last look at herself and inhaled deeply. It had been a long time since she'd felt this stunning. She pursed her lips as she remembered a daddy daughter dance from her elementary school years. Shaking her head to clear away the memory, she exited the closet. Now was not the time to reminisce on things that would probably make her cry.

As Kaeli opened the door leading to her bedroom, she ran smack into Lukka's chest. Almost tripping over the back of her heels, she had to step back a moment to regain her bearings. She glared up at Lukka. He crossed his arms as a smug smile played across his face. She flared her nostrils as she let out a huff of air.

"And why is it that you're standing right in front of my bathroom door... inside of *my* bedroom," she stared him down, and her sudden flash of anger faded as she took in the sight of him. He still had that stupid pompous look on his face, but he looked amazing. He wore fitted black slacks with a button-down shirt that was left just a little open at the top. Over the shirt, he wore a silky orange vest that not only perfectly complemented his decently muscled figure, but also happened to perfectly match the color of her outfit. Despite the impeccable style, however, her eyes were drawn to his forearms. The sleeves of his shirt rolled up to his elbows, revealing gnarled, raised scars, starting from his wrists and traveling up until they were concealed by the shirt.

You're staring. The thought occurred to her, and she tore her eyes away from Lukka, shaking her head. She refocused her gaze to his face and a rush of heat bloomed in her cheeks. There was a mischievous glint in his eyes that told Kaeli he had very much noticed her attention to his burns.

"Aries yelled at me to come get you," Lukka chuckled. "The big guys are saying we need to go." The smirky smile on his face was infuriating. "Not gonna lie though, I'm totally willing to linger a little longer if you need more time." He winked. Her cheeks flushed even more. She stood up a little straighter and rolled her shoulders back, trying to regain some semblance of her confidence.

"I'm *more* than ready to leave." She propped a hand on her hip and motioned for Lukka to step aside. The grin on Lukka's face grew wider as he stepped aside and swooped his arms toward the entrance. Kaeli held her head high as she stalked past him toward her bedroom door.

"Do you know why I don't care if people stare at them?" he called after her as she was just about to leave the room. She stood frozen in place with her hand on the doorknob and tried not to cringe. She was hoping he would just let the whole situation slide, but apparently that wasn't really his style. Kaeli let out a slow exhale and relaxed her shoulders.

"No, not really," she replied through pursed lips.

"Well, do you want to know?" Kaeli could hear his footsteps approaching, but she didn't turn around. Not even when he moved in close to whisper, "Aren't you at least a little curious?" Kaeli sighed. He was fishing for something. She didn't know what, but she did know she didn't want him to get any closer than he already was. She turned around to face him. Her back pressed up against the door. He placed one of his hands just above her head against the door frame, effectively making her feel even smaller compared to his height than she already was, even with the inch or two she had gained from the heels. Her gaze flickered to his scarred arm before she stared him dead in the eyes.

"Alright, I'll bite." She cocked her head to the side. She couldn't tell whether his arrogant attitude was sexy or annoying as hell. "Why don't you care if people stare?"

"Cause chicks dig scars," Lukka said with a huge grin on his face. He looked like he had just delivered the best punchline to the funniest joke ever. Kaeli rolled her eyes. She didn't know what she was supposed to expect from Lukka, but she thought he would at least be a little more intelligent than that.

"For the love of…" She turned away from him and opened the door, forcing him to back up so he didn't fall forward. "We have to go." She stepped through the doorway. Joseph lounged on the couch. He turned his head slightly to acknowledge them.

"Are you two finished?" A small grin formed on the corners of his mouth. Kaeli's stomach lurched.

"We—we weren't… it—it wasn't…" The words weren't working. Joseph laughed as he hopped up off the couch. His outfit was the same as Lukka's except that his vest was a deep red.

"I'm kidding," he said. Lukka came out of the bedroom, and Joseph gave him a nod.

"You both suck." Kaeli scrunched up her nose and brushed past the boys to the door that would lead her out of the embarrassing hellhole. Joseph and Lukka trailed after her.

★ ★ ★

They met Aries, Leo, and Sagittarius at the entrance with a giant centaur carved into the door and, together, the six of them walked to the same portal Kaeli and Leo had originally taken to the house. She braced herself in anticipation for the nausea that inevitably came with teleporting. They stepped to the center of the portal runes. Kaeli shot a glance at Lukka. He fiddled with his shirt sleeves and shifted ever so slightly from side to side. Maybe he had issues with teleportation too.

When everyone stood safely within the circle of the runes, Leo said the name of the destination, and Kaeli lurched as they tumbled through the familiar, all-encompassing darkness. It lasted for only a few moments before a rush of cool wind caressed her face. The bridge of swirling colors arched before her. Leo stepped ahead and turned to face the recruits.

"Alright, so tonight the three of you need to be on your best behavior. You're going to be meeting the other Western Zodiacs as well as their recruits, and we need to make a good impression." Leo stepped over to Lukka and straightened out his tie.

"But don't let people push you around either," Aries chimed in. "Some of the other signs… They like to get a little cocky. If they try anything with you, don't be afraid to shut that down immediately."

"This is supposed to be a civil gathering," Sagittarius sighed. "I'm sure *everyone* will behave appropriately." He raised both of his eyebrows and looked pointedly at Aries. "And that there will be no problems."

Aries widened her eyes to an unnatural size and placed a hand over her chest.

"Are—are you referring to me?" She let out half a gasp and then laughed before making her way to the bridge. She waved for everyone to follow her. "You don't have to worry about me, Fabio. I can't promise the same for everyone else though."

It wasn't long before Kaeli spotted the platform. A lightness filled her chest as they approached. Her pulse quickened. The platform had completely transformed from the last time she'd seen it. Tall torches lined the perimeter of the circle, their flames an array of vibrant colors ranging from the typical oranges and reds, all the way to crystal blue, deep purple, and emerald greens. Smaller lights, twinkling like tiny stars made of diamonds, were strung between the torches, refracting the light from the fire into a colorful aura of rainbow that encompassed the platform. As they stepped off the bridge and into the glow, a warm sensation ran through Kaeli's fingertips and down her whole body. A soft melody from instruments she couldn't place tickled her ears. She smiled. For the first time, in a very long time, Kaeli felt content. Someone stepped next to her, but she was too entranced by the beauty of the platform to acknowledge it.

"The Celestial Spirits really have a gift when it comes to setting up for parties." It was Leo. Kaeli turned her head to him and blinked. She had been so entranced by the view, she hadn't realized she'd stopped at the base of the bridge. Lukka, Joseph, and the other signs were already mingling with the other recruits and zodiacs. Celestial Spirits of all different colors floated around the platters of food and drink. Leo chuckled as he looped his arm around her shoulders.

"We only have parties like this for special occasions. The last time the platform looked like this was when some of the current zodiacs finished their recruitment process over... I don't even remember how many years ago." He looked around before refocusing his gaze on Kaeli. "It's been too long." He took a step back and extended an arm to her. "Shall we make our grand entrance?" An infectious grin spread across his face. Kaeli couldn't help but smile back. She snaked her own arm through Leo's.

"Yes, let's."

As they made their way to the center of the circle, Leo pointed out the other zodiacs and their recruits. Libra she recognized from when she first arrived. She stood next to Gemini. At first glance, there didn't seem to be anything striking about him. He was tall, had dark hair that seemed to spike in every different direction, and a smile that was almost as charming as Leo's, but Kaeli couldn't seem to look away from him. It wasn't until she made brief eye contact that she realized why. In shape and size, his eyes were the same, but everything else about them was different. His left eye was a pale cerulean blue with a rather large pupil. His right eye was almost completely black with only the slightest hint of white surrounding the darkened iris. In the center, where a normal pupil should have been, was a yellow slit closely resembling that of a snake. Kaeli stepped a little closer to Leo. Gemini's smile split into a grin, revealing a sharp pointed right canine tooth. She tore her gaze away and looked around at the zodiacs as Leo continued to talk.

"And then that other woman standing with them is Aquarius. The woman over there by Scorpio is Pisces, and the man is Cancer." He motioned to the opposite rim of the platform. Pisces had slick straight hair, so dark and shiny it reflected the faces of the people standing near her. She was small and fragile looking with wide, slanted, almond-shaped eyes that were a deep crystal blue. Cancer seemed out of place with his two companions. Everything about him radiated friendliness, from his messy, short-cropped hair, to the lazy smile on his face. Leo turned as the earth zodiacs entered the platform. They were the last to arrive. Leo pointed at the man and woman walking closely to each other at the head of the trio.

"That man and woman are Virgo and Taurus. They have this on-again, off-again thing with each other. The tall man trailing them is Capricorn. He stays quiet and mostly keeps to himself, but it's best not to get on his bad side. For the most part, if you leave him alone, he leaves you alone too," he grinned. "And that's all of the zodiacs. I haven't had a chance to meet all of the recruits yet, so you'll have to meet them on your own." The music changed from a soft lulling melody to an upbeat rhythm.

"YES!" Aries jumped to the center of the circle and started pumping her fist in time to the beat. "Dance party!"

"She gets excited easily." Leo turned to Kaeli and winked. "Shall we dance?" He offered her a hand. Kaeli grinned. Her heart pounded in her chest as she took his hand. He spun her in circles until they found their way to the center, where he lowered her into a dramatic dip. The rainbow colors turned into a kaleidoscope around her as her vision refocused. The music crescendoed in waves, consuming the platform in an infectious melody that worked deep into her bones. Judging by the reckless, abandoned way everyone else around her danced, the music had devoured them as well. Kaeli closed her eyes and threw her head back, letting the sounds wash over her as she moved and swayed in time with the rhythm. A light touch on her shoulder and opened her eyes to find herself in the arms of a man she hadn't yet met.

He was tall, well-built, and had a square jawline. His narrow eyes looked like pools of honey when the light caught them just right. His thick black hair was perfectly coiffed to the side. Not a shred of this man seemed out of place or unintentional, which made the plethora of tattoos peeking out from under his silky sapphire dress shirt seem all the more intriguing. A water recruit, most likely. Kaeli held eye contact as he assessed her. She lifted her chin ever so slightly. A coy smile played on her lips.

"Are you going to stand there gawking at me, or would you like to dance."

A serpentine grin broke out onto the man's face as he closed the gap between the two of them. Kaeli became acutely aware of just how prominent his muscles really were as she placed her hands on his shoulders and trailed them lightly down his arms until their hands touched. Like a spring trap, he spun her into a cross-body turn that ended with his arms wrapped around her as she faced away from him. Adrenaline pumped through Kaeli's veins and she couldn't help but giggle. He drew her in closer. His breath caressed her ear.

"What's your name, gorgeous?" His voice was deep and velvety. A shiver ran down her spine. Before she could answer, he unfurled their arms so they were facing each other once more. Kaeli cocked her head to the side as she looked deep into his eyes. The music swayed them in perfect sync.

"Yours first."

"Niko."

"Niko." Kaeli tasted the name on her tongue. She decided it suited him. "My name is Kaeli. Although if you want to call me 'gorgeous,' I won't object." Niko chuckled as he took a step back and, raising one of Kaeli's hands to his lips, brushed a light kiss over her knuckles.

"It's a pleasure to meet you, Kaeli."

Kaeli couldn't stop the rush of heat that flooded her cheeks.

And just like that, he disappeared in the throng of dancing bodies.

As the night wore on, Kaeli met the rest of the recruits. Selena, Randi, and Alex and Ryan would be the new air zodiacs; Alex and Ryan the gemini twins. Eryn, Jamal, and Shaina were the earth recruits. Daniel, and Anya were the new water recruits. Through the process of elimination, Kaeli found out that Niko was training under Scorpio.

It seemed like barely anytime had passed by at all before the music started to fade, and the Celestial Spirits appeared around the perimeter of the circle. Some held platters of food, others, pitchers of brightly colored beverages. Leo and Libra made their way to the center of the platform. Leo held out a hand, and a crystal glass appeared out of thin air. He brandished a knife in his other hand and clinked it against the glass. The music went silent, and every eye turned to look at Leo.

"Welcome, new recruits and future zodiacs!" He spread his arms wide and spun in a slow circle to look at all of the newcomers individually... or to make sure that everyone could get a good look at the absolute radiance that emanated from him. Keali couldn't tell if he was being hospitable or vain. Maybe both. "Tonight we want to celebrate and honor you for accepting this journey."

Libra took a step closer to Leo, subtly taking her place at the epicenter of the crowd.

"I'm sure all of you have been made aware as to why you were chosen and the purpose of your being here, and although tonight we are celebrating, you have been brought here to be trained." Her gaze was hard. "Starting tomorrow morning, each of you will begin personal training sessions with your zodiac mentors as well as group training sessions with each other. Together, we, the current and future zodiacs, form a complete whole. No one person here can thrive solely on their own. We all have our individual strengths, but taken too far, those strengths can become weaknesses. Because of this, we must all strive to be balanced—"

"Hurry it up, cupcake!" Aries hollered from her spot in the circle. "Some of us are starving. There'll be plenty of time to hear your ramblings about the balance of the universe *after* food."

Some of the zodiacs threw piercing glares at Aries, including Libra, but none of the recruits protested the interruption. As if in response, several stomachs grumbled their agreement to Aries's suggestion. Libra let out a sigh.

"After your initial personal training sessions, we will reconvene here at the platform to reveal your groups."

"Now let's eat!" Aries bellowed. As she spoke, she snapped her fingers and a large round table fell from the sky so quickly that Libra dove out of the way in order to avoid being crushed. She glared at Aries. Aries flashed her a devilish grin. Once the table landed firmly on the platform, the perfect number of chairs appeared around it. Aries and Lukka were among the first to seat themselves. As soon as the spirits started approaching with platters of food, all of the recruits rushed to the table. Leo pulled out a chair for Kaeli and motioned for her to sit. She did so without hesitation.

She barely had time to sit before a light-blue Celestial Spirit placed a plate of food in front of her. Her eyes widened as she was suddenly overwhelmed by the savory scent of spices. Rolls of bread, savory stews, sizzling vegetables—the spirits continue to place food around the table until it couldn't hold anymore. As much as she wanted to dive headfirst into the feast, she found herself hesitating, overwhelmed by the sheer volume and sensory overload.

"What are you waiting for?" Leo asked, a bite of rare meat hanging out of his mouth muffled the question. She arched an eyebrow at him. He grinned and finished chewing. "Don't be shy. Eat as much as you want. Just enjoy the food." He stabbed at his plate and stuffed another forkful into his mouth. Kaeli chuckled and took a bite of the lentil stew nearest to her. She closed her eyes as the savory blend of spices played on her tongue. She dug her spoon in for another bite, then another, and another.

The spirits continued to bring more food as the zodiacs and their recruits ate through plate after plate. As Kaeli continued to sample the dishes around her, she caught a glimpse of Libra. While her recruit, Randi, eagerly enjoyed the food, Libra glared murderously at Aries. Kaeli kept her eyes on the air zodiacs as she took another bite of her food. Her gaze flickered to Gemini whispering something to the twins who sat on either side of him. As they talked, a small but mischievous smile crept onto his face, revealing the one sharpened canine. Kaeli thought she saw his slitted pupil widen, turning his yellow eye almost completely black. He snapped his fingers once, and then resumed eating. As he did, Keali caught his gaze. His smile widened just a little as he discreetly raised a finger to his lips, indicating for her to keep quiet. She raised her eyebrows as she moved her fork to get another bite of food.

It was at the moment she noticed the smallest little whirlwind forming behind Libra. It continued to grow until it was almost the size of a baseball. Before she even had a chance to blink, it shot toward Aries's food, splattering it all over her face. Everyone at the table froze. Next to her, Leo dropped his fork, sending it clattering to the table.

Aries took in a deep breath and exhaled slowly through pursed lips as she grabbed a napkin from the table and proceeded to wipe the food off her face. Lukka looked at his suit in disgust. A bit of sauce had splattered onto him as well. He stuck the corner of his napkin into a water glass and began dabbing at the splotch. A strand of Aries hair plastered to her face, dripping with something viscous and orange.

"What the *hell* was that?" Her eyes lit up with literal fire as her focus lasered in on Libra. Libra looked at Gemini, defeat in her eyes. He simply shrugged as if he had no idea what was happening. Libra looked back at Aries, but this time with a smirk on her face.

"No idea. I didn't do it. You might want to keep curry in your hair though. It's a great compliment to your skin tone."

"*You bitch!*" Aries snapped her fingers, and a Celestial Spirit appeared at her side with a platter, on top of which was a perfect looking cream pie. Aries yanked away the platter, lit it on fire, and flung it at Libra's head. A wind shifted the flaming pie mid-air, and it landed smack in Scorpio's face. Every muscle in his body tensed as the fire fizzled out on impact. The silence that followed was so thick, Kaeli felt like she could cut it with a knife. The cream pie slowly dripped down Scorpio's face, sizzling with steam. Murder glinted in his eyes. He took in a deep breath, not even attempting to wipe anything off his skin. Cream pie had never looked so threatening.

"Speaking of bitches…" he growled.

"Food fight!" Gemini jumped with surprising grace to stand on the seat of his chair. With his arms outstretched, he summoned a forceful wind that raised several dishes of food into the air and flung them in various directions.

Chaos exploded around the table.

"Shield!" Leo hollered at Kaeli as he picked up his own plate to block the onslaught of food flying toward his face. Celestial Spirits vanished into thin air before they could be caught in the crossfire. Kaeli narrowly dodged a bowl of soup that whizzed past her head. She crawled under the table. The twins were there too, forming little whirlwinds of their own and launching them over the table. One of them noticed her and tapped his brother on the shoulder. The brother turned to look at her and grinned wickedly.

"Fun dinner, huh?"

"What's going on down here?" Lukka, holding a creampuff in each hand, popped his head under the table. Some type of liquid ran through his hair, but he didn't seem to care anymore. Without warning, he flung the cream puffs at Kaeli. She dodged one, but the other hit her shoulder. The pastry splattered on impact, and cream smudged all over her top. She caught a glimpse of the twins as they disappeared above the table. Lukka cackled and returned to the surface as well.

"Oh, you are so dead!" Kaeli crawled back out from underneath the table and grabbed onto the first piece of food she could find. Her eyes scanned the frenzy for Lukka. It was a mess. Everyone was splattered in a cacophony of colors. The whole thing looked like a Jackson Pollock painting.

Most everyone was having fun, except for Libra, Aries, and Scorpio who had ditched the food and now resorted to using their elements to actually kill each other. At least, that's what it looked like.

Kaeli zeroed in on Lukka amidst the chaos and launched her ammunition. A wide grin spread across her face as her food hit her mark. A glop of mashed potatoes ran down Lukka's neck.

"Watch out!" a warning cry sounded next to her. Kaeli barely had time to react before someone using a chair as a shield stepped in front of her. It was Niko. Food and dishes hit the bottom of the chair with a loud thunk, clattering to the ground. Niko turned his head and looked at her with a mischievous expression.

"It's all fun and games until the dishes get involved." He cracked a grin as he gave her a once over. His eyes lingered over the smeared cream on her shoulder. "You seem to have gotten out of this fairly unscathed." His grin grew wider. "We should probably do something about that."

"What are you—" Before she could finish, Niko had flicked a soupy something at her face. Her eyes shut, and she scrunched up her nose as she frantically wiped away the mess.

"You do *not* want to start that game with me." Her eyes narrowed, but she kept a smile on her face as she scooped a dollop of the cream off her shoulder and smooshed it into Niko's perfectly styled hair. His jaw nearly dropped, but he still held onto the chair shield.

"I *know* you did not just do that to my hair." Something wicked, dangerous, and exciting flickered through his eyes, but it faded just as quickly as it had come, replaced by shock. "What's that?" He nodded toward the ground. Kaeli jumped back. A thick fog rose from the ground around them. Niko dropped the chair.

Before she had a chance to reply, the colorful lights fluttered out, and a crack of lightning struck the table in the center. The table vanished. A searing pain shot through Kaeli's shoulder, and black spots clouded her vision. She doubled over, losing her balance.

"Whoa." Niko caught her before she staggered to the ground. "You okay?"

Kaeli nodded as she clutched her shoulder.

"I'll be fine," she rasped. The pain didn't make sense. Her stomach flipped somersaults as she remembered the incident with the door. She'd felt the same pain there as well. The fog rose higher, and with it, a growing sense of terror. Most of the recruits shifted uneasily. Niko held her in a firm grasp as she leaned into him for support. The sharpness of the pain ebbed ever-so-slightly.

"What's going on?" an unidentified female voice asked from somewhere within the thick fog. As if in response to her question, the darkness stirred at the center of the circle, taking on the form of a snake.

"No way…" Lukka's voice sounded from somewhere close, causing her to jump. The fog solidified, and electric purple eyes shot open, staring right at her and Niko. The wind left Kaeli's lungs as tremors took hold of her body. Without warning, the snake uncoiled and lunged toward them. Someone screamed. Before Kaeli even had a chance to blink, a fireball the size of the snake's head came flying from her left, chasing away the shadowy fog. The snake slithered to the outskirts of the platform, hissing in distaste at the light.

"Ophiuchusss will sssoon return," it's voice echoed, vibrating through the air. "The few have been chosssen. It'sss only a matter of time." The snake once again locked its gaze onto Niko and Kaeli. She watched, frozen in horror, as more oncoming fireballs glinted against the purple of the snake's eyes before it dissipated into nothingness.

"Could you maybe loosen your grip?" Niko grunted. Air rushed back into her lungs, and Kaeli, suddenly able to breathe again, realized she was digging her nails into Niko's arm. She retracted her fingers and stepped away from him.

"Sorry," she murmured as her gaze flitted across the diameter of the platform where the snake had been circling them. Lukka was at her side in an instant, grabbing her shoulders and facing her toward him.

"Are you okay?" he demanded. Kaeli kept her gaze cast over his shoulder, but nodded her head.

"We need to get back to the houses," Leo said, his voice wavering just slightly. The recruits were silent, but the zodiacs muttered their agreement. No one spoke as they crossed the rainbow bridge and made their way to the portal.

Kaeli felt lightheaded as Leo, Aries, and Sagittarius ushered her, Lukka, and Joseph back into House Ignis. Before she had a chance to really process what happened, she found herself back in the shared living quarters with the boys. She vaguely heard Leo mention something about training in the morning and trying to get some sleep before he left, but visions of the snake replaying in her head kept her from remembering the details. She walked over to the couch and sank into the plush cushions. Her eyes fluttered closed.

"You sure you don't want to change first?" Lukka asked quietly. He sounded like he was trying to make a joke but didn't have the energy. Kaeli looked down at her skirt and realized she was still covered in cream puff and speckles of whatever soup Niko had flung at her.

"Right," she said as she stood up and made her way to her room. She stepped into her bathroom to wash off. Folded on the counter was a pair of silky pajama bottoms and a loose cotton tank top. A note on top of them read, *Heard what happened at the dinner. Hope you are okay. Things will be better in the morning. -Liani.* Kaeli bit back a faint smile as she stepped into the shower, quickly rinsed away the grit, and slipped into the pajamas. As she made her way to her bed, she could hear Joseph and Lukka talking to each other in hushed voices about the snake, but she was too exhausted to join the conversation. She threw herself onto the bed, buried herself under the thick blankets, and closed her eyes. As she drifted off into sleep, a soft voice whispered to her.

Opeeen the doooor.

CHAPTER 10

*B*ang *Bang Bang!* Kaeli shot out of bed at the harsh sound of metal clanging against metal.

"Wake up, you lazy maggots!" Aries's booming voice echoed through the common room. "First day of training starts now!" Kaeli heard her kick open a door.

"AH! What are you doing?!" Lukka sounded mortified. "You don't just *do* that to a guy first thing in the morning!" Aries howled with laughter. Kaeli rolled over into her thick comforter and groaned face first into her pillow.

"Why did we have to get placed in the same element as Aries?" she mumbled.

"What was that?" Aries busted through the door to Kaeli's room. Kaeli immediately sat upright and attempted to make her blurry eyes seem as alert as possible.

"Nothing, ma'am." She hopped out of bed and stumbled a little as her sleepy limbs struggled to find balance. From her entryway she saw Leo and Sagittarius enter the living quarters. Leo popped his head up behind Aries.

"You didn't have to go all boot camp on them the first day," he said. "Especially after what happened last night."

Aries spun to face Leo, propping both hands on her hips.

"They need to adjust to waking up at early hours. It's precisely because of last night that we need to take this training seriously."

"Making training a priority and torturing our recruits are different," Sagittarius chimed in from the common room. Aries rolled her eyes and huffed.

"Well, maybe next time one of you can pop in and bring them breakfast in bed to start their day. That'll teach them resilience," she snorted and stomped past Leo back to Lukka's room. Leo shook his head.

"Sorry about that. She kind of got away from us before we could stop her. Are you ready to start training?"

"Ready isn't exactly the word I would use," Kaeli said, bringing a hand to her mouth as she stifled a yawn.

"Being ready to save the world doesn't happen overnight," he said, "but the sooner we finish our sessions, the sooner we eat!"

"That's not exactly a motivator for me this early in the morning." Kaeli squeezed her eyes shut as she stretched her arms and stifled another yawn.

"Trust me, by the time we're finished, it will be." Leo chucked something in Kaeli's general direction. She attempted to block it, but her sleepy reflexes weren't fast enough, and it hit her in the face. Thankfully, it was soft. Leo laughed. "Put those on and meet me at the training arena. If you can't remember how to get there, ask a spirit for help." He turned his back and shut the door. Kaeli sighed but pushed herself out of bed and stumbled toward the bathroom, clothes in hand.

When she stepped into the bathroom, she found a pair of lightweight combat boots on the floor and a heavy-duty sports bra on the counter, with a note written in familiar handwriting.

Thought these might be useful for today! Hope you're ready to kick some ass! -Liani

Kaeli didn't know whether to groan or smile. She appreciated the gesture but didn't feel like kicking any ass after the events from last night. Still, a small smile grew on her as she placed the note to the side and examined what it was that Leo had thrown in her face. Inside the package was a pair of black pants made out of a resistant stretchy material, a red tank top, and an intricately designed jacket. She would have found the outfit to be extraordinarily boring if it hadn't been for the jacket. It was made of a lightweight, insulated material. The base of the jacket was black in color, but along the shoulder, sides of the arms, and the elbows was a red, leathery material. On the back of the jacket was a flame engulfing a circular symbol that had the leo, aries, and sagittarius insignias stitched in white threading. She dressed as quickly as she could and tied her hair up into a ponytail, taking only a couple of brief moments to examine herself before rushing out the door.

Kaeli wandered in circles through several corridors for what she was sure was way too long. There were so many staircases and tunnels in this place, and the quick tour Leo had taken her on yesterday wasn't enough to orient her location. Just as she considered giving up, Liani turned down the hallway. They locked eyes for less than a second before Liani's face burst into a dazzling grin.

"There you are!" She bounced over to Kaeli and wrapped her a hug. Kaeli froze, not sure how to react, but still happy to find someone who could help her get to the training arena. Liani unlatched and held Kaeli away at arm's length, making intense eye contact. "Leo sent me looking for you when you didn't show up. I still can't believe he wouldn't wait for you and just take you to the arena himself, but maybe he had something he needed to prep. Or *maybe*—" she gasped, her mouth hanging open, "—maybe this was supposed to be *part* of the training. Maybe he's testing you *right now*."

Kaeli shook her head and blinked rapidly, trying to process everything Liani had just spewed out. Liani chuckled and looped her arm through Kaeli's as she started walking down the hallway.

"Don't worry about it. You were actually getting pretty close, we just need to go down this stairwell, through another tunnel, and then we'll be at the arena!"

Kaeli walked with Liani as the excitable fire spirit went on about how she was so happy to have new recruits in the house, and how hanging out with Kaeli was so much more exciting than maintaining weapons that really hadn't been used in about a century anyway. Kaeli nodded occasionally and offered little bits of input here and there, but mostly she tried to stay focused on where exactly they were walking, noting interesting looking hallways and landmarks, so she hopefully wouldn't get so lost again.

It didn't take long before they descended a staircase that led to a wide tunnel. The light from the arena shone in the distance. As they neared the entrance, a cool breeze blew through the air, and Kaeli suddenly gained an extra appreciation for the insulated jacket. Leo stood at the center tapping his foot and looking up toward the sky.

"Well, that's the cue for me to leave," Liani whispered as they stood at the mouth of the tunnel. "I don't like Leo when he gets all huffy."

"What do you mean all huff—" But before Kaeli could finish asking her question, Liani had disappeared in a puff of red smoke. She sighed and slumped her shoulders. "Never mind." She shook her head and took in a deep breath before making her way toward Leo. As she approached, he regarded her with arched eyebrows. Kaeli pursed her lips together and steeled herself for a lecture. To her surprise, Leo only shook his head and let out a long exhale.

"I guess if I expected you to be here earlier, I should have waited to walk you to the arena instead of leaving you with the likes of Liani." He grimaced before a slow smile grew on his face. "You're here now though, and that's what matters, so let's get to work! During these sessions we're going to cover a lot of things, but mostly we'll focus on developing your celestial abilities."

"Celestial abilities?" Kaeli's eyebrows knit together as she cocked her head to the side. "You mean like being able to control fire?"

"Yes! But there's a lot more to our celestial abilities than just control of the elements. Each zodiac has a specific set. Some of them you already started using while you were on Earth without even realizing."

"Like what?"

"Well, for leos in particular, we have a type of charmed influence over people. You may have noticed at the party last night, a lot of the recruits couldn't keep their eyes off you. That was you inherently using your ability. It presents as a type of radiant glow that draws people in unconsciously. This was the first ability I saw you using on Earth, and it's the one I think you might have the most aptitude for."

"When was I using this on Earth?" Kaeli bit her lip and flinched as she remembered growing up with Trent and her mother. If she was able to charm people, why had her brother tried to physically harm her? Why would her mom never try to protect her? Her throat grew tight and a slight tremor shook her arms. Leo didn't fail to notice her change and gently placed his hands on her shoulders. The light touch was enough to snap her out of the past.

"Remember Luis at the coffee shop?" Leo's smile was soft. Kaeli blinked a few times. Truth be told, she was often so stuck in her own world, she didn't often notice the people around her. But now that she thought about it, Luis had always clung to her whenever she ordered coffee. And that one elderly couple had paid for her drink the day she met Leo… it wasn't necessarily an uncommon experience. Her thoughts drifted back to when she'd first met Leo and the magnetizing pull he seemed to have. She tilted her head to the side.

"Were you using that when you first met me?"

"Not intentionally," Leo chuckled. "When you're a full-fledged zodiac, some of these natural abilities have a stronger influence over humans while we're on Earth."

"We have other abilities too." Leo puffed out his chest ever so slightly. "Other than our charm and fire, we can also control light, have healing abilities to an extent, and can shapeshift into lions. With this comes acute predatory instincts related to hunting—seeing in the dark, exceptional hearing and sense of smell, increased strength—all of which can be utilized in our non-shifted form as well when honed properly. Based on my observations of you so far, I think this may be your weak link, so that's what I want to focus on this morning."

Kaeli nodded resolutely. "So, how are we doing this?"

Leo's eyes lit up with an enthusiastic fire. "We're playing hide and seek." He grinned. Kaeli arched an eyebrow as she stared at Leo in disbelief.

"Really..." Her voice was flat. "A kid's game. You woke me up before the ass crack of dawn to play a kid's game."

Leo nodded.

"You've already shown me you can use both fire and charm. Controlling light is really similar to using fire, but just requires more focus. Healing can come later. Instincts are a critical function, and I've yet to see you display any ability for it. The first step of the hunt is to track down your prey. If you can't even do that in this obstacle arena, you're going to have a hell of a time using any predatory abilities in combat."

Kaeli frowned and crossed her arms. Although his explanation made sense, the whole situation seemed... silly.

"Alright." Leo pointed at her. "Close your eyes. Count to ten. When you're finished try to use your senses to find me."

"Only ten?" Kaeli smirked. "You sure that will give you enough time to get away from me?"

"Oh, trust me." Leo crossed his arms and winked. "I don't even need ten seconds." He leaned in close to Kaeli's face. She held eye contact even when they were almost nose to nose. "The only way you'll find me is if I want you to. This is just to see how close you can get." He took both of her hands in his, and placed them over her eyes. "Now count to ten!" Wind rushed as he disappeared. She sighed.

"One, two, three..."

Kaeli quickly discovered that this game of hide and seek was not the simplistic game she remembered playing as a child. It seemed like hours had passed, and she had searched the entire arena multiple times, without the slightest hint of Leo. Occasionally, she would hear her name whispered on the wind, only to spin around and find nothing. She was getting sick of it. She sighed as she glared at the arena. There were the obstacles, but it wasn't like there were that many good hiding places. Most of it was open. A low growl escaped her throat as she stomped over to a nearby bench and plopped down on it.

Closing her eyes, she tried to focus on her using her senses. That was what people always did in movies. It seemed kind of ridiculous, but she was willing to try at this point. Quieting her frustrated thoughts, she honed in on her surroundings—the way the morning light warmed her skin, the firm support of the bench underneath her. She listened. Sniffed the air. Nothing. This was stupid. She opened her eyes and slumped back.

"I give up!" she yelled, cringing as the words escaped her. They felt so wrong. Her jaw clenched and she kicked the dirt. The arena stayed silent. Wherever Leo was, it didn't seem like he was in a hurry to reveal himself. A heat built at the base of her neck. Why did they need to play this ridiculous game to figure out how much instinctual ability she had? He was freaking Leo of the zodiac. Shouldn't he just *know* these things? She snorted, blowing out hot air.

"Where are you?" she yelled again at the empty air.

Silence.

Kaeli let out a frustrated cry, and her arms erupted into fire.

"Whoa there." The voice came from behind her. Kaeli spun. Leo stood, hands up in the air.

"Where were you?" she snarled. The flames rose higher up her arms. "I searched every inch of this arena at least three times, and you weren't anywhere!"

Leo cautiously placed a hand on her arm. The fire powered down. The anger, however, did not subside.

"It's part of the hunt. Moving silently. Blending in. I'll teach you more about this later," he said, his voice was calm, not smug like Kaeli had expected he would be. "For now, you need to cool off. Let's go get some food before all of the groups meet at the platform."

Kaeli crossed her arms and glared at him.

"Fine," she sighed, "but you *will* be teaching me how to disappear like that."

Leo cracked a smile.

"That's why I'm here."

✳ ✳ ✳

Trent laid on his cot in the meager living quarters Elethia had given him and stared at the stone ceiling above him. Living wasn't quite the right word to describe it. It was barely larger than a prison cell and hardly better furnished. At least he had plenty of blankets to keep warm in the unrelenting damp chill. There was also an attached bathroom, but that was where the niceties ended. Thin slivers of candlelight from the hallway peeked through the grated opening on the door. If it weren't for those candles, Trent would be in complete darkness. Elethia had said he was free to roam if he wished but advised against it. Something about nightmares roaming the halls.

He sighed. He'd lost count of how long he'd been in here with nothing to do. He glanced down his body and arched an eyebrow. Well, there was something he could do. Just as he got up to walk to the bathroom, the door to his room opened with an ear-piercing creak. His eyes scrunched shut, and his hands covered his ears until the horrible noise eased. Elethia stood silhouetted in the doorway. Her long, lithe fingers tapped against the cold steel.

"It's time." Her face was neutral, but she spoke through slightly pursed lips. She turned and motioned for Trent to follow her into the hallway.

Trent grunted. She might be beautiful, but she acted like an entitled bitch. She turned her head and regarded him with an amused smile.

"You should watch your thoughts while you walk these halls." Her purple eyes flashed with something dark. "Some of us in this castle can hear such things." She winked, then continued walking without giving Trent a second glance. He frowned and folded his arms across his chest as he did his best to keep his thoughts from yelling a stream of curse words.

Elethia ushered him through a series of winding hallways that led down to the depths of the castle. Trent quickly learned that it was in his best interest to keep his gaze trained on Elethia's back. Strange, grotesque creatures walked the halls. Monsters that looked like they were stitched together piece by piece. Some moaned as if they were in pain. Others paced back and forth only to scream every couple of seconds. And then there was the brood of shadowy snakes that seemed to slither around the walls and ceilings whenever Elethia was present. She ignored them all. Even casually brushed away a monster that got a little too close for comfort.

The deeper they went into the heart of the castle, the more disturbing the creatures became. Red demonic eyes glared at him, and he felt like he'd just walked into the pits of hell. Trent swallowed as his pulse raced, and he attempted to keep down the sense of rising terror. The sound of his thrashing heart pounded in his ears.

Elethia motioned for Trent to stop as they approached a floor to ceiling metal gate. At the center of the gate was a circle. Intricate swirls shooting off from the circle cut through the metal like small, dry riverbeds. Elethia placed her hand in the middle and muttered a phrase in some language Trent had never heard. As soon as she finished speaking, her eyes glowed with a vibrant light, and shocks of purple lightning shot through the swirls, lighting the gate with color. She removed her hand and turned toward Trent.

"We may enter now," she smiled, but it didn't reach her eyes. Trent's gaze flashed down to her hands which trembled just slightly. An empty feeling sank to the pit of his stomach. If even she was afraid of whatever was beyond these gates... What did that mean for him?

"*Now,*" Elethia snapped, and Trent's gaze immediately flickered to her face. Her smile disappeared and she clenched her hands into fists. She turned on her heel and continued through the gates. Trent followed.

Every step she took seemed to light another segment of the hallway. Other than that, they were immersed in complete darkness. No monsters roamed this corridor, but as they approached a series of doors, Trent almost turned and fled as scream after agonizing scream shook the walls. Elethia stopped in front of a door at the end of the hallway, and Trent used every ounce of his willpower not to turn and run in the opposite direction. Elethia knocked on the door. She barely got through the first tap before it swung open.

"Come in."

Trent found himself rooted to the floor, unable to twitch a muscle, even as his legs grew weak. That internal thought. It was so deep it reverberated through his bones. It carried both a terrifying and calming tone all at once. Elethia wrapped her hand around Trent's. The cool feel of her touch seemed to snap something in his muscles, and he found himself walking forward through the entryway with her.

Trent couldn't stop the tremble that took his body, or the clammy sweat that formed on his brow as the powerful being before him moved to shut the door once they were inside. This... thing... looked like a man, but he had to be something else entirely. His dark, golden brown eyes stared at him through slitted black pupils. He didn't make a move toward Elethia or Trent, but only tilted his head to the side. His pale gold skin shimmered in the faint light of the room, and a few strands of his long, midnight black hair fell over his shoulder.

"So this is the one you've told me so much about," he murmured. A small smile crawled to the corners of his thin lips, revealing sharpened fangs.

"Yes," Elethia said. Her voice was barely louder than a whisper, almost as if her throat were parched. Faster than Trent could blink, the man moved, and suddenly stood right in front of him.

"Excellent," he grinned, hand extended. "My name is Samael. We'll be working very... closely... with each other for the next couple of days." He motioned to a medical chair with restraining straps in the far corner of the room. Next to it was a table lined with all manner of surgical material and knives in nearly every shape imaginable. The adrenaline coursed through his veins as he spun toward Elethia.

"What in the *hell* is this?!" he bellowed. He didn't wait for her to answer as he bolted for the door. Consequences be damned. He just needed to get *out*. He groped for a handle. When he didn't find one, he pounded on the iron. The sound echoed off the walls.

"I'm afraid that will do you no good," Samael chuckled. Trent spun around to face the monster, keeping his back pressed against the wall. Samael turned to Elethia.

"You may go now, my dear. Thank you for bringing me this one. He will serve us well."

Elethia pressed her full lips into a thin line and merely nodded before vanishing in a cloud of shadow. Samael focused his full attention on Trent.

"Let's begin, shall we?"

CHAPTER 11

Kaeli shifted from one foot to the other as she stood in between Lukka and Joseph on the meeting platform. Aries, Leo, and Sagittarius stood not too far off with some of the other zodiac signs. Aquarius, Libra, and Virgo were already at the platform with their recruits. The others started to materialize at the portal in the distance. Kaeli stuffed her hands into her jacket pockets and let her gaze wander so that she wasn't really looking at anything.

This morning's training session had really gotten under her skin. It was all she could think about during breakfast, and the negative thoughts still wouldn't leave her alone. Even though she *knew* in her mind it was okay to be a beginner as she'd never done any of this before, she still felt like a failure. The other abilities, well the charm and fire anyway, had come so easily to her. Sure, she needed training to learn how to control them properly, but they had manifested naturally. Why couldn't she do the same for her instincts? A sharp nudge to her ribs snapped her out of her thoughts, and Lukka's jarring voice broke through her consciousness.

"What's up with you? You've barely said a word all morning." He looked down at her with a ridiculous grin on his face. Kaeli let out an exasperated sigh. From the corner of her eye, she spotted Joseph assessing her, a thoughtful expression on his face.

"It's nothing," she said, wrinkling her nose as she took a step away from Lukka.

"Well, you're not acting like it's nothing. Maybe... and I'm just taking a shot in the dark here... *maybe* someone wasn't as talented during her first training session as she thought she would be?" The ridiculous grin on Lukka's face grew wider, and Kaeli felt an overwhelming urge to sear his mouth shut on his face. Her fists clenched tighter in her pockets. Heat built in the palm of her hands.

"You shouldn't have said anything." Joseph shook his head.

"How did you find out about that?" Kaeli growled through gritted teeth. The heat grew. Whether it was from embarrassment or anger, she couldn't really tell. The last thing she wanted to do, however, was burst into flames. This was their first day of group training. She wanted to leave a good impression. She exhaled and a puff of smoke blew through her lips.

"Told you to keep your mouth shut," Joseph said to Lukka. Kaeli whirled to face him. She couldn't spend one more second looking at Lukka's smug face, or she was going to lose control.

"You knew about this too?" Her voice came out much harsher than she intended. Joseph looked at her with raised eyebrows, cautiously amused, as if he found her reaction interesting, but didn't want to tip her over the edge.

"We may have overheard Leo talking to Aries and Sagittarius about the best way to proceed with your instinct training," he answered. Kaeli closed her eyes and inhaled deeply, trying to calm the rising fire inside of her. Thankfully, Lukka didn't say anything else. She opened her eyes and took her hands out of her pockets. They sizzled a little, but the threat of combustion was gone. She focused on the group of zodiacs standing together, her gaze drawn to Leo. She didn't blame him for consulting Aries and Sagittarius, but it sucked that Lukka and Joseph knew about her failure.

Almost everyone was gathered on the platform now. Scorpio and Niko approached. Kaeli thought she heard one of the zodiacs complain they were late, but she didn't have enough time to dwell on it before Libra turned to face the recruits.

"Okay! Now that everyone has finally shown up..." She side-eyed Scorpio who just stood with his arms crossed and legs spread apart. Niko glanced around the platform, clearly uninterested in anything Libra had to say. He caught Kaeli's eye contact, and a faint smile played on his mouth. Kaeli returned the gesture before refocusing her attention on Libra who continued talking.

"We are going to divide all of you into groups. These will be the cohorts with which you will receive specialized training and the education needed to be a full-fledged zodiac. When I call your names, stand together. Group one! Kaeli, Ryan, Alex, Niko, and Shaina. Group two! Lukka, Selena, Daniel, and Eryn. Group three! Joseph, Randi, Anya, and Jamal." The recruits shuffled away from the others in their house groups to the zodiacs who already stood in the newly formed cohorts. Kaeli stepped toward Leo who waited with Gemini, Scorpio, and Virgo. Still bitter about her failure during the morning training session, she tried not to acknowledge Leo's presence, but he didn't seem to notice her anyway. He kept his gaze trained on Scorpio, who looked totally oblivious and uninterested in anything Leo might do or say. Niko sidled up to Kaeli.

"You clean up well," he smirked. Kaeli arched an eyebrow as she gave Niko a once over.

"Did you have fun cleaning all that crap out of your hair?" She smiled sweetly. His only response was a chuckle. Kaeli stood a little taller as she took notice of the other recruits joining their group.

Alex and Ryan, the gemini twins, approached the group. The only way Kaeli could tell them apart was because one had facial hair, and the other was clean shaven. Other than that, they both had the same thick, black, short hair and the same caramel skin. Their golden brown eyes twinkled mischievously as they approached the group. Behind them was Shaina. Her skin had more of a honey hue, and dark, layered hair fell just below her shoulders. Her eyes reminded Kaeli of a doe. All of the recruits were dressed in the same uniform Leo had given Kaeli earlier, except for the accent colors and zodiac insignias on the jackets, which matched the representative elements from each house.

"Alright, everyone, it's time to go over a few of the ground rules." Leo's voice commanded attention. All of the recruits turned toward him. "First off, over these next few months, you will be taking various classes from the other zodiacs as well as some of the Celestial Spirits that work here on the island. This will be in addition to your morning mentor sessions. Your group lessons will be aimed at building teamwork and problem-solving skills with your cohort, as well as preparing you for combat and the more political aspects of ruling the Western portion of the Celestial Realm and protecting our quadrant of Earth. Now, I know for a fact you're not all going to get along with each other at first." Leo flashed an almost indiscernible glance at Scorpio before returning his attention to the recruits. "Possibly ever," he muttered and cleared his throat, "but during your training you *will* act civilly with each other. At the first sign of unsupervised fighting, whether it be physical or with excessive language, there will be consequences for *all* of you. So keep each other accountable.

"Second! You're a team. That means you help each other. If one of you is having a hard time, then the rest of you help out and make sure the person can catch up. No one gets left behind. Third! If you're having a problem that absolutely cannot be helped or solved through your teammates, you come to Scorpio, Virgo, Gemini, or myself. It doesn't matter whom; we're all here for you. Fourth. We're going to be taking a tour of the Celestial Island very soon. During this tour, we will be informing you of the forbidden sections of our Western quarter of the Celestial Realm. You are *not* permitted to go to these sections *ever*. They are off limits for a reason, and should you be caught trespassing, we will immediately wipe your memories and you will be sent back to Earth with no recollection of your time here.... This will only be if you are still alive after trespassing. Does anyone have any questions?"

The recruits all shook their heads.

"Excellent!" Leo clapped his hands together. "Let's get this tour started!" He, along with the other zodiacs turned their backs and made their way across the bridge toward the teleportation runes that were becoming very familiar at this point. Kaeli's mind spun as she tried to recall all of Leo's ground rules. It was all a little much. For the first time since coming here, she was hit with the realization that this was now her home. Her pulse quickened, and she tried to focus her attention on the sound of Virgo's voice as he talked.

"We have four zones on the island, each of which are named after the four elements present in our quarter of the Celestial Realm," he explained. They were almost to the rune circle. "Central to everything is the library. You can see it from here," he said as he pointed ahead as everyone started to gather at the center. Kaeli's eyes widened as she saw the library. It was by far the most magnanimous building she had ever laid eyes on. Built entirely from white stone and marble, the library loomed above everything. It had graceful arches and spires reminiscent of gothic style architecture. Virgo continued his speech.

"You will have some of your more academic style classes there. The library contains a copy of every book and every story ever told. Books related to our civilizations are located on the lower floors. Books related to other civilizations are on the upper floors. The Celestial Spirits who work in the library will teach you how to access the books later. For now, we are going to Terra. "

Kaeli was not prepared for the nauseating darkness that enveloped them as soon as Virgo uttered the word. The feeling lasted for only a second before they reappeared. She stumbled slightly, bumping into Niko. He turned to her and offered a small smile.

"Still not used to teleporting, huh?"

Kaeli straightened her shoulders and tilted her chin upwards. "I'm getting used to it."

The zodiacs ushered the recruits out of the runes, and Kaeli took in a deep breath as she looked at the scenery before her. Terra certainly lived up to its name. The runes were at the top of a plateau overlooking colorful canyons and spacious, hilly plains. Virgo continued to walk the path leading down the plateau. Both he and Shaina had wide smiles on their faces. Ryan yawned as he leaned his head against his brother's shoulder. Niko kept an impassive expression on his face. Kaeli wondered what it would take to get the guy to react to something. He seemed so composed *all* the time. She found herself staring at Niko, and quickly forced her thoughts to focus back on Virgo's voice. She didn't want to miss any important information... especially if he said anything about the forbidden zones.

As they made their way down the plateau, the foliage thickened. Huge trees with thick trunks created a canopy of shade, shadowing a cobblestone path. Celestial Spirits with green and brown skin tended to the colorful flowers and bushes on the wayside.

"The main feature of Terra is the botanical gardens. Being part of the earth element, we like to make things grow and flourish. The gardens are open to anyone as long as you do not destroy or damage any property. Unlike other places in this realm, the gardens are susceptible to celestial fire. So fire signs especially need to be extra cautious. We don't want another... incident... happening."

Ryan's head popped up off of Alex's shoulder. His eyes lit with a dangerously mischievous glint.

"What incident?" he asked. Alex groaned.

"It really wasn't that big of a deal," Leo shrugged. "Pisces was able to put it out in minutes."

"She *shouldn't* have had to put anything out *at all*." Virgo closed his eyes and took a couple of deep breaths. "We won't tour the gardens now, but if any of you would like someone to show you around sometime, you can ask me, one of the other earth zodiacs, or any of the other earth spirits. Shaina will know these grounds soon as well, so you can ask her too in a couple of weeks." He quickly ushered them across the cobblestone path to a set of portal runes situated in the center of a willow grove. The dangling willow branches danced lazily in the breeze, and Kaeli caught sight of more earth spirits meandering through the flora. Scorpio made his way to the center of the circle.

"Aquae."

Kaeli once again found herself stumbling through a void of nothingness, but at least this time, the nausea held itself at bay. When she materialized again, she didn't even fall into Niko, much to her relief. Niko flashed her a grin.

"You are getting used to it."

Kaeli stuck her tongue out at him, and he chuckled. Their banter was cut short, however, as Kaeli was soon overtaken by the beauty of Aquae. They had teleported to runes that were cocooned in a cove of waterfalls. The ancient stone itself was a small island in the center of a lake that reflected near perfect replicas of the glittering starlight above them. A narrow stone pathway led the way out of the cove to an open expanse of flat land that almost looked like glass. Waterfalls framed the pathway looking like walls of shimmering blue glass. The mist from the waterfalls sent refractions of colorful light dancing over the smooth, dark stone. Everything about it emanated magic.

"Whoa," Kaeli said as her jaw dropped open as she walked in a slow circle, trying to take in the beauty of everything.

"Eh, it's alright," Ryan shrugged. "What are those mountains over there?" He pointed across the open expanse. Kaeli tilted her head and squinted her eyes as she looked off into the distance. She hadn't noticed before, but near the end of the open pathway were a cluster of mountains shrouded in fog.

"That is the first of the forbidden zones," Scorpio said. "Within them are portals that lead to other realms that none of you have any business visiting." His eyes narrowed as he stared down all of the recruits. "Should any of you have the bright idea to try, however, we do have Celestial Spirits guarding the portals. It would not be prudent to test their compassion."

"So, hypothetically, what happens if someone does end up getting past the guards and enters a portal?" Ryan asked, even as Alex elbowed him in the ribs, causing him to flinch. The zodiacs fell silent, and Leo fixed Scorpio with a hard stare. Scorpio arched an eyebrow. Leo turned to Ryan.

"The last zodiac who saw what was beyond those portals... never returned. That's all you need to know." He cleared his throat as he flashed another pointed stare at Scorpio. "Shall we continue the tour?" A lazy smile spread across Scorpio's face as he led the way across the lake. The bridge was only wide enough to let them cross in a single file. They continued to the next set of runes in relative silence. Kaeli didn't see as many spirits, but she did see more animals. Different varieties of colorful fish and sea creatures swam through the vertical walls of water, and as they passed by a pond, she thought she saw the head of what looked like a mermaid pop up for a split second before disappearing under the silky blue water. When they approached the runes, Leo stepped in the center.

"Ignis."

Kaeli once again found herself overwhelmed by the sudden change of scenery. Ignis was the complete opposite of Aquae, but no less stunning. It was filled with volcanoes, rich red soil, and natural hot springs interspersed with colorful plants and flowers. Leo led them through all of it to the outskirts where there was a huge combat arena similar to the one in House Ignis. As they walked past it, Leo explained that this was where they would have their combat lessons. Occasionally, the zodiacs also liked to hold tournaments to pit their strength against each other. The winner got bragging rights until the next tournament. Attached to the side of the combat arena was the armory. Only the zodiacs and fire spirits were permitted access for the time being, but after they received some training, the recruits would be allowed access as well.

Lastly, Gemini took them to Aera. The portal runes brought them to a pathway framed by looming mountains. Flying above, high in the mountain tops were strange, cat-like dragon creatures that let out eerily musical calls as they passed overhead. The echoes wove together and created an intricate harmony of tones that easily out-performed any symphony. Kaeli arched backward to get a better look at the creatures, her eyes wide with wonder. Even Niko looked stunned. Gemini cupped his hands and his mouth and mimicked their call before holding out his arm. A small dragon creature flew down and landed expertly on his forearm.

"These are the Yantari. Although they will sometimes travel around the Celestial Realm, for some reason they've seemed to have dubbed these mountains in Aera their home," Gemini said. Kaeli shifted a little uneasily. This was the first time she'd ever heard Gemini talk, and his voice had the same dual qualities as the rest of his appearance. When he spoke, it sounded like two voices talking in unison with each other. He gave the creature a small kiss on its forehead, and it let out a noise that sounded like a cross between a coo and a purr.

"The Yantari are unlike any other creature in the Celestial Realm. No one knows how they came here or from whence they came. Their existence predates all historical records we have of this world. I would strongly advise you to stay away from them unless you receive special training on how to interact with them. They are extremely intelligent and don't appreciate being treated as lesser beings. For the most part, if you leave them alone, they will leave you alone, but not all of them are as friendly as this little one." He pet the creature on the head, and it nuzzled into the palm of his hand. In one swift movement, he raised his forearm to the sky and the Yantari took off into flight.

"Beyond that way," Gemini motioned toward the tapering path leading deeper into the mountain range, "are more portals leading to other parts of the Celestial Realm ruled by other zodiacs. You will get to meet them after you are fully trained, but for now, I suggest you stay away, or else…" Gemini let out a high, sharp pitched whistle that had Kaeli covering her ears and squeezing her eyes shut tight. As if on cue, a huge shadow passed over them. Kaeli looked up and saw a massive dragon flying overhead. It wasn't a Yantari but shared some of the similar sleek characteristics. The larger Yantari didn't seem phased by the new presence, but the smaller ones scurried behind craggy rocks. The dragon let out a terrifying roar, and Kaeli once again covered her ears. Fire burst from the dragon's mouth, setting the mountain peaks ablaze. As soon as the dragon closed its mouth, the flame extinguished.

"You'll be barbeque," Gemini finished his sentence. "He and a couple of his friends guard the portals and they've been given express instructions not to allow any of you through." Kaeli stared with wide eyes as the dragon circled around and flew back toward the direction of the portals. Some of the smaller Yantari skittered out from behind the rocks, and she smiled. She liked these little cat dragons. Hopefully, she would be able to do the interactive training Gemini mentioned.

Together the group made their way to another circle of runes that brought them back to the platform. There wasn't much discussion as they crossed the rainbow bridge. Ryan talked to Alex in hushed tones, while Niko and Shaina kept mostly to themselves. Kaeli didn't blame them. She didn't really feel like talking herself. This whole tour was a lot to process. The layout of the island seemed simple enough as long as you knew the name of where you wanted to go, but the scenery was all so overwhelming. She wondered how long it would take to get island fever here. Sure, it didn't seem so bad if you could go back to Earth and get away from the vastness of space, but, beautiful as it was, there was only so much to do. Although she could probably spend an eternity in the library reading all of the books. That didn't sound so bad. She glanced over her shoulder to look back at the massive book haven. She couldn't wait to go inside.

When all of the groups had rejoined at the platform, Aries stood at the center.

"Alright, kiddos, that's where we're ending things today. Starting tomorrow, your groups will begin their rotation with us after your regularly scheduled mentor sessions. During your lessons with the other zodiacs, you will be learning the things necessary not only to fulfill your duty as a zodiac, but also the skills necessary to eventually rule this realm. Your mentors will tell you with whom your first class will be in the morning. You are dismissed and may return to your houses. Or don't. You've had the tour of the place now. I don't really care where you go." With those last inspiring words, Aries made her way toward Lukka's group.

"Alright! I guess that means we'll be seeing more of each other tomorrow!" Ryan sauntered his way in between Shaina and Kaeli and slung an arm over both of them. Shaina's nose scrunched up, and she let out a small snarl. Kaeli gingerly peeled Ryan's hand off her shoulder and dropped it.

"I think we're going to have to do a lot more team building before either of the ladies are comfortable with you like that," Niko snorted.

"I apologize for him," Alex said, shaking his head.

"You shouldn't be the one apologizing. He should!" Shaina shoved Ryan slightly away from her and glared at him. The sign of aggression was only met with a dazzling smile. Kaeli watched the scene unfold with a hint of amusement. Out of the corner of her eye, she saw Lukka heading toward the portal runes.

"I'll see you all tomorrow," she said as she followed after him.

"Ah, leaving so soon?" Ryan had a mock pout on his face. "But we were just starting to get to know each other."

"You don't need to be so heartbroken about it. You'll get to see more of me tomorrow," she smiled with a sickly sweetness before jogging off after Lukka.

✳ ✳ ✳

Trent groaned. His eyelids felt so heavy he couldn't open them. Every muscle in his body ached. Pain. That was all he knew. He didn't know how long he'd been down in this hellhole, or even what Samael had done to him. He just knew if his limbs hadn't been strapped down, he would be doing everything in his power to end this.

Mobility slowly returned to his body. He tried curling and uncurling his fingers, but the sensation was awkward. They didn't *feel* like his. His eyes darted from side to side, trying to look through his peripheral vision, but his head too was fixated in one position. He winced as a streak of light fell across his face. Even with his eyes closed, the soft glow hurt. Light footsteps sounded across the floor and the door squeaked closed. A syrupy sweet smell hit his senses and almost made him gag. He heard a soft chuckle.

"You've been enhanced." It was Samael's voice. Every muscle in Trent's body tensed, as if some separate entity instinctively knew what Samael had done and wanted to stay as far away as possible. A shadow fell over his eyes. Trent mustered the strength to just barely pry his eyelids open. He kept his features neutral as he stared into the face of the demon before him. Even though he knew it was nearly pitch black in this little torture chamber, he could see every detail as if he stood in broad daylight. Samael cocked his head to the side. A devilish grin spread across his face as he looked Trent over. He brushed his fingers across Trent's jawline. His skin felt cool and scaly. Anger roiled in the pit of Trent's stomach at the touch.

"I haven't made anyone like you for quite some time," he murmured. He stepped away and arched his brows. "Elethia should be pleased with the results." He paused. "It might be too soon for this, but would you like to see your new self?"

Trent growled an utterly unearthly, foreign growl. Samael's grin grew wider, and his slitted pupils expanded, almost turning the whole of his eyes black.

"I'll take that as a yes." He flourished his hand and a floor to ceiling obsidian mirror appeared in front of Trent. If it weren't for the similar facial features, Trent would not have recognized his own reflection. The general shape of his face and his eyes were the same, although his pupils were now slitted. Other than that, he didn't recognize the monster in front of him. His skin was tight, stretched taut over his muscular body and hairless skull. Scales covered him from head to toe. His brow bones were accentuated, and his mouth was a thin slit that stretched from one side of his face to the other in a mocking curl. His jaw dropped in surprise almost splitting his face in two, and a forked tongue slithered out before he quickly snapped it shut. Trent's gaze traveled down his body taking in the monstrous sight. His fingers were elongated and sharpened to points… perfect for stabbing. He barely had a chance to process his new body before the mirror disappeared.

"You'll get used to it soon enough." Samael patted Trent on the head. If he hadn't been trapped, he would have snapped Samael's hand clean off. Samael chuckled. "I'll be back soon. Now that you're awake, I'm going to give you some time alone to adjust to your new body." He turned his back and stepped out of the room without a second glance toward Trent. As soon as the door shut, the bonds holding Trent in place disappeared. Trent rushed to the door, tripping over his own speed. He slammed into the door and pounded it with a strength that should have dented the thing in half, screaming all the while. Shadows swirled around him, engulfing him in darkness.

Alyssa Markins

CHAPTER 12

*T*hat night, Kaeli jolted up in bed as she heard a faint whisper in her ear.

"Ooopeeen the doooor."

    A chilling wind seeped through her bones, and she pulled her blankets tighter around her shoulders. Her eyes darted back and forth, scanning the room for the bearer of the voice. Nothing. Silence settled into the darkness. She ducked her head under the pillows and clamped them against her ears. Her chest rose and fell with rapid, shallow breaths as every one of her senses were on alert, straining to pick up any abnormality.

    Minutes passed.

    Silence continued.

    Kaeli let out a steady sigh as her heavy eyelids fell closed.

    "Open the door!" The whisper turned to a demanding hiss.

    Kaeli's eyes shot open. She flung the pillow away from her face and sat upright, her hands splayed out on either side of her. Every muscle in her body tensed. Her fingers curled around the sheets in an iron grip. Wrapped around her bedposts was a shadow snake with electric purple eyes. Kaeli's heart dropped as the snake slithered off the post and onto her bed, making its way toward her, then winding behind her back. Kaeli squeezed her eyes shut. Her chest constricted, choking out the air in her lungs. A tingling sensation radiated from her head down her shoulders. She couldn't find the voice to scream.

"Ooopeeen the doooor."

The snake nudged her out of bed and goaded her to the doorway. As she took step after reluctant step, the whisper became louder and more forceful. Kaeli found herself slipping back into a familiar trancelike state as the shadows of the dark room pressed around her, moving her legs against her will. It only took two more steps before she lost all conscious control of her body. Her mind thrashed and raged against the shadows, but her body just gave in. She opened the door and stepped out into the shared living quarters.

Lukka and Joseph were nowhere to be seen. If only someone would bust out of their room and help fight off this snake. It was wishful thinking. Kaeli crossed the room in silence, completely alone with the snake that slithered around her feet and shadows that coaxed her onward.

As the snake led her through House Ignis, the strain between her mind and body became so tense that pinpricks of pain shot through her muscles. With every footfall, she internally screamed at her feet to stop moving, but to no avail. Where was everyone? The corridors were completely empty as the snake led her to the training arena. As they approached one of the arched openings, the shadows stopped pushing. Kaeli twitched her fingers, regaining slight control over her limbs. The snake continued to slide along the floor to the center of the arena.

A faint outline of a door started to materialize in the midst of the obstacle courses. Blood thrashed through Kaeli's veins. It was the same door she'd seen a couple of days ago. She stared at it—wide-eyed, legs trembling. The door rattled with sounds of tortured screaming. The shadows nudged Kaeli forward again. One curled around her hand and lifted it in front of her face. Kaeli gritted her teeth as she struggled to maintain the little control she had. Heat built in her core, but she couldn't release the pressure. Small sparks danced around her fingers, but she couldn't summon enough fire to fight back against the shadows. The snake turned to face her as she moved closer. Its head tilted inquisitively.

"Let. Me. Go." Kaeli found control over her voice again, but her demanding pleas did nothing to stop her from walking. The sparks grew to flames, but more shadows leaked out of the door, covering the open sky in inky darkness. Her flame responded in defiance, licking up her arms to encase her entire body, but still the shadows urged her onward. The ear-splitting screams reverberated through her skull as she got closer.

"OPEN IT!!!"

The shriek pulsated through Kaeli's entire body as she struggled to keep her outreached hand from making contact with the door handle. The tips of her fingers barely grazed the door before the pressure of her fire exploded in a last ditch effort for control. She flew backwards. Her head hit the packed dirt of the arena floor, and the last thing she saw before passing out was the shape of the snake slithering slowly toward her.

"Kaeli! What the hell! WAKE UP!"

Kaeli awakened to Lukka shaking her so hard she almost fell out of the bed. She flailed, grabbing onto anything she could to steady herself. Her heart pounded in her chest as she took deep breaths. The shadows were gone. Streaks of sunlight peered through the windows. She hesitantly brought her gaze to Lukka.

"What the hell is wrong with you?"

Kaeli rubbed her eyes, trying to orient herself. Then it hit her. The pain. Her head was throbbing and her arms ached. Kaeli moaned as she pressed her palms against her temples.

"What are you talking about…" She tried to swat Lukka away, but she didn't have the energy. Then the memories came crashing all at once. The door. The snake. She froze. In her peripheral vision, she noticed her arms were darkened with soot. She looked up at Lukka, and her breath caught in her throat. He had the same markings on his face. Her eyes widened as her heart raced.

"What happened?" she squeaked.

"You were shooting fire all over the place in your sleep," Lukka said, breathing heavily as he took slow, steady breaths. His eyes flickered frantically but otherwise he appeared calm. "But it was… hot fire. It didn't exactly catch onto anything, but it left marks." He motioned to her arms and his face.

"I… did that?" Kaeli's arms fell to her sides. She looked around the room. The walls and furniture had not escaped unscathed either.

"Yeah, and it hurt like a bitch."

"We only noticed because of the smoke that started billowing into the common room," Joseph said as he entered through the doorway. Leo rushed in not far behind.

"Kaeli, are you—" He paused when he saw the marks all over the room. His gaze rested on Kaeli, and the expression on his face darkened. Kaeli sank away from the glower, unintentionally pressing herself closer to Lukka. Lukka placed a hand on her shoulder.

"She was sleeping," he said.

"Get dressed and meet me in the training arena." Leo pressed his lips into a thin line. Kaeli didn't think the anger in his voice was directed at her, but his tone frightened her nonetheless. He turned, leaving the room, and she let out a shaky exhale. She looked up to see Lukka staring down at her. He removed his hand from her shoulder and lifted the edge of his shirt to wipe away the soot from his face. Kaeli couldn't stop her faze from flickering to his toned abs. When Lukka dropped the shirt, a playful grin spread across his face.

"Somebody's in trouuuble."

Kaeli pushed herself away from him, grabbed a pillow, and smacked him in the face, which only elicited a laugh from both him and Joseph. She threw a pillow at Joseph who caught it expertly midair with one hand.

"Out of my room. Now!" She pushed herself off the bed and made her way to her bathroom, slamming the door behind her without giving a second glance to see if Lukka and Joseph had actually listened to her.

Less than an hour later, Kaeli faced Leo in the training arena. His expression softened slightly, but he still did not seem pleased. Kaeli wished she could sink into nothingness as she approached him. He sat down on one of the nearby obstacles and motioned for her to join him.

"What happened? I need you to tell me everything you can remember." His brows were drawn down in a serious expression, but his voice was soft. Kaeli took in a shaky breath as she recounted the details of her dream. The snake, the door, the fiery explosion—it was all so vivid in her mind. And the soot. There was no way this had been just a dream. Leo stayed silent as she talked. Her shoulders dropped as she traced meaningless squiggles in the sandy floor.

"What's going on?" she whispered. "These snakes keep… following… me around, and I've been hearing those whispers in my head way more often than I feel comfortable with."

"I wish I had all the answers," Leo sighed. "We know part of the story, but there's still a lot of details we're trying to figure out. There's only so much I could tell you at this point."

"Well, what can you tell me?" Kaeli ran her foot through the sand, ruining her little doodles.

"I do know how your fire was able to leave physical marks on you and Lukka," Leo said as he stood up, "and it's one of the reasons we're focusing on your elemental control today instead of your instinct. Honestly, I should have considered this earlier given how quickly you took to fire, but I never thought it would go to this extent."

"Just tell me already."

"How do I explain this?" Leo gnawed at the inside of his lip. "You know how we've referred to this place as the Celestial Realm? Well, this isn't the only alternate 'realm,' so to speak. One of those realms is the Dream Realm, and for the zodiacs, dream and physical realms can often… intermix."

"So… when we're dreaming, we're actually in another realm?"

"In a manner of speaking, yes. On Earth, dreams are a manifestation of the subconscious mind. Here, the subconscious mind has the power to create and enter reality if you allow it. The collective creation of many minds over time has led to the formation of the Dream Realm. Pisces probably has the most experience dealing with it, but occasionally the rest of us get a little taste as well. In the process of becoming a zodiac, it's much more likely for you to enter by accident."

He paused, taking in a deep breath as he gazed out at the expanse of galaxy above them. "In the Dream Realm, you retain all of the abilities you have in the waking realms. If you don't have full control over your abilities in the waking worlds, you don't have control over them in the sleeping ones either. The problem is that, unless you are very aware, the Dream Realm isn't 'element proof.'" He did air quotes. "The fire you produce there can still affect you here because you're not a full zodiac." Leo fell silent for a couple of moments. "What concerns me is that your fire not only appeared to affect you, but also Lukka and your entire room. That means you were somehow able to conjure the fire in the Dream Realm and replicate it in the Celestial Realm in some form that could actually cause damage," Leo said, punctuating the realization with a heavy sigh. Kaeli pursed her lips as she focused her attention on her ruined sand doodles. Leo clapped her on the back and stood. She looked at him to see a genuine smile on his face.

"I'll figure out how to deal with this later. For now, we need to make sure you have this fire completely under control to prevent anything like this from happening again."

✱✱✱

The training session left Kaeli feeling out of breath and exhausted. Since they had started early, and Leo thought she'd made adequate progress during their training session, he had let Kaeli go back to her room with extra time to shower. She just finished putting on her uniform when Aries came bursting through the door. Kaeli jumped and tried to hold back a groan. Aries grinned from ear to ear, showing off her perfectly pearl white teeth.

"Hope you're ready for today!" She leaned her forearm against the doorframe. "Your group is having a class with me." Her grin turned into a sadistic smile. Kaeli struggled to keep the disappointment off her face. A class with Aries was not how she wanted to start her first day of formal group training. Aries stepped closer and lowered her voice, "Now look, kid, I'm only telling you this because you're training to be a fire sign, and Leo seems to like you, but you'll be using your elemental power to fight today. So you better kick ass. If you make our element look bad, I'll never live it down. We're consistently the best at everything, so you better be too. Got it?"

Aries had gotten so close Kaeli could feel the heat of her breath trailing after the question. She backed up a couple steps to put some distance between herself and the intimidating zodiac. She averted her gaze toward the floor to avoid the intense eye contact.

"Got it," she said with an awkward mix of determination and fear.

"Good," Aries said as she turned on her heel and walked toward the door. She paused at the bathroom entrance and turned her head back to look at Kaeli. "This'll be fun!"

"So... much... fun..." Kaeli bit her lip. Aries smiled, then left.

"Jeez, no pressure," Kaeli muttered. She walked over to the mirror and checked herself one more time, making sure she had everything before following in Aries's footsteps and leaving.

Kaeli caught sight of Niko as she made her way to the portal at the center of the houses. He grinned as they approached the circle of runes, neither of them crossing over into the center just yet.

"Are you ready for our first class with Sagittarius today?" he asked.

Kaeli returned the smile. After her morning training session with Leo, and the strange dreams, she was more than ready. Sagittarius was going to give them the grand tour of the library. A thrill of anticipation rushed beneath her skin as she thought about the beautiful building she'd only seen glimpses of until today.

"Definitely ready," she said, taking a step closer toward the portal runes. She paused before putting her foot all the way over the border. Up to this point, one of the zodiacs had always used the portals to teleport. This would be the first time they did it on their own. She looked down at her foot and then up at Niko. "We just step in the center and say the name of where we want to go?"

Niko stepped all the way in and shrugged.

"I would assume so, based on how the zodiacs have been using it. Get your other foot in here. The last thing we need is one of us saying the name of our destination, and only half your body teleporting."

Kaeli's eyes widened as she hurriedly pulled her other foot into the circle.

"Library," Niko said. A whoosh of air engulfed the two of them.

Before Kaeli could blink, she and Niko stood in front of the massive stone library. Sagittarius paced in front of the entrance, turning to face them as they materialized. He waved them over. Another rush of air sounded behind Kaeli. She turned to see Shaina and the twins standing behind her. She nodded her head in greeting and made her way to the entrance where Sagittarius stood.

"You're all on time. Good." Sagittarius straightened his shoulders and said, "In our lesson today, I will be giving you a tour of our Celestial Library. Other lessons here will concern learning about the inner societal workings of the Celestial Realm and the political responsibilities you will all bear as future zodiacs, but it all starts with learning the basics of this library. Come." He walked toward the double glass doors and they slid open before him. Together, the group walked through the entrance.

Kaeli's breath stalled. Her lips parted as her eyes blinked rapidly before she stared wide eyed at the huge expanse of book filled space before her. The interior of the library was even more impressive than its intricately stone-carved exterior, and Sagittarius had not been exaggerating when he called it a labyrinth. Warm sunlight spilled into the open foyer framed by white marble arches leading to pathway upon pathway of books. At the very center of everything was a spiral staircase surrounded by a white stone counter with a single opening. Kaeli craned her neck to try to see where it ended, but it towered too tall. Platforms extended out from the staircase at each floor, leading to more marble arches.

"How long do you think it would take to get to the top of that thing?" Ryan asked. He didn't bother lowering his voice.

"Precisely forty-eight hours for a human with average endurance and no breaks," Sagittarius answered, "but that is hardly of consequence. The staircase is here mostly to add a sense of grandiosity. Everything you will need to access is located here on the first floor. If, perchance, there is a book you need from one of the upper floors, one of the Celestial Spirits working in this establishment can retrieve it for you." He cleared his throat and then, as if summoned by the cough, a spirit entered the foyer from one of the shadowed corridors. Kaeli's eyes widened. While she was still not used to the spirits and their translucent skin, the one that came before them was more otherworldly than any she had met. Her skin was a faded shade of lavender, and her eyes and hair glowed with a muted white light. As she moved through the aisles of books, her long hair billowed behind her as if she moved through water, swaying in some unseen force. Sagittarius folded both of his arms behind his back, making his already muscled chest seem even larger. As she approached the group, she offered Sagittarius a slight smile.

Kaeli didn't fail to notice the corner of his mouth twitch upward before he schooled his features into a neutral expression.

"This is Aurae," he stated. "She is the head librarian of our Celestial Library."

Aurae inclined her head the tiniest bit to the group.

"It is a pleasure to meet you all." Her voice was silky smooth. Keali found herself at a loss for words. Ryan stepped forward and bowed deeply.

"The pleasure is all mine, m'lady," he said, winking as he rose. Sagittarius raised his eyebrows. Shaina crossed both her arms and snickered. Ryan straightened back his shoulders and shot her a glare. Aurae kept the small smile on her face.

"As Sagittarius has just said, I am the head librarian here. You can see this library is vast and has a large selection of books. If there is something you want to look for specifically, I can provide you with the titles that fall under the category. I can also retrieve books from sections that may be too difficult to reach. If you would simply like to browse, I can direct you to sections based on your interests. Should you find yourself in need of my assistance, come to this front counter and ring the bell." She moved toward the marble counter and delicately tapped the top of a silver bell that Kaeli hadn't noticed when they came in. The crisp, clear sound echoed throughout the lobby in waves of hypnotic chimes. It only stopped when Aurae placed her hand over it. "You may not remove anything from this library, but you are welcome to spend as much time here as you would like, when you are not partaking in your training activities, of course."

"As... much time as we... want?" Kaeli's face parted into a wide grin. Niko snorted, snapping her out of the brief moment of euphoria. She turned to face him.

"What?"

"Nothing. Just didn't take you to be a book nerd."

Kaeli made a face. "Shut up. This is awesome."

"We must have different ideas for what qualifies as awesome," he said, an amused smirk on his face. Kaeli was about to open her mouth in protest, but before she could get out a single word, a strong wind blew through the space straight toward Niko, making him stumble back a couple of feet. By the time the wind vanished, Niko's hair stuck out in all different directions. He stood frozen, blinking his eyes rapidly. Aurae clasped her hands behind her back and smiled sweetly.

"I am *certain* you were not referring to *my* library, because it is indeed 'awesome.' If you would like to continue using the resources here, I would suggest you," she paused as her eyes narrowed and started glowing with a pale lavender light, "watch yourself." She cleared her throat, her eyes returning to their normal white color. "Now then, it was a pleasure meeting all of you. I know Sagittarius must continue on with your lesson, but we shall be seeing more of each other later." She threw one more side-eyed glance at Niko before nodding politely to Sagittarius and disappearing down one of the book aisles. Ryan lightly punched Niko's arm.

"Way to go, man. Pissing off the hot librarian on your first visit."

Without warning, a gust of wind rushed toward Ryan, hitting him at the knees. He caught himself in a push up position just before his face smashed into the ground.

"Looks like he's not the only one," Shaina laughed.

"Enough." Sagittarius's voice was quiet, but the strength of it rumbled through the air. "There's a great amount of knowledge within these walls. Knowledge is power. I suggest you start acting as if you are in the presence of such." He eyed Ryan as he pushed himself up to his feet. "Are we clear?" Everyone collectively nodded. "Good. Now if you will follow me, there is one section of this library you will need to become very acquainted with today." He turned his back and walked past the front desk toward the back of the building. The recruits followed after him.

At the far end of the foyer stood a dark, obsidian door with shimmering silver constellations etched into it. The markings actually seemed to twinkle, as if some force had taken the stars from the sky and set them into the dark stone. Sagittarius stopped and turned to face the group.

"This is the Room of Records," he said, motioning to the door, "and it is the only section of the library that any of you should attempt to access without assistance until you become full-fledged zodiacs."

Alex raised his hand.

"Yes, Alex?"

"Why?"

"Because if you try to access any other section unassisted, you will undeniably become horribly lost." Sagittarius arched an eyebrow and a small smile crept onto his face. "I remember when Aries was still in training. She tried to run off on her own during a tour. She was stuck running in circles for three days before Aurae was able to locate her." The smile immediately vanished from his face and a fire lit behind his eyes. "But none of you will *ever* repeat that story or I will personally see to it that you are put on Krillig cleaning duty for the remainder of your training."

"What the hell's a Krillig?" Ryan asked.

"And what's so bad about Krillig cleaning duty?" Alex echoed.

"I've seen them before," Shaina interjected. "They're raised in the Terra region and kind of look like a cross between an anteater and an armadillo. Apparently, their waste makes the most amazing fertilizer or something like that. They're basically just kept around for their poop."

"And believe me when I say it *does not* smell pleasant." Sagittarius cleared his throat. "Now then." He grasped the door handle and pulled, splitting the star speckled obsidian stone in two. "Welcome to the Room of Records." With his free hand, he motioned for them to step inside.

Kaeli's breath hitched as she stepped through the entrance. The room was circular with a domed skylight embedded into the ceiling that let in refractions of the kaleidoscope sky beyond the library walls. A round table made of the same inky black stone as the door sat in the center of the room. Chairs with plush cushions representing all of the colors from the different houses surrounded it. It was the shelves upon shelves of books, however, that filled Kaeli with giddy excitement. She could almost hear them calling to her. Faint whispers of words murmured too quietly to distinguish.

"You look like you're going to burst," Niko said. Kaeli tore her gaze away from the impressive collection to find him studying her with an amused gaze.

"I get that you may not be so interested in matters of refined culture, but that doesn't mean I have to stoop to such brutish instincts." She batted her lashes, then rolled her eyes. Niko tried to stifle a laugh.

"Well, despite my brutish instincts, even I have to admit that at least this section of the library might be… awesome," he stuffed his hands in his pockets as he craned his neck to take in the whole view of the room. Kaeli felt a slight nudge to her arm and turned to find Ryan standing a little too close.

"He's just saying that to get on the librarian's good side," he whispered to her just loud enough for Niko to hear. Niko's eyes darted to Ryan, a scowl planted on his face. Ryan's eyes sparkled as he grinned.

"Does anyone else hear voices?" Shaina asked. She looked at Ryan and Niko with raised eyebrows. "And no, I don't mean your inane chatter."

"I do," Kaeli said.

"That would be the records," Sagittarius said as he closed the door behind them. With the entryway shut off, the colored lights streaming in through the window become more vibrant, and the whispers more amplified. A slight shudder ran down Kaeli's spine as the voices tickled her ears.

"The Room of Records is unlike any other section of the library." Sagittarius sauntered to the table and turned to face the recruits. "As you may have deduced, it contains recordings from every zodiac hailing from our Western territory. These books are not read as you might typically read a book." He paused, as if musing on his thoughts. "It would be much easier to show you how this works than to explain it to you. Kaeli."

Kaeli stood upright at the mention of her name.

Sagittarius smiled. "Pick a book from one of the shelves and open it here on the table."

Kaeli's heart skipped a beat as she looked around the room, perusing the shelves. As her attention focused solely on the books, the whispers seemed to get louder, calling to her, begging almost, to be taken from their tucked-away posts. She brushed her fingers over a few of the spines and noticed that a small zodiac constellation marked each one. Below the constellation was an inscribed word that changed from book to book.

"If we could do this sometime today, that would be great," Ryan said. Kaeli shot him a dirty look before turning back to the shelves and pulling out a book with an Aries constellation. She brought it to the table and set it down. As soon as the cover made contact with the smooth, dark surface, the matching constellation on the map lit up with a brilliant silver glow. Kaeli opened the book to the first page and almost went blind with the burst of red and yellow light. She jumped back as a roar rattled the shelves, resonating off the walls.

When the light dissipated, she found herself trembling in front of a massive being standing in front of the table. He must have been nearly seven feet tall and was built like a rhinoceros. She heard Sagittarius sigh from somewhere nearby.

"Of all the books, you had to choose this savage," he murmured.

"FREE AT LAST!" the giant bellowed. He looked down at Kaeli and grinned at her with a wolfish smile. Kaeli's eyes widened as her feet rooted themselves to the floor. Her brain told her to flee in the face of this terrifying person, but her limbs refused to move, so she stared at him head-on. The being before her was decked out in a full suit of ancient, Roman-style armor complete with a sword and helmet that cast a dark shadow over his glowing orange eyes.

"He looks like the actual god of war," Alex said.

"Ares," Shaina breathed.

"That's my name." The former aries propped his fists on his waist and surveyed the recruits. "Now what are you tiny humans doing in my library?"

"They are training." Sagittarius stepped between Kaeli and the spirit. "This is their first time in the library, and I'm showing them the Room of Records. I thought the demonstration of how these records work would serve better than an explanation. And your name is no longer Aries, Cassius."

Cassius. That was the word Kaeli had read on the spine of the book. She looked up to consider the giant again. It was difficult to tell with the glowing eyes, but she could have sworn a flash of disappointment fell across his face.

"So I am to be a mere tour guide." He slammed a fist on the obsidian table. A vibration rumbled through the floor with the force of the hit. "Oh, the fall from glory! I used to slay armies with this sword!" He unsheathed the weapon strapped to his waist and swung it forward, making all of the recruits jump back. "Now I have been reduced to a spectacle." He dropped the sword at his side as he took a seat at the table and sunk his head into his hands. Sagittarius sighed and rubbed his temples before turning to face the recruits.

"Each of these books contains apparitions of the previous zodiacs. When we die, or are replaced, our memories and personalities are preserved in these records. You can glean a great amount of wisdom and insight from these books."

"Who are you calling a book?!" Cassius bellowed as he violently pushed himself up from his seat. Sagittarius paused and arched an eyebrow before continuing on with his speech.

"They exist as a means for you to seek counsel. Although be warned," he said, looking Cassius up and down. "Some provide better counsel than others."

"You take that ba—" before Cassius could finish his sentence, Sagittarius closed the book on the table. There was another flash of warm light. When it dissipated, the giant warrior was gone. Sagittarius slid the book back onto the shelf.

"You may access the Room of Records any time you'd like. In fact, we encourage you to learn as much as you can from the former zodiacs. There are millenia of insights contained in these records that will serve you well in times to come. Are there any questions?"

Dead silence filled the room. Sagittarius nodded his head in approval.

"Alright then, follow me to your next class."

He led them out of the library to the portal. Whispered words barely left his lips before the loud rush of wind sounded in Kaeli's ears and everything turned to a blur. When the world righted itself again, they stood in front of the arena in Ignis. Aries materialized at the entrance in a cloud of orange and red smoke. The smoke trailed behind her as she walked toward them.

"Welcome to combat training!" Her face twisted into a devilish grin. She nodded to Sagittarius. "You can head out, big boy. I got it from here."

Sagittarius scowled at her, but didn't retort as he disappeared in a cloud of orange smoke.

A sharp cough interrupted Aries's speech before she could even start. Everyone turned to see Aquarius walking through the entrance. Aquarius was on the short side compared to the other zodiacs. She had short jet-black hair styled in an A-line cut, with full red lips set on her small face. A cloud of icy indigo smoke trailed after her, disappearing into the orange haze of the arena.

"This is not combat training," she said, emphasizing each word. "It is an evaluation of the recruits' elemental capability." Aries crossed her arms and rolled her eyes.

"Buzzkill," she muttered. Shaina let out what sounded like a sigh of relief. Aries returned her attention to the recruits. "Regardless, in order to evaluate your powers and abilities, we actually have to see you use them," she said with a wicked grin across her face. "And that means we need to see you suckers fight."

"That is absolutely *not* what that means." Aquarius stared at Aries through furrowed brows. Aries inhaled and exhaled slowly as she pursed her lips. Aries looked like she might pop if she heard Aquarius contradict her one more time, although Kaeli was secretly glad Aquarius was here to intercede. Aries crossed her arms and glared at Aquarius.

"Alright then, what do you suggest would be the best way to test their untapped, raw potential?" She cocked her head to the side. "You and I both know that untrained recruits need an adrenaline rush to reveal their true potential. Maybe you want to do it the way the previous zodiacs tested us? Throw them into life or death scenarios where they will be forced to defend themselves or die? That sounds *so much* more reasonable than a supervised fight."

Aquarius paused, running a hand over the back of her neck, before nodding decisively. "You make a good point."

"How is that a good point?" Shaina blurted. Everyone turned their attention to her. Shaina's gaze flitted from person to person. She cleared her throat. "There *has* to be some other way to test our potential than putting us in life or death situations or making us fight each other."

Aries and Aquarius looked at each other thoughtfully.

"Well maybe..." Aquarius said.

"That could possibly..." Aries scratched her chin. They blinked.

"Nah," they said in unison.

"Well, I tried." Shaina kicked her toe into the ground. A cloud of red dust puffed around her shoe. Ryan patted her on the shoulder. She shot him a hard glare. He grinned and stuffed his hand back into his pocket.

"Alright." Aries clapped her hands together. "This is how it's going down. As we're testing your elemental potential, you will not be allowed to use any physical contact." She brushed a strand of her wild hair away from her face. "Unless you have a fist wrapped in your element, then I guess maybe you could punch somebody, but we want to see more creative fighting uses than that."

Shaina opened her mouth to protest, but Aries cut her off.

"If any of you lay so much as a single finger on your sparring partner, be prepared to feel my wrath. But go as all out with your element as you possibly can. We need to see what you're capable of."

Kaeli's stomach started flipping circles. She didn't mind showing off what she could do with her powers, but using them to actually fight another person… She didn't know if she was ready for that. Her gaze flickered to Aries. Aries had a wide grin on her face.

"We're going to do this bracket style. Two teams, and then the winners of the two teams will duel it out against each other. We'll start with elemental opposites. You!" She pointed at Shaina. "I want you to go up against the twins. Kaeli, you're fighting Niko."

Kaeli bit her lip as her gaze met Niko's. He stood straight, hands loosely tucked into his pockets, shoulders squared off. Kaeli couldn't help the grimace that crossed her face. How could he be so serene about this? Kaeli closed her eyes and took a calming breath before letting a lazy smile play over her lips. If he wasn't going to show physical signs of stress, neither would she. She couldn't let him think he had an advantage over her—even if water did normally extinguish fire. Maybe that's why he looked so nonchalant.

"The arena will change environments between fights so each of you will have a tactical terrain advantage. The fight ends when either Aquarius or I say it does… or if someone passes out." Aries had a fire burning in her eyes. Kaeli shook her head and blinked again. A literal fire burned where Aries's pupils were supposed to be. "Shaina and the twins will go first." Aries turned to Kaeli and Niko. "The two of you can sit in the bleachers and enjoy the show." She clapped her hands together and sparks flew from her fingers as she rubbed them together. "Let the games begin!"

Aquarius shook her head. "You're always so dramatic about these things."

CHAPTER 13

By the time the fight between Shaina and the twins ended, Kaeli's heart was beating so fast, she felt like it would burst out of her chest. The twins had won. Well one of them had won. Ryan had all but collapsed on a rock platform that floated in the air. Alex was winded but still standing. Shaina was in the same state as Ryan. Really the odds had been stacked against her, having to hold her own against both of them. Aquarius had called the fight just as Shaina and Ryan almost passed out.

"Alright, Kaeli! Niko! You're up!" Aries bellowed. The words barely left her lips when the arena changed. The floor morphed into a glittering lake. A circle platform rose from the center, water cascading off the edge. In the middle of the platform was a ring of fire. The contrast of the fiery reflections dancing on the water would have been beautiful if Kaeli didn't have the weight of impending dread hanging over her. Before she even had time to properly assess the situation, the familiar unwelcome whoosh of teleportation washed over her, and she found herself standing on top of the platform. She glanced across the fire pit and saw Niko standing on the opposite side—arms crossed, cocky smirk smugly in place. She straightened her stance and squared off her shoulders, tilting her head in such a way that she knew the fire light would gleam off her hair and eyes. Niko's smile grew even wider.

"Okay, you know the rules! The fight starts when someone makes the first move!" Aries's voice echoed throughout the arena. Kaeli barely had time to register the words before a giant geyser shot up from the water behind her and came crashing toward her with supernatural speed. Without thinking, she reached toward the flames at the center of the platform. The fire leapt toward her fingers and swirled around her in a protective shield just as the stream of water came crashing down on her. The water hissed as it made contact with the heat and evaporated into sizzling steam. Kaeli whirled to face Niko. He smiled at her mockingly.

"Nice reflexes," he said, his voice dripping with arrogance.

Kaeli's blood boiled beneath her skin as she gritted her teeth. She hadn't wanted to start this fight on the defensive, but Niko had more control than she anticipated. She let out a low growl and the flames at the center of the platform rose higher in response.

"Feisty." Niko's voice was unbearably cocky.

Kaeli knew he was trying to bait her, but despite her best efforts to remain calm, her temper rose to the surface. If he wasn't going to take this easy, neither was she.

She rushed straight toward the fire.

Niko wasted no time. He held his arms out to the side, palms facing upward. Water shot up in columns around him. Kaeli emerged from the fire, flames encasing her like armor. Niko stretched out his arms, and spikes of water flew toward Kaeli. She willed the temperature of the fire to increase and held her hands up to block. The water evaporated on impact, but she wasn't making any headway. Steam plastered wisps of hair against her face. She needed to *do* something. The last thing she wanted was to block onslaughts of water for the entire fight.

Kaeli spun away from an oncoming water spike, the fire dancing with her movements. The living armor became an extension of her arm, whipping out toward Niko. He dove out of the way, but the distraction caused him to lose control of the water. The geysers plunged back into the lake. Kaeli grinned but didn't pause as she placed both hands on the ground and sent a wall of fire rushing toward Niko.

The flames circled him, trapping him and cutting off any direct access to water. Kaeli stood up, not entirely sure what to do. The strength of her fire should have been enough to neutralize any water Niko could generate himself, but Aries hadn't called the match. A stray pebble bouncing on the ground caught her attention in her peripheral vision.

The ground fell out from under her, flattening down to an island at water level. She flailed as she fell midair before twisting her body into an upright position and extending her arms downward. She shot fire out like a thrust, cushioning her landing.

Niko, on the other hand, twisted so he fell away from the newly formed land mass, and dove straight into the water. Kaeli's stomach dropped. This couldn't be good. Letting out a sigh, she let her eyes flutter closed. Instincts. Leo told her she had talent for predatory instincts. If she could just focus, maybe she would be able to sense where Niko would surface. She kept the fire burning in a low blaze around her fists as she steadied her breathing. The heat danced in anticipation under her skin. Building. Waiting. Itching to be released.

* * *

Niko relaxed his muscles as the cool water enveloped him. He honestly hadn't expected Kaeli to be this much of a challenge. He'd been holding back, but if he wanted this fight to end, he'd have to start putting some effort into it. Sweeping his arms through the water, he started to form currents. He manipulated the streams until they swirled around him in a protective bubble. The sound of thrashing water roared in his ears, and a smile crossed his face. Now.

He shot his hands upward and the bubble followed suit, blasting through the surface of the lake into the sky and landing on the edge of the island. Kaeli was sitting at the center, legs folded in a crossed position. If she wanted to go down as a sitting target, Niko wasn't about to stop her. He extended an arm and tendrils of water whipped out from his bubble toward her, like a giant deadly octopus about to devour its prey.

Columns of fire shot to the sky, evaporating Niko's water as if it were nothing. Kaeli opened her eyes. Niko's heart thrummed as he fought to keep his features schooled in an illusion of calm.

The columns of fire swirled around the arena, encasing Kaeli and himself in a hallway of fire. It didn't burn, but the heat was intense enough that it tingled over Niko's skin. *That shouldn't be possible.* He refocused his attention on Kaeli and she let out a scream so shattering he had to cover his ears. Her eyes were completely ablaze, and her golden hair had turned to licks of flame. She would have been terrifyingly beautiful if it wasn't for the fact that he was almost positive she was trying to kill him—whether it was intentional or she'd just lost control. The fire built behind her, taking the form of a lion's head. Niko's pulse raced. Tremors started to overtake his hands.

"That's not good," he whispered. Just as the lion's was about to open its mouth, Aries's voice reverberated throughout the arena.

"ENOUGH!" She held out her hand, and instantly Kaeli's fire sucked into some unseen vortex and dissipated.

The combat arena returned to its original form. Aquarius snapped her fingers, and within the blink of an eye, she, Aries, Shaina, and the twins were all on the ground level. Kaeli's scream died out as the flames in her eyes and hair extinguished. Her legs trembled so violently she fell to the ground. Niko instinctively caught her before she hit her head on the rocky floor.

He stared at her with wide eyes, swallowing her up in his gaze. When he'd first met her at the welcome dinner, he'd thought she was pretentious. Beautiful, yes, but pretentious nonetheless, smiling like she owned the world and could get anything she wanted. Looking at her now, however, the soft glow emanated around her unconscious being, she felt different. Maybe she wasn't the person he'd first perceived. She certainly had a lot of potential when it came to her element. She could possibly be even more powerful than him. He absentmindedly caressed her hair. It was soft, silky, and warm from the fire. He would have to keep an eye on this one. Kaeli's eyes fluttered closed, and she moaned as he gently lowered her all the way to the ground. Aries shoved him out of the way as she rushed to huddle over Kaeli. Her hands glowed with a soft orange light as they hovered over Kaeli's body.

"Shit, shit, shit," she muttered under her breath. "This wasn't supposed to happen. You!" She snapped at Niko. "How much has Scorpio taught you about water healing?"

Niko cocked his head to the side and asked, "Water healing?"

"*Ugh*! Not much apparently." Aries's muscles were so tense, Niko could practically see her veins popping out of her neck. Aquarius approached Aries and lightly placed a hand on her shoulder.

"Let's just teleport her to the infirmary in Aquae before Leo—"

Leo materialized next to her. Aquarius's gaze darted between him and Aries.

"You're here," she stated. Leo's face was hard as stone as he looked down at Kaeli.

"What. Happened." His voice came out in a low, dark rumble.

"We need to test their elemental potential... so we had them fight—"

"*Are you crazy*? After what she did last night? You really thought pushing her to her limits in elemental combat was a good idea?!" He pushed past Aries and scooped up Kaeli from the floor. "I'm taking her to the infirmary. Try to make sure none of the other recruits dangerously over-exert themselves." With Kaeli in his arms, he disappeared. Niko looked awkwardly around at the others in the group. Aries slowly rose to her feet. Aquarius cleared her throat.

"Seems like an inappropriate time to say 'I told you so,' but—"

The glare she received from Aries was enough to make her mouth shut. Ryan tentatively raised a hand.

"What exactly just happ—"

"Shut it," Aries snapped. Ryan pursed his lips and took a step behind his brother. Aries sighed as she rubbed her temples. "I... maybe I underestimated the consequences of certain individuals going all out with their powers. And after... well... never mind." She turned to Aquarius. "I'm going to go make sure they don't need anything. You've seen what they can do. Give them exercises to work on their weak spots until they need to leave."

Aquarius nodded, and Aries disappeared in a puff of orange smoke. Aquarius faced the recruits, a grim expression on her face.

"Alright, kiddos, let's get back to the lesson."

***

Kaeli groaned as her eyelids fluttered open. Her whole body was wracked with pain and her limbs were so stiff she didn't know if she could move. As the fuzzies subsided from her peripheral vision and her eyes began to focus, she saw a very concerned looking Leo and Pisces standing over her.

"What happened?" she rasped. Her throat was parched, like she had no water in the last three days. Her eyes darted around as she took in her surroundings. She laid in a cushioned bed with pale green, fluffy blankets. Slivered rays of sunlight danced on the walls. Wooden wicker chairs covered in a palm frond fabric were shoved into two corners on either side of a white stone waterfall decorated with polished seashells. "Where am I?"

"How are you feeling?" Leo asked instead of answering her question. His mouth formed a small, tight scowl, but his voice sounded worried.

"Like I fell out of a tree and then got punched in the gut," Kaeli said as she tried to push herself up to a sitting position, but when she moved her arms, decided it would be best to stay lying down. She positioned herself to see Leo more clearly. "Now you answer my questions."

Leo shot a glance at Pisces before letting out a sigh and turning back to Kaeli.

"We're not exactly sure," he said quietly. "Part of it was you overexerted your power. The fire took control of you, rather than you controlling it, but..." His voice trailed off as if he were searching for the words to say next. "I think part of it may have had to do with the dream you had. We don't have an exact correlation yet, but the snakes that seem to be following you—"

Pisces placed a gentle hand on Leo's shoulder.

"We shouldn't be spreading speculation until we know for sure." Her voice was soothing, like a quiet stream. She smiled at Kaeli as she explained, "This is the infirmary in Aquae. It's where we bring badly injured zodiacs or spirits." She held her hands out in front of Kaeli, and they lit up with a pale blue light. She hovered them over Kaeli's body. Pinpricks tingled on her skin.

"You've been asleep for quite a few hours," Pisces continued in her soft voice. "That's helped, but you weren't in good condition when Leo brought you here. Your temperature was much higher than it should have been, and your vital signs were skyrocketing. I could barely sense any brain activity."

"You can sense stuff like that?" Kaeli asked. Her throat still scratched as she spoke, but at least she had regained a little bit of her voice back. The stiffness in her muscles had started to ease as well.

"Yes, dear," Pisces smiled. "All of the water signs have a gift for healing. It comes with the water element, but I'm especially gifted with these sorts of things. Now I need you to be quiet. Kio and I were able to bring your consciousness back, but your body is still very weak, and you need to save as much energy as you can."

"Kio?" Kaeli couldn't stop the question.

"He's a water spirit. The head healer here at the infirmary. Now please, dear, for your own sake, no more questions. There will be plenty of time to catch you up on everything once you've healed." Pisces gave her a semi-reproachful look. Leo made his way to one of the corner chairs and dropped into it with a heavy thud. He let out a long sigh.

"I shouldn't have let this happen."

From her peripheral vision, Kaeli could see him thumping a clenched fist against his forehead.

"There's nothing you could have done about it," Pisces said quietly.

"Yes, there was," Leo said, his voice sharp and angry. "I should have kept her out of Aries's class today. I knew what they were going to do. I should have done more one-on-one training."

"She needs to work with her group just as much as she needs to work with you," Pisces said. Her voice grew louder, but it was still calm and collected, dancing like a lulling melody. "She's awake and stabilized. Now she just needs a little rest and recovery. And now we have a clear understanding of her elemental potential." The glowing light from her hands disappeared as she propped them on her hips and turned to face Leo. "Now honestly, Leo, I'm going to need you to either calm down or get out. Your agitation and anxiety are not going to help Kaeli get better."

Leo sighed as he propped an elbow up on the arm of the chair and rested his chin on his fist. Pisces smiled.

"Good boy. Kaeli's going to be fine. Don't worry."

Kaeli couldn't help but smile too as she allowed herself to fully sink into the plush bedding. She let her eyes slowly close. Her mind drifted off into thoughts of dancing flames and lions as she floated off to sleep once more.

✳ ✳ ✳

Kaeli yelped when she woke up again. She had opened her eyes only to see a stoic, chiseled face with beady onyx eyes staring intently down at her. Her own eyes widened as she took in the being before her. Judging from the deep hue of his transparent blue skin, he was a water spirit. His dark hair cast a slight shadow over his eyes. He wore a long white tunic tied at the waist with a pale blue sash and a long chestnut colored overcoat with sleeves that billowed out near the wrists. He regarded her with a cold, steel gaze and cocked his head to the side. Kaeli gulped as she tried to regain some amount of composure.

"Are you..." her mind searched back to the conversation she'd had with Pisces, "Kio?" she asked. The spirit nodded.

"I have instructions to prepare you to return to House Ignis." He crossed his arms, the long billows of his sleeves folding over each other. "Although if it were up to me, and it really should be, I would have you here for at least another day. Maybe two." He snorted. Kaeli pushed herself up to a sitting position. Her muscles were still a little stiff, but nothing worse than if she'd had a strenuous workout.

"I feel fine," she said. Kio narrowed his eyes and snorted.

"You may *feel* fine, but there is something off with your..." His voice trailed off. He squinted his eyes as if he could peer inside of her. "Energy."

Kaeli tilted her head. "What do you mean?"

"I'm not at liberty to discuss it with you." Kio unfolded his arms and scowled. "It's inane, really. You should be able to know about things that directly affect you." He huffed. "The truth always comes out eventually. I just have to do one more diagnostic check on you before you can be released." He sighed, "Although, I don't really understand the point. If they want me to release you before you're ready, why bother getting cleared? Zodiacs are insufferable sometimes."

Kaeli stiffened and raised her eyebrows. She'd heard Pyronius complain about his job before, but none of the spirits ever complained about the zodiacs directly. And what did Kio mean something was off with her energy? Kaeli internally scanned her body. Everything felt fine, at least for now. Kio smirked, clearly pleased with her reaction.

"You'll understand what I mean soon enough. If you haven't experienced it already. There's a certain... lack of consideration... that comes with being incredibly old and nearly immortal. Now sit back." He held his hands out, and a soft blue light, similar to the light Kaeli had seen on Pisces, emanated from his fingertips. Kaeli did what he said without another word. Kio gave her the distinct impression he was not to be questioned. As he hovered his fingers just inches away from her skin, the darkness in his eyes intensified. They began to look more like a never-ending abyss rather than polished obsidian. It was as if he was looking past her physical body and straight into the essence of her.

As Kio's hands roamed near her neck, Kaeli flinched and let out a yelp. A sudden burning sensation overtook her senses and a stabbing pain pierced her temples. Kio immediately retracted his hands and clenched his fists. Kaeli started breathing easier as the pain slowly subsided. Her heart pounded in her chest. Kio grimaced as he flexed his fingers.

"That's what I thought," he muttered.

"What... was that..." Kaeli winced as she struggled to get the words out. Kio pursed his lips and narrowed his eyes, his stare shooting daggers through Kaeli as if he gazed upon some unholy force.

"That's what is off with your energy." His expression twisted as if he had a bad taste in his mouth. "You've been marked with some sort of darkness." He let out a frustrated sigh and shook his head. "But other than that, you're fine. I need to attend to some other spirits in the infirmary, but I will be back shortly to return you back to House Ignis."

As he left the room, Kaeli rubbed the spot on her neck where the pain had died down to a dull ache. Marked by darkness. And the snakes. There had to be a correlation. She leaned back into the pillows, thoughts spinning at a hundred miles an hour. She would get to the bottom of this.

CHAPTER 14

Lukka paced back and forth in the common room, his mind racing a mile a minute. Kaeli had been gone for days and Aries wouldn't tell him anything other than that she'd experience minor injuries during the elemental training session and they expected her to make a full recovery. Lukka sensed her bullshit the minute she told him, but everyone else refused to divulge any more details. Minor injuries his ass. If it was minor, Kaeli would be back by now.

His heart thrummed in his chest. A familiar heat grew in his gut. Through his snooping, mostly eavesdropping, he'd found out the "minor injury" had happened during a practice fight with Niko.

Lukka snarled. The next time he saw Niko, he would make him pay for what he'd done. Maybe he could lure that bastard to the meeting platform and push him over the edge. He stopped pacing in front of the couch and punched a pillow, letting out a cry of frustration. A flicker of flame jumped from his fist but dissipated upon contact with the plush cushion. Lukka sighed, his nostrils flaring as he sank down into the couch. He didn't even know why he cared so much, but every time he thought of Kaeli lying injured... a growl escaped his throat. His temples throbbed. A door to his left opened. His head whipped around to check if it was Kaeli. When he saw Joseph step through the entryway, he couldn't stop his expression from falling a little. Joseph arched an eyebrow.

"Expecting someone else?"

Lukka huffed in response and turned away to continue his brooding.

"I just don't get why she isn't back yet if she only had 'minor injuries.'" He spat the words out as if they were poison. Joseph was silent as he walked around the couch and plopped down on the other side.

"I might have heard some more information, but I'm not exactly sure what it means," he sighed.

Those words snapped Lukka out of his brooding as his gaze shot toward Joseph. "Tell. Me."

Joseph swallowed, his features set in a neutral expression, as he continued to look at the fireplace at the far end of the room.

"I didn't catch the whole conversation, but I heard Leo and Pisces talking about a mark they found on Kaeli... something to do with the snakes," he said, turning to face Lukka. "You wouldn't know anything about that, would you?"

Lukka's limbs felt like they suddenly weighed a hundred pounds as heat traveled down from the top of his head to his spine. His mind flashed back to when he'd first met Kaeli and they had found the door. He rubbed his neck absentmindedly. That was the only time he could think of that they'd had direct contact with a snake… but he was pretty sure there was no mark left on him. He made a mental note to check with Kaeli about this.

"No," he lied.

Joseph narrowed his eyes, then shrugged. "If you say so."

The door opened, interrupting their conversation. Lukka and Joseph whirled around. A lean, muscular blue spirit in a tunic stood at the entryway, one arm around Kaeli's waist. She had an arm slung around his broad shoulders. Down the hall, Liani's head popped out from behind a column.

"You're back!" Lukka shoved himself up from the couch, and then cleared his throat, darting his eyes around the room, trying not to look too concerned. Kaeli smiled weakly.

"I'm back." Her voice was hoarse. The spirit holding her up clicked his tongue disapprovingly.

"As touching as this reunion may be, Kaeli will need to rest undisturbed for the next few hours. She really shouldn't even have left the infirmary yet, but I'm under orders to return her to House Ignis." He flashed a pointed look toward Lukka and said, "You can ask her more questions *after* she's had more time to rest." He frowned as he looked around. "Which one is her room?" Joseph pointed toward a door at the far corner with the leo insignia. The spirit grunted as he ushered Kaeli through the room.

"I'm pretty sure I can walk on my own." Kaeli pushed herself away from him. The spirit arched his brow as he looked at her.

"Even though you almost collapsed after teleporting?"

Kaeli's cheeks flushed a light pink, but she quickly cleared her throat and brushed her hair back from her face.

"I'll be fine," she said, unhooking his arm from her waist and making her way past the couch, hobbling only a little.

"Make sure you sleep." The spirit kept his eyes trained on her until she disappeared into her room. Kaeli peeked her head out and gave him a thumbs up before closing the door behind her.

Only then did the spirit acknowledge Lukka and Joseph's presence. He gave them both a curt nod before turning on his heel and exiting the room. Lukka glared after him.

"Who was that jerk anyway?" he grumbled.

"That was Kio!"

Lukka heard the high-pitched voice before he saw Liani's small frame practically bounce through the door to the common room. "He's the Head Healer at the infirmary." She brought both her hands to her cheeks and started swaying back and forth, saying, "I've mostly only heard stories about his breakthroughs in the healing arts, or seen glimpses of him in passing, but to actually see him *here* at House Ignis… Ahh!" she squeaked. The next second her expression fell. "Although, I guess it's not a good thing. He basically only comes out of the infirmary when it's a really serious case." She looked at the door to Kaeli's room. "I hope Kaeli is going to be okay."

"She said she would be fine," Lukka said a little too forcefully. Liani turned to him, placed one hand on her heart and cocked her head to the side. A knowing smile grew on her face. Lukka scrunched his nose. He didn't like that expression.

"I'm sure she will be." Her voice bordered on mocking. Joseph sniggered. Lukka frowned and glared at both of them, the muscles in his hands twitching slightly.

"I'm going to train with Pyronius," he growled. Without giving so much as a second glance to Joseph and Liani, he stalked out of the room and slammed the door.

＊ ＊ ＊

Kaeli woke up with a throbbing headache and a slight pain at the back of her neck. She slowly blinked heavy eyelids open and pushed herself to a sitting position. She had no idea how long she'd been asleep, but judging by how groggy she felt, it'd been too long. She blinked a couple more times and looked around her room. Her eyes widened and she almost jumped when she noticed Lukka standing by the doorway, staring at her with an amused smile on his face. She took one of her pillows and threw it at him.

"What the hell are you smiling at, creeper?"

Lukka chuckled as he caught the pillow and hugged it to his chest.

"I swear, I was just coming in to check on how you were doing." His smile grew a little wider. "But then you started talking, and I decided to stay. You say some interesting things in your sleep."

Kaeli groaned and pulled the heavy cover blanket over her head.

"What did I say?"

"If I was following your storyline correctly," Lukka said as he shuffled back and forth, "it sounded like you were having an argument with a crime boss. You did multiple voices and everything." He paused. When he spoke again, his voice sounded more serious. "What happened to you? Aries wouldn't tell me anything, and I couldn't get much information out of anyone else."

Kaeli popped her head out from under the blanket. Lukka shifted and refused to look her in the eye. Kaeli had a sneaking suspicion that the little information he had found out wasn't good. She threw the covers down to her waist and squared her shoulders as she sat a little taller.

"Aries had us fighting tournament style to test the extent of our elemental abilities. I was paired up against Niko." She paused, noting the shadow of a scowl that crossed Lukka's face. "And, I don't know, it was like this uncontrollable heat wave just took over, and it felt like... I *became* fire." She leaned back against the headboard of the bed and looked up to the vaulted ceiling as she tried to pull what happened next from the depths of her subconscious. "I don't really know what happened for the rest of the fight. I blacked out, and when I woke up, I was at the infirmary in Aquae. Kio didn't think I was ready to leave yet, but apparently the zodiacs wanted me back here." She returned her gaze to Lukka's face and stared him dead in the eyes. "Now spill. What information *were* you able to find out?"

Lukka cleared his throat, and Kaeli caught his grip tightening around the pillow that he now held at his side. He raised his chin a little before speaking.

"Joseph said he overheard Leo and Pisces..." He cleared his throat again and transferred the pillow to his other hand. "He didn't really know what they were talking about, but he said they think your... episode or whatever you want to call it... may have had something to do with... the snakes," he said, the last word barely louder than a whisper. Kaeli froze as a chill of ice ran down her spine. Leo had said something similar. Memories of the attack at the welcome feast, and the door... *the door.* She raised a hand to the base of her neck and gingerly brushed her fingertips where the dull ache still pulled at her muscles. The same place she had felt that agonizing pain when she and Lukka had found the door.

"Lukka... is there... something on my neck?" She hopped out of the bed and crossed the floor in a matter of steps. She pulled at the collar of her shirt, baring the back of her neck to Lukka. Her inquiry was met with an uncomfortable silence. She yanked the top of her collar back in place and whirled around to face him.

"Well?" She noticed an almost imperceptible twitch in the muscles of his cheek. He gave her a terse nod.

"It's a snake," he said through pursed lips. "Like a tiny tribal snake tattoo or something." Kaeli cringed as her stomach twisted in knots. While she'd been expecting the answer, it didn't make the reality any less unsettling.

"Do you think…" she trailed off, not wanting to give voice to the thoughts inside her head.

"Do I have one?" Lukka turned around and pulled at the neck of his shirt. Kaeli's eyes grazed his muscled back, perhaps lingering longer than they should, before looking at his neck. There was no mark.

"No," she said, shaking her head.

Lukka pressed his lips into a thin line as he scratched at his chin. Kaeli massaged her neck as she made her way back to her bed, sinking into the down comforter. She wondered if this had anything to do with the information Kio refused to tell her.

"I think there's something going on. Something the zodiacs aren't telling us," she murmured. "When I was at the infirmary, Kio said there was something off with my energy, whatever that means, and that he wasn't at liberty to discuss what was going on with me. He wanted me to stay at the infirmary for a few more days, but apparently the zodiacs wanted me to come back here instead."

Both she and Lukka fell silent.

"Seems like we might need to find out more about these snakes and the door we found earlier," Lukka said. The sound of a cough coming from the entryway had both of them whirling toward the door. Joseph stood leaning against the door frame, arms crossed over his chest.

"What door?" he asked. Lukka and Kaeli shared a look before scrambling over each other to relay the story of what happened when Kaeli first met Lukka in the Celestial Realm.

"And apparently, going through all that left me with this creepy—albeit cool looking— tattoo." Kaeli pulled the edge of her collar down so that Joseph could see. "I just found out about it."

Joseph scowled in concentration as he digested Kaeli and Lukka's messy storytelling.

"And you want to actively go searching for these snakes. Why?" He pushed himself away from the door frame.

"Because obviously there's some kind of danger and people aren't telling us about it!" Lukka said a little too loudly.

Kaeli brought a finger to her lips and shushed him. He shut his mouth, his eyes flickering back and forth making sure he hadn't summoned any unwanted ears. When they were all sure no one had heard anything, Kaeli spoke up.

"Look, it's not like we want to go hunting for the snakes or anything," she said as she side-eyed Lukka. "Or at least I don't want to yet, but we need to find out more about what we're up against. Clearly these snakes aren't going away, and based on the few encounters we've had, they're out for blood. It definitely can't hurt to at least get more information on them."

Joseph chewed at his lip but nodded in agreement. "That's a fair point."

"So you'll help us?" Lukka pushed. Joseph ran a hand through his hair and sighed.

"Yeah."

"Awesome." Kaeli smiled. Having Joseph on their side would make this so much easier.

"But—" Joseph interjected before either of them could get too excited. He locked eyes with Lukka. "We *really* need to know what we're up against before charging into anything. That means we do our due diligence at the library."

"I knew you'd find a way to ruin it," Lukka muttered.

Kaeli flashed him a piercing glare. "What do you have against the library?"

"Nothing… it's just… books…"

Kaeli arched an eyebrow. Lukka shook his head.

"Nothing, nothing. The library is a great place to start."

"Alright, then it's settled." Joseph pushed himself off the wall. "As soon as you're feeling better," he shot Kaeli a pointed glance, "and I mean, actually better, we'll start looking up more information. For now, you need to rest more, and Lukka and I have classes."

"Forgot." Lukka muttered a stream of curse words under his breath. Kaeli chuckled as she crawled back under the blankets. Joseph shook his head.

"I don't know how you've been managing, man." He smirked and exited the room. Lukka went to follow after him but paused at the doorway. He turned to look back at Kaeli.

"Get better soon," he said before gently closing the door behind him.

✷✷✷

Trent gasped for air as he bent to rest his entirely too large hands on his knees, sweat dripping down his clammy skin. It all felt foreign. The feel of the moisture. The scaly skin itself. Everything about his being had been fundamentally changed. He had no idea how those monsters had done it, but they had, and now he needed to adjust.

Still panting heavily from the obstacle course he had just completed, Trent rose to his full height—at least a good two inches taller than when he was human. Trying to look like he was barely winded, he raised his gaze to the observation box where Elethia watched him with that freak. Samael. His gaze narrowed and an involuntary gravelly noise rose from the depths of his gut as he made eye contact.

It had taken a few days before he could look at that demon without his muscles instinctually recoiling. Now, however, the innate fear gave way to pure, undiluted hatred for the monster. He still didn't know where to stand with Elethia. She had led him here… but she had this irresistible, deadly grace about her that was magnetic, even more so now than when he had first met her. His gaze flitted to his scaly skin. Snakes did seem to be drawn to her. Maybe that was why.

He watched as the two discussed his performance from their elevated deck. For weeks now, they had put him through this deadly obstacle training, evaluating the way his body reacted and adjusted each time. Never mind there were times when he had legitimately almost died. The two turned away from each other and faced him. Even though there was a great amount of distance separating them, he could hear Elethia's soothing voice crystal clear.

"Well done, Trent. You are finished for the day. I will speak to you inside the castle."

Trent let out a satisfied breath as a grin crossed his face. His lungs still burned from the physical testing, but Elethia's affirmation always made the near-death experience feel worth it. He smirked as Samael turned and vanished in a puff of black smoke. If he never saw that monster again, it would be too soon. With a contented huff, Trent turned his back from the observation deck and headed toward the tunnel that would lead to the castle he had started to recognize as home.

Hours later, Trent lay staring at the ceiling, on his bed in the new stone-cobbled cell that was his room. It wasn't a bed so much as a rocky outcropping outfitted with a couple of threadbare blankets and a straw stuffed pillow. In his other body, he would have found the accommodations torturous, but in this new skin… the stone felt soothing. The room was drafty at times, but it had everything he needed. His fingers absentmindedly curled around a stray pebble. He threw it up into the air and caught it expertly between two fingers just centimeters from his face before throwing it in the air again.

This had become his new routine. Train. Avoid dying. Come back to the room. Wait for further instructions. His head twitched slightly toward the door. Footsteps approached outside before he heard the click of the lock and the slight screech of the hinges. At first the noises had driven him to near insanity. Every. Little. Thing. Sometimes he could identify the noise, and sometimes it was just a prickle of foreboding—an itch under his scales. He could identify a bug crawling in the next room if he focused hard enough. These days most of his efforts went into defocusing.

He could smell her sweet lavender scent before he saw her glide through the doorway like a goddamn angel. His eyes drank her in as the prickling sensation tickled under his scales. His mouth dried out and he pushed himself up to a sitting position as Elethia approached. She smiled.

"Mind if I have a seat?" She gestured to the now empty spot on Trent's bed. Her soft voice caressed his ears, and it was all he could do to keep from shuddering. Somehow, he managed to nod his head. Her smile wavered slightly as she took a seat. Trent frowned as his stomach quivered uncomfortably.

"What is it?" his voice rasped. He flinched a little at the husky noise. Of all the changes that had been made, his voice had been the hardest to adjust to. Probably because he didn't use it often. Elethia's smile steadied as she placed a gentle hand on his leg. She brought her gaze to meet his, staring straight into his soul.

"I need you to do something for me." Her voice was cautious, but the words did not waver. Trent resisted the urge to lean into her touch. Every fiber of his being wanted to serve her. He would do anything, and she knew it. He hated it.

"What is it?" his voice rasped again. The smile completely dropped from Elethia's face.

"It's Kaeli," she said, and her voice fell as she stared directly into Trent's eyes, as if she really could see through his soul. For a moment, when he heard his sister's name, the world went still. His jaw clenched and every muscle in his body tensed. Then, like a bursting dam, a roar filled his ears. He saw his sister's face in the midst of burning flames, and she laughed at him, at the monster he'd become, or maybe that he'd always been. He gripped the edge of the bed, knuckles white. The rough stone dug into his scaly, clawed hands.

"What. About. Kaeli." He barely uttered the words through gritted teeth. Elethia placed a cooling hand against his jawline, gently, but firmly guided him to look at her, momentarily snapping him out of the rage that coursed through his veins. He could feel his heart thudding in his chest as if it was trying to break free.

"I need you to kill her."

CHAPTER 15

K aeli groaned as her alarm blared, jolting her from her deep sleep. She was starting to regret procuring the dreadful device from Liani. With a huff, she rolled over and slammed the button. The jarring noise instantly cut out. She lay face down in the pillows for a couple of moments before pushing herself to a sitting position and rubbing the sleep from her eyes. It had been three days since she'd been confined to bed rest after the fighting incident, and Leo finally said today would be the day she could leave and resume her training activities. She threw the heavy blankets away from her legs and immediately regretted the decision. The morning air was cold, even in the house of fire. Unfortunately, *early* morning was the only time she, Lukka, and Joseph were able to coordinate their search of the library without drawing attention. While Kaeli was grateful to have a chance to dig into this snake and door mystery with Lukka and Joseph, a part of her would miss the lazy mornings in bed.

"But there's more important things to do than sleeping," she murmured to herself as she made her way to the bathroom. Slipping into her regular training clothes, Kaeli took a moment to observe herself in the mirror and adjust her hair before heading to the library.

Her stomach quivered as she approached the massive building. Lukka and Joseph were already standing at the entrance, deep in conversation about something. She grabbed the edge of her sleeves and fiddled with the hem as she walked up to them.

"Miss me?" Her light voice didn't betray the growing unease in her gut as she interrupted their conversation.

"Look who decided to join the land of the living!" Lukka grinned. "We've been waiting out here for like—"

"One minute." Joseph glanced down at the watch strapped around his wrist before saying, "We literally got here a minute ago." He arched a disapproving eyebrow at Lukka who rolled his eyes.

"You *literally* ruin all the fun." He sighed, but the playful grin instantly returned to his face. "So, we ready to do this thing or what?"

"You realize we're primarily here for research, don't you?" Joseph kept the look of disapproving skepticism pinned to his face.

"Dude, stop! I'm just trying to make this interesting. You think I want to be here this early in morning for *research*?" Lukka walked up to the library doors. They shot open. He scrunched his nose as he flung a look back at Joseph before turning on his heel and disappearing through the doors. Kaeli chuckled.

"He can be so dramatic," she said, and her eyes sparkled as she looked at Joseph. "Don't tell him I said that though, or he'll flip out."

Joseph smirked. "Secret's safe with me."

They followed after Lukka.

Inside, Lukka leaned against the front desk, talking casually to Aurae who had a stack of books in her arms that towered over her head. Her face was held in a pinched expression as she drummed a finger restlessly against one of the books. As Kaeli and Joseph approached, she cleared her throat, cutting Lukka off mid-sentence.

"While I would love to continue this conversation with you, I have a job to do. Search the sections in the left quadrant of the library. You'll most likely find what you're looking for there." She let out a heavy sigh and muttered unintelligible words under her breath as she walked away. Lukka turned to Kaeli and Joseph and grinned. The faintest hint of a smile played onto Joseph's face.

"What did you do to the librarian?"

"Oh nothing." Lukka flexed his hand out in front of him and examined his fingertips as if they were the most interesting thing in the world. "Just asked a couple of questions and, you know, made sure she wouldn't want to follow us around during our little research mission." His grin grew mischievously wicked. "If anyone is wondering, she's single, *but* I got this sense she might be into someone."

Joseph barked out a laugh. Kaeli rolled her eyes.

"As if you would know anything about what women want." She pinned Lukka with a hard stare. He clutched his chest and stumbled backwards as if he'd just been wounded.

"I never said my tactics were orthodox, but they are effective," he said with a wink. "Now come on, I did my part. Let's get to the left quadrant so you nerds can get to researching."

They roamed the shelves for what seemed like hours but came up with nothing. Kaeli turned down yet another aisle and let out a sigh as she surveyed the titles on the spines. They had found books ranging from flora and fauna in the Celestial Realm to incurable viruses, but had found absolutely nothing about shadow snakes with electric eyes. Blood pounded behind her temples and she raked a hand through her hair, shaking her head as she stared at all of the useless information. They would have to leave for training soon and had made zero headway.

"It's hopeless!" Lukka walked from a couple of aisles over, his whine followed by a loud thunk. "I've spent my entire morning on a wild goose chase in the *library* when I could have been sleeping!"

"Get over yourself." Joseph's voice sounded from nearby. The boys continued to argue, but their voices faded into the background as a chill ran down Kaeli's spine... like a wisp of smoke grazing her shoulder.

"Guys, *shut up,*" she hissed. She didn't know where they were at, but she hoped her fierce whisper carried far enough for them to hear. The chill returned, but this time it seemed to graze her ear. She shivered. Lukka peeked his head around the corner of the aisle.

"Everything okay?" he asked. Kaeli's eyes flitted back and forth. She couldn't shake the feeling that something was there.

"I found something..." Joseph's voice trailed off from a couple of rows over. Lukka motioned for Kaeli to come with him. Following the sound of Joseph's voice, they made their way to an aisle that sloped into an underground tunnel. Joseph stood about halfway down.

Kaeli took in a shaky breath when she saw what Joseph had found. At the end of the aisle was an opening in the floor emanating tendrils of shadow. The three stood staring at it, paralyzed, until Joseph broke the silence.

"What do you make of that...?"

"We should go in!" Lukka answered a little too quickly. Every muscle in her body tensed.

"You can't think that's a good idea," she said, turning to Joseph. "Tell him that's not a good idea."

"It's not a good idea."

"But we came to the library looking for answers, and this looks like it has answers!"

"We came to the library for *research*." Kaeli tried to keep her voice under control and continued, saying, "Even if there are answers down there, we have no idea what we're really dealing with yet. We're not going down a creepy hole. It's dangerous and we all... know... it..." The last words stuck in her throat as a thick black fog rolled up from the opening. Her pulse raced as a shiver rushed through her body. Her gaze darted to Joseph. His eyes widened as his jaw dropped. Lukka had turned to face them, completely unaware of the danger.

"Come on, Kaeli, relax! You don't have to be so worried. We're fire signs! Strongest in the zodiac." He spread his arms wide, a lackadaisical grin on his face as he walked backwards down the aisle, closer to the shadows. The fog rose higher toward the ceiling. Lukka continued walking toward it, completely unaware.

"Um, dude." Joseph snapped out of his stupor long enough to get out the words.

"We've been searching for hours, and now that we've finally found something that might be a lead, you want to leave it behind. I don't think so." The shadows snuck down the aisle, curling through the books, getting closer and closer to Lukka.

"Lukka, RUN!" Kaeli finally found her voice and it came out in a shrieking rush of emotion. Lukka turned to see what had her so terrified. His eyes widened in fear as the shadows approached. They were about a foot away from him now, but they suddenly stopped, forming a thick wall of darkness.

Who'sss there? A hiss echoed from the darkness. Kaeli froze as the world seemed to spin. It was the same voice she'd heard when she and Lukka first stumbled into the mysterious hallway. *You...* One tendril of shadow snaked out of the wall toward Lukka. He stood completely paralyzed. The tendril wrapped itself around his torso, winding its way up to his neck until it was eye level and caressed his cheek. Lukka's eyes glazed over. The tendril uncoiled from his body, but beckoned Lukka to step closer toward the wall of shadow. Lukka shuffled after it as if in a trance.

Open the door.

"Lukka, no." Kaeli's throat closed up, like something was strangling her. In a few steps, Lukka would be swallowed by the darkness. This couldn't be happening. She shouldn't let this happen. "LUKKA, STOP!" She outstretched her hands as if she could grab onto him and pull him away from the danger, even though she was too far away.

Bright spots dotted her vision and fire erupted from her outstretched hand. The flame took the form of a huge lion that let out a roar. Kaeli immediately pulled back her hand and covered her ears. She could practically see the sound waves as they pulsed toward the wall of shadow. It cracked and shattered as if it were glass. At the same instant, Lukka snapped out of his trance. Joseph made a lunge for him, grabbing his arm.

"Let's get out of here," he said, pulling Lukka away from the shards of shattered fog and the two stumbled toward Kaeli. Her mind went numb. Lukka grabbed onto her wrist as he and Joseph passed by, and the three ran away as the fire lion dissipated into a plume of smoke. Kaeli cast a glance over her shoulder, only to see the fog reassemble itself and slink back into the dark hole.

It was only when they had returned above ground and into the main lobby of the library that they slowed their pace. Panting hard for breath, they stopped running. Trying their best to maintain a calm appearance, they walked out of the library without looking back. When she was sure they were out of sight, Kaeli rested her hands on her knees as she gulped in breaths of oxygen.

"Remind me to *never* entertain any of your bright ideas ever again," she spat. Lukka clutched his side as he walked in slow circles.

"I'll admit... not the best idea I've ever had," he said.

"Dude, you could have died." Joseph let out a bitter chuckle. "We could have all died."

"I know. I know," Lukka spoke with a forceful authority, but Kaeli caught the slight shakiness behind his words. "This is my fault. I take full responsibility. I promise it won't happen again, but the important thing is that we're all safe." He paused. "And no one is going to say anything about this because if we do, I'm pretty sure Aries, Sagittarius, and Leo would kill us, or worse..." He turned to Kaeli and held her gaze with a piercing stare. "You were amazing." His facial features softened. Goosebumps rose on her arms. "You saved my life."

"Yea, well... don't mention it. I just want to forget this happened." She hugged herself as she said the words, knowing that doing so would be pretty much impossible.

"Forget what happened?" An unknown voice came out of nowhere causing Kaeli, Lukka, and Joseph to all jump. Gemini materialized out of thin air, a wicked, knowing smile on his face. Kaeli's heart pounded so fast she thought it might burst out of her chest.

"Um, how did you do that?" Joseph asked in a shaky voice.

"I'm an air sign," Gemini laughed. "We can materialize anywhere there is air. So watch out. You never know when we could be listening." He winked. Kaeli gulped.

"Now," Gemini said, taking a slow step forward. "What are three fire recruits doing outside the library so early in the morning? You," he pointed at Kaeli, "I can understand. You've seemed to have really taken a liking to this place, but these two. . ." His eyes narrowed as he looked between Joseph and Lukka. The boys shifted uncomfortably. "Seems like a bit of an odd place for the three of you to be hanging out together before your training even starts."

Kaeli opened her mouth to make a half-hearted excuse when Lukka doubled over and started violently coughing.

"Whoa, man, you okay?" Joseph put a hand on Lukka's back, trying to steady him. Gemini just looked at them, his head slightly tilted to the side, eyebrows raised in mild interest. Lukka took in a couple of wheezing breaths before spitting out a viscous black liquid. Joseph grimaced. Kaeli turned back to Gemini, her heart sinking straight to her stomach. How in the world were they going to explain this?

"Lukka had this weird cough, so we were trying to see if we could find any information to help him." She looked down at the black gunk on the floor. It almost seemed like it was writhing. She cringed as she looked back up at Gemini. "This is the first time that happened. Clearly he needs more help." It was bad. She knew the lie was bad. She just hoped it was enough to convince Gemini to get off their case. Gemini only smiled a bemused smirk.

"Clearly." He paused, holding the three of them captive with his stare. Kaeli stopped breathing. Gemini laughed and asked, "Well, what are you waiting for? He needs help. Get him back to House Ignis." He turned to leave. Kaeli sucked in a refreshing breath of air as relief washed over her. She motioned for Joseph to take Lukka while she ran after Gemini.

"Actually!" she called out to him. "There was something I wanted to ask you about."

Gemini paused and turned around. He raised an eyebrow.

"Yes?"

"Earlier, when you were showing my group through Aera, you said you could teach us more about those dragon creatures."

"The Yantari." Gemini's eyes brightened as he smiled. "Yes, I did say that."

"Do you think you could teach me?" Kaeli asked. Gemini examined her momentarily before answering.

"It would be my pleasure," he said. "Interesting. It's not often a fire sign takes an interest in the creatures of the air." He placed a hand on Kaeli's shoulder and said, "You must be special." His fingers hovered disturbingly close to the snake tattoo Kaeli had covered. She resisted the urge to squirm away from his touch. Gemini removed his hand. "You can come to the lessons with Ryan and Alex. I'll get in contact with you when they start. I'm still trying to get them to master the basics of handling air." A wide grin spread across his face. "From what I've heard, you seem to be adapting to your element *quite* well." Kaeli felt heat rising to her cheeks. She was hoping the details from her training in the arena hadn't made it out to the public... but perhaps that was asking too much.

"Uh, yeah... I guess you could say that," she said, followed by a nervous chuckle. Gemini's eyes twinkled.

"Well, I'll leave you to your friends so you can get Lukka some... help," he said. He turned to go but paused and looked over his shoulder "Oh and Kaeli." He lowered his voice so only she could hear what he said next:

"Tell those boys not to go gallivanting down any more secret passages in the library. It would be really disappointing if anyone were to find the three of you dead." With those parting words, he disappeared in a poof of lavender light.

Kaeli stood rooted to the ground in horror. Gemini knew everything. The three of them could be sent back to Earth for this. She shook her head, trying to clear her mind. Gemini didn't seem angry with them or like he planned on telling anyone. She just had to make sure none of them gave him any motivation to do so. She jogged back to the portal. She couldn't focus on this predicament right now. Right now, she needed to make sure Lukka was going to be okay... and get to the training arena to meet with Leo.

Kaeli chewed at her inner lip as she walked through the dark tunnel leading to the training arena. She couldn't stop thinking about Lukka. She'd stopped by the room to check on him before leaving for her training session, and he was definitely worse for wear. His normally olive complexion had turned pale and dark circles rimmed his eyes, like he'd been punched in the face. Lukka had crashed out on the couch and was in a deep sleep, but Joseph said he'd vomited up more of the black gunk before passing out. Gemini's words rang through her head.

Kaeli absentmindedly fiddled with the ends of her jacket sleeves. He hadn't given any indication that he would tell the other zodiacs what happened, but he wasn't exactly the easiest person to read. Kaeli approached the end of the tunnel and let out a deep breath before stepping out and shielding her eyes from the bright light in the training arena. Leo stood at the center, facing away from her. She approached and coughed uncomfortably to announce her presence. Leo turned and smiled. Kaeli's shoulders relaxed and she stopped fiddling with her jacket as she swung her arms and returned the smile. He didn't look like he wanted to bite her head off. That was a good sign.

"Everything okay?" he asked. He tilted his head to the side as he walked toward her. "You look preoccupied."

"It's nothing," Kaeli answered, maybe a little too quickly. Leo raised his eyebrows and looked like he was about to ask a question. Her heart skipped a beat as her mind rushed to cobble together a convincing story. There was no way she could tell him about what happened at the library. Before he could get out another word, Kaeli let out what she hoped sounded like a dejected sigh and made a show of drooping her shoulders.

"I guess… I can't stop thinking about the fight with Niko and how I completely lost control." There. That should be believable. It was, after all, her first day being back to training since she'd been sentenced to bed rest. Leo offered her a small smile and placed a comforting hand on her shoulder.

"Believe me when I say it's happened to the best of us. Fire is one of the hardest elements to control, second only to air, and Aries should have known better than to put you in that situation this early on." His smile grew a little wider. "And that's why today we're going to focus on your elemental control." As he guided her to the center of the arena, Kaeli let out an internal sigh of relief. She knew she and Joseph would have to find a way to explain what happened to Lukka soon enough, but at least for this training session, she could focus solely on the lesson.

Leo deemed the training finished about an hour later. The training session had been exceedingly easy. Leo tiptoed around her, not wanting to accidently trigger anything, but still… she could have handled more. It wasn't like she was a fragile baby. Although, in comparison to beings who had been alive for hundreds of years, maybe that's how they saw her.

Kaeli bit her lip as she walked toward the portal runes. She still had some time before her next class with Scorpio and she wanted to spend it in the library, doing some of her own research. Her chest tightened as her thoughts flickered to Lukka. She'd stopped by the room to see him right after her training session with Leo. Aries had furiously paced back and forth across their common room muttering swear words. Lukka was still passed out on the couch. Wanting to skip the interrogation with Aries, Kaeli thought it best not to linger. It served as another excuse for her to be at the library.

She held her head high, her gaze trained straight ahead as she entered the doors to the library and walked directly to the Room of Records. Thankfully, there weren't any spirits wandering around in the front lobby. The more covert she could keep this visit, the better. She didn't want anyone asking questions about what had happened earlier. She crossed the lobby floor as quickly and quietly as she could.

When she closed the door behind her, she let out a sigh and slumped against the cool slab of obsidian, allowing the rapid beating of her heart to slow a little before venturing further into the room.

"Where do I even start in here?" she whispered, eyes grazing over the shelves. It was strange to think that they all contained a personality with the life experience and personality of a former zodiac. A particularly unloved corner of the room shrouded in cobwebs caught her gaze.

"If you're looking for hard to find answers, might as well try opening a book with a hard-to-find title." She walked around the giant table toward the shelf and brushed away the cobwebs, tracing her hand across the surface of the book titles. Her fingers tracked a clear path through the layers of dust on the spines, revealing the inscribed name titles.

"Let's try… this one!" Kaeli pulled out the book her hand hovered over and looked at the title. *Elethia.* Distressed scuff marks made the book look more worn than the others surround it. Kaeli squinted as she tried to make out the constellation, but the weathered condition made it impossible. "Alright, Elethia, let's see if you can help me figure out what's going on in this crazy realm."

She placed the book on the table and opened to the first page. A soft purple glow emanated throughout the room. It faded to reveal a stunningly beautiful woman. She had long, dark hair that fell in careless waves to the middle of her waist and she wore a tight-fitting formal gown that was the same soft purple color that preceded her. Her eyes were narrow and the most vibrant hazel Kaeli had ever seen. Kaeli stood dumbstruck. She had come to the library searching for answers, but now that she was standing one on one with a former zodiac who was who-knew-how-many-millennia old, she wasn't quite sure how to move forward. Elethia stretched her arms and cracked her neck before focusing her attention to Kaeli.

"Oh, it feels so lovely to be out of that book. You can't even begin to imagine what it's like to live in a two dimensional blank space for… goodness. I don't even know how long it's been." She looked Kaeli up and down before smirking and taking a seat at the table, motioning for Kaeli to follow her lead. "Go on, sit. I can see you have a lot of questions."

Kaeli did as the woman commanded and tried to organize her thoughts so she could form coherent words, but before she could do so, she heard herself say, "Who are you?"

A small, sly smile tugged at the corners of the woman's lips and she gracefully leaned back in her chair.

"That's a stupid question. You read my book title before opening it." Her eyes glimmered in amusement. Kaeli clenched her jaw and held her chin a little higher, trying not to betray the humiliation she felt. She didn't have time for this sort of conversation before her first class of the day. She was just about to get up and close the book when Elethia's voice stopped her.

"I apologize if I come off a bit brash. I've been stuck in that book for a very, very long time. Solitary confinement tends to bring out the worst in me, I'm afraid."

Kaeli glared at her but didn't close the book. Elethia's words were nice, but her tone and facial expression were insincere.

"What zodiac sign were you?" Her question came out as more of a demand through Kaeli's gritted teeth, but she didn't care. If this woman wasn't going to be pleasant, Kaeli wasn't going to try either. Elethia straightened her shoulders and tilted her head to the side as if she seriously had to consider her answer. A darkness shadowed her features.

"To give that answer, I would have to recall stories from a life that has long since passed… ones I would rather not relive," she sighed, and refocused her attention to Kaeli. "But," Elethia said as she elegantly placed her elbows on the table and leaned in closer toward Kaeli. Her stare so intense, Kaeli thought it might bore holes straight through her skull into her mind. "You're not here to learn about my past life. You want information about something that is relevant to *you*. So, why are you here?"

Kaeli hesitated. She didn't completely trust this woman, and yet the urgency of needing information pressed stronger than her distrust.

"Do you know anything about the talking shadows and snakes that are trying to kill people?" Even as she said the words, Kaeli realized how strange the question sounded. She fought to keep down the heat that threatened to send a flush to her cheeks. Elethia leaned back, a genuine smile playing upon her lips.

"I've heard whispers from the librarians here and there." She flourished her hand and another book materialized on the table. "This should point you in the right direction." She pushed the book toward Kaeli. Kaeli's eyes widened when she read the title—*Mythos of the Stars*. It was the same book she'd been reading when she first met Leo. Her eyes flickered between the book and Elethia, her jaw going slightly slack.

"How did you—how?"

"The Celestial Realm is full of mystery." Elethia chuckled as she tapped the cover of the book and said, "I suggest researching the Serpent Bearer." She cocked her head to the side. "It sounds like more people have entered the library. That book doesn't belong here, so feel free to take it with you. I should go now."

Before Kaeli could ask even one more question, Elethia stood up and placed her hand at the center of her open book. The soft purple glow once again enveloped her, and when it faded, her book was gone. Kaeli furrowed her eyebrows together and let out a discontented sigh, but she pulled *Mythos of the Stars* closer to her and searched the table of contents for "Serpent Bearer."

She turned to the page, and her eyes landed on an image of a man holding a snake double his size. The snake draped itself around the man's body, lying its head down in the man's left palm. In his right hand, the man held the serpent's tail. Kaeli's eyes ran over the words as she read.

Ophiuchus, known in Greek as Asklepios, was born to the son of Apollo. When he was a baby, Ophiuchus's mother committed infidelity. She was killed because of this (some legends say it was at the hands of Apollo, others say it was at the hands of his vengeful sister, Artemis). Apollo took his son and gave him to the centaurs. It was the centaurs that taught Ophiuchus the art of medicine from an early age.

Ophiuchus became a very talented healer under the instruction of the centaurs, but it was an incident with two snakes that gave Ophiuchus the reputation of being the greatest healer known to humankind. The legend goes that one day, while Ophiuchus practiced his medicinal brews, a poisonous snake came upon him. Ophiuchus killed the snake in self-defense. Soon after, however, another snake came, holding an herb in its mouth. The snake placed the herb near his dead comrade and brought it back to life. Together the two snakes slithered away, leaving the herb behind. Amazed by what he had just witnessed, Ophiuchus took the herb. Through his studies, he was able to find the cure for life's most difficult malady—death.

"Is he the one behind the attacks?" Kaeli whispered.

"Who's behind the attacks?" A sudden voice came out of nowhere causing Kaeli to almost jump out of her seat, shutting the book with a hard thwack.

"Sorry! Didn't mean to scare you!"

Kaeli turned to face the intruder and let out a sigh of relief as she braced her hand against the table to steady herself. It was only Alex.

"It's okay," she said, trying to subtly move her hand over the title of the book so Alex wouldn't see what she'd been reading. "What are you doing here?" She stood and took the book off the table, holding it down by her thigh, cover facing toward her leg. Thankfully the lighting in the room was dim. She walked past Alex toward the door and turned to face him.

"Oh, I've been in the library for a few hours now." Alex grinned as he walked over to the table and leaned against it, saying, "Gemini always has Ryan and me up at the crack of dawn for lessons, so we get some free time afterwards. I like to come here and read. Or," he gestured to the books lining the room, "talk."

"Yeah, it's a cool place." Kaeli schooled her features into a passive calm. Internally, however, her thoughts were shrieking at her. What if he'd been there during the incident with Lukka? What if he'd *seen* the incident with Lukka? She edged closer toward the door. She needed to get out before Alex found out more than he possibly already knew. She didn't have anything against him, but he had daily contact with Gemini and she wasn't about to let the zodiac get wind of any of this.

"What book are you reading?" Alex nodded his head toward Kaeli's hand. "You know you can't take any of the zodiac books out of the Room of Records, right?"

"Oh, this isn't… it's not a zodiac book. It's mine. I brought it here with me." She lifted the book to hold it close to her chest, but before she could, a hand reached over her shoulder and swiped it away from her. "Hey!" She whirled around to see Ryan standing behind her, a stupidly mischievous grin plastered on his face. He turned the book over in his hands a couple of times as he examined the cover.

"*Mythos of the Stars*, huh?" Ryan looked down at the book and then back up to Kaeli. "Discussing constellation mythology with former zodiacs? Why would you be doing that?"

Kaeli lunged forward and snatched the book away from Ryan.

"None of your business," she hissed as she pulled the book in tight. Not that it mattered anyway. Ryan pressed a fist against his lips before making eye contact with his brother.

"She's feisty," he chuckled. Kaeli scoffed.

"Keep talking about me like that in the third person, and I'll show you a hell of a lot more than feisty." Her retort only seemed to amuse Ryan more. His mocking smile grew into a wicked grin.

"I have absolutely *no* problem with that."

"Okay, that's enough." Alex stepped between the two, separating them before Kaeli had a chance to whack Ryan over the head with her book. Alex shot Ryan a death glare. "Knock it off."

Ryan rolled his eyes.

"Fiiiiine," he whined, winking at Kaeli. "You'll have to show me your 'more than feisty' side some other time."

Kaeli pursed her lips into a thin line but refused to take the bait. Clearly, any show of outer frustration just fueled his amusement.

"You should be so lucky."

She swore Ryan's eyes danced with delight.

"What's going on here?" Shaina popped her head through the door. The trio turned to look at her. Alex grabbed Ryan's arm and started tugging him toward the entryway.

"We were just leaving," he said in a firm voice. "We need to go to Aquae for Scorpio's class." He looked back at Kaeli. "I really do apologize for him."

Kaeli offered him a smile. She felt bad for Alex. It had to be hard being a decent person with a twin who always tried to find the most amusing way to piss people off. Shaina stepped aside as Alex dragged his brother away before entering the room.

"I came here looking to see what was holding up the twins. I didn't know you'd be in here too! How are you? We were super worried after Leo took you away. The zodiacs wouldn't tell us anything other than that you would be okay but needed rest."

Kaeli let out a heavy sigh. "They wouldn't tell me much either, other than that I lost control. But I'm feeling a lot better now. I was really weak initially, but resting has really helped."

"Well, I'm glad you're feeling better now." Shaina smiled and asked, "Want to go to class together?'

"You can go ahead." Kaeli looked down at her book. Part of her wanted to say yes, but the other part of her wanted alone time to ruminate over everything she'd just read. "I need to return this book anyway."

Shaina nodded. "Alright then, I'll see you soon." She offered a little wave before leaving. Kaeli sighed and turned the book over in her hand. Hopefully the twins hadn't heard anything too incriminating. If they did, Gemini would probably find her sooner rather than later. She tucked the book under her jacket. She would just drop it off at House Ignis before going to Aquae for her next lesson.

Alyssa Markins

CHAPTER 16

Kaeli mentally kicked herself for not going to class with Shaina. They had been instructed to meet at some sort of reflection pool. Kaeli took one step out of the circle and realized she had no idea where to go. The others must have received directions while she'd been confined to bed rest.

"This is just great," she muttered as she kicked at the dirt, contemplating which direction she should try first.

"Lost?" Niko's voice sounded from behind her. Kaeli's stomach instantly twisted into knots. She hadn't seen Niko since she'd passed out in the middle of the fight, and after everything that had already happened this morning, she really didn't feel like rehashing any of the events.

"I'll take that prolonged silence as a 'yes.'" Niko chuckled. Kaeli arched an eyebrow.

"I mean, I wouldn't entirely say I'm lost because I know exactly where I am." Kaeli's shoulders slumped a little as she kicked at the dirt again and said, "I just don't know where we're supposed to be going."

"I thought that might be the case," Niko chuckled. Kaeli tilted her head in an unasked question. Niko smiled and shrugged. "You've been gone three days and weren't there when they told us about class today. I thought I would hang back until you got here in case you needed help." Kaeli's jaw went slack as she stared at Niko with wide eyes.

"Thank you." She cleared her throat as she broke the awkward eye contact. The smile on Niko's face grew wider as he motioned to a narrow stone path leading to a grove of trees.

"It's this way," he said.

They walked along the path for all of two seconds before the trees cleared to a willow grove. Kaeli's eyes widened as she inhaled deeply as she took in the view. Large, wispy willow trees surrounded three small pools of water that were so blue and still, they reflected an exact portrait of the sky in their midst.

"I could have found this on my own you know."

"Maybe." Niko shrugged. A wide grin spread across his face as he said, "But it would have been a shame for you to get lost. There's some nasty creatures that live in these forests."

"And I'm oh so defenseless against nasty creatures," Kaeli retorted, rolling her eyes. Niko snickered. Kaeli opened her mouth to retort, but sharp voices diverted her attention.

"If you don't shut up, I swear I will open up the ground you're standing on and swallow you whole!" Shaina yelled. Kaeli turned toward the center pool of water to see Shaina standing across from Ryan. Except Ryan wasn't fully Ryan. He had somehow managed to change his face to look like the spitting image of Shaina, although he still had his regular body. Kaeli cringed. It didn't look right. Not at all.

"I'm gonna open the earth and swallow you whole," Ryan mimicked back. His voice even sounded like Shaina's. This must be one of his abilities that he hadn't mastered yet. His face shifted, and he once again appeared as himself. "That's not going to do a whole lot of damage if I can fly." He winked and said, "Might want to consider revising your plan."

"You are *incredibly* annoying." Shaina stared at him with a deadpan expression. Ryan looked away from her to casually examine the back of his hand while he shifted it into a series of different skin colors.

"Why thank you. I do what I can."

"I do not want to see the type of damage he is going to do when he fully masters that ability," Kaeli muttered.

"Me either," Niko agreed.

"Ryan, cut it out," Alex said, his voice low and foreboding. He folded his arms across his chest, and his face twitched. Ryan spun to face his brother, about to protest, but Alex flashed him one vicious look and Ryan closed his mouth. A rustling noise came from the willow trees and Kaeli turned to see Scorpio enter the clearing. A dark power rippled off of him and everyone fell silent. Kaeli shuddered and shifted ever slightly closer to Niko. Even he seemed unnerved by his mentor's presence.

"Glad to see everyone is having a good time here." A slow smile crept across Scorpio's face as he surveyed each of the recruits. His gaze pierced straight to the soul. The smile instantly dropped and his eyes narrowed. "I can assure you that will not be the case by the time we're done with our lesson. I can't say I have high expectations for many of you, but if you all could do me a favor and not pass out by the end of our training today, I would greatly appreciate it." He gave Kaeli a pointed look. Heat involuntarily rose to her cheeks. Scorpio cleared his throat.

"Now that we've gotten all of the pleasantries out of the way, let's get to the good stuff." Scorpio walked past Niko and Kaeli, motioning for them to follow him toward the center pool. Shaina, Ryan, and Alex all stiffened as he neared them. He walked to the edge of the water before turning to face the recruits. Kaeli's stomach turned in somersaults.

"I have the ability to uncover and manipulate what lies hidden in the subconscious, both of the living and the deceased." Scorpio was definitely in his element, standing amidst the calmness of the water. His voice and posture perfectly mimicked the control and poise of the still crystal blue pools. "If you are all to become your true selves, there are subconscious issues you will need to address, many of which you do not yet even know. You may not like what you see, but this is a very necessary part of your training. I suggest mentally preparing yourselves for the worst before we begin."

Kaeli took in a steady inhale and hardened her stare. She couldn't think of anything in her life that could be *that* bad. She hadn't had the easiest childhood, but she'd survived all of it. She'd always been able to handle everything life threw at her… which was quite a lot considering she grew up with Trent. Scorpio continued his speech.

"For this exercise, you simply have to kneel over the pools and stare at your reflection. The water and I will do the rest." Scorpio pointed toward the pool to his right. "Niko and Kaeli, you'll be here. Shaina and Alex, the two of you will be at this center pool. Ryan, you get that pool all to yourself."

Ryan shuffled his feet, breaking up the mossy ground as he moved away from his brother. Kaeli flashed Niko an uncertain look as they walked to the pool. Niko grinned in what looked like a lame attempt to ease the tension that was so palpable in the air.

"You think you can handle this?" he whispered. Kaeli rolled her eyes as she knelt at the edge of the pool and looked into the water. Her mirrored reflection was sharper than any image she'd ever seen of herself. She could see every line in her skin, every strand of long golden hair. She instantly recoiled, her head spinning. She wasn't the only one. Everyone besides Niko was looking away from the water, mixed expressions of shock and disbelief written all over their faces. Kaeli looked up toward Scorpio. He had an amused smile on his face.

"The water will allow you to see things about yourself that you've never seen before," he cautioned. "Now look back into the pools, and we'll begin." Kaeli blinked and rubbed her eyes a couple of times before staring back into the water. She tried not to get too wrapped up in the sharpened details of her face as Scorpio continued speaking.

"Now look deeply into your eyes." His voice took on that deep, alluring tone it'd had when Kaeli first met him. Her gaze locked onto her image even though every instinct she had warned her to run. "Try to see through them, to your own soul." Scorpio's voice continued to drone on in the back of her mind. "Get lost in the colors of your skin, the slight movement of your nostrils as you breathe in… and out…" His voice began to fade and a shadow rolled in over the pools. As she unwillingly stared at herself in the water, she couldn't tell if she was seeing through her reflection, or if her reflection was seeing through her. Her mirrored self seemed so… alive. Kaeli couldn't look away.

The water image shifted. Her facial features started to change, becoming younger and younger, until Kaeli recognized her face as it was when she was eight years old. Little Kaeli looked up through the water and let out a soft giggle that echoed throughout the pool, making small ripples. A fire formed behind her, the orange and yellow colors shining through the blue. Her gaze shifted away from her younger self and into the flame. A gust of air hit her and she gasped as she struggled to breath. She wasn't in the willow grove by the water anymore. She was in a car. With her father. A crackling voice talked through the radio.

In recent news, another earthquake in Japan has triggered tsunami warnings for nearby coastal regions. As of now, there are 67 confirmed dead, with over 50 reported missing and...

No, no, no, no, no. Kaeli's heart skipped a beat and nausea roiled in her stomach. Not here. Anywhere but here. She knew exactly where and when this was, and she would rather relive *any* day involving Trent's torture than this day. Her father turned to her and smiled.

"Want me to change the station, honey?" he asked. Tears sprang to Kaeli's eyes as soon as she heard his voice. It had been so long. She'd forgotten how warm and comforting it sounded.

"Dad…" It was the only word she could utter through her constricted vocal cords.

"Ugh, Kaeli, you're acting weird again." Trent. He sat in the back seat. Kaeli looked back to her brother. He was only fifteen years old at the time of their father's death. Kaeli started to hyperventilate as the overwhelming feeling to *get out now* consumed every thought. She looked away from Trent and back toward the front windshield. Every single muscle in her body froze. This time she was able to clearly see the car approaching. Time moved in slow motion as she stared at the oncoming car, unable to look away. Stared as it rammed into the front of their vehicle. Stared as the impact of the crash caused her head to snap backwards. Stared as the glass shattered, grazing the skin of her arms and face.

The pain of that glass roared through her body and brought time back to full speed as Kaeli came back to her senses and released an ear-piercing scream. She was vaguely aware of Trent scrambling to unbuckle his seat belt as he crawled out of the car. He would be fine. Kaeli knew that.

What she wasn't expecting was the soothing voice of her father, telling her to calm down, assuring her that everything would be alright. Something was wrong. He was supposed to have died on impact. Bile rose in her throat and she fumbled for her seat belt as a realization began to dawn on her. A burning heat roiled in her gut. The pressure of her fear, burning, building in her chest until she couldn't contain it anymore. She let out another screech. All of her limbs exploded with a shooting fire. The force engulfed her father and sent her flying out of the car. Kaeli skidded on the pavement, taking in shaky, uneven breaths as she stared at the burning car in abject horror. She made eye contact with Trent, crouching not too far away, and could see it in the twisted look of panic and hatred on his face.

It wasn't the car accident that had killed her father.

It was her.

Alyssa Markins

CHAPTER 17

Kaeli's consciousness snapped back into her body as she gasped for breath. She scrambled to push herself as far away from the pool as she could before weakness overtook her muscles and she collapsed in the mossy grass. She hugged her knees close to her chest as she looked around, doing everything she could to distract herself from replaying the memory of the car crash in her mind. The others still gazed in the water, a mixture of different emotions playing on their faces. She closed her eyes and inhaled deeply, focusing on the slight rustle of the trees, the stillness of the air... anything to forget, to shove the memory down where she couldn't remember it. *Head-on collision. Fuel leakage. Engine combustion. Everything went up in flames.* That's what the news had reported. This memory had to be a trick.

An uneasy presence settled over her, and she opened her eyes to see Scorpio. The scorpion tattoo peeking out from underneath his shirt glowed with a mystical, cerulean blue light as a foggy mist swirled around him. Her eyes started to burn, threatening to tear up, as she glared at him.

"What the hell did you do to me?" she whispered. Scorpio pursed his lips into what looked like a grim, almost apologetic smile.

"That was the moment you first discovered your powers," he said, his voice low and cautious, as if something he said could break her more than she'd already been shattered. "You were the youngest out of all the recruits when you first wielded your element. Unfortunately, the event was traumatic for you. Your mind buried the experience deep into your subconscious and interpreted it through a different story so you could cope. Burying that memory is also why your fire was so suppressed growing up and why it bursts out of control in the Celestial Realm."

"No." Kaeli shook her head as if that could erase everything she'd just witnessed.

"Yes."

"But... the incident report from... from the crash..." Her throat tightened, and her vision started to blur. She tried to take deep breaths to calm the rising panic, but her heart beat so rapidly the blood pounded in her head. "It said... it said he died on impact." Scorpio sighed as a pained look danced through his eyes. Pity. He pitied her. She hated him. Hated him for showing her this.

"No one would believe an incident report that said he died because his own daughter exploded into flames and somehow came out unscathed except for minor scratches from the shattered glass. Elementals hadn't surfaced at that point. Your brother was the only witness. The other driver was knocked unconscious and taken to the hospital."

"No." Kaeli's pulse hammered against her temples. Her vision lit up with blazing orange light as flames erupted around her hands. She charged Scorpio in desperate fury. She didn't know why. She just had so much anger and hurt and pain, and it was all because of him. Scorpio caught her wrists and immediately extinguished them with a douse of water. Kaeli couldn't stop the flood of tears any longer as they poured down her cheeks.

"You're upset. That's understandable." Scorpio held so tightly to her wrists that Kaeli winced a little at the pain. "But you experienced that memory for a reason." His voice was stern. Kaeli tried to pull away, tried to shut out the words, but his grip was too strong. "Look at me!" Scorpio placed one hand on her shoulder and used the other to tilt her head up so she had no choice but to look into his sapphire blue eyes. "I can see *you*, Kaeli. It's part of my gift. I know your strengths, your weaknesses, what brings you happiness, and what you fear, and Kaeli, I know you have been *afraid*. Afraid of what you are and what you're capable of. You need to accept that this is you. This has always been you. Stop trying to hide it. When you bottle your power, it explodes and ends up either hurting you or those around you. That's what fire does if you don't embrace it and learn how to channel it. That's what happened during your fight with Niko. That's what happened when you were eight years old and *killed your father*. You need to come to grips with reality. Take that lesson. Learn from it. Don't let his death be in vain." He let go of her chin. Kaeli's shoulders heaved as she took in a couple of shaky breaths, but the tears began to stop. "You're stronger than you realize, Kaeli." Scorpio looked over his shoulder. "The others are starting to come out of their memories as well."

"Did Leo know…" Kaeli whispered under breath. Her voice was so quiet she didn't even know if Scorpio could hear her. He turned back to her, a grim smile on his face.

"Yes," he spoke evenly. "We all knew. It's one of the reasons you were chosen."

With those words, he made his way over to the other recruits. A shaky exhale escaped her chest. She had killed her father. Scorpio had known. Leo had known. All of the zodiacs knew. Even Trent knew, although he may not exactly have understood the how. No wonder he had hated her so much. She hated herself.

✳ ✳ ✳

Scorpio's lesson had left all of the recruits in utter shambles. All of the recruits besides Niko. The experience had left him a little shaken, but since coming to the Celestial Realm, Scorpio had taken him through so many exercises similar to this that when he witnessed his brother's murder and relived how he'd slaughtered over 30 men in a fury of sharpened icicles, it hadn't come as a complete shock. He'd still felt all of the emotions in the moment… but now that it was over, it was just that. Over.

As they walked back to the teleportation portal, Niko analyzed his teammates. The twins were unnaturally quiet, whispering among themselves. Shaina hugged her arms around her waist, avoiding eye contact with anyone by looking at the ground as she shuffled away from the grove. And Kaeli. She hadn't moved since he'd come out of the memory. She still sat in front of the pool, knees drawn close into her chest as she stared off into the trees. He couldn't see her face, but he knew the type of defeat that would be in her eyes. He didn't know what she'd seen, but he could read her reaction. He'd been through the same thing, a long time ago, after the death of his brother. Niko looked back at the twins and Shaina as they disappeared through the portal with a flash of light, then made his way to Kaeli.

When he approached, he put a gentle hand on her shoulder, grazing her silky hair as he sat down beside her. Kaeli didn't even acknowledge the touch. She just stared into the willow grove. Her eyes glazed over.

"Hey," he said quietly. She shifted slightly and turned to look at him. The corners of her eyes glittered with unshed tears and her lower lip trembled. Niko suddenly grew a strong awareness of his pounding heartbeat as a long-lost warmth rushed through him. He wanted to help her, to be the one who rescued her from the devastating events she had witnessed. To be her savior. A part of him knew this was all coming from her uncanny ability to emanate leo's charm, and the other part of him didn't care. In that moment, he had to be her everything.

"Are you okay?" He found himself making very firm, intense eye contact with her as he fought the urge to wrap her in his arms and pull her close to his chest. Kaeli inhaled and exhaled a shaky breath.

"Not right now." Her voice cracked. She took the edge of her sleeve and wiped at her eyes. Niko moved a little closer to her. Kaeli blinked a few times, her lashes clumped together with the moisture from her tears. "You seem fine," she whispered. Niko let out a heavy sigh.

"This isn't the first time I've gone through training like this," he said. Even before he'd come to the Celestial Realm. His life on Earth hadn't exactly been pleasant. Kaeli raised her eyes to look at him, *really* look at him. Niko's heart started pounding even harder.

"How do you... move on... from stuff like this?"

"You acknowledge that it's in the past and you work to make things right for the future," Niko said and pursed his lips into a thin line. He didn't know what else to say, what words he could possibly give that would make her feel any form of better. So they sat. And they stared into each other's eyes. Tightness gripped his chest at the pain dancing in her gaze, as he reached out to pull Kaeli in close. To his surprise, and relief, she didn't move away. Instead she melted into him, wrapping her arms around his waist and hiding her face in the crook of his neck. Time stopped. There was only her skin against his. Her trembling body enveloped in his sturdy embrace. He placed a hand on top of her head and stroked her hair. He didn't know how long they held each other, or who might stumble upon them. He just knew that right now, he would stay like this for as long as Kaeli needed.

Lukka paced the common room, grinding his teeth and kicking at the unfortunate objects that happened to be in his way. He had just been about to leave for a training session with Aries at the arena in Ignis. After his last horrific bout of sludge vomit, the last thing he remembered was that overly pompous water spirit, Kio, standing over him and doing some weird healing magic thing. Whatever it was, Lukka had fallen into a deep sleep that kept him out of his morning classes, and Aries had ordered him to train with her that afternoon. He wasn't exactly looking forward to the session.

But then, he saw Kaeli and Niko materialize onto the portal circle at the center of the houses. They were standing close to each other... *too* close, and Niko had his arm slung around her shoulders like she friggin belonged to him. Lukka's first instinct had been to tackle Niko, football style and send him flying over the side of the platform into the vastness of outer space, but before he'd gotten the chance, he saw Kaeli's face. She had clearly been crying. *Crying!* Her eyes were red and puffy. She had the occasional sniffle. The sight had left him completely out of sorts and he had no idea how to react.

So instead of going toward the platform to meet Aries for his one-on-one training session, Lukka had immediately turned and made a mad dash back to their room in House Ignis, anticipating that Kaeli would likely show up... eventually. Aries would be furious with him, again, but he had to figure out what was wrong with Kaeli and then kill whatever bastard had made her cry. Lukka crossed his fingers hoping it was Niko. That jerk deserved to get beat up after what had happened to Kaeli during their fight three days ago.

He heard the rustle of the doorknob turning and spun around to confront Kaeli.

"Hey, man, what's up?" Joseph waved his hand in greeting. "Glad to see you're looking better." *No, not him!* Lukka's thoughts screamed. He needed to talk to Kaeli alone. There was no way she'd show any sign of weakness if they were in a group. A part of him felt bad for what he was about to do. He really liked the guy. But this was too important.

"Out!" Lukka pushed Joseph back toward the door.

"But—"

"OUT!" As soon as Joseph crossed the line, Lukka slammed the door in his face, and turned the lock for good measure. Then, realizing Kaeli might not be able to get in either, promptly unlocked it. He still leaned against the doorframe though, just in case Joseph tried to bust back in. He tapped his foot as he waited for Kaeli to arrive.

"Joseph? Why are you sitting out here?"

Kaeli! Lukka's pulse quickened. His gaze darted across the room as he tried to think. He hadn't expected Joseph to just sit outside the room and wait for Kaeli to show up. He had to figure out a way to fix this.

"Lukka kicked me out. He's being weird… but he's walking around now so I *guess* maybe that's a good sign?"

Lukka pressed his hands against his ears, muffling Joseph's voice. He needed to focus. Needed to come up with a plan. Should he bust open the door and drag Kaeli inside before Joseph had a chance to find out what happened between her and Niko? That sounded like a logical course of action. Just as he was about to place his hand on the doorknob, it turned and Kaeli peeked her head inside.

"Are you alright?" she asked. "Joseph said you were acting weird." Lukka looked over the top of Kaeli's head. His friend raised his eyebrows, demanding a silent explanation. Explanations could come later.

"Yes, yes, I'm fine. Get inside!" He grabbed Kaeli by the upper part of her arm and dragged her through the door, swiftly closing it before Joseph could sneak in.

"*Ow!* Lukka!" Kaeli yanked her arm away and rubbed it vigorously. "I'm cutting you some slack because this morning you vomited black sludge, but seriously, you can't just grab people like that."

"Oh, uh, sorry!" Lukka ran a hand through his shaggy hair. This was *not* the start he wanted to have in this conversation. The room suddenly spun and he stumbled over to the couch for support. Kaeli tilted her head and furrowed her eyebrows together.

"Lukka, are you really okay?"

"I'm... fine." He made his way around the couch and sank down into the plush cushions. With a heavy sigh, he leaned his head against the back pillow, and closed his eyes. The dizziness started to subside a little. "Don't worry about it. That weirdo Kio did some woowoo water healing thing on me. Are you okay?" He opened his eyes and craned his neck to look at Kaeli. She moved around the couch and sat down next to him. "I saw you at the portal with Niko..."

Kaeli's facial features softened.

"You saw that?" Her voice was quiet. Too quiet.

"Yeah." Lukka paused, not entirely sure how to continue the conversation. "What was that all about?"

"Nothing," Kaeli said, her voice a raspy whisper. For the first time since she entered the room, Lukka really looked at her. Her eyes were red, not like the fire red he was used to seeing when she burst into flame, but the kind of red people got when they finished bawling their eyes out. And there were bags around them. Big bags. Dark circles that left her looking totally exhausted. If Niko had done anything to hurt her... Lukka clenched his fist so tightly his knuckles turned white.

"Nothing, huh?"

Kaeli bit her lip, then face-planted into the couch, obscuring her face from his view. Her golden blonde hair sprawled out in all directions. Lukka resisted the urge to stroke it. He cleared his throat.

"It doesn't look like nothing," he said. Kaeli shot up, flipping her hair as she did. Lukka bobbed his head out of the way to avoid the whiplash. She turned to face him. He noted the almost imperceptible quiver in her lower lip and made a mental note to try not to set her off. Dealing with emotions was not his area of expertise.

"Have you had your class with Scorpio yet?" Kaeli asked.

"No," Lukka shook his head. "Why? Did he hurt you? Do I need to kick his ass?" Taking on Scorpio would be a lot more difficult than taking on Niko, but if he could factor in the element of surprise, maybe he could do it. Heat could evaporate water after all. Lukka's attention snapped back toward Kaeli as a small smile tugged her beautiful, perfect lips.

"No, it's nothing like that," Kaeli said, shaking her head. She let out a heavy sigh. She inched slightly closer to him. Lukka became acutely aware of the warmth emanating from her body as their legs nearly touched. Maybe he should talk more about kicking ass.

"Lukka, I... I killed my dad." Her voice trembled a little, but she said the words with a resolved tone. Lukka instinctively reached out to hold her hand. Kaeli didn't pull away. "Scorpio has this ability to hack into people's subconscious, so today in class he… he made us relive our most painful memory. I… I didn't even know I was the one who… the one who killed him." She raised her eyes to meet his gaze, and Lukka's heart melted into a puddle. He slung an arm around her shoulder. Kaeli let out a shaky exhale. "I panicked during the crash and I used my fire…" Her voice trailed off and she leaned in the crook of Lukka's arm as she stared off into the distance. "I understand why I needed to see it… why I needed to know… but… my dad would still be alive if it weren't for me."

Lukka pursed his lips and stared off into the fire. His chin quaked as a lump formed in his throat. He tucked Kaeli closer into his side.

"I know what that's like," he whispered. "I… I killed both my parents when I first got my fire. Unintentionally burned down the entire house." He let out a strangled cough. Kaeli shifted to sit upright and placed a light hand on his shoulder. Lukka tilted his head to look at her. Her eyelashes, wet from tears, clung to each other as she rapidly blinked. She chewed at her bottom lip. For once, Lukka didn't have any words to say, and Kaeli showed no indication of moving. So he tucked her into his side again and together they sat on the couch staring into the fire.

✱ ✱ ✱

Leo entered the arena at House Ignis to meet with Aries and Sagittarius. Classes were finished for the day and the recruits were safe in their rooms. Leo looked out at the galaxy sky, thinking about Kaeli. He hadn't talked to her after her class with Scorpio, but he knew what the class entailed and worried Kaeli might not have been ready for it. Judging from the eerie silence coming from her room, and his brief encounter with Joseph who had been hanging out with Liani since Lukka had apparently locked him out, the class had taken a turn for the worse. Leo clenched his fists together as he tried to suppress the rising anger in his chest. Things were getting out of hand. First Lukka's mysterious illness this morning, and now this. If Scorpio had done anything to hurt Kaeli...

"What's bothering you?" Aries's voice cut through Leo's thoughts. Leo shook his head. They were meeting to discuss training strategy and he had to be thinking clearly.

"I'm just worried about Kaeli. I haven't seen her at all since she finished Scorpio's class."

"Oooooh," Aries said, half to herself and half to Leo. "Maybe *that's* why Lukka never showed up for our training session this afternoon."

"What do you mean?"

"You haven't noticed?!" Aries pulled at Leo's shoulder, making him stop mid-step as she put an over-dramatic hand to her heart. "The budding romance between two young loves? Please tell me you've at least sensed *something*. He was probably trying to make her feel better.*"

Leo shifted his gaze back and forth and pursed his lips.

"No. Kaeli hasn't said anything about Lukka during any of our sessions... or otherwise."

"Of course she hasn't told you anything." Aries firmly planted her hands on her hips. "You have to learn to read between the lines on these things. Hmmmm." She stroked her chin as a mischievous smile played onto her face and said, "Maybe I should plan a girls night. Me, Kaeli, Liani. I could get a few of the other spirits. We'll have *lots* of wine, and maybe I can get Kaeli to open up about her feelings for Lukka!"

"You are *not* doing that." Leo frowned. Aries winked. "While this is a fascinating conversation," Leo said, "training strategy should be our focus right now."

"Fine, fine, fine, let's talk business." Aries shook her head and sighed as she moved to a bench and sat down. "I already know how I want to move forward." She crossed her legs and leaned forward. "Lukka's really talented with fire. He's progressing with the other abilities at higher than average pace. I'd say in about a week, I want to introduce him to his celestial form."

Leo froze.

"Already? Isn't it a little early for that?"

"After seeing what happened to him today," Aries clasped her hands together and leaned back, "absolutely not. The barrier is getting weaker, Leo. The more snakes and shadows that leak through from the dream realm, the more important it will be for our recruits to be able to defend themselves— and that means learning celestial forms."

"But celestial forms are also the only way to open the door." Leo paced. Centuries ago, when Ophiuchus had been locked away, the zodiacs had needed to access their celestial forms to create the door and seal it. An eternal oath prevented them from ever unlocking it… but a recruit who wasn't a fully-fledged zodiac yet… He shook his head. "It's too soon. Too dangerous. We know that Ophiuchus has already started distributing marks. If the recruits stumble on the door again…"

"Lukka doesn't have a mark, thank the stars. I was worried after this morning, but Kio says he's clean." Aries stood and said, "Look, Leo, I get that you want to be careful about training Kaeli, and maybe a celestial form isn't right for her at the moment, but when it comes down to it, this is a necessary skill that they will *all* have to learn eventually." She looked deeply into his eyes. "Shit's about to hit the fan. The world could *end* if we don't play our cards right. I understand you want to protect Kaeli, but the truth is, we picked them knowing how wrong things could go. You'll have to tell her sooner or later." Aries let out a heavy breath. "I'm not going to tell you what your next move should be, but I know mine." She clapped Leo on the back. "Now, I'm going to go find a beer. Talking about the end of the world makes me thirsty."

Leo shook his head and she walked off toward the exit. He'd hoped this meeting would help give him more clarity about what to do with Kaeli. Instead, he just felt more conflicted. Becoming a zodiac always came with risk, but now, with so much at stake, it was especially dangerous. He needed Kaeli to be prepared, but he also wanted to keep her alive. He tilted his head up to look at the sky.

"I hope I don't screw this up."

Alyssa Markins

CHAPTER 18

K aeli shuffled through the tunnels toward the House Ignis arena for her morning training session with Leo. It had been a struggle to leave her room at all that morning. She hadn't slept well the night after Scorpio's class. Her feet dragged along the stone floor, kicking bits of gravel out of her way as she neared the arena entrance. Kaeli took in a deep breath and wrapped her arms around herself. Her dreams had been filled with snakes and shadows and fire… and death. A shiver ran down her spine as she noticed the stairwell where Lukka had first shown her the door. She found herself staring into the dark abyss as she thought about Lukka. He sat with her for hours the other day after she told him what happened until he'd finally just fallen asleep on the couch. She felt bad. He was the one who had been in real danger that day, and yet he showed more concern about what had happened to her.

Shaking her head, she dismissed any further thoughts. She needed to at least try to pull it together before meeting Leo. Letting out a long, low sigh, she dropped her hands to her sides. She could do this. What was done was done. There was nothing to do now but move forward. She took the last few steps toward the arena.

Leo stood, as he usually did, with his back facing away from the entrance, but there was something about his posture that was different this morning. His shoulders were slightly drawn in and a tense energy filled the air. She barely took one step into the arena before he turned toward her. Kaeli's nose twitched. She wished she could master the instinctual side of her abilities… but unlike the fire, that part of her power did not come easily.

As she approached, she could see the wary edge in Leo's eyes. She had no doubt it had to do with Scorpio's lesson, and she cringed in anticipation of the looming questions. Kaeli had no desire to talk about it. She'd spent enough time baring her soul yesterday. Today, she wanted to focus on mastering her abilities so nothing like that would *ever* happen again. She needed to get stronger, to develop more control. He scratched at his chin while tilting his head to examine her. She met his gaze, trying to telepathically communicate with her eyes that all she really wanted to do was train. She noticed the almost imperceptible clench in Leo's jaw as if he understood but wasn't happy about it. He let out a heavy sigh.

"I was talking to Aries about your training last night." His voice didn't hold its usual enthusiasm. "Given everything that's happened just within the last week, it's become clear that we need to accelerate your proficiency in your unique abilities." Kaeli stiffened as a knot formed in her stomach. "Today we're going to work on developing your instincts." Leo scratched the back of his neck. "That way you'll be better able to sense when danger is coming and prepare yourself." He cocked his head to the side, eyes studying her. Kaeli stared right back.

"But I think we might need to do more than play a game hide and seek this time," Leo said, his voice low. He nodded to something behind

Kaeli. She turned to see Pyronius walking toward them with strong, purposeful steps. Leo cleared his throat and said, "Lions learn to develop and hone their instincts by watching their mothers hunt. While I strongly discourage you from calling Pyronius your mother, he's known as the fiercest warrior in the Celestial Realm." The small smile cracked his lips. "Just don't tell Aries I said that."

Kaeli quickly turned to look back at Leo.

"You can't seriously expect me to go hunting with him," she said. She hadn't interacted with Pyronius much, but he definitely came off as a do-or-die type of teacher, and Kaeli didn't get the impression he cared much about the later part. Leo shoved his hands into his pockets.

"I admit, it's not ideal. I would rather try our hand at hide-and-go-seek again, but desperate times call for desperate measures."

Kaeli scrunched up her nose as she glared at Leo through squinted eyes. Leo chuckled.

"You'll be fine. I promise."

Kaeli rolled her eyes. Pyronius's large shadow loomed over her as he approached. She turned to face him, her shoulders tensing as a heaviness dropped to the pit of her stomach. Pyronius had his usual scowl and judging glare plastered to his face. She didn't even try to offer a weak smile. He came to a stop in front of her, stance spread wide and thick, tree trunk arms crossed over his chest. Kaeli couldn't think of a worse way to start the day. Their eyes stayed locked in the most intimidating staring contest Kaeli had ever participated in before Pyronius shifted his unimpressed gaze to Leo.

"On second thought, I'm not sure she's ready for this." His tone was blunt. That just made the words cut deeper.

"Excuse me?" Kaeli propped both of her hands on her hips and tried her best to stare daggers straight through Pyronius. A dangerous warmth lurked just beneath the skin of her fingers. She closed her eyes briefly and took in a slow deep breath.

"She'll be fine," Leo said. Pyronious shrugged and redirected his attention to Kaeli.

"If you say so. Come on, kid." He jerked his head toward the tunnel that led out of the training arena. "I guess we're going on a field trip." Without another word, he turned and started walking out. Kaeli turned one last time to Leo.

"If I die, I'm completely blaming you. I hope you can live with that."

A playful smirk spread across his face. "You'd better follow after him," he said. "Pyronius doesn't have a reputation for waiting." Kaeli huffed her disapproval, but ran to catch up to Pyronius anyway.

The warrior fire spirit was not known for his conversational skills, and he apparently had no intention of changing that perception. Kaeli followed him in silence as they navigated the corridors in House Ignis until she had completely lost her sense of direction and had no idea where they were. He stopped in front of a door and opened it to reveal a small room, more of a closet really, with a single teleportation portal at the center. Pyronius entered the closet, his huge frame barely able to fit through the doorway. He hunched over and had to tilt his head to the side just to fit all the way inside. A pinched expression crossed his face and Kaeli noticed the muscles in his neck twitch as his jaw clenched.

"Get inside," he ordered. Kaeli's eyes widened as they roamed the width and height of the closet.

"How?" she asked tentatively. Pyronius let out a huff. Despite his cramped shoulders, his hand shot out, closing around Kaeli's wrist as he yanked her into the tiny space. Her disgruntled protest was immediately smothered by his rock-hard abdomen. His arms settled around her as he mumbled something under his breath. Before she could even squirm uncomfortably, the whole world swirled into a conglomeration of colors. As soon as her feet touched solid ground and the world began to settle, Pyronius shoved her away. Kaeli stumbled backward, holding her hands out for balance, barely able to regain her footing before falling to the ground.

What is your problem?! Kaeli wanted to lash out the words but kept them contained as the heat built in her gut. Pyronius could squash her like a bug. He pulled himself back up to his full height and cracked his neck.

Kaeli let out a couple of deep breaths and took a moment to look at her surroundings. The same celestial sky was still above her, but the terrain was completely different. They stood in the middle of a hilly grassland that seemed to expand endlessly in all directions. The greenery was sporadically interrupted by large rock formations jutting out of the ground, as well as sectioned off areas of what looked like farmland. Spirits with brown and green skin roamed between the sections of farmland, bent over the crops. They wore tunics cinched at the waist and draped over one shoulder, and wide brimmed hats with pointed tops cast shadows over their faces. Around the perimeter of the farms stood red- and orange-skinned spirits wearing leather armor similar to Pyronius's garb. Kaeli had never seen so many spirits gathered in one place.

"Where... are we?"

"In Regio Terra," Pyronius answered. "This is the land below the zodiac's ivory tower, where the spirits really live. You can only get from there to here via the hidden portal in each of the houses, unless you're a zodiac."

Kaeli blinked slowly as her brain worked to process all the new sensory information. The land was so serene, yet the spirits moved with an air of tenseness.

"Why are we here?" she asked. The scowl on Pyronius's face deepened.

"It's gaisk mating season," he growled. Kaeli's eyes widened.

"It's *what now?*"

Pyronius looked down at her and a hint of a chuckle escaped as he saw the shock on her face.

"I probably should've given you more context," he smirked. The hairs on her arm stood on end as a shiver ran down her spine. "The gaisk are a type of beast that dwell here in the Celestial Realm. They are large, winged, and stinging creatures that live and hide underground but pop out to hunt their prey. We typically allow them to live in peace around the farmlands because they kill and eat other small pests that try to destroy the crops, but during mating season…" Pyronius actually cringed. "During mating season they are so desperate to lay their eggs in a host, they don't care who or what the host is."

"Ummmm… lay their eggs *in* a host?" Her chest tightened, constricting her breath. If Pyronius was worried about these things, she didn't even want to imagine what kind of creature they might be. Pyronius nodded his head.

"They use their stingers to paralyze their victims with a poison and then inject their eggs. After that, they drag the host back to their underground cell where the eggs incubate. When the eggs hatch, the larvae devour the host alive." His face twisted into a disgusted expression as he said, "Normally the earth spirits tend to the farmlands themselves… but during gaisk mating season, a battalion of fire spirits is sent to help protect them."

"So, let me get this straight." Kaeli's limbs trembled, but she didn't know if it was from fear or anger. Probably a mixture of both. "Every year a battalion of *trained fire spirits* is sent to kill these monsters, and Leo thought it would be a *good idea* for me to do this as a *TRAINING* exercise?" She clenched her fists so tightly her knuckles turned white.

"Actually, I'm the one who thought it was a good idea." He reached for a baton-like stick hanging at his side, unlatching it. With a swift flick of his wrist, it expanded into a wing-tipped spear that was almost as tall as him. "These things burst out of the ground with nearly no warning. You have to be able to sense them before they're coming if you're going to protect yourself, giving you an excellent opportunity to develop your instinctual abilities."

Kaeli was sure her heart would burst out of her chest at any moment. Or maybe her eyes would pop out of her skull. He couldn't be serious. This couldn't be happening. She had no idea how to even access this part of her ability and they expected her to somehow fight off these terrifying monsters.

"You don't have anything to worry about." A cocky grin crossed Pyronius's face. "You're with me. Leo only agreed to let you come here because I promised to personally protect you. I will be able to sense where they are coming from, but I want you to try to tell me before it happens." He spun the spear so that the blunt end pointed toward Kaeli's face. She tried not to flinch as it stopped just inches away from her nose. "Before they pop out of the ground, there is a slight vibration in the earth. If you're able to unlock your instinctual abilities, you should be able to use your other senses to figure out where they are moving before they decide to surface." His eyes narrowed in warning. "Under *no* circumstances are you allowed to use your fire. The only way to kill a gaisk is to stab it in the soft part of its abdomen. It would take hours for a gaisk to die from fire due to their resilient exoskeletons and the last thing we need are horny gaisks flying around setting fire to all of the crops, got it?"

Kaeli clenched her jaw but nodded her head. Pyronius let out a satisfied grunt. "Good." He moved the spear away from her face and reached for a metallic, baton-like object strapped to his other side. He pressed an unseen button and it also extended into a spear. "This is only for an emergency. A gaisk would kill you before you could get close enough to stab one so don't go running toward danger. You shouldn't have to use it, but just in case." He handed it to her and held his spear out horizontally, clicking another mechanism. Another sharpened point shot out the other end. "Stay close to me and try to pinpoint where the gaisk are coming from before they surface." Kaeli bit her lip and nodded again as she moved closer to Pyronius.

She didn't take a full step before the slightest tremble in the earth made her stop cold in her tracks. A wicked smile crossed Pyronius's face.

"You felt it. Good. Now where do you think it's coming from?"

Kaeli took in a shaky breath as the vibrations made the blades of grass quiver. Before she could locate the source, a thundering, buzzing hum sounded from behind her as the ground split. Kaeli spun around and jumped back toward Pyronius. The sound of her pulse hammered through her ears. A gaisk hovered in front of them, the powerful beat of its wings making Kaeli's hair fly back. She squinted her eyes against the wind. It was about half the size of an average human with three quarters of its body comprising the lower abdomen and a menacing stinger the size of her forearm. Six barbed legs dangled from the body of the creature. It stared at them with small, beady black eyes. Kaeli started hyperventilating. She wanted to scream, but her throat closed up as she gasped for breath. The gaisk only stayed in place for a second before lunging, stinger first, straight toward her. Kaeli didn't even have time to react before Pyronius shot out his spear, stabbing the monster with precision in its fleshy, unprotected center. The gaisk let out a hissing sound before falling limp over the weapon. Pyronius gave his spear one solid shake and the dead creature slid to the ground, a pale amber color leaking from the gash in its body. Kaeli tore her eyes away from the gruesome scene. A metallic blue vapor oozed from the wound, letting out a pungent smell. Her lips curled in disgust as she pressed her hands over her nose. Pyronius tensed behind her as he coughed.

"Please tell me that's not poison gas," Kaeli squeaked.

"Worse." Pyronius curled his lip in disgust and said, "That's the death pheromone. We'll be seeing a lot more of these guys real soon." A chill shot down Kaeli's spine and she fought the urge to run. Right now, she was in the safest place she could be, considering that she was here at all. Not to mention she had no idea where she would even go or how to get back to House Ignis.

She tried to steady her breathing and focus. If she could just start using her instinctual abilities, maybe Pyronius would get them out of this hell. The ground trembled again and this time, Kaeli closed her eyes, trying to detect the direction. She focused on the vibrations, but every time she thought she could sense the gaisk, the vibrations seemed to shift. She squeezed her eyes even tighter, attempting to ignore the tingling sensation in her chest.

"Fear can heighten your senses if you use it correctly," Pyronius said softly. "Let the adrenaline fuel you. Expand your focus outward."

Kaeli exhaled and did as Pyronius said, pushing past the panic pressing in on her and focusing on the ground, on the terrifying creatures lurking underneath. Her eyes shot open as a sense of nausea overtook her. She turned to Pyronius, her legs quaking.

"There's five of them," she murmured, "and they're surrounding us." The cocky smile returned to Pyronius's face.

"That's close, kid." As if on cue, the gaisk burst from the ground, the sound of their wings nearly deafening. "There's six!" Pyronius bellowed, his voice barely audible over the thundering buzz. He flourished the spear above his head in a graceful arc, out of place with his large frame. The gaisk all charged at once. More burst out from the grounds closer to the farmlands. The earth spirits shrieked and made a run for it while the fire spirits screamed their war cries. The familiar heat of her fire smoldered in Kaeli's gut. *No no no, this can't be happening.* She clutched her arms around her torso as if that would physically contain the fire that wanted to explode. Pyronius stabbed a gaisk and spun the spear to stab another with the other end, sending the first of his victims flying into another charging wasp and knocking it off course.

"Control it," he growled. Kaeli dropped her to her knees and squeezed her eyes shut. *Don't explode.* She repeated the mantra over and over in her brain. It was then, close to the ground, that she sensed another vibration through the earth. This one was different from the others. It was clearer, like a beacon shining a light. The fire building in Kaeli tugged toward it. It wasn't trying to explode outward. It was trying to warn her. She focused on the sensation and placed her hand on the ground, allowing the warmth of her power to guide her senses. It shot straight down. She opened her eyes.

"There's one right und—"

The ground between her and Pyronius erupted, sending her reeling several feet. The gaisk hovered over the ground facing Pyronius who fended off the remaining three gaisk. The newcomer lunged toward him.

"NO!" Kaeli yelled. Without fully registering the situation, she thrust her spear at the gaisk. The gaisk hissed as it lurched mid-air before falling to the ground. The weight of it tore the spear from Kaeli's hands. Pyronius stabbed the last of the gaisk attacking him and flipped it over, smashing it into a nearby rock. He turned toward Kaeli. Excitement danced in his eyes as he ran an arm across his forehead, wiping away the faintest trace of sweat.

"Good job, kid." he smiled. Kaeli sat back on the ground, her chest heaving. The blue vapor from the dead gaisk started to form a cloud of stench around them and she choked. Pyronius walked toward her and hauled her back up to her feet.

"That was a good start," he said. "I wish we could stay longer, but I promised Leo I'd have you back at the house with enough time to get a hold of yourself before your first class." He let Kaeli grip his arm to hold herself upright. The stench distorted her senses. The adrenaline completely overloaded her system. She was light-headed and black specks dotted her vision. Thankfully, they hadn't ventured too far away from the portal. Pyronius guided her toward it, and within moments, the world turned upside down as they returned back to the house.

Once they were back at House Ignis, Pyronius led her through the confusing maze of corridors, back to the upper levels of the house. Liana had waited in front of her room, demanding to know all of the details about her training session, but Kaeli didn't have the energy to deal with her dynamic personality. Only a little guilty, she brushed past the spirit and headed straight to her bathroom to take shower. She needed to get the stench of the gaisk death pheromone out of her hair.

✴ ✴ ✴

After she'd washed up and changed into a fresh set of training clothes, she still had a little time before her first official class for the day. Swiping her copy of *Mythos of the Stars* and peeking her head out the door to make sure no one else laid in wait to ask her prying questions, she snuck out the room and made her way to the portal. She wanted to find a place to read where she could do so uninterrupted. Based on recent events, the library didn't seem like the best location.

"Terra," she said as she stepped into the portal.

Seconds later she appeared in the lush gardens. Floral fragrances assaulted her senses in the best possible way as she inhaled deeply. It was still fairly quiet. The birds chirped in the trees, but there weren't many spirits out tending to the gardens like when they'd first taken the tour. She walked down the cobblestone path leading deeper into the foliage and spotted a small alcove with a stone bench situated in the center. Smiling, she hurried over to sit and cracked open the book to where she'd left off.

Ophiuchus became so adept with the herb that many were soon coming to him, pleading with him to heal their dead loved ones. Hades, the god of the underworld, saw this as a direct assault to his domain as his subjects were now being taken away to resume life with the living. He brought his complaints to Zeus and demanded that Ophiuchus be disposed of on account of his new power. While Zeus favored Ophiuchus, he realized the complications that came with being able to bring the dead back to life. Even if Ophiuchus's intentions were good, the power could not be trusted. He banished Ophiuchus to the realm of no return, but left a memorial of him in the stars.

Outside of Greek mythology, Ophiuchus is also known as the omitted thirteenth sign of the tropical (Western) zodiac. He typically falls under the element of water, although he does contain a variety of personal qualities that embody several signs from several elements. Descriptions of Ophiuchus differentiate greatly, but overall, it is agreed that he not only has the power to give and take life, but also has the power to interpret dreams.

"Hello, Kaeli." A jarring voice snapped her attention away from the page. Kaeli's eyes shot up as she slammed the book shut, only to see Gemini standing at the entrance, his lithe frame silhouetted in the light of the doorway. As he started walking toward her, Kaeli noted the wide, disturbingly knowing grin on his face. "What book do you have there?" Kaeli looked down at the book for a split second before hugging the cover into her chest so that Gemini couldn't get a decent look at the title.

"It's nothing." She cringed at the sound of her own voice. She was acting the exact opposite of casual, but he caught her off guard. Gemini slid into the seat at the table opposite of her and snapped his fingers. The book vanished from her grasp and appeared into his with a puff of smoke. Kaeli opened her mouth in protest, but the words didn't come.

"How... how did you..."

Gemini turned the book over in his hands as he examined the cover.

"Teleportation, my dear. Air Signs can generally apply it to objects as well. Did you forget what kind of spirit the head librarian is?" He looked up from the cover and winked before setting the book back down onto the table and sliding it back over to Kaeli. "*Mythos of the Stars,* eh? Any constellation you were studying in particular?" Kaeli's shoulders sagged as she took the book back into her lap.

"Do you really need to ask that question?"

"Well," Gemini's grin grew wider as he crossed his arms over his chest and settled back into the chair, "if I had to make a completely random, off-the-wall, shot-in-the-dark guess, I would say your research perhaps has something to do with the snakes? Considering everything that's happened here with you and your friends recently." Kaeli flinched. "Oh, relax." Gemini leaned forward, placing his elbows on the table and crossing his hands under his chin. "I haven't told anyone about your little secret, and, as interesting as this conversation is playing out to be, this isn't why I've come to find you."

Kaeli blinked several times, unsure of how to respond. She fidgeted with the edges of the book cover.

"Then… why did you come to find me?"

"So glad you asked!" Gemini unfolded his hands and settled back into his seat, crossing an ankle over his knee. "When I found you and your friends leaving the library the other day—" he said, winking again as Kaeli gulped nervously, "—which by the way, I haven't told anyone. You mentioned that you wanted to learn more about the Yantari. I'm having a lesson with Alex and Ryan today. Would you care to join?" Kaeli's eyes widened. She stopped fidgeting with the book. She didn't know whether or not she should breath out a sigh of relief or squeal with excitement.

"Yes!" It was all she could do to keep from jumping out of her seat. She looked down at the book and frowned. She didn't exactly know what she was going to do with it. Elethia was the one who had given it to her, so she didn't think it belonged to the library, but at the same time, she didn't have anywhere to stash it. "I just need to… return this book."

"Done and done." Gemini stood up from the table and snapped his fingers. The book once again vanished in a cloud of smoke. "Now let's go. We have a limited amount of time before the three of you will have to go to your first class and I want to make sure we get through the proper introductions with Yantari." A twinkle danced in his eyes. "They can be very particular about these sorts of things."

＊＊＊

Together they walked back to the portal in silence. Gemini barely whispered the word "Aera" before they materialized in front of a gorge flanked between two towering cliffs. Ryan and Alex stood at the entrance, bickering about something. Kaeli couldn't make out the words, but judging by Alex's angry gestures and Ryan's hardened stare as he crossed his arms over his chest, it wasn't anything good. Gemini sighed as he made his way over to the twins.

"What is it with you two this time?"

They paused as they turned to their mentor.

"Ryan was—" Alex cut himself off as he caught sight of Kaeli. He shook his head. "We can talk about it later. It was nothing serious."

Ryan locked eyes with Kaeli and his grin grew so wide it threatened to split his face in two. "Come to join the dark side? Finally realized that air is the best element and you're trying to convert?"

Kaeli smirked. "Only if it's true you have cookies."

"Kaeli is here to learn about the Yantari, same as the two of you." Gemini shook his head as he guided her past the twins. They followed close behind. "Although the Yantari seem to prefer living with the air dwellers, they are native to the Celestial Realm before we were even chosen to be guardians of the zodiac. Because of this, they do not belong to any one element. They simply align with those they feel most compatible." As he talked, the four walked through the depths of the canyon. Kaeli couldn't help her mind from wandering as she looked up at the towering rocks surrounding them. Vibrant green foliage covered certain sections of the chasm, but it was the colors in the bedrock that took her breath away. Purples, oranges, reds— the grand canyon on Earth absolutely paled in comparison to the stimulating beauty currently surrounding her.

"Here," Gemini said and stopped, holding out a hand to prevent them from walking any further. He paused, and for a moment the only sound Kaeli could hear was the wind as it passed through the gorge. Then, Gemini let out a long, low whistle—similar to a bird call, but with an ancient, haunting melody. The eerie sound echoed off the walls of the canyon, building to an unnatural crescendo until it became so loud that Kaeli fought the urge to cover her ears.

Then, she saw them. Dozens of cat-like faces peeked out from various rocky crevices. One of them crawled out, and Kaeli took in a deep breath, her eyes unblinking as she found herself utterly transfixed by the creature before her.

It crawled… more like glided down the rocky terrain on its four padded feet. Its gait was similar to that of a cat, as was its face, but its body was unmistakably that of a dragon—if a dragon were the stature of a mid-size dog. Although this particular Yantari looked much smaller than the others. It sat right at Kaeli's feet and looked up, eyes wide with curiosity as it examined her and tilted its head to the side. Kaeli couldn't break eye contact.

Then the little beast opened its mouth and let out the most god-awful wailing howl Kaeli ever heard. Her hands flew to her ears as she tried to block out the horrendous noises. Ryan and Alex followed suit. The noise seemed to be a signal to the other Yantari because they came down from their rock perches in hordes. Some slithered down the edges of the cliff while others took to the sky. The gust from their wings blew Kaeli's hair wildly around her face and she struggled with whether to pull it back or to dim the sound of the howl. The ground shook as the Yantari landed. Kaeli, Ryan, and Alex could do nothing but stare in awe. The largest of the Yantari was nearly the size of a house. Each had different shiny, cool-toned scales that refracted the light into colorful patterns on the surrounding rocks.

"These are our friends, the Yantari." Gemini smiled at the stunned expressions on the recruits faces. "Well, don't be rude! Introduce yourselves. The Yantari are sticklers for manners." The largest of the Yantari snorted as if confirming Gemini's words. Kaeli looked down at the little Yantari sitting in front of her. It nodded its head ever so slightly while looking up at her with its almond-shaped eyes.

"Uh... hi." The words sounded awkward to her own ears. "My name is Kaeli... Thanks for letting us come see you today." Her gaze flickered to Gemini, searching for some sign of approval. He gave her a reassuring thumbs up. The little Yantari nuzzled against her leg and Kaeli froze, unsure if she should be worried or give the adorable thing a hug.

"Ryu seems to have taken a liking to you," Gemini said.

"Ry-who?" Ryan asked "You named all these guys?" Ryu snapped its head toward Ryan and bared its teeth, letting out the tiniest of growls before turning back to Kaeli and nuzzling her leg again. Kaeli couldn't resist the urge any longer. She reached down and scratched behind Ryu's pointed ears. Ryu let out a cooing purr.

"Ryu is actually female," Gemini chuckled. "And no. I didn't name them. I've simply known them long enough to learn their names."

"You talk with them?" Alex asked.

"Yes and no," Gemini answered. "When you become close enough with the Yantari, it's as if there is another realm of communication that opens up. Of course, they exhibit body language, as Ryu is doing with Kaeli, but they can also project mental images to beings with whom they wish to communicate. It's like telepathy, but with pictures."

"Whoa..." the twins said.

Gemini smiled at his mentees. "Today, however, we will not be doing much with the Yantari other than introductions, which, by the way, the two of you have yet to do." One of the larger Yantari huffed and stomped a massive paw impatiently, creating a cloud of dust.

"Sorry," Alex apologized to the beasts,\. "My name is Alex and this is—"

"Ryan." Ryan finished Alex's sentence. Ryu's lip curled over her sharp teeth as she growled at Ryan.

Kaeli couldn't help the amused smile tugging at her mouth as she looked between the ferocious little beast and Ryan. "She *really* doesn't like you."

Ryan glared at Ryu as he mimicked her aggressive expression. "Well no one said I had to like her either," he scoffed. Ryu let out a small cough from which a puff of smoke escaped her throat. Ryan arched an eyebrow. "Oh, was that supposed to be a little fireball?"

Ryu let out a noise that sounded like a cross between a hiss and a growl before turning her back to Ryan and walking to the rest of the Yantari. Kaeli elbowed him in the side.

"Be nice! She's cute. It's not her fault you're an obnoxious jerk."

Ryan opened his mouth to protest, but Gemini interrupted before he could start talking. "Ryan, I'm afraid… due to… your nature… you may not get along well with most of the Yantari."

"What?! Why? I'm so darn loveable…"

Kaeli didn't mean to laugh, but she couldn't stop herself. Alex laughed as well, but much louder. Ryan glared at both of them.

"Sorry, bro." Alex shrugged. A few of the Yantari approached him out of curiosity. "But let's face it, most of the people that hang out around you are there because of me."

"It's not your fault… necessarily," Gemini said. "You and Alex are like two sides of the same coin. Alex embodies the 'light' qualities, and you embody the 'shadow.' Together, the two of you make one whole gemini. The Yantari just so happen to have a natural aversion to shadow. They are very sensitive to it, and for many millennia, they were seen as guardians of the light, before they relocated to this particular location on the Celestial Island."

"Well then why are they so chill with you?" Ryan crossed his arms. "You have both sides in you."

"I have had many years to learn balance, Ryan." Gemini smiled, but a tinge of sadness flashed his eyes. "It's not that you'll never be able to interact with the Yantari, but if you want them to be comfortable with you, you really should be standing closer to your brother." Ryan huffed in protest but went to join Alex anyway.

"Being a gemini sounds complicated," Kaeli said, mostly to herself, as she watched the Yantari stretch out their necks to sniff at Ryan. She heard a cooing noise to her left and turned to see Ryu standing next to her again.

"Hey there." She smiled as she bent down to be eye level with Ryu. Ryu seemed pleased with this as she pounced and wrapped herself around Kaeli. Kaeli circled her arms around Ryu as the Yantari nuzzled under her neck. "You're so sweet." A shadow loomed over her, and she looked up to see Gemini standing behind her, stroking his chin. Kaeli stood up.

"This *is* interesting," he mused. "I've never seen a Yantari grow so attached to anyone so quickly before... much less Ryu. She's normally a little skittish."

"Skittish?" Kaeli looked down at Ryu as she wove circles between her legs. Gemini nodded.

"You wouldn't know it looking at her right now, but yes." He paused and tilted his head. "Kaeli, I want you to try something. Just to see if it will work."

"Um, okay. What is it?"

Gemini bent down to one knee so that he was eye level with Ryu. Ryu took one step back, hunching her head into her shoulders. Her eyes flickered apprehensively between Kaeli and Gemini, but she didn't show any overt signs of hostility. Gemini held out his hand, palm down, in front of her.

"Don't be silly," he said in a soothing voice. "You know me." Ryu straightened out and cocked her head to the side before inching a little closer and nudging her head under Gemini's hand. Gemini flipped his hand so that he coddled her head in his palm. He closed his eyes, and after a moment, smiled. He looked at Kaeli. "Ryu wants to try talking to you. Hold out your hand like this."

"Okay…" Kaeli mimicked his gesture, and Ryu immediately laid her head on it.

The instant her head made contact, Kaeli's mind turned to a blank canvas. Everything around her morphed into a white background. Ryu's image blurred and shifted until Kaeli was standing in front of her house on Earth. Nausea swirled in her stomach. It was the scene from right after the earthquake, right before Leo had taken her to the Celestial Realm. The shadow snake erupted from the ruins of her house, and all the air left Kaeli's lungs. Some alternate part of her brain that wasn't immersed in this experience tried to pull her hand away from Ryu, but an invisible force kept her frozen in place.

A series of scenes progressed in her mind's eye, all instances where she had seen the shadow snakes. The images flew by as if they were in fast forward, until they came to a stop in a desert terrain Kaeli had never seen. Kaeli looked around and saw a shadowed image of a person standing next to her. She tried to make out the details of who it was, but before she could pin down any solid features, the person shifted, growing horns and bursting into flames. Then, the person blew apart into pieces and from its center jumped a lion. Just as the lion was about to pounce on her, Kaeli was able to pull her hand away, and her vision returned to normal. Her entire body shook as she took a deep, slow breath and turned to Gemini.

"What. The hell. Was that."

"I don't know what you saw," Gemini shrugged. "I just know Ryu wanted to tell you something." Kaeli looked at Ryu who held her head high as she strutted around in a circle looking pleased with herself.

"She showed me the shadow snakes," Kaeli said under her breath, "and then a lion destroying a… fire devil." Gemini clasped his hands together and placed them in front of his mouth as a pensive expression fell over his face. He looked intently at Ryu before turning his attention back to Kaeli.

"Sometimes the message a Yantari wants to send isn't always clear," he said slowly. "Because they communicate in images, it is oftentimes difficult for us to understand the full meaning. Like I said before, however, the Yantari have a natural aversion to shadow. It could have been a warning, or Ryu could have been trying to tell you something else entirely."

"CUT IT OUT!" Ryan's shout interrupted their conversation. A large purple Yantari shot sparks of lightning at Ryan's feet, making him dance around trying to avoid it. Gemini's serious tone turned into a light-hearted smile.

"And that's our cue to cut these introductions short," he said. He started walking toward the twins but paused to look over his shoulder at Kaeli. "I do hope this doesn't deter you from coming to our next session. It really is quite rare to find someone who has such a natural way with the Yantari."

Kaeli hesitated before answering. She looked at Ryu who, she could swear, smiled at her through her cat-shaped dragon mouth. The sight was both endearing and disturbing at the same time. Kaeli returned the smile. Ryu let out a happy coo.

"I'll be back," she said more to Ryu than Gemini. Ryu jumped into the air and flew circles around Kaeli's head. A laugh escaped Kaeli's lips.

"Good." Gemini nodded his approval before turning to help Ryan escape the tortures of the other Yantari.

CHAPTER 19

Lukka walked into the common room only to be greeted by the sound of soft snoring. He made his way to the couch. A relaxed smile crossed his face and he ran a hand through his shaggy curls as he saw Kaeli sprawled out on the cushions. She'd managed to gather all the pillows and build the perfectly cushioned nest. She still wore her training clothes so she must have returned from her classes recently. Probably from a class with Aries. That's how he always felt after finishing a class or training session with his mentor. Poor thing. It would be a shame if something were to wake her up.

"Hey." He poked at her side. "Hey, Kaeli, you alive?"

Kaeli groaned as she swatted at his hand. "Go awaaay."

"I want to sit here." He went to move her outstretched legs to the floor when something soft and fluffy smacked him square in the jaw. He froze, eyes blinking rapidly as he processed what happened. Kaeli had twisted her torso around and was holding one of the couch pillows in her hand. She glared at him, but her eyes twinkled with the slightest glint of mischief. He clenched his hand into a fist as he moved ever so slightly toward another pillow that was propped against the back of the couch near her feet. Surely, Kaeli knew she was inciting war. He kept his eyes trained on her as she hopped up to her knees, pillow still firmly in her grip. Her gaze flickered toward his hand that slowly reached for the pillow. She was expecting retaliation. If he was going to land an effective strike, he'd have to opt for speed instead of stealth. He could do that.

"That's what you get for—"

Lukka launched his attack, delivering the fluffy blow to her gut. She grabbed the pillow as it made contact, yanking it out of his hand and leaving him weaponless. Still, he couldn't stop the grin that crept onto his face. Kaeli legitimately looked like she wanted to kill him, but he didn't care. The fun was just beginning.

"You're going to regret that," she growled, throwing one of her pillows at him. Lukka moved to catch it, but Kaeli used his momentary distraction to lunge forward and land a strike at his stomach with her remaining pillow. As soon as he had possession of the pillow, Lukka wasted no time in delivering his counterstrike, which Kaeli parried. They continued in a crazy flurry of pillow punches and flying feathers that ended with both of them lying on the floor in fits of laughter.

The creak of the door opening snapped them out of their fit. Joseph stood at the entryway, his eyes widened as he surveyed the damage in the common room.

"Is this… a bad time?"

Heat rose to Lukka's face, but before he could react any further, Kaeli shoved him away from her.

"No! Absolutely not a bad time at all!" She pushed herself up off the floor, brushing her clothes free of feathers. "Lukka woke me up from a nap and well…" She sighed as she looked around at the mess. Her lips pursed into a thin line. Without saying another word, she started picking up some of the nearby pillows and put them back on the couch. Lukka decided to stay on the floor and see how things played out. Joseph looked at Kaeli, then at Lukka, then back to Kaeli.

"Ooo-kay then, I'm just gonna take a shower," he said before disappearing into his room. Lukka waited until he heard the sound of running water before venturing a look at Kaeli. Thankfully, the heat had left his face. Kaeli now sat cross legged on the couch, clutching one of the pillows close to her chest and staring hard at the floor. Lukka couldn't help but smile. Her hair was teased up in different directions. Definitely a rare sight, but one he didn't mind. Imperfection looked cute on her. He pushed himself off the ground and sat down next to her.

"You look like you're thinking about something," he said.

"I am." Kaeli sighed as she leaned her head back against the couch and said, "Gemini introduced me and twins to the Yantari today…" She paused. Lukka waited for her to say something else, but she didn't. He stretched his arms out over the back of the couch and lolled his head to the side so he could look at her.

"Aaaaaand," he prompted. A small smile played onto Kaeli's face.

"Well, there's this one adorable Yantari named Ryu—"

"Hold up," Lukka interrupted. "Adorable? You are talking about the humongous elemental-breathing beasts that live in the Aera cliffs right?"

"Yes! Except Ryu isn't a giant like some of the other ones. She probably comes up to the middle of my leg and acts just like a cat. Anyway, that's beside the point. She really took a liking to me and ended up showing me some sort of… vision. Apparently they communicate by projecting mental images, and Ryu kept showing me different scenarios with the shadow snakes—" She clenched both of her hands into fists and slammed them down on the couch. "I got an idea!" She whipped her head to the side and made direct eye contact with Lukka. The grin on his face grew wide as he noted the excitement glinting in her eyes. "While we were there, Gemini said the Yantari have a natural aversion to shadow…" Her voice trailed off. Lukka could practically see the ideas turning in her head as she processed her thoughts. "Maybe Ryu could help us track down the snakes so we can find where they're coming from and figure out why they're coming after us!"

"Shadow snake hunting? Oh, I am so in."

The door to Joseph's room opened. Both Kaeli and Lukka turned their heads to see Joseph peeking his head out. He had a towel wrapped around his waist and beads of water dotted his olive skin. Lukka had been so enraptured in his conversation with Kaeli he hadn't noticed the shower turn off.

"The two of you are not going on a snake destroying mission without me," he said. Tendrils of steam curled around him.

"Wouldn't dream of it," Kaeli grinned. "We'll definitely have to do more research to figure out how to actually get the Yantari to start tracking them. We also need to figure out how to kill them. I'll focus on learning more about the Yantari since I'm taking lessons with them. Joseph, how about you work on figuring out how to kill the snakes?"

"Sounds good." Joseph nodded before withdrawing his head and shutting the door. Lukka propped his feet up on the coffee table and folded his arms behind his head as he sank a little deeper into the couch. He low-key—okay, high-key—hoped his bulging biceps would catch Kaeli's attention.

"I'm assuming that means you don't expect me to do any of the actual information gathering?"

"Well… no. It would be helpful, but no, I really wasn't expecting you to do that."

"Good," Lukka winked. "This is going to be fun."

Alyssa Markins

CHAPTER 20

The next morning, Kaeli woke up before the first light and slipped her way into the Room of Records. Going straight for Elethia's book, she removed it from its space on the shelf and opened it on the table. When the purple light cleared, Elethia stood completely nonchalant, rotating her wrist as she examined her nails before turning to look at Kaeli.

"My, we certainly have been seeing a lot of each other lately." Her usual sassy smile made its way onto her face. "Come to pester me with more questions, dear?" She motioned to one of the chairs at the table as if she had just invited Kaeli into her home. "Please, have a seat." Kaeli raised her eyebrows, but with a sigh and a shake of her head, did as Elethia requested. She was useful, but so brass. The combination was infuriating... in the most confusing sort of way. Once Kaeli sat down, Elethia took a seat opposite her.

"So, what can I answer for you today?" She propped her elbows on the table and gracefully intertwined her fingers. Kaeli leaned back in her chair and tilted her head.

"I finished reading the section about Ophiuchus's constellation in *Mythos of the Stars* and it was really interesting, but I need more concrete answers. I don't have time to piece together some abstract puzzle." She placed her hands on the table and leaned forward, asking, "Where can I find the snakes that are attacking us, and how can I kill them?"

"Well, someone is feeling rather ambitious today," Elethia smirked. She clapped her hands together and held them under her chin as she looked Kaeli over with an evaluating gaze. "No one can kill the snakes in exactly the same way. They are extremely adaptive to elemental skill sets. I'm going to need to know a bit more about *you* before I can give you that information. What sign are you training for?"

"I'm training with Leo."

"Ah, Leo." Elethia tilted her head as she cast an unfocused gaze to the wall behind Kaeli. The nostalgia quickly faded from her face as she cleared her throat and schooled her features into a neutral expression. "Alright then, you're training to be a leo. Have you mastered your instinctual abilities yet?" Kaeli pursed her lips as an embarrassing heat rose to her cheeks. She'd definitely improved, but the likelihood she would be able to track a shadow was not high. Elethia chuckled. "I'll take that as a no. How then, exactly, were you planning on finding the snakes if you don't have a means for tracking? Or were you expecting I would just have all of the answers ready at your disposal?"

"I was thinking the Yantari could help." Kaeli kept her voice steady as she focused on breathing in and out slowly to calm the flush in her face.

"The Yantari?" Elethia arched an eyebrow. "Perhaps you know more about this realm than I originally presumed. Yes, they would be able to find the snakes, if you can manage to get them away from their canyon. They have a tendency to stay rooted to their home."

"But if I can, will it work?" Kaeli asked. Her breath bottled in her chest at the anticipation.

"Yes, the Yantari are highly intelligent creatures. If you can get them to leave the cliffs, they will be predisposed to helping you, but you must be cautious. The Yantari are very social creatures with an aptitude for communication. You will need to be sure that the Yantari who decides to help you knows not to tell its kin… or any of the air signs. I imagine this little adventure you have planned is not something Leo has suggested you do."

Kaeli nodded. "So once I find a snake, how do I kill it?"

"Well, judging by your expertise, you won't be able to kill it alone," Elethia laughed. The heat crept back into Kaeli's face. She clenched her jaw to refrain from making any snappy comments. She needed this information. Elethia's eyes narrowed mischievously as if she knew exactly the type of reaction she created. "You were planning on bringing someone with you, yes?"

"Lukka and Joseph… Aries's and Sagittarius's recruits," Kaeli replied.

"If you want something killed, take an aries," Elethia muttered to herself before returning her attention to Kaeli. She sighed and plastered a smile onto her face. "Has the aries recruit mastered the berserker state?"

"I… ummm. I don't know… Berserker state?" Kaeli asked.

Elethia shook her head as she rubbed her temples. "What has this Leo even been teaching you? You have so much to learn. How do I explain this? Each sign has its own set of unique abilities, of course you would know that by now, but as part of the abilities, each sign also has… I guess you could call it a special ability for lack of a better word. Aries's happens to be a berserker state where they completely lose all control and go absolutely insane." She smiled. "Leo can harness the essence of the sun, which is blindingly brilliant if you ever get a chance to witness it. Also extremely effective against shadow snakes, I might add. I can tell by the look on your face you had no idea of your own ability, but do you know about your aries friend? Don't bother with the sagittarius. Their form is more suited for healing, believe it or not."

Kaeli held her mouth halfway open before letting out a defeated sigh. "I... have never even heard of this," she admitted.

"Stars above." Elethia rolled her eyes. "Well, if he doesn't, then there is no way you will be able to kill the snakes. The best you'll be able to do is use your fire to make them disappear for a bit, but they will come back. A zodiac would need to have at least partial mastery of their celestial form to kill certain snakes, full mastery to kill some of the stronger ones, much less an entire brood. If you plan on hunting those creatures, I suggest you find someone with enough power to do so. Are there any other questions?"

Kaeli opened her mouth, then shut it and shook her head. Now that she knew what needed to be done, she could follow up with other people who could actually train her later.

A coy smile played on Elethia's lips before she said, "I'm sure I will be seeing you again. If you survive this ridiculous endeavor, that is." She disappeared in a flash of her signature purple light. Kaeli picked up the book and studied the cover for a couple seconds before walking over to the shelf and sliding it back into place. She needed to find out if Lukka could go into his berserker form.

If Niko had the capability to dread something, it would be this first and only class of the day with Capricorn. But he didn't feel such strong emotions. Not anymore.

Out of habit, he scanned the perimeter as he stepped into the library lobby. Capricorn had told them all to meet here for the lesson, but the lobby was empty. He must have been the first to arrive. Good. The creak of a heavy door echoed through the room and Niko's stare shot to the obsidian doors leading to the Room of Records. He arched an eyebrow as Kaeli poked her head through the entrance. Never mind. Shame. Although if he had to choose anyone to be alone with in the group while waiting for the others, it would be her. Despite the fact that she was his natural opposite element, he found her intriguing. And after Scorpio's lesson at the water pools... Niko closed his eyes and shook his head. He would not let his mind wander.

Kaeli seemed to take great offense to this gesture as her face immediately fell into a frown and her brows furrowed together. She locked him into a hard stare as she marched over to the main lobby. The door silently closed behind her. Niko tilted his head back and pasted a cocky grin on his face. This type of expression always seemed to pull out feisty reactions from her, and he quite enjoyed those.

"You're here early," Kaeli greeted him with terse words.

"Not as early as you." Niko leaned against a nearby pillar and said, "You seem to spend a lot of your free time here. Does Leo have you working on a special research project?"

"Something like that..." Kaeli bit her lip as she glanced around the lobby. "Are you the first one here for class?"

Niko noted the sudden change in conversation topic, but he decided to file it away as an interesting fact for later. Ever since she'd broke down crying in front of him at the pools, it just didn't feel right to mess with her in the same way.

"Yeah, well, aside from you."

The clack of sharp footsteps approaching caused Niko to turn. Capricorn strode into the library. The twins and Shaina followed close behind. Niko pushed off the pillar and made his way to the center of the lobby. His gaze flitted toward Kaeli as she went to stand by Shaina. Capricorn removed his glasses and stuck them into his front coat pocket. Niko blinked several times but flattened his features into a neutral expression. He'd never seen Capricorn without dark shades before. His eyes were the most unnerving shade of cloudy pale blue. It wasn't the color that was unnerving so much as the intensity of his stare—as if he could see straight through all outer exteriors and directly into the essence of a thing. Niko looked around at his teammates. They all seemed to have similar initial apprehensive reactions… other than Ryan who squinted his eyes almost as if he was trying to stare into Capricorn's soul right back.

"You're all on time. Good."

Everyone let out a collective sigh of relief. Capricorn folded his arms behind his back and lazily lolled his head to the right.

"Today, we will be building trust and cultivating teamwork amongst your group. These two elements are *crucial* to fulfilling the responsibilities of a zodiac. Come." He turned on his heel and started walking toward the left wing of the library. The group exchanged shifty glances with each other before following after Capricorn.

Niko lost track of the turns and corridors as Capricorn led them deeper and deeper into the library labyrinth. He dug his nails into the palm of his hand and clenched his jaw as he thought back to all the lefts and rights, but there were too many at this point. Capricorn did not want them to know where they were going. Something Niko did *not* appreciate.

They came to a stop at a hallway. At the end was a nondescript door with a single moon insignia etched into the center. The tiniest twinge of a smile played onto Niko's lips as Kaeli nearly ran into him. She muttered an apology and stepped away. Capricorn flashed a judgmental side eye over his shoulder before motioning to the door ahead of them.

"Your training will take place inside of this room." His voice was flat. "This particular exercise will be familiar in that it is similar to the initial testing you had before you were officially accepted as a recruit. In order to leave the exercise, you will need to complete the challenge." He paused and took a moment to stare into the eyes of every single recruit. "Except this time, the danger will be very, *very* real. If you cannot complete this training, you *will* die."

Nervous energy rolled off his teammates as if it were a tangible force. It was one of his gifts—physically sensing the emotions of those around him.

"What kind of crap training exercise is that?!" Ryan protested. Capricorn directed all of his searing attention toward him. To Ryan's credit, he didn't flinch, even as a fresh wave of fear rushed off of him.

"One that will determine if you are truly eligible to take on the magnitude of a zodiac's responsibility," Capricorn hissed through gritted teeth. "Do you have any other pointless questions?"

Ryan pursed his lips into a thin line but shook his head.

"Good," Capricorn said and then folded his arms behind his back and paced in front of the door. "This will be an escape room type of situation that will require all of you to work together. You will have one hour to solve the puzzle and find the way out. If you cannot, well… then you'll have put your zodiac mentors at an extreme disadvantage as they will need to find another human to replace you and catch them up to speed." He placed two fingers at the center of the moon insignia on the door and it sprang open. Niko squinted to try to get a better look at what was inside, but there was only a dark void.

"You may proceed," Capricorn said, waving a flippant hand toward the entrance.

Niko exchanged glances with the other recruits. No one was particularly eager to be the first to enter. Kaeli let out a deep exhale and pushed her way to the front of the group, taking the first step into the darkness. Niko watched as the black swallowed her. Not willing to let her be in that room alone for more than a couple of seconds, he quickly followed suit.

Niko caught his breath the moment he stepped through the doorway. What had appeared like a dark void from the outside was a kaleidoscope of blue hues and stars on the inside of a circular room. Kaeli stood at the center, spinning in a slow circle and looking up at the ceiling. Niko followed the direction of her gaze. Pinpoints of silver light formed various constellations that ran down the length of the room, although something was off about their formations. His gaze returned to eye level as he took in the rest of the surroundings.

At the far end of the room was a bicycle connected to a power meter that led upward to the letter *S*. On the walls were six square shapes consisting of nine holes. The square directly to the right of the bicycle had small pinpoints of light that formed a zigzag pattern. Shaina and the twins entered the room. Capricorn stood silhouetted in the doorway.

"Your hour starts now," he said before turning on his heel and slamming the door behind him.

Nothing changed. Niko didn't know exactly what he expected to happen when the challenge officially started, but this wasn't it. The recruits all stood in the middle of the room, scoping out the scenery in silence.

"How do you think we die if we don't figure this out?" Ryan asked, his voice completely nonchalant.

"Hopefully, we never find out," Shaina said. Alex walked over to the bicycle.

"Clearly, it has something to do with this." He climbed onto the seat and started pedaling. One by one, the meter bars started to light up until they reached the letter at the top. The *S* illuminated, matching the silver light of the constellations. Nothing happened. Alex stopped pedaling and the light faded. He hopped off the bike.

"Maybe it's a decoy," Ryan said as he scratched his chin.

The words barely left his mouth before a creaking groan of moving machinery sounded from the ceiling. Niko looked up, his pulse quickening and his eyes widening as the entire ceiling shifted down, obscuring the top half of the constellations on the wall. Fear and shock rolled off his teammates in waves, making the hairs on his arms stand on end. Kaeli took a step closer toward him.

"So if we don't figure this out… we get crushed to death?" Her voice shook slightly, but it was nothing compared to the actual terror coming from her. He closed the gap between them and placed a hand on her arm, slightly tugging at that terrified emotion and siphoning some of it into himself. Her terror instantly muted to a normal level of fear as his own pulse quickened.

"That's not going to happen," he said, keeping his voice stable to mask his own fear. The last thing they needed was for everyone to break out into a panic.

"Well, it will if we don't figure this out," Ryan said. "We need a plan. A strategy. This bike may or may not have something to do with the key, but we know that lighting up that word on its own doesn't do anything."

Shaina walked over to the zigzag pattern in the box and crossed her arms over her chest as she stared at it. "This has to mean something," she whispered to herself. She turned back to the group. "Maybe it's a letter?"

"An *S*!" Alex exclaimed. "It's the same pattern as the one above the bike! Maybe we're supposed to spell something?" They all jumped as the ceiling groaned again, dropping another foot.

"A word that starts and ends with *S*," Niko said as he looked around the room, "and has eight letters." Niko looked at Kaeli as she broke away from his touch and made her way toward the wall. Kaeli bit her lip as she ran a hand over the constellations.

"Or more than one word that still uses eight letters," Shaina pointed out.

"But how would we even spell the word?" Ryan flashed a side glance to Shaina. "Or words. Those two *S*'s are both already in place."

"I think I…" Kaeli started muttering as her fingers fiddled with one of the silver pinpoints in the sagittarius constellation. She let out a frustrated grunt and then loosened one of the lights from a groove in the wall. As soon as it was removed from its position, the silver light flickered out, revealing a regular miniature light bulb. She broke out into a dazzling grin. "These come out!" She flashed a glare toward the wall. "Though not very easily." She moved to one of the empty square spaces on the wall and screwed the small light into one of the nine vacant spots. As soon as she had it secured, it lit up again.

"So we can move the lights to shape the words!" Shaina squealed.

"Now we just have to figure out what to spell," Niko said. The ceiling groaned and dropped again.

Ryan laced his fingers behind his head and tilted back to look up. "Anyone happen to have a watch and see what time it was when we got in here? Capricorn said we have an hour."

"Judging by the height of this room and how far that ceiling has dropped, I think we need to figure this sooner than in an hour." Shaina nearly spat out the words, "I think he meant we have an hour before we *die*."

Ryan moved next to her and linked arms. "Hey, at least we'll go out together!"

Shaina shot him a deadpan glare and deliberately unlinked her arm from his. She turned to face the rest of the group and said, "We need to solve this *now*."

Alex muttered under his breath as he turned in a circle, pointing to each empty square.

"What about the word 'searches?'" he said.

Ryan arched an eyebrow as he quickly scanned the room. "It has all the right letters. Why 'searches?'"

Alex shrugged his shoulders and explained, "Because we're looking for the answer... searching..."

Niko couldn't stop his mocking scoff. "It *can't* be that easy."

"At least Alex came up with an idea," Kaeli said.

He let out a sigh. "If no one can think of anything better, it's worth a shot."

"Well then, what's everyone waiting for!" Shaina was already unscrewing light bulbs from the constellations. "I'll get letters *H* and *E* closest to the bicycle."

"I'll take the *C* right next to the *H*." Ryan winked at Shaina as he moved closer to her and began unscrewing light bulbs as well. Shaina pursed her lips and inhaled deeply.

"I'll take *R*, but not because it's next to *C*!" Kaeli was quick to cut off Ryan before he could open his mouth. "I'm just standing closest to it is all."

"Whatever you say, Kaeli." Ryan grinned. "You don't have to try to hide your feelings from me."

Rage started to boil in the pit of Niko's stomach, but he held it in. Schooling his face into a practiced, relaxed expression, he moved toward the letter *E*. Alex started building the *A*.

When they finished forming the letters, everyone met back in the middle. Nothing happened. Niko scratched the back of his neck with one hand as he let out a long sigh. His gaze flickered up to the ceiling as it groaned again, lowering another foot.

"Nothing is happening..." Shaina's voice trailed off.

"Maybe we need to light up the letter *S* with the bicycle?" Kaeli's eyes widened. A small wave of hope came off her, like a comforting hug. He mentally latched on to that feeling. They would all need it if they were going to figure this puzzle out.

"On it!" Alex ran back over to the bike and started pedaling like his life depended on it. In a manner of seconds, the *S* illuminated. Niko kept his eyes open to see if anything would change. A flicker of light caught his eye as the *R* lit up.

Alex climbed off of the bicycle and the *S* faded back into darkness. "I guess 'searches' wasn't the right word." He was obviously trying to bite back the disappointment that threatened to show itself.

"But the *R* was!" Kaeli pointed to the illuminated letter. "So we know that whatever this spells, it begins and ends with *S* and has an *R* as the fourth letter."

Ryan scratched his chin. "Maybe it has something to do with the word 'star.' There's a lot of constellations in this room."

Niko bit his lip and nodded his head as he looked upwards and scanned the constellations. There had to be something they were missing. "We should search the constellations. Maybe they have some sort of clue." Everyone nodded their heads and looked around the room. Niko furrowed his eyebrows and crossed his arms. His fingers drummed against his tense muscles as he searched for a pattern. Examining the room, he noticed some of the constellations repeated, but he didn't know all of them. He recognized Libra and Sagittarius. They showed up a couple of times. There were a few standalone lights that were bigger than the others. Those could potentially be planets. Did any of the planets have the right letters? Maybe if he took out the first letter of the names it would spell something.

"Oh!" Kaeli's enthusiastic exclamation snapped Niko from his thoughts. Everyone turned to face her. The pure radiant joy that emanated from her being was intoxicating. Niko let out a slow controlled breath. *It's her charm ability. Don't let her get in your head.* While Kaeli seemed naturally inclined to this particular leo gifting, it was worse for him because he could literally *feel* the attraction like it was a living entity beckoning to just get closer, to—Niko shook his head. This was not the time. Kaeli was talking. He forced his attention onto her words.

"There was something off about the constellation patterns. At first I thought they were in the wrong order but then I noticed something."

"Spit it out, woman!" Ryan yelled.

"The constellation Scorpius is missing!" Kaeli blurted. Niko noticed her pulse quickening. Her infectious adrenaline permeated the room and took effect on the others. Shaina was nearly bouncing on her toes.

"Say no more!" Ryan started mouthing and pointing at the letters, rushing to the one nearest him. Everyone ran to the nearest letter and furiously began unscrewing and rearranging the light bulbs. The ceiling groaned, dropping yet another foot. Niko, the tallest in the group, found himself having to tilt his head ever so slightly so that he didn't hit the ceiling. When they finished, Alex sprinted to the bicycle and pedaled faster than he ever had. This time when the letter *S* illuminated, all of the other letters lit up as well. Shaina and Kaeli both squealed. The sound of clicking mechanism echoed throughout the room and a trap door on the floor at the center of the room sprang open.

"It's the way out!" Ryan rushed to the open door. He looked at the others and told them, "There are stairs going downwards."

"Let's get out of here!" Niko said. Ryan disappeared down the steps. One by one they followed his descent, the sound of the ceiling dropping behind them a reminder of what they had just escaped.

The stairwell was dark, lit only by a sporadically suspended blue light. It was unfortunate that powers didn't work in the library. Kaeli could have made a flame to light the way. Not that any of them were in a hurry. After making it out of that infuriating puzzle, rushing down a poorly lit stairway just to get injured was not something that any of the recruits wanted to do.

Faint light illuminated the steps as they neared the end of the stairs. In the distance, Niko could see another room, but thankfully, this one looked like a normal part of the library. A wave of relief rolled off his teammates.

He allowed himself to soak in it, never thinking he'd be so happy to see books.

Capricorn stood at the center of the room. His head tilted to the side and his mouth curled in an infuriating smirk. He clapped as they entered the room. The sound bounced off the library walls, mocking them. Niko clenched his fists as a tremble overtook his muscles. This *psychopath* deliberately put them through a lethal training session, one that was absolutely ridiculous, and then had the *gall* to clap for them after they escaped. Pounding sounded in his ears as blood rushed through his veins and red started to dot the edges of his vision. Zodiac or no… if Capricorn said one wrong thing, Niko would end him right here in the library.

A cool sensation brushed his arm, and Niko blinked rapidly. Kaeli stood at his side, looking up at him. Her eyes were like crystal pools of refreshing water. Niko found himself drawn into them. The fury began to dissipate until the only thing he could see was her.

"Congratulations." The sound of Capricorn's voice snapped him back to reality. Niko took in a deep breath and let it out. "I honestly didn't know if you would be able to pass. I'm glad to see you did."

"What kind of *fucked up* training session was that?!" Ryan exploded. Capricorn tilted back and raised both of his eyebrows as he regarded Ryan. "What?" Ryan crossed his arms. "We're all thinking it. I just said it."

A slow smile grew Capricorn's face. He laughed. An actually jovial laugh. The sound disturbed Niko to his core. "The goal was to get you to all operate as a team. It appears this training may have done that in more ways than one." He turned his back and flippantly waved as if shooing away some annoying fly. "That is all for today. Some of your mentors weren't exactly pleased with the training methods I had planned for today, so I've been strongly encouraged to give you the rest of the day off. You may spend the remainder of the day however you choose." Without giving the recruits a second glance, he stalked off. They all stood in several minutes before Shaina finally spoke up and broke the silence.

"For once... I actually agree with Ryan," she muttered.

Ryan sidled up to her and slung an arm around her shoulders. "That's my girl! What are we going to do to celebrate?" He turned and cast a sly gaze toward Shaina and Kaeli. "I can think of a couple things—OW!"

Alex yanked Ryan by ear, tearing him away from Shaina. *"We're going to meet up with Gemini."* He hissed, "Or did you forget he instructed us to see him after we completed training with Capricorn?" Ryan pushed Alex away, muttering a cacophony of curse words under his breath.

"Yeah, yeah, yeah," he sighed. "Fine, let's go." Alex looked back at Shaina and Kaeli flashing them an apologetic glance.

Shaina bit her tongue and shook her head. "Poor Alex. It can't be easy having a twin that exasperating." She turned to Niko and Kaeli and asked, "Do either of you have any plans? Virgo didn't give me any instructions for after the training, so I'd be down to celebrate." Niko's heart skipped a beat at the prospect of potentially doing something with Kaeli that *wasn't* related to training. He immediately checked himself. He *could not* get attached. Any attraction he felt, it was just her ability. It wasn't *him,* and until he could be sure of his own feelings, he *would not* let himself get attached. Still, he couldn't stop the disappointment from dropping to the pit of his stomach when Kaeli shook her head.

"I really shouldn't. I don't know when Lukka's training gets out, and there's something I really need to ask him."

"Lukka?" Shaina's voice took on a mischievous tease as a smirk played across her face. Niko had to stop himself from gagging. *Lukka?!*

Kaeli would rather spend time with that hothead than him? He closed his eyes. Calm. He needed to be calm.

"Yeah." Kaeli looked down as she kicked at the ground with the toe of her shoe. "It's nothing like that though. Just a special project we're working on. I need his input on it."

Niko hated himself for the relief that instantly soothed the rising anger. It was a project. Nothing personal.

"Well, I could definitely use a nap," Shaina said. "Maybe we can all celebrate when we've put this almost dying business behind us. Wanna walk back to the houses together?" Niko nodded his head in agreement. Kaeli smiled and nodded as well. In an awkward, but relieved silence, the three made their way out of the library and over to the portal that would take them to the houses.

When they reappeared at the portal, Niko instinctively reached for Kaeli. He had gotten so used to her stumbling over every time they used the portal, but this time she was perfectly steady. Not knowing what to do, he kept his hand on her back. Shaina looked at them with raised eyebrows before flashing Niko a knowing smile. The look in her eyes made him uneasy.

"See you two tomorrow." She gave a halfhearted salute before walking toward House Terra. Niko and Kaeli stood alone at the center of the portal. Kaeli turned to face Niko.

"Thank you," she said in a quiet voice.

Niko arched an eyebrow. "For what?"

Kaeli sighed. "I almost lost it in that training room… but when you touched my arm, I don't know. It almost felt like you took some of that sheer terror away and replaced it with something else." She paused as she looked up at him. Niko found himself getting lost in those eyes again. "I assume that was on purpose, so thank you. I wouldn't have had the clarity of mind to solve the puzzle if it weren't for you." A surge of pride welled in Niko's chest and a compelling urge to gather Kaeli up in his arms and hold her close beckoned him to pull her into an embrace, but instead, he nodded.

"You're welcome." The words sounded harsh to his ears as he reined in his emotions. Kaeli smiled.

"I'll see you tomorrow." And with those parting words, she turned and walked away. Niko stood at the center of the portal and watched her until she disappeared through the doors of House Ignis.

CHAPTER 21

Kaeli entered the common room looking around to see if either Lukka or Joseph had arrived back from training. They hadn't. Kaeli pressed the palms of her hands into her eyes as an overwhelming exhaustion overtook her body. Today had been too much.

"Everything okay?" Liani's chipper voice sounded from the doorway. Kaeli turned to face the spirit. Liani's eyes widened as she brought a hand to her mouth. "You don't look okay. At all. What happened?"

"Rough day training with Capricorn," Kaeli said and offered a weak smile. Liani dropped her hand and pursed her lips, nodding her head slowly.

"I've heard of his tactics. Those zodiacs can be such bullies! I don't see how putting you all through trauma is supposed to make you learn more effectively. There's gotta be a better way." She propped a hand on her hip. "They should let us spirits do more training with you! Although Pyronious isn't much better… they should let you do more training with me! I could teach all of you about different weapons and how to use them in combat—"

she cut herself off, mouth hanging open for a half second before she snapped it shut and let out a huffing sigh. "I'm rambling. You've had a tough day. Is there anything I can do?" She held her arms open. "Want a hug?"

Kaeli smiled despite the exhaustion and stepped into Liani's embrace. Liani squeezed her tight—much stronger than her slight frame suggested was possible—before letting go. "Thanks, Liani. There is actually something you could do for me, if you don't mind."

Liani stood a little straighter. A smile beaming off her face, she exclaimed, "It would be my pleasure! Depending on what it is, of course."

Kaeli chuckled. "Nothing crazy, I promise. Could you let Lukka know I need to talk to him? I'm gonna spend a little bit of time in my room, but I need to talk to him as soon as possible. Can you tell him to come get me if I happen to fall asleep or something?"

"I most definitely can." Liani nodded so deeply her entire body almost bowed. "Now go get some rest!" She started ushering Kaeli toward her room. Kaeli couldn't stop the chuckle that escaped her throat.

"Thank you," she said before walking through the entryway.

"You are most welcome." Liani smiled as she shut Kaeli's door.

Kaeli leaned her back against the doorway and sagged all of her body weight into it. She took a moment to decompress before kicking off her shoes and heading toward the bathroom. A warm bath was *exactly* what she needed right now.

A pair of bath slippers rested near the sink. Kaeli slipped her feet inside, the soft fleece embracing them in the most welcoming sensation of fluff. She made her way to the giant clawfoot bathtub and turned on the lionhead faucet. Steaming water poured out of the lion's mouth. As the water ran, Kaeli walked over to a nearby cabinet filled with scented oils and soaps and picked out a silver bottle that was the shape of a mermaid. This was one of her favorites. It smelled of lavender and jasmine and changed the water texture to a bubbly silk. She uncorked the bottle and poured a little of the magical concoction into the running bath water.

As the water bubbled up, Kaeli walked out to the big bookcase in the common room. Her eyes roved over the titles until one caught her attention. It was an old book that was made of some type of hardened, dark clay. Instead of a title on the spine, a carved snake looked as if it were winding around the book, holding it together. Standing on her tiptoes, Kaeli reached to grab the book and went back to her bedroom.

The tub was nearly full of water. She turned off the faucet, disrobed, and slipped into the luxurious bath, letting out a sigh as the water hugged her body, soothing the tension from her muscles. Relaxing back into the water, she opened the book up to the first page. Her eyes widened as she saw a hand drawn depiction of the Ophiuchus constellation on the front. Turning the page, she scanned the forward.

According to legend, Ophiuchus was destined to be a water sign in the original zodiac system. Due to his unique status as the serpent bearer, however, he was able to easily influence the snakes in the Chinese, Celtic, and Incan Zodiac systems, among others, giving him an unparalleled level of power. Refusing to step down from his position within the Western Zodiac system, the other signs were forced to—

"KAELI!" Lukka's voice sounded precisely two seconds before he basically kicked down the bathroom door. "I heard you were looking for me!" Kaeli yelped and threw the book, missing Lukka's head by a hair breadth. She sank deeper into the water so only her eyes peered over the rim of the tub. *Thank goodness* there were so many bubbles.

"WHAT THE HELL IS WRONG WITH YOU?! You don't randomly kick the door open when someone is in the bathroom!" Kaeli didn't have a clear view of Lukka from her vantage point, but she sure could hear his mocking laughter. She should have aimed more precisely with the book.

"Sorry, Liani made it sound super urgent. I thought you might be in trouble." His laughter died down and he let out a couple of breaths before saying, "I'll be waiting in the common room whenever you decide you wanna get out. Unless…" He paused and Kaeli could practically hear the smirk growing on his face.

"Unless what?" she hissed.

"Well, if you want some company—"

"OUT!"

The sound of Lukka's laughter faded as he ran out and shut the door before Kaeli found something else to throw at his insufferable head. When she was sure that he was well and gone, she relaxed back into the water, splashing some of the water over the edge as she gave a frustrated kick. She already knew Lukka could be obnoxious, but cutting into her relaxing bath time, and then having the *audacity* to suggest what he had just suggested… it was a new low. Not that the thought of him was *so* repulsive, but… Kaeli squeezed her eyes shut and shook her head, trying to clear the mental image out of her head. There wasn't time for thoughts like that. She could worry about relationships when and if there was ever a practical opportunity.

Kaeli finished her bath, dressed in a comfortable jogger outfit, and opened the door to the common room. Lukka sat on the couch, legs stretched out on the ottoman and one arm draped over the back. The stupid fool lolled his head back to look at her, a wide smirk on his face. Kaeli's eyes narrowed. He was clearly fishing for a reaction. She wasn't about to give it to him. Letting out a sigh, she straightened her posture ever so slightly and plastered what she hoped looked like a casual, unimpressed expression on her face.

"A little advice," she said as she sauntered over to the couch and sat down next to Lukka. She turned her head so that she made direct eye contact with him, leaning forward so that their faces were only inches away from each other. She knew the lavender and jasmine scent from the bath mixture wafted off her... mingling with her charm which she consciously amplified toward Lukka. "If you're trying to get intimate with someone, there are *much* more effective ways to do so." Kaeli smiled, not breaking eye contact as Lukka's eyes widened and he audibly gulped. The stupid smirk fell off his face. *Perfect.* Just the reaction she'd been hoping for. Lukka backed away a couple of inches and reached for a pillow. He then proceeded to hold it up as if it were a feeble shield between them.

"Sooo, what was it exactly that you wanted to talk to me about?" He cleared his throat.

"I learned about something interesting today." Kaeli leaned back into the couch cushions. Enough playtime. She thought back to her conversation with Elethia earlier that morning. "Apparently there's only one way to kill the snakes..." Her voice trailed off.

"And that is?"

"I guess we have these... special forms? I don't know much about them. Leo never told me about mine, but maybe Aries taught you more. It's—"

"My berserker state. Aries has had me training on that for the last couple of weeks now. She says it's one of my only redeeming qualities... whatever that's supposed to mean. Wait a second..." He paused as a slow grin started to grow across his face. "So, you're saying you haven't learned anything about your special form... at all?" Kaeli's heart dropped to her stomach. She could practically see the thoughts processing through his brain and she did not like where this conversation was headed. Lukka continued talking. "Which means…"

"Oh, brother."

"I'm stronger than you!" Lukka laughed as he repeatedly poked Kaeli in the shoulder. "Oh, you're so weak! You wouldn't even be able to go after these snakes if it wasn't for me!"

Kaeli pursed her lips into a thin line. Fire roiled under her skin. She swatted Lukka's hand away and mustered up the most intimidating glare she could manage.

"You are on your *last* straw with me, Lukka," she hissed. "Do you want me to bring you on this mission or not? I can try to do this on my own if I absolutely *have* to."

"Yeah, yeah, yeah." Lukka smirked and crossed his arms across his chest and settled back into the cushions. He closed his eyes and then cracked one open to look at Kaeli. "I swear, I'll lay off the jokes for a bit."

The door to the common room opened and the pair turned as Joseph entered the room. He paused at the entryway looking from Kaeli to Lukka and then back to Kaeli before letting out an audible sigh.

"Well, at least the two of you aren't in a mess of feathers on the floor this time." He made his way to the couch and sat down next to Lukka. "Do I even want to know what you're up to this time?" The smile on Lukka's face widened and he lightly nudged Joseph in the arm. Joseph smirked. Kaeli rolled her eyes.

"I was telling Lukka about what I learned at the library today," she sighed. "Have you learned about your special sagittarius form yet?"

Joseph nodded. "A bit. Not a lot. Sagittarius has kind of… introduced me to it."

"Great," Kaeli huffed. "Apparently, Leo's been holding out on me."

Lukka put a hand up to his mouth and leaned over toward Joseph. "She's bitter because she just found out she's the weakest out of the three of us." Joseph arched an eyebrow. Kaeli bit her lip. *Don't react. Don't react. Don't react.* She mentally counted to three before inclining her head to Lukka. She plastered a sickly sweet smile on her face but deadened her gaze to a flat stare.

"Last. Straw." She raised an eyebrow and the fire in the hearth jumped about six feet, the face of a lion emerging. Lukka's gaze flickered toward the fireplace, then back to Kaeli.

"Could I maybe get one more?" he asked. Joseph bust out laughing. Kaeli waved the fire down and it relaxed to its normal, cheerful, crackling state.

"*One* more. And you're going to teach me everything you can about getting into the celestial state."

Lukka firmly nodded his head. "Deal."

Alyssa Markins

CHAPTER 22

After a few weeks of practicing, the three thought they had a good enough handle on their celestial states to kill a snake. They waited for nightfall before sneaking out of the house and heading to the canyons in Aera to meet with Ryu. At first, Ryu had been ecstatic to see Kaeli. She was a little cautious around Joseph, but when she saw Lukka, she made a strange noise that sounded like a cross between a hiss and a growl. It later became clear that the small Yantari just wanted Lukka to keep a certain amount of distance away from Kaeli. After several angry glares and near kerfuffles, Kaeli, doing the best she could with mental projections, was finally able to communicate to Ryu that Lukka was harmless and asked if she could help them find where the shadow snakes were hiding. Ryu eventually understood and now guided the three through Terra.

The erratic trail Ryu had them follow led them to particularly rough terrain dotted with an assortment of human-sized succulents. Celestial Realm succulents were quite different from the ones on Earth and not just because of the size. They still had the desert flower look, but now, in the dim light of the evening stars, they started glowing. Vibrant hues of pinks, yellows, blues, and greens filled the air with a mystical energy that almost made Kaeli lose track of why they had come here in the first place.

"It's so beautiful," she whispered. Ryu let out an affirmative coo. Lukka nudged Kaeli.

"If it was just the two of us this would almost be a romantic date," he winked. Kaeli arched an eyebrow in an unimpressed stare. Ryu snarled and moved protectively into position between Lukka and Kaeli. Joseph clapped Lukka on the back.

"Didn't know you felt that way about me, bro."

A look of surprise overtook Lukka's face before he scrunched his facial features together. "I *was not* talking about you and you know it." Kaeli couldn't contain the laughter that came out. Lukka turned his scowl toward her and she shut her mouth.

"Sorry," she said, offering an apologetic smile. A far-off sound caught her attention. Ryu's ears flattened and she let out a long, low growl. Lukka spun to face the Yantari.

"What is your *deal* with me," he demanded. "I'm a nice guy. Loveable. Charming. Get off my case already!"

"Shh!" Kaeli held up a hand to silence Lukka. "Ryu wasn't growling at you." Lukka opened his mouth to respond, but then actually shut it for once. Kaeli let out an internal sigh of relief. She squinted her eyes as she strained to concentrate on the voices, but they were still too far away to hear clearly. She was, however, able to pinpoint the direction they came from. Keeping a finger to her lips indicating to Lukka and Joseph that they should stay quiet, she motioned for them to keep moving forward, but to stay close to the surrounding boulders. Lukka and Joseph followed her and Ryu's lead. Eventually, they came close enough to where Kaeli could distinctly hear what the voices said. Her eyes widened as she realized who was talking. Although she couldn't see them, she could distinctly hear Scorpio and Capricorn deep in an intense discussion. She turned to Lukka and Joseph, her face twisted into an expression of surprise. Lukka mouthed something vulgar. The three of them pressed closer to the rocks.

"How much longer will we need to prepare?" Capricorn asked.

Scorpio let out an impatient sigh and said, "You know as well as I do that the timing depends entirely on how quickly Kaeli is ready, which Leo somehow seems to be actively stopping."

Kaeli stiffened against the boulder at the mention of her name, her hand shooting to cover her mouth before she could make any noise. A million questions flooded her mind. She flashed a look at Lukka and Joseph. Following the sound of their voices had been a mistake. They needed to find out how to get away from the zodiacs without being noticed. She jerked her head, indicating they needed to go. Lukka shook his head in response. Evidently, he wanted to stay and finish hearing out the conversation. Idiot. But she couldn't leave him alone. The last thing she wanted to do was split from the group. Joseph's gaze flickered between the two of them, but he stayed put—completely neutral.

"Well if he doesn't teach her, we need to find a way for her to learn it on her own." Capricorn continued, "We're running out of time to open the door for Ophiuchus, and we have all the signs other than fire."

Every limb started to tremble as Kaeli's head spun in a delirious confusion. All they needed was a fire sign? Did that mean other signs or recruits were already working for Ophiuchus? Despite the unanswered questions, it was too risky to stay much longer. Each second they stayed only put them in more danger of being exposed. They had to leave. She wasn't about to get caught by Scorpio or Capricorn. She'd suffered during their training sessions. She didn't even want to imagine what they were capable of if they actually tried to torture someone. A shiver ran down her spine. Her foot shifted in the sand brushing against the sparse vegetation just enough to make the slightest rustling noise.

Capricorn and Scorpio went silent.

Kaeli shriveled against the rock as she choked out a silent breath. She frantically glanced around, searching for potential escape routes, but none appeared imminently obvious. Lukka shot her a look that said he was about ready to chop off her head. Ryu nervously bobbed her head back and forth.

"Did you hear that?" Scorpio asked. Capricorn didn't respond.

"Hey, boss." A third voice joined the conversation. One which didn't immediately register with her. Kaeli sniffed at the air. It was Jamal, Capricorn's recruit. She felt the zodiac's attention shift away from their general direction. She looked point-blank at Lukka and motioned that they needed to leave now. Lukka nodded. As silently as they possibly could, they slipped away.

The three continued to follow behind Ryu as the Yantari led them deeper and deeper into the desert terrain, which now grew rockier. No one said a word about the conversation they just overheard, but that didn't stop Kaeli from thinking about it. At least two of the zodiacs and one of their recruits worked for Ophiuchus. Did Niko know? Was he in on it? How the hell was she going to pretend she hadn't heard Scorpio say anything when they were in their training group? Scorpios had mind manipulation abilities. What if he looked into her mind and found out?

"Hey." Lukka's voice broke through her thoughts. "Ryu stopped." Kaeli came to an abrupt halt, blinked, and turned around to see that she'd walked several paces past Ryu, Joseph, and Lukka. Her skin prickled and unease tightened her gut. She couldn't feel any of the distinct signs that something was nearby. There were no vibrations in the ground, no smells or sounds out of the ordinary, but there was a different energy that settled in, almost like a cloud of static shock. She made her way back to the group and looked around. It was well into the night, and the glowing plants were few and far between, accentuating the shadows from the rocks that surrounded them. Dread washed over her.

"Are you sure it's here?" she asked Ryu in a soft voice, already knowing the answer to her question. Ryu let out a low growl in response. Kaeli stiffened, every muscle in her body going tense. Lukka and Joseph shifted closer to her. Ryu wasn't growling at any of them. She growled at a rocky outcropping nearby. A midnight shadow slithered out from behind one of the boulders. It would almost have been invisible if not for its lightning eyes. Ryu made a noise that sounded like a cross between a dog bark and a lion roar. She opened her mouth and started shooting streams of blue lightning at the snake, but it dodged every strike. Ryu whimpered and hid behind Kaeli, Joseph, and Lukka. The snake let out a hissing laugh.

"Foolisssh baby ssspiritsss." It's voice crackled with the sound of static. "I'm one of the ancientsss. There isss no way you will live to sssee the daylight."

"We'll see about that," Lukka growled. He turned to face the group. "You guys might want to stand back. I can't exactly control what happens in this form." Kaeli nodded and coaxed Ryu to follow her to another rock outcropping. As she was still less skilled than either of the boys in her celestial state, the plan was for her to hold back unless absolutely necessary.

Joseph followed not far behind. It wasn't so far away that she wouldn't be able to help Lukka if he needed it, but it put enough distance between them so if Lukka lost complete control, he wouldn't be able to kill them. At least not easily. The snake laughed again as it considered Lukka.

"Only one of you plansss to fight?" It shifted its focus to Kaeli and Joseph. "You have sssent him to die!"

"Hey, ugly," Lukka snapped. "Leave 'em alone! This is going to be between you and me!" Kaeli's jaw dropped open as Lukka slowly began to transform before her eyes. Ram horns sprouted from his head and his eyes glossed over until they were completely red. He grew about two times his size, and fire engulfed his hands. Kaeli's breath hitched in her throat as he turned to face her and shot her a feral grin before returning his attention to the snake. During their training sessions, Lukka had refused to fully enter his berserker state because he didn't want to risk hurting anyone. She now understood why. He looked like a demon straight out of hell.

"DIE." Lukka's voice had changed too, had dropped by three octaves. It echoed off the rocks. He lunged toward the snake. The snake didn't seem to expect the power coming from Lukka because Kaeli could have sworn it recoiled, if only for a split second. Sharp nails protruded from the fire consuming Lukka's hands. He swiped at the snake, grazing the shadowy surface of its being as it dodged. The snake hissed. A black, viscous substance oozed out of the cut and its eyes flared with electricity. Lukka laughed. The sound shook the ground and sent a chill running down Kaeli's spine. She shifted closer to Joseph and Ryu.

Lukka lunged at the snake, pounding it again and again. Each hit he landed made him faster. More vicious. Coarse hair grew from his body. His facial features shifted. Soon, he looked more like a beast than a man—a beast consumed by raging fire.

The snake was injured, but it was by no means finished fighting. It struck out with its tail and wrapped around Lukka's wrist just as he tried to block it. Using its momentum, the snake pulled Lukka in close to itself and opened its mouth. From the light of Lukka's flame, Kaeli could see the pointed fangs dripping with green poison. It attempted to clamp down around Lukka's neck, but Lukka dodged and used his now massive weight to shift the balance. He rammed into the snake, crushing it against a boulder. The snake relinquished its hold around Lukka's wrist and opened its mouth again as if it were about to take a chunk out of Lukka's neck. Lukka moved to dodge. The snake shot out a stream of purple electricity. Lukka absorbed the full force of the attack with his face and staggered back. His berserker form faded until he looked like his normal human self. He faced off the snake. Fire still burned in his eyes, but he panted and his clothes were tattered. Kaeli edged closer to the fight, her heart pounding in her chest. The snake seemed to have forgotten about the others and focused all of its attention on Lukka.

"Foolisssh boy," it hissed. The snake cracked its tail on the ground before whipping it toward Lukka's now completely human body. The force from its tail battered Lukka away as if he was nothing more than a rag doll.

Kaeli heard a sickening snap as Lukka's limp body smacked into a boulder and he fell to the ground. Panic and anger surged through her veins. Her arms trembled with adrenaline. No. Lukka couldn't die. She wouldn't let him, but this snake sure as hell would. A burning heat roiled in the pit of her stomach, then exploded. She roared louder than any lion and everything within her vision turned into bright light. Everything glowed in varying shades of blue and white, except for the snake. It was the only form of darkness Kaeli could see—a black spot in her field of vision. That infernal creature loomed before her, flickering its tongue in and out.

She heard a groan sound from behind her and spun. Lukka pushed himself up against the boulder. Blood trickled down the sides of his face and one of his legs bent in an unnatural direction. A fresh surge of anger rushed through her body and the white-hot light surrounding her pulsed in response as she turned back to face the snake. She was going to *destroy* it.

Lukka groaned as his eyes fluttered open. His head pounded with a splitting pain, making it difficult to open his eyes all the way. That and the *light*. Everything was too damn bright. Why was everything so bright? Wasn't it supposed to be nighttime? Moving as much as his muscles would let him, he looked around and spotted a figure standing before him. His eyes widened when he realized it was Kaeli. For half a second, he forgot his pain as his jaw dropped. This was not any Kaeli he had ever seen before. Her golden hair flowed around her face like a lion's mane, and tentacles of blue and white energy whipped around her. She had become the sun incarnate.

All Lukka could do was watch as Kaeli lunged for the snake so fast that she nearly disappeared. The snake dodged, matching her speed. The two forces of darkness and light clashed again and again until Kaeli got a hold of the snake. It tried to struggle away, but Kaeli held it securely in a throttle hold. She roared, the sound deafening and unearthly as light exploded out of her. A small crack formed in the snake's head, running all the way to the base of its tail. The snake burst open, shattering into a million pieces of darkness that scattered away in the wind.

Ryu whimpered next to him and the sharp pain immediately returned to his head. He put a hand to his head and yanked it away in shock. It was wet. He looked at his hand. A coat of red liquid ran down his fingers. Ryu whimpered again and licked at a wound on his temple. How embarrassing. A shadow loomed over him. Lukka adjusted his position to see Joseph standing near him, except this didn't look like Joseph. He had turned into a giant centaur. His eyes were pure orange and a tangible energy moved around him like water. He gave off a warmth, like standing by a fire on a cold night. From his peripheral vision, Lukka saw Kaeli walking toward them, still in her light form. The thought occurred to Lukka that she might not know how to get out of it. She'd never gone full sun goddess during any of their training sessions and snapping out of his berserker form had been one of the hardest things for him to do when Aries first taught him about it. Aries had needed to go into her berserker form and knock him out.

Kaeli now stood in front of him. She knelt down and looked intently at his wounds, glancing at his leg before returning her attention to his face. She looked at Joseph.

"He's bleeding," she whispered. Lukka made his best attempt at a charming grin, but the pain in his head turned it into a wince.

"I'll be fine," he said. Ryu still licked his head. He wasn't sure if the Yantari was trying to help or if it had developed a taste for human blood. He tried to shoo it away. Kaeli placed a hand on the Yantari's head and started stroking it. Ryu cooed and moved away from Lukka to nuzzle against her.

"He will be fine," Joseph said. His voice was much deeper than it normally was. It vibrated down to the depths of Lukka's soul. He knelt down and brought both of his hands to Lukka's temple. They started glowing with a warm, orange light. A tingling sensation ran through Lukka's head all the way down to his toes. His eyes involuntarily fell closed as he rested his head against the rock behind him. The sensation was gone within seconds, and when Lukka opened his eyes, every ache had disappeared. He raised a hand to touch the side of his head. Aside from the Yantari slobber, there was nothing that would have indicated that he'd just suffered major head trauma.

"All better," Joseph grinned.

"Damn." Lukka pushed himself up to his feet. He looked at Joseph, then at Kaeli. She looked like her normal self again, save for a glow lighting her skin. "Next time I'm saving you guys." Kaeli offered a half-hearted smile. Lukka chuckled. He was only half joking. If Aries found out how many times Kaeli had actually saved his ass, he would get a beating for sure.

"Let's get out of here," Kaeli said. "We need to get Ryu back to the canyon, and then we have to get back to the house before people realize we're gone."

Kill Kaeli. Those had been Trent's last directives before the snakes caught him up in a swirl of shadow and dropped him back on Earth. In the dead of night. In his old neighborhood. It had been months, but no one had bothered to rebuild. While the streets had been cleared of the wreckage, buildings still lay leveled in small heaps of brick and rubble. The sound of something rustling caught his attention as his head whipped toward the noise. His tongue flickered out to sniff the air, one of his many new oddities thanks to Samael, and his face instantly crinkled in disgust.

"Rats," he muttered. Their smell tasted like rotten sludge. He grunted and kicked a nearby rock with enough force to send it flying into one of the heaps. The rock landed with a thud quickly followed by a sickening crack and a squeak.

"Gotcha." A ferocious grin crossed Trent's face. He stuffed his awkwardly sharp hands into his pockets and looked around. The snakes had dropped him off in the last place he had seen Kaeli. The objective was for him to catch her scent, track her down, and kill her.

He meandered over to the location of his mother's old apartment complex, flicking his tongue in and out every so often. Since his transformation, he had gained the ability to move through shadows... almost like walking through a portal from one to another, but he still preferred to walk the old fashion way if given the choice. Made him feel like less of a freak.

He reached the destroyed apartment complex, or at least what was left of it. With a heavy sigh, he stepped into the wreckage and shifted around the rubble, tasting the air as he unearthed beams and bricks.

It wasn't even fifteen minutes before he caught her scent. Cinnamon, cloves, and honey. As soon as he tasted it, the scent was everywhere. Like a fiery orange thread weaving through every place Kaeli had been. Trent couldn't tell *how* he knew it was her. He just did.

He followed that trace, that thread, through the rubble, around the street, until it came to an abrupt stop. It ended in the middle of the street, as if Kaeli had just simply *disappeared.* A growl surfaced in Trent's chest as he fought to maintain composure. He looked to the sky. The first traces of pink and orange daylight peaked out from behind the clouds. He slinked over to the shadows. He would have to stay within them for the remainder of the day. It was harder to travel in the daylight. Fewer shadows. Not to mention his new skin seemed to have an adverse reaction to the sun. Come nightfall, he would resume the search for his sister.

Alyssa Markins

CHAPTER 23

The next morning when Kaeli woke up, her entire body ached. She felt like someone pounded the inside of her head with a sledgehammer. She massaged her temples and groaned as she pushed herself to a seated position. Was this because she had entered her celestial form last night? She crawled out of the bed and stumbled toward the bathroom. Her eyes widened when she saw herself in the mirror. Either someone had switched up the lighting overnight or her vision was way off. She blinked several times and vigorously rubbed her eyes before looking at her reflection again. It wasn't the lighting. Her skin was still glowing.

"How the hell am I going to explain this to Leo?" She reached for her foundation and dabbed a little on her arm, just to see if it would help cover up the light radiating from her skin. Nothing.

"Crap."

She finished putting on her makeup, made her way to the closet, pulled on her training clothes, and stepped out into the common room.

Joseph sat on the couch, reading a book. As she entered, he looked up and inclined his head.

"You're shiny today," he greeted. Kaeli tilted her head to the crook of her arm as she yawned.

"I know." Kaeli slapped at her skin as if that would help. "I can't get rid of it. Hoping that it fades before I have to train with Leo. Speaking of which, what time is it? Shouldn't you be out training with Sagittarius?"

"Already finished," Joseph said, putting his book down. "Leo came by around twenty minutes ago saying he would meet you for training in fifteen. We thought you were awake because you gave a muffled response through the door."

"Shit!" Kaeli slammed her bedroom door as she rushed out to the training arena.

Her iridescent shimmer had mostly faded by the time she reached the tunnels, so that was a plus. Kaeli slowed her pace as she drew closer to the arena. She could see Leo standing, arms crossed, foot tapping impatiently. Kaeli cringed but forced herself to keep walking forward.

"You're late," he stated. His lips pursed to a thin line and his gaze was hard, but his voice didn't sound terribly angry. Maybe this would be okay.

"Sorry... I... well I found out from Joseph you came to the room and told me to meet you here. Apparently I was sleep talking and woke up late."

Leo looked her over. His nose twitched slightly as if he sniffed the air. "You smell different."

Heat rushed to Kaeli's cheeks. She hadn't showered this morning, but she didn't think it would be noticeable. She had put on deodorant. Leo furrowed his eyebrows.

"Where were you last night?"

The heat in Kaeli's cheeks immediately drained, leaving her sheet white. It hadn't occurred to her that Leo would still be able to smell the snake or Ryu. She should have prepared for this. Of course she would smell different to someone with senses as advanced as Leo's. She stood in place, eyes downcast to the floor as her feet drew nervous circles in the dirt. She had no idea what to say.

"You did something last night you weren't supposed to," Leo said. "I already know that. I just don't know what it is. So you might as well tell me." Kaeli exhaled a shaky breath as she relayed the events of last night to Leo: everything from the conversation they had overheard between Capricorn and Scorpio to the battle they had with the shadow snake. She left out the bits about meeting with Elethia in the library and how exactly she learned about the celestial form. Something in her gut told her Leo wouldn't exactly be thrilled to learn she was talking to previous zodiacs in order to figure out what was going on with Ophiuchus and these snakes. When she finished telling what happened, he remained silent for several moments, stroking his chin. Kaeli didn't know whether he looked furious or concerned. Maybe both. When he did speak, his voice was low and cold.

"Kaeli, don't *ever* do anything like that again. You have no idea how dangerous your celestial form is when you don't know how to use it. You could have killed yourself, not to mention Lukka, Ryu, or Joseph. And Lukka could have easily killed all of you! Not even Aries has full control when she's berserk."

Kaeli shrank back, wishing she could melt into the floor. She didn't like being reprimanded, and she certainly didn't like thinking about how she and Lukka could have killed each other.

"As for Scorpio and Capricorn," Leo placed both of his hands on Kaeli's shoulders and forced her to look at him, "you *must* forget you ever heard anything from them. Scorpio has mind manipulation abilities. If he so much as suspects you overheard that conversation, there's no telling how he would mess up your brain. Got it?" Kaeli started shaking, but she nodded her head. Leo released his grip. "Good." He exhaled and put half a semblance of a grin on his face. "I was going to teach you some fire handling techniques today, but since you've activated your celestial form, we need to focus on that. If you don't learn how to control it, it can randomly take over, and then there's no telling what you could do." He paused and raised his eyebrows as he fixed an intent stare on her. "Now, show me what you got."

A mischievous smile played onto Kaeli's face as she closed her eyes and turned her focus inward to transform. She delved deep into her mind, into her soul, until she found the core of her fire. Reaching out to touch it, she barely grazed the surface before it enveloped her like a glove. The warmth continued to build from the inside out until Kaeli couldn't hold it any longer. She opened her eyes and roared. The sound was distant, almost as if it were coming from someone else.

She looked around, everything appearing in shades of light, until her gaze landed on Leo. Her eyes widened. A giant flaming lion surrounded him. Its mane whipped out like rays of sunlight. She blinked a couple of times to make sure it was real. A giant grin crossed Leo's face.

"Yes, that lion is always there. When you become a fully-fledged zodiac, there's an imprint of your sign that stays with you. Only spirits and other zodiacs are able to see it. And recruits in their celestial forms." He crossed his arms and tilted his head. "You transformed fairly quickly... have you been practicing?" Kaeli nodded and felt her light shift around her as she did so. Leo's grin pressed to a thin line, although he didn't mention his distaste. He let out a sigh. "Well, if I'm going to see the extent of your power, I guess that means I better transform too." His eyes flashed with a blazing golden fire. For a split second, a flare of pure white light encompassed everything. Kaeli squeezed her eyes and tucked her head under her arm to shield herself against it. By the time she opened her eyes, Leo was a completely different being about three times his normal height. Golden fire consumed his eyes. He still looked like Leo, but his facial features had morphed into something more animalistic, and his fingernails had turned into sharpened claws encased by fire that ran up his beefed up arms. A mane of pure light crowned his head. Kaeli's heart skipped a beat and she took a step back, bowing her head in instinctual submission. Leo chuckled and the sound reverberated throughout the entire arena. Kaeli looked up at him. A feral grin crossed his face. Her heart started pounding. Maybe she wasn't ready for this. Her fire wavered.

"Tsk, tsk, tsk." Leo shook his head. "When in your celestial form, it is extremely dangerous to let your emotions take hold of your power. If you're in this state, it's likely because you are facing dire circumstances. You must wield the fire with precision and control. Now," he said as he stepped to the side and flourished his hand. At the opposite side of the arena, a column shot up from the ground toward the open sky. "I want you to unleash as much power as you possibly can at that column."

Kaeli inhaled and bit her lip as she strengthened her resolve. She narrowed her eyes as she focused all of her energy at the target. She gathered fire into her hand and, with a roar, sent it shooting toward the column.

Only it didn't go toward the column.

It exploded out around her.

The shockwave rippled out in a wall of flame that expanded the radius of the arena. Leo crossed his arms and held them in front of his face, creating a shield that pushed the rapidly encroaching fire around him. When he uncrossed his arms, twin flame swords extended out from his hands, sucking in Kaeli's fire. Almost as suddenly as the fire appeared, it was gone. Kaeli looked around at the destruction, her eyes wide. She'd leveled every obstacle and reduced them to charred rubble. Leo cleared his throat and snapped his fingers. Instantly, the arena rebuilt itself as if nothing had happened.

"How exactly did Joseph and Lukka manage to go unscathed from your snake fight?"

"I… I'm not sure. I just remember Lukka was hurt and I was angry, but I knew I couldn't fail because if I did…" Her voice trailed off.

"Ah," Leo nodded in understanding. He flourished his hand and the column reappeared in the same spot. "Well, let's teach you how to yield this power when the stakes aren't life and death. Again."

Kaeli returned to her room several hours later, totally drained. Her legs wobbled so badly, she didn't know how she was going to complete the rest of her training for the day. She'd finally gotten to the point where she could purposefully concentrate her power into a focused blast and hit the column without destroying everything in the surrounding area, but it had taken all of her strength. Trying to rein in all that power to a concentrated blast was like trying to hold back a tidal wave. But she'd done it. Even if she had collapsed on the ground afterwards.

She had about an hour to gather herself before she had to leave. Apparently there was an important meeting with all of the zodiacs and recruits. Kaeli stepped into her bathroom and started the shower. She was gross and sweaty and smelled like day-old gym socks. There was no way she was going to a big meeting without washing first.

A half hour later, she was nearly at the bridge leading to the platform, still tired but feeling slightly more rejuvenated. Alex stood at the base of the bridge, his eyes locking onto Kaeli's with a deadpan stare. He crossed his arms and shifted his weight to the side as she approached. Kaeli ran a hand through her hair, moving it away from her face.

"Everything okay here?" she asked. Alex uncrossed his arms and stuffed his hands into his pockets. Something wasn't right. The way he moved, how he held himself, he just looked… off. Maybe he wasn't feeling well.

"I heard about yesterday." His voice cracked, just a little. Kaeli's muscles tensed and her heart started pounding, but she reined in the rising panic as she cleared her throat.

"What are you talking about?"

Alex sighed and kicked at the dirt with the toe of his shoe. "Kaeli, look… there's no easy way to say this, so I'll just…" He took a step closer to Kaeli. Kaeli didn't back away, but she flashed him a confused warning glance. Alex let out a breath, placed both of his hands on either side of her face, and kissed her straight on the lips. Kaeli's eyes widened. She placed her hands on his chest and pushed him with enough force to break the kiss, but not enough to pull away from his grasp.

"Alex, what the hell!"

A mischievous glint flashed through his eyes before he leaned in for another kiss. Kaeli kneed him in the crotch and pushed herself away. He crumpled to the ground in pain, but to Kaeli's surprise he was also… laughing? His face changed subtly—the shift indistinct until the facial hair came through. Kaeli's stare hardened as she realized what was happening. She crossed her arms.

"Ryan?! Are you freaking kidding me?"

"Gemini said… I should practice… my abilities more often." He groaned and chuckled simultaneously as he clutched his midsection. "What do you think? Pretty cool, huh?"

"I think you're a damn idiot," Kaeli muttered. She heard laughter coming from behind her and turned to see Shaina and Niko approaching the bridge. Shaina stared daggers at Ryan and Niko had an amused smirk on his face. Kaeli nudged Ryan with her foot for good measure before straightening her shoulders and crossing her arms. "How much of that did you guys see?"

"All of it," Niko winked. "Don't worry. You don't have to try to hide your feelings from us. You and Ryan can just be open with your relationship. It doesn't matter to me what kind of freaky twin stuff you're into." Shaina punched him in the arm. To Kaeli's disappointment, he only winced slightly. She arched an eyebrow and shifted her weight as she tilted her head a little to the right.

"Is that a hint of jealousy I detect?"

The smirk on Niko's face grew to a playful grin. He just winked again. Kaeli pursed her lips as she attempted to control the flush that threatened to color her cheeks.

"I pulled it off, man," Ryan said to Niko as he pushed himself to a seated position. He held his hand out, palm facing upward. "Pay up."

"I find it disconcerting what you're willing to do for some extra snacks." Niko dug into his pocket and pulled out a small package. "But you were right."

"You're both pigs," Shaina growled in frustration, kicking Ryan as she walked past him.

"Love you too, Shaina," he yelled after her. Niko chuckled, shook his head, and followed after her.

"Hey, guys!" Alex waved as he came running up to the bridge. His pace slowed as he approached Kaeli still standing next to Ryan who was sitting on the ground. His eyes flitted between the two of them. "Is, uh… is everything okay?"

"I'm sorry, Alex." Kaeli sighed as she took Alex's hand in both of hers and shook her head. "This is through no fault of your own… but I just can't look at or be around you for a couple hours." She clapped him on the back and released his hand before turning to follow Shaina and Niko over the bridge. Alex looked down at his brother who pushed himself up to a standing position.

"What did you do?" he asked.

"Don't worry about it, bro." He slung an arm across Alex's shoulders. "Now help me get across this bridge. It kind of hurts to move right now." Alex sighed.

"LISTEN UP, BITCHES!" Aries exploded into a ball of flame once everyone was gathered at the platform. "ANNOUNCEMENT!" Everyone snapped to attention and went to stand at their place around the circle. Although Aries's antics were… unorthodox… and definitely damaging to the ears, Kaeli had to admit, she knew how to work a room. Or at least how to get everyone to shut up and listen. It seemed like a job Aries seemed to enjoy immensely. Kaeli wouldn't be surprised if she'd selected herself to do announcements. She was probably the only one who could shout that loud without tearing any vocal cords.

"Thanks for that." Libra clenched her jaw as she removed her hands from her ears. She smoothed her hair before stepping to the center of the circle and cleared her throat to say, "I know it's been a while since we've all been gathered here, but we have a very special announcement today."

"I *just* said that," Aries interjected. Libra let out an exasperated sigh.

"We're going on a trip!" Leo said before the two started fighting. The recruits immediately broke out into chatter. Kaeli spotted Lukka standing on the other side of the platform. He flashed a smile at her. Kaeli couldn't stop herself from smiling back.

"Quiet, quiet, quiet!" Libra shouted. Thankfully, everyone listened to her before Aries decided to light the place up in flames.

"Where are we going?" Ryan asked.

"We're going to be spending some time on Earth," Libra continued. "You've all been training and developing your powers here for a while now, and it's time to do the same on Earth. Your abilities are much easier to control here in the Celestial Realm. If you are to become fully-fledged zodiacs, you will need even more mastery, if not more, over them on Earth. We will need to put you through real life pressures to ensure you have control of your powers."

"Won't that put other people in danger?" Daniel, Cancer's recruit, asked.

"Sometimes danger is necessary, kid." A wicked grin crossed Aries's face. Daniel gulped and widened his eyes but didn't say anything else. The platform erupted in a cacophony of questions. Kaeli stood quietly in her spot and allowed the noise from the slew of voices to wash over her. An uneasy sensation quivered in her stomach at the thought of going back to Earth. She wasn't necessarily afraid of hurting anyone. As long as she didn't enter her celestial form, she was confident in her ability to control her fire. But the Celestial Realm was *home* now. It was comfortable. Earth was only full of hurtful memories, and she had no desire to return. Leo placed a steadying hand on her shoulder.

"You alright?" he asked. Kaeli shook her head.

"I don't want to go back to Earth yet," she said. Her voice barely rose above a whisper. Leo pulled her into his side.

"Everything will be fine," he said. "It's a necessary part of your training, but we won't be there forever. You'll be okay."

"If you say so." Kaeli bit her lip.

"Everyone be QUIET!" Aries's voice rose above the confused conversation. "We won't be leaving until tomorrow morning, so you'll have plenty of time to get all of your little questions answered. Now go get ready for a full day of training. Just because we're going to Earth tomorrow doesn't mean you get to slack off today."

A collective groan rose up from the recruits.

Alyssa Markins

CHAPTER 24

Kaeli woke up the next morning, disoriented and drenched in sweat. She glanced sideways at her alarm. Fifteen more minutes before it would go off. She'd planned to wake up early to sneak away to the library before everyone met at the platform to leave for their trip back to Earth, but the nightmare she'd just had preemptively did the same job. Groaning, she reached over, turned off the alarm, and curled the comforter around herself as she took deep breaths to steady her heart rate.

The dream had been a twisted flashback of Trent. A lump rose in her throat as images played on loop in her mind. The look on Trent's face after their dad died. The glittering hatred in his eyes as he stared at her through the flames of the car accident. Her mom's screams when Trent tried to shove Kaeli into oncoming traffic, whispering that she deserved to die the same way their father had. The thought of going back to Earth, of returning to the world where he existed...

She grasped the sides of her head and squeezed her eyes shut, trying to force logic to override the irrational panic. The odds of running into her only remaining family were slim, but just the fact that it was a possibility made her stomach turn. Exhaling a heavy sigh, she rolled out of bed to get dressed. Maybe if she hid long enough in the library, they would give up and leave without her. Statistically, she knew those odds weren't great, but the thought still brought a small amount of comfort.

She crept through the library doors, keeping as low of a profile as she could. She cringed when the large doors creaked shut. Sticking to the aisles to avoid the wide-open space by the front desk, Kaeli made her way to the Room of Records.

She pulled Elethia's book off the shelf and opened it on the obsidian table. Purple light shot out toward the ceiling. Elethia stepped out and stretched her arms as she let out a long-winded yawn.

"Do you have any idea what time it is?" She cracked her neck from side to side before pausing to consider Kaeli. "I see you survived the fight with the shadow snake." She sat down at the table and propped her head up on both her hands and commanded, "Give me all the details." Kaeli was a little taken aback by Elethia's enthusiasm, but she relayed the story anyway. Elethia listened with rapt attention. When Kaeli finished telling the events, how she and Lukka had shifted into their forms to kill the snake, Elethia smiled.

"Well done. Honestly, I wasn't sure if you would be able to pull it off. But I'm proud of you." She stood up and looked at Kaeli with a calculated stare. "So, why did you come back? Not that I don't appreciate being let out of my book, but you know how to kill the snakes now. Why do you need me?" Kaeli bit her lip.

"We're taking an extended field trip to Earth," she said. It was weird thinking of going back to Earth as a field trip. Even though she'd lived nearly her entire life there, it wasn't home. She shook her head as she continued talking. "I'm not ready to go back. I wasn't exactly in a good place when I left, and I only *just* learned how to shift into my celestial state here. They said it's harder to control our abilities on Earth. What if I can't control shifting, and I end up blowing everything... or *everyone* up. Leo said everything would be okay... but I don't *feel* like it will be." Elethia stood up from the table and placed a gentle hand on Kaeli's shoulder.

"You are extremely gifted, Kaeli. The fact that you have the mastery you *do* have over your abilities is impressive. Still, your concern is understandable and even warranted. I know a bit about shifting into the celestial state, and I have something that might help you." Elethia removed her hand from Kaeli's shoulder and extended it in front of her. A soft purple glow danced around her fingers. When it disappeared, a gold coiled ring with an amethyst stone in the center appeared in the middle of her palm. "Leo was right. You most likely will have nothing to worry about while you're on Earth, but if you find yourself in a desperate situation, use this ring. It absorbs celestial power in a way. If you feel yourself about to shift and you don't have control, put this on. It will take just enough of your energy to keep you looking human. *Do not* wear this all the time. It's for emergencies only. If you wear it for too long, it will absorb all of your power and you won't be able to return to the Celestial Realm until you've had adequate time to recover. You only need to wear this for about a minute before taking it off. Do you understand?"

"Yes... " Kaeli nodded her head slowly but eyed the ring with caution. She didn't think the records could materialize anything. Sagittarius had said these were just preservations of past zodiacs. Still… if it could help her to *not* kill anyone with her powers…

"Good," Elethia said and pressed the ring into the palm of Kaeli's hand, closing her fingers over it. She held Kaeli's hand in both of hers and assured her, "Everything will be okay. This is a necessary part of your training and will only help you to become stronger in both a physical and emotional capacity. Your life before coming to the Celestial Realm may not have been the best, but I think you'll find things can change drastically over time."

Footsteps clattered outside of the room. Kaeli and Elethia snapped their heads toward the door.

"KAELI! KAELI! WHERE ARE YOU?? WE GOTTA GO!" It was Lukka. Kaeli pulled her hands away from Elethia and stuffed the ring into her pocket.

"That would be my cue to leave," Elethia said. The light from her book vanished just as Lukka entered the room.

"There you are! Why are you always in the library? Come on!" He grabbed Kaeli's wrist just as she finished tucking Elethia's book back into its spot on the shelf. "We need to go. Everybody is almost gathered at the platform already."

"Okay, okay, calm down." Kaeli yanked her wrist away from Lukka's grasp and rubbed it. "I'm perfectly capable of walking there without you dragging me, thank you very much!"

"Sorry." Lukka flashed her a cheeky grin.

As they neared the meeting platform, Kaeli found her thoughts flitting back to memories of her family. Lukka nudged her arm.

"Everything okay?"

"Hm? Yeah." Kaeli shook her head trying to clear her mind of the paranoid thoughts. Her shoulders sagged as Lukka's stare settled onto her.

"You don't look okay," he said. Kaeli sighed.

"I'll be fine." Her fingers toyed with the ring hiding in her pocket.

"If you say so," Lukka shrugged. "I don't believe you, but if you don't want to talk about it, that's fine." Kaeli smiled slightly to herself. They walked the rest of the way in silence.

Almost everyone already gathered by the time they arrived. Kaeli nonchalantly walked over to her group, perfectly attaching herself to their conversation without adding many words. She caught Lukka staring at her a couple of times, but she avoided making any direct eye contact.

"Okay, everybody, listen up!" Aries's voice put an end to every conversation. She stood near Leo and spittle flew from her mouth onto his face. Leo arched an eyebrow and wiped it away with the edge of his sleeve.

"Thanks for that," he said, his lips curled into a disgusted grimace. Aries smiled as if it was her greatest pleasure. Leo rolled his eyes and announced, "Alright, everyone, we're going to go over some ground rules before we teleport to Earth. First off, we'll be arriving in what is known as a safe zone. These are located all over Earth. They're pockets of space that are completely inaccessible to regular humans. The particular safe zone we're going to is located on an island—a portion of which is a popular destination for tourists. You all will be allotted free time to explore in between training sessions. When you are around humans, you are *under no circumstances* to use your elemental or special abilities unless you are under the specific direction and supervision of your mentor. Are we clear?" Everyone nodded their heads with a couple of 'yeah, sure's.' Leo sighed and shook his head.

"I said ARE WE CLEAR?!" he bellowed as flames burst from all around him. This time everyone snapped to attention and responded with a collective 'yes, sir!' Leo smiled. "Good. Then we're ready to take off." He moved next to Kaeli and motioned for her to follow him to their spot on the zodiac ring. Each of the zodiacs took their spot with their recruits.

"Okay, everyone, hold hands," Libra said. Kaeli took Leo's hand to her right and turned to her left to see Shaina. They smiled at each other before joining hands. The zodiacs started to chant in low voices, creating a lull that made Kaeli want to shut her eyes and fall asleep. Then, just as she didn't think she could stay conscious much longer, the world flipped upside down and everything turned into a swirl of color.

When the kaleidoscope faded and her stomach stopped threatening to leave her body, Kaeli groaned. She was on a hard floor surface. Her head felt like it had slammed into a brick wall. She raised a hand to her temple, running her fingers through her hair to feel for any bumps or bruising but found nothing amiss. Although that did nothing to stop the throbbing headache. Sporadic groans echoed across the room. Kaeli opened her eyes and pushed herself up to a seated position. They were in what looked like a large, empty warehouse. Metal beams supported an expansive ceiling dimly lit with scattered LED lights. The floor was bare concrete. The zodiacs all stood perfectly unfazed. Most of the recruits lay flat on their faces. Except for Niko, who casually leaned against a pillar as if nothing happened. He caught her gaze and flashed her a smirk. A sneer crossed her face as she pushed herself up off the floor to a standing position.

"I am *not* your landing cushion!" Lukka said from across the room. Kaeli turned her head just in time to see him shove Eryn, the taurus recruit, off his back.

"Alright, you lazy asses, get up!" Aries demanded.

"You're being a little harsh," Libra intervened. "We didn't exactly prepare them for inter-realm teleportation."

"Well, they already did it once when they came to the Celestial Realm," Aries said as she propped her fists on her hips. Libra let out a sigh and shook her head as she muttered something indistinguishable under her breath. Kaeli dug around in her pocket to make sure the ring hadn't gotten lost in the interdimensional travel. She let out a sigh as her fingertips made contact with the warm, smooth metal.

"You okay?" Shaina's voice snapped Kaeli back into her surroundings. She suddenly became very aware of the pounding headache again and squeezed her eyes shut. This was not what she imagined her first few moments back on Earth would be like at all.

"Yeah, just a headache," she responded.

"Girl, me too. I still hate teleporting in the Celestial Realm. Forget about this whole 'inter-realm' nonsense."

Despite the throbbing pain, Kaeli cracked a smile. It was nice to know she wasn't alone. When the recruits had more or less shaken off the effects of teleporting, the zodiacs ushered them out of the warehouse.

The sun blinded Kaeli the moment she stepped outside. She squinted and raised a hand to shade her face as she tried to figure out her surroundings in the bright white light. She could hear the waves crashing and smell the salt. Her eyes adjusted as her vision gradually returned. She gasped as she took in the scenery. The water lapping onto the sandy shore was the purest form of crystal blue. It sparkled in the sunlight as if the foam was made from diamonds. A few feet from the shoreline was a bonfire pit surrounded by large rocks and logs that served as benches. A docking pier shot out toward the ocean. Several colorful kayaks, bobbing up and down in the water, were tethered to it.

"Alright, dingbats, you'll have plenty of time to stare at the pretty view later. Right now, we need to get settled! Follow me!"

Kaeli sighed as she turned away from the peaceful picture to follow Aries. The zodiacs led them up a steep dirt hill. Kaeli looked around as they walked. They were surrounded by mountains and pine trees. Small birds chirped between the branches. Kaeli took in a deep breath and exhaled with a smile. This was one thing she hadn't realized she missed about Earth. The air out in nature was so… crisp. Refreshing. The air in the Celestial Realm didn't have quite the same revitalizing quality.

A large lodge-style hotel building rose in the distance. It blended in perfectly with the scenery while also looking elegantly elaborate with its arched wooden entryways and towering pointed rooftops. When they walked inside, Kaeli's eyes widened. Celestial Spirits wearing matching uniforms bustled around, some working at a reception desk, others pushing around hospitality carts. Libra and Aries stood at the reception desk, talking to an earth spirit. Kaeli turned in a slow circle. All of the spirits working at the lodge were earth spirits.

"I didn't know spirits could live on Earth," Kaeli murmured. Leo moved next to her.

"A few of the safe zones are used as meeting points for other zodiac systems. We had our annual Earth summit here last year." He propped his hands on his hips and shook his head slightly as he laughed to himself and said, "That was a crazy summit." Kaeli tilted her head as she looked up at Leo.

"You actually meet with the other zodiac systems?"

"Yup." Leo patted her on the back. "You'll learn about diplomatic interactions with them after you've had more training."

"Alright, everybody, listen up!" Aries's voice cut through the conversation. "We got your room keys. You have to stay with at least one other person from your training group." She slid a side eye toward the earth spirit receptionist and explained, "Because apparently some of the punks from the Lunar system decided to take a vacay. If you see any strange looking beings, ignore them *at all costs*. The last thing we need is for one of you to piss off Gold Dragon and end up getting eaten. Now grab your buddy and come get your room key from either me or Libra."

Kaeli and Shaina took one look at the mischievous glint in Ryan's eyes and instantly clung to each other like glue. There was no way either of them would get near Ryan, and after what she'd heard from Scorpio, Kaeli wasn't about to share a room with Niko either.

Obnoxious giggling from the other side of the lobby immediately diverted Kaeli's attention. Her stare hardened and her jaw clenched as she saw Salena, Aquarius's recruit, trying to cozy up to Lukka. The hair on the back of her neck raised and a heat rose in her stomach. A familiar warmth started to tingle in her fingers, and she immediately shook her head and took a deep breath. She wasn't in the Celestial Realm. If she let her fire out, it would definitely cause some damage to the wooden lodge. Staring daggers would have to suffice. Shaina coughed and nudged her gently in the ribs.

"We should get our room key," she said under her breath. Kaeli shook her head and snapped back to the present reality.

"Right." She bit her tongue as she moved toward Aries.

"Okay let's see, you get room... 528. Right across from Lukka and Daniel." She winked. Kaeli blinked several times before silently taking the key card and turning back to Shaina. Aries sniggered. Shaina arched an eyebrow. Kaeli shook her head and let herself get lost in the details of the key. In general, it had the same appearance as an ordinary card key, but it glittered and reflected the light when she turned it over in her hands, like it was made out of pure stardust. Kaeli sighed as she slipped the key into her pocket. The tip of her pinky finger slipped into the ring for half a second, sending an electric shock shooting up her arm. Kaeli yanked her hand out of the pocket and examined her fingers briefly before turning to Shaina.

"Let's go check out the room."

Despite the impressive exterior, the room was rather basic: two full-sized beds, cozy decor, and lots of neutral beige accented by deep maroon. Kaeli flung herself onto one of the beds and let her body sink into the cushioned surface. The bed, at least, was incredible. Shaina walked around the room, opening all of the drawers and cabinets. She squealed, and Kaeli sat up on her bed.

"What is it?"

"They have coffee!" Shaina stepped aside so Kaeli could see the little kiosk. "And cocoa and tea!" Kaeli raised her eyebrows and nodded her head in approval. A knock sounded at the door. Shaina went to go open it. Leo and Virgo stood at the entrance, smiles on their faces. Kaeli stood from the bed.

"Are you two finding everything okay?" Virgo asked.

"Yup!" Shaina answered.

"We have something for the two of you." The smile on Leo's face widened as he produced two cards from his pocket. Kaeli tilted her head.

"What are those?"

"Credit cards!" Leo stepped forward to give one to Shaina and then one to Kaeli.

"Sort of credit cards," Virgo corrected. "They operate as a credit card on Earth, but they were made in the Celestial Realm." Kaeli and Shaina shared a glance with each other.

"So that means…" Shaina's eyes sparkled as a smile grew across her face.

"You have unlimited access to an infinite amount of funding and you won't be racking up any debt or interest rates!" Virgo beamed. Kaeli couldn't stop her jaw from dropping. Shaina squealed again.

"You have the rest of the day to yourselves," Leo said. "But you have to stay at or near the lodge." He gave Kaeli a pointed stare. Kaeli rolled her eyes, but still had a smile on her face. There was no way she would be mad at Leo's condescending tone when he'd just given her an unlimited amount of money to spend. Leo continued, "We'll let you do some more exploring later, but for now we need to make sure you have enough control over your abilities before setting you loose near other humans. We'll begin training early tomorrow morning so make sure you get plenty of rest. It's going to be unlike anything you've done in the Celestial Realm."

Shaina nodded her head vigorously. "Got it."

"We'll behave don't worry," Kaeli winked. Leo sighed and shook his head. He turned his back and headed toward the door.

"We'll see you tomorrow," he said and waved a lackadaisical farewell. Virgo followed him out the door. As soon as the zodiacs left, Shaina plopped down on her bed and propped her chin up in her hands to look at Kaeli.

"So, what exactly is going on between you and Lukka?" she asked. Kaeli froze. She took a steady breath to calm her rising heart rate.

"I, uh, well… what do you mean?" She stammered over her words. Shaina chuckled as she moved to a seated position, propping herself on top of the many pillows garnishing the bed.

"Seriously? You were glaring at Salena and Lukka so hard, I could practically see smoke coming out of your ears. Come to think of it… it could have been literal smoke."

"I…" Kaeli shut her mouth and pursed her lips. The truth was, she didn't really know what to feel about Lukka. He was definitely one of the people she'd connected with and trusted the most since coming to the Celestial Realm. His crazy antics drove her up the wall sometimes, but at the same time, she found them equally endearing. She definitely felt a protective possessiveness about him… but did she *like* him in that way? Kaeli rubbed her neck as she let out a heavy sigh. These were thoughts she preferred not explore at the moment. There were other, more important things to focus on that didn't revolve around grade school topics of who-liked-whom.

"I don't know how I feel," she replied.

"Well, for what it's worth," Shaina said as she leaned back against the headboard of her bed and grabbed a remote sitting on the nightstand situated between them, "I think the two of you would be a good couple. I don't know Lukka very well, but I've seen the way he looks at you, and I'm pretty darn sure he knows how he feels." She turned on the TV and started flipping through channels before settling on pro-wrestling. Kaeli stared at the screen but didn't really watch as she mulled over Shaina's words. No one had really forced her to confront these feelings before, but now that they'd been brought up, she couldn't get them to leave her brain. A series of loud thumps coming from the wall directly behind the beds snapped her out of her head.

"What in the hell!" Shaina yelped. Muffled mischievous laughter danced through the wall.

"That's definitely, Ryan." Kaeli rolled her eyes.

"SHUT IT!" Shaina threw a pillow at the wall and then sank back into the bed, clutching another one of the pillows to her chest. "This should drown him out," she said, grabbing the remote and bumping the volume on the TV up several notches. Kaeli smiled to herself as she settled back into her own bed. This was what she needed—a few hours of extremely fit men being ridiculous as they fake fought each other. She craned her neck toward Shaina.

"Should we room service some ice cream up here?"

"Absolutely, yes."

Kaeli smiled as she reached for the menu. Despite her initial thoughts this morning, today was going to turn out just fine.

Alyssa Markins

CHAPTER 25

*B*ang bang bang!
"TIME TO WAKE UP, SLEEPING BEAUTIES! GET YOUR BUTTS
DOWN TO THE LOBBY IN TEN!"

Kaeli jolted out of her bed, shocked out of blissful sleep, although
her heart rate stayed fairly steady. Over the last several months, Kaeli had
gotten used to Aries's wake up calls, even if they were mostly directed
toward Lukka. Shaina, however, had no such training. She awakened with a
startled scream and immediately flipped on the lights, blinding Kaeli in the
process.

"It's okay! We're okay!" Kaeli shouted over Shaina's screams.
Shaina placed a hand over her heart as her chest heaved up and down with
labored breaths.

"What the hell was that?!" She let out a long sigh and rested against
the headboard of her bed. Her head rolled to the side so that she could get a

look at the clock on the nightstand adjacent to her bed: "It's four-friggin-thirty in the morning!"

"That would be Aries," Kaeli said as she threw off her blankets and stood up, stretching her arms high into the air as she let out a sleepy moan. She walked over to the closet and pulled out her leo training uniform. "She didn't cuss us out this morning. She must be in a good mood." She yawned as she stepped into the bathroom. Blinking rapidly as she flipped on the light, she stuck her head out to look at Shaina and warned her, "You should really get ready though. When Aries says to be somewhere in ten, it's best to get there in five." Shaina let out a frustrated groan and threw one of her pillows to the floor.

"Stupid," she muttered. Kaeli let out a half-hearted chuckle before closing the bathroom.

By the time Shaina and Kaeli arrived, the zodiacs were already gathered at the center of the lobby. Other recruits started filing in from different entrances. Most of them looked like sleepwalking zombies. Kaeli took in a whiff of air and whirled toward the reception desk. Coffee. The comforting aroma of roasted beans filled the air and she made no hesitation in walking up to the small, but elaborately designed, self-serve cart to pour herself a cup. Shaina followed close behind. The two stood close to the cart, sipping away at the life-giving beverage as the rest of the recruits came into the room. Ryan spotted them from across the room, raised his hand, and opened his mouth as if he was about to say something cheery, but Shaina shot him such a look of half-asleep disgust that he promptly shut it and wandered over to another group of recruits.

Aries made her way to the center of the crowd precisely at the ten-minute mark. Kaeli squeezed her eyes shut, anticipating the signature abrasive shout, but to her surprise, it never came. Instead, Aries simply cleared her throat, then stretched her arms wide as she let out a roaring yawn. It wasn't her usual attention-grabbing tactic, but the sound was still startling enough to make the half-asleep recruits widen their eyes, if only a little. Aries motioned toward Kaeli and Shaina.

"Kaeli, dear, get me some coffee."

The room was completely silent as Kaeli filled up a cup and brought it over to Aries. The instant she had possession of the cup, Aries knocked it back in one shot, completely oblivious to the boiling temperature of the beverage. Kaeli stood rooted to the floor, mouth agape and eyes wide as Aries shoved the cup back into her hands.

"Thanks for that, hun. Alright, kiddos! Here's how today is going to go! We're all taking a hike to a series of caves. Each will have a special artifact your team will need to retrieve. This will require minimal use of your powers, however, you will find it much more difficult to retain control. Whichever team finds and brings back their artifact first doesn't have to go through boot camp training this evening. Any questions?" All of the recruits shook their heads. Even without regular daily interactions with her, everyone knew that when it came to Aries, it was best to smile and nod, then ask a different zodiac any questions later.

"Good!" Aries's mouth curled up in an approving smile. "Alright then, everybody, roll out!" She marched through the lobby and headed toward the doors. Sleepy recruits reluctantly followed after her. Kaeli took a moment to walk back to the coffee cart and return Aries's cup. As she turned around to follow the rest of the group out the door, a flash of light caught her eye from one of the upper balconies. She looked up and caught a glimpse of what appeared to be a strangely disfigured man. His elongated features were partially obscured by his flowing white hair, and he had... horns? He wore long, golden robes, and leaned casually over the balcony railing, watching the recruits. She saw him for about two seconds before he turned on his heel and disappeared through a doorway. Kaeli blinked and rubbed her eyes before shaking her head and jogging out the door to catch up with the rest of the group.

The zodiacs led them to a narrow dirt trail that wound up the mountain through a thicket of trees and shrubs. The trail was clear, but the hike itself was rough. After the first hour, Kaeli found herself short of breath and struggling to continue up the steep incline. She wasn't the only one. Several paces behind her, Ryan had all but collapsed on a pile of bushes. Lukka was just a couple paces ahead, but he was cussing out the stupid rocks that were somehow at fault for making his life miserable. Kaeli took a moment to pause. For once not caring about the cleanliness of her training uniform, she sat down on the dirt and leaned back on her forearms. Looking up the trail ahead, she saw Shaina, Niko, and Alex. Niko looked like he might be starting to get tired, but Shaina and Alex were just fine. Kaeli cocked her head to the side as she examined her three teammates. That made no sense. They all received the same type of training, so there was no reason they should have a significantly higher level of endurance.

She squinted her eyes, and upon further scrutinization, noticed that Alex's feet hovered just above the ground and how Shaina would intermittently shift the ground so that it pushed her up. Kaeli scrunched up her nose. That was just unfair. There was no way she could even try to use her abilities in this environment. She'd just start a forest fire and that was the last thing they needed.

She looked back down the trail at Ryan. He was still collapsed in the bushes. With a heavy sigh, she pushed herself up from the ground and backtracked over to his makeshift bed.

"You doing okay?" she asked, lightly kicking one of his feet to get his attention. Ryan let out a disgruntled moan.

"Just leave me to die. This isn't worth it."

"Stop being a drama queen," Kaeli sighed. "I have an idea that will help both of us get up this mountain a lot faster, but I need you to help me with it." This got Ryan's attention. He propped himself up in his bush pile and shielded his eyes from the sun as he looked up at Kaeli.

"Is that so?"

Kaeli's mouth flatlined. She might regret this decision... but it was either ask Ryan for help or spend who knew how long trekking up the rest of the mountain.

"Yes," she sighed. A mischievous grin played onto Ryan's face.

"And how, my dear lady, might I be of assistance?"

Kaeli rolled her eyes. "Your brother is using his abilities to help him up the trail..."

Ryan's smile grew wider. "And you want me to do the same for us." He lounged back in his pile of bushes which now somehow seemed like a throne. "Interesting proposition, Kaeli. What are you willing to give me in return for this service?"

Kaeli narrowed her eyes and gave Ryan a piercing stare. "A friend would do it for free."

"Yes, yes, yes, but I'm an opportunist," he said as he stood up and looked to the sky, scratching at his chin before flashing Kaeli a sly look out of the corner of his eye. "I mean if you really want my help, I could think of a couple ways—"

"You know what? Forget it! I expected this from you, but I don't have to put up with it. I'll just go up this mountain the hard way. See you at the top, whenever that happens." Kaeli turned on her heel and started to walk away, but Ryan's hand shot out and grabbed a hold of her wrist.

"Kaeli, you're right. I'm sorry. I was just messing with you. You want my help, you got it." Kaeli arched an eyebrow, not exactly sure how to receive the apology. Ryan's signature grin returned to his face. Kaeli opened her mouth to protest, but Ryan pulled her close to his chest and wrapped his arms around her waist.

"Hold on tight," he whispered. Before Kaeli could squirm away from his grip, they both shot straight into the air. Kaeli yelped, squeezed her eyes shut, and tucked her head into Ryan's chest, wrapping her arms around him for dear life. A chuckle rumbled deep in his chest. She would have pinched him... but she had absolutely no interest in falling to her death.

They made it to the top in a manner of minutes. As soon as they touched down, Kaeli pushed herself away from Ryan, stumbling over her feet as she did so. Ryan spread his arms wide, a look of mock hurt crossing his face.

"Ah, come on, I helped you up the mountain, didn't I? You don't have to act like I'm a repulsive monster."

Kaeli's face scrunched up as she ran a hand through her hair. Her fingers caught on the tangled strands and she let out a frustrated grunt.

"You ruined my hair," she said through gritted teeth. She stuffed a hand in her pocket and fished around for a hair tie. She normally had one on her just in case. Ryan looked her up and down.

"Honestly, though, the tousled bed head look is *definitely* working for you," he grinned. "But I swear that wasn't my intention. The zodiacs weren't kidding when they said the elemental abilities would be harder to control. I was just trying to pick up a little bit of speed." Kaeli glared at him from the corner of her eye as she pulled her hair up into a messy bun. She'd give him the benefit of the doubt this time… if only because she had almost lit the lodge on fire the day before after looking at Selena and Lukka. She sat down on a rock and looked up at the sky, envying Shaina and Alex's ability to so expertly control their elements.

Other recruits must have caught on to Ryan and Kaeli's tactics because less than a minute passed before the sky was dotted with air recruits carrying their peers. Ryan looked up at the sky and sighed.

"Ah man, there goes our alone time together."

Kaeli kicked at some stray rocks. "As if anything was going to happen in the first place."

Ryan shrugged and replied, "You never know."

Kaeli dropped her shoulders and tilted her head to the side as she looked up at Ryan. "Yes, Ryan, yes I do. I would have burned this forest to the ground before letting you make a pass at me."

Ryan opened his mouth to retort but shut it as other recruits started to touch down. The zodiacs were not far behind. Aries crossed her arms as her feet hit the ground, her eyebrows furrowed in displeasure.

"While I admire the innovativeness of your tactics, using your powers for this segment of today's training completely negated the purpose of developing discipline and endurance!" She let out a sigh and said, "But I guess there's something to be said for innovation. BEHOLD!" she said and gestured to three cave entrances that gaped open off in the distance.

"Alright, everybody, you heard my directions earlier. Each team, pick a cave and find your artifact. You'll know what it is when you see it. First team back doesn't have boot camp training at the end of the day. GO!"

The recruits scrambled, each trying to find their team members and head to the same cave before the others.

* * *

Kaeli's group chose to go through the cave on the right. The moment they entered, a thick darkness enveloped them, shutting out any light even from the entrance. Kaeli held her arms out to steady herself. This was not a normal type of darkness: it was a physical entity pressing in around her. Encircled by the void and unable to recognize any physical markers, she felt like she was falling in suspended darkness. Vertigo overwhelmed her sense.

"Kaeli, do your fire ball thing so we can see!" Ryan's voice echoed off the cave walls, making it impossible to identify his location.

"I can, but you all need to make sure you're not standing near me," Kaeli answered. "I have no idea what's going to happen if I try to use my powers, and I'd rather not burn anybody to a crisp." She waited a couple of seconds for the sound of shifting feet to quiet down before closing her eyes to focus inward and take a deep breath. She held out her hand and envisioned a ball of fire the size of a tennis ball—only the size of a tennis ball—forming in her palm. She turned her attention to the warmth roiling in her gut. It danced, begging to be set free and expand. She gently tugged at the power, trying to keep it from overtaking her. She let out a slow, steady breath and opened her eyes. Fire exploded in her hand. She clenched her fist and focused on molding it, struggling to rein in the power that yearned to erupt and consume.

"Come on…" she gritted her teeth as she clenched her fist even tighter, digging her fingernails into her skin. Slowly, the fire began to compress and form to her will. By the time she was able to get it to the size of a basketball, she breathed heavily. Sweat formed on her forehead. This would have to do it. She looked around and saw Ryan, Alex, and Shaina pressed against the far side of the cave wall, staring at her with wide eyes.

Niko stood right in front of her, water dancing between his fingertips, ready to douse her at any moment.

"I got it," she said, trying her best to look as relaxed and nonchalant as possible. Niko arched an eyebrow as he eyed the ball of fire roaring around her fist.

"If it's all the same to you, I'm going to keep my water out anyway," he said. Kaeli sighed, but a part of her was relieved.

They continued to walk deeper into the cave in relative silence. Kaeli was inwardly grateful. It was taking up almost all of her concentration to keep the fire at a manageable size, and if she heard one snide remark from Ryan or Niko, she knew she would lose it. That didn't keep her from admiring the beauty of the cave, however. The light of her fire revealed an expanse of sloped ceilings. Striations accented the arches leading to different passageways made inaccessible by a lake of murky water, separating them from the path.

After walking for what seemed like hours, they came upon a clearing in the rock formation. The rocky path turned to a loamy semicircle of dirt enclosed by a rock wall extending up for miles. At the very top was a hole, dropping a stream of sunlight down onto a podium situated at the center of the semicircle. On top of the podium was an ancient chest.

"I bet that's what we're looking for!" Ryan blurted as rushed toward the podium.

"Noooo… really?" Shaina's voice dripped with sarcasm. Ryan smirked and then stuck his tongue out at her. Kaeli unclenched her fist in an attempt to snuff her fire out. Unfortunately, the action seemed to have the opposite effect. The basketball sized ball blew up to the size of a beach ball before Niko shot a stream of water at her, completely drenching her arm and most of her shirt. Kaeli scrunched up her nose, her mouth twisting into a grimace as she shook the excess water away.

"Was that really necessary?"

"I thought so," Niko shrugged nonchalantly, but an amused grin grew across his face. Alex approached the chest and fiddled with the latch before focusing his gaze on Shaina.

"The lock is made out of solid rock," he said. "I think you're supposed to break it."

Shaina cracked her knuckles as she approached the podium. "Not a problem!" She barely took the lock into her hand when a low rumbling noise reverberated across the cavern wall. Everyone froze.

"Pleeeaaasse tell me somebody is just really hungry because we didn't eat breakfast this morning." Ryan's voice held the faintest bit of hope behind the implausible statement. The rumble sounded again. Everyone stepped a little bit closer to each other.

"That is definitely *not* someone's stomach," Alex said.

At the mouth of the cavern, a terrifying creature appeared. It was two times the size of an elephant and looked like a mutated cross between a beetle and an armadillo. It had a rough, armored shell and large, spiked mandibles protruding from its face. Small, beady, black eyes fixated on the group as it crouched low to the ground on six segmented legs. The creature emitted an aggressive growl.

"I don't think that thing wants us in this cave." Ryan shifted ever so slightly closer to the back of the cave wall.

"Is this supposed to be part of the training?" Shaina whispered.

"I don't think so," Kaeli said.

"If we all remain calm and *don't freak out* we might be able to fight it off," Niko said quietly. They stood, locked into the beast's stare for what seemed like an eternity, before the creature let out an ear-splitting shriek and launched itself toward the group.

"Get out of the way!" Niko shoved Kaeli and Shaina to the side. Shaina yelped as she tripped over Kaeli. They both tumbled to the ground.

Kaeli pushed herself up just in time to see Niko shoot a beam of ice, freezing the monster in place. Kaeli let out a sigh of relief, but the feeling of safety didn't last long. The creature let out a grunt as it thrashed against the ice shackles rooting it to the ground.

"We either need to find a way to get out now or kill this thing!" Alex shouted.

Next to her, Kaeli could feel Shaina start to shake. A couple of rocks from the cave wall shook loose and tumbled to the ground. Shaina curled into a tight ball, hugging her knees to her chest, and squeezed her eyes shut. Her frantic breathing echoed off the rock wall. She knelt near her friend and placed a gentle hand on her back. If Shaina lost it, the whole cave could come down and then they would definitely die.

"Alex, Ryan," Niko shouted at the twins. "You two create some type of wind vortex to keep that thing away from us. Shaina!" Niko stepped toward her with a commanding presence. He knelt down in front of her and put a strong hand on her shoulder. "You need to calm down," he growled.

"I'm—trying—" Shaina said through gritted teeth. Kaeli locked eyes with Niko.

"Can you do your scorpio emotion manipulation thing to make her stop?"

Niko looked at Shaina, but hesitated. Shaina didn't give any indication that she'd even heard Kaeli's suggestion. Her hands were balled into fists and almost every inch of her body trembled. The ground started to shake, tipping the twins and the monster to the ground.

"You don't have time to waste to get permission!" Kaeli shouted. Niko glanced at her, nodded his head, and placed both of his hands on Shaina's shoulders. His eyes started to glow a deep blue, but it was too late. Shaina screamed. The ground in front of the artifact split. Kaeli's heart dropped to her stomach and her eyes widened in horror as three shadow snakes sprang from the hole. They snapped at the creature struggling to right itself from the ground and tore it to pieces, dropping the remains into the expansive abyss.

"Shit," she muttered. Larger chunks of rock fell to the ground as the shaking increased. There was only one thing she could do now. She fished through her jacket pocket until her fingers latched onto the ring Elethia had given her. The snakes started slithering toward the recruits. Kaeli grabbed Shaina's hand and pried open her clenched fist. Another tremor knocked Niko away from them, but Kaeli held onto Shaina with a vice grip. She slipped the ring onto one of Shaina's fingers. The purple stone in the center emitted a soft glow, and instantly the tremors started to settle. Kaeli locked eyes with one of the snakes. Its tongue flickered in and out of its mouth before an unnerving smile formed on its face. Kaeli looked down at the ring, now shining brightly, and tugged it off of Shaina's finger. The snake slithered closer to them, taking its time—a predator hunting its prey.

Then a thunderclap split the air with a flash of light. The snakes instantly turned tail and slithered back into the dark abyss. Kaeli barely had a chance to blink before the bright light faded. In its place stood Leo, Gemini, Scorpio, and Virgo.

The moment the light dissipated, the zodiacs sprang into action. Virgo closed the hole, sealing in the snakes. Gemini summoned the wind to reinforce the cave walls. Scorpio walked directly toward Shaina and placed a hand on her head. Shaina fell limp to the ground, unconscious.

"Hmm…" Scorpio tilted his head as he considered Shaina. "Interesting." He brought his gaze up to Kaeli and locked eyes with her. "What did you do to her?"

Kaeli's heart raced as Scorpio's inky presence started to probe her mind. Before he could completely infiltrate her thoughts, however, Leo placed a hand on Scorpio's shoulder and spun him around.

"We need to leave *now,*" he said. There was a quiet tone to his voice that sounded more threatening than any lion's roar. Scorpio nodded.

"Yes, of course,." He picked up Shaina. Leo motioned for Kaeli to join him. She did so without any questions. Leo held Shaina in close to his side with one arm, stretching the other out above his head. The same bright light surrounded them, and then they were gone.

They reemerged in a penthouse suite at the lodge. Scorpio transferred Shaina to Virgo who immediately took her out of the room. Gemini hissed something at the twins and they left as well. The room spun around Kaeli and her legs trembled, threatening to give out at any moment. She moved to position herself near the huge sectional couch. If she collapsed, she wouldn't hit anything hard. Had using the ring on Shaina been a mistake? It wasn't something she had wanted to do, but she hadn't been able to think of any other options at the time. Her hand went to her jacket pocket, but it was empty. She must have dropped it in the cave. Kaeli shivered as she remembered the feeling of Scorpio's *presence* trying to encroach upon her mind. Maybe leaving the ring in the cave was for the best. She sank down into the cushions. It was now just her, Niko, Leo, and Scorpio in the room. Leo turned to her and Niko.

"Scorpio and I need to go back to the training site and make sure everything is okay," he said. "You two *wait here* until further notice. Somebody will come back for you when everything is under control."

Kaeli didn't look at him, but she could feel Scorpio's gaze trained on her until he and Leo disappeared in another flash of light. Kaeli let out a shaky breath as her head relaxed back into the cushions and her eyes closed. The cushion sank as Niko sat down next to her, and she tried not to tense as she realized she was in the room alone with someone who could very well be working for Ophiuchus.

"What the *fuck* just happened?" Niko asked. Kaeli let her eyes flutter open. Natural. She just had to act natural. Niko hadn't given any indication of knowing that she had overheard the conversation between Scoprio and Capricorn.

"I have no idea," she said quietly. Niko shifted so that he faced her. His eyes stared intensely into her own.

"Are you okay?" he asked.

Kaeli pursed her lips. No, she was not okay. How could anyone be okay after what just happened. She didn't want to talk about her feelings... especially not with Niko right now.

"I'm fine."

They sat in silence for a couple of minutes before Niko let out a heavy sigh.

"I heard about your little adventure with Lukka and Joseph..." His voice trailed off. He didn't sound sinister or threatening, but every muscle in Kaeli's body went rigid. She inhaled and exhaled steadily, trying to keep panic from overtaking her senses.

"What adventure?"

Niko arched an eyebrow and smiled ever so slightly. He draped an arm over the back of the couch. "Really? Okay, I'll put it this way. I saw the three of you kill that shadow snake in the Celestial Realm. Do you know what I'm talking about now?"

Kaeli clenched her jaw. She had thought they had been alone when that happened. Her sensory instincts may have not developed to their full potential yet, but she was sure she'd mastered them enough to know when someone was following her.

"Oh. That adventure." The only words she could manage to say.

"Yes, that adventure." The smile on Niko's face grew a little wider. He sighed and the smile disappeared off his face. "Kaeli, whatever it is that you're doing, I want to help."

Kaeli fell silent, not exactly knowing how to react. As far she could tell, Niko hadn't been present for the conversation with Scorpio and Capricorn, but that didn't he mean he wasn't conspiring with Scorpio. He was either telling the truth or trying to trick her, and unfortunately, it was very difficult to get a read on where he stood.

"I really want to trust you, Niko," she said. Her lower lip quivered. She took in a steadying breath. "Honestly, after everything we've gone through together, I really do. But I don't know if I can, and your close proximity to Scorpio makes you dangerous even if you don't intend to be."

Something like hurt flashed through Niko's eyes, but he nodded his head.

"I understand, but Kaeli…" His hand touched her arm as he gazed deeply into her eyes.

A warm sensation of peace washed over her. Her muscles relaxed under that simple touch. This time she didn't try to hide the shaking. This all felt like too much. The lack of control over her fire. The monsters. The snakes. Putting Shaina in danger. Niko's fingers lazily traced the length of her forearm. She sank into that feeling, letting him take away the stress.

"I would do anything for you," he whispered. Kaeli met his gaze with her own. Her stomach twisted in knots as a deep yearning settled into her. Niko's hand wandered upward from her arm to caress her cheek, pushing her hair away from her face. Kaeli melted into the touch.

"I honestly don't know what's going on." She let out a shaky breath. "I know the snakes are connected to Ophiuchus. That night with Lukka and Joseph... we were trying to see if it was possible for us to kill them. But I still don't know why they keep coming after us or where they're coming from."

"Let me help you," Niko said. "I promise I won't put you in danger, but my connection to Scorpio could be extremely helpful in uncovering the bigger plot of all this." His thumb ran back and forth across her cheek.

"Promise?" she asked. Niko nodded his head and smiled. Kaeli inched closer to him, tucking herself under his arm and leaning into him. His chest rose and fell beneath her head, the sound of his heartbeat reverberating through her body in a soothing rhythm. He wrapped his arms around her and pulled her in closer. Kaeli let her eyes flutter closed as an exhaustion fell over her.

"Okay, I'll trust you," she murmured.

The light from outside cast the faint glow of sunset by the time Virgo materialized into the room with Shaina. Niko and Kaeli were sitting on the couch watching TV. Niko grabbed the remote and turned it off. Kaeli hopped to her knees and leaned over the back of the couch so she could see them. Shaina didn't look like she was in great shape. Bags under her eyes cast a darkness over the rest of her face, but she was conscious at least... even if she leaned heavily on Virgo for support.

"Are you okay?" Kaeli asked. Virgo helped Shaina to the couch. Shaina cracked a shadow of a smile.

"I've definitely been better."

"Are we free to go yet?" Niko asked. Virgo shook his head as he adjusted the cushions on the couch to support Shaina a little more.

"Not yet," he said. "Soon. I just brought Shaina back here because she needs a safe place to be for a bit while we settle some more things."

"What kind of things?" Niko pressed. He turned to face Virgo and asked, "Why did those snakes appear and attack us? None of you have told us anything about what's going on."

Virgo's eyes hardened into a dead stare. "I can't tell you. Someone will be back soon to escort you to your rooms." He placed a hand on Shaina's shoulder. "Just rest here for a bit." Shaina nodded as she closed her eyes and let out a heavy breath. Virgo disappeared in an earthy green light. Kaeli turned to face Shaina.

"What happened?"

Shaina leaned her head into the couch. "I wish I could forget." Her shoulders drooped. She opened her eyes but didn't make eye contact with either Kaeli or Niko. "Let's just say that Virgo kind of freaks out when I royally fuck up. He did bring me to a hospital wing, though. There were some water spirits there who helped bring me back to consciousness." She rubbed at her temple with her forefingers. "I completely blacked out. I just remember feeling like the earth was about to tear me apart and then… nothing."

"Did you see the snakes?" Kaeli asked. Shaina pursed her lips together and started kicking at the ground.

"I didn't see them, but… I could *feel* them." She shuddered. "It was like… a rot in the earth. It's a type of decay I can normally sense around graveyards, but this… it moved with them." Kaeli fell silent. She glanced at Niko, trying to decide if she should pull Shaina in on her snake-destroyer task force. As if he was reading her mind—which she *really* hoped he wasn't—Niko nodded his head.

"I found out how to kill the snakes," Kaeli said. Shaina's eyes perked up, and a slight hint of life seemed to return to her features. "I've been researching them with Lukka and Joseph. There's something bigger going on that the zodiacs aren't telling us. I don't know what it is exactly, but I know the snakes are related to it. It's dangerous, but I think if we can get close enough to them, we might be able to figure out why the zodiacs have been pushing to train us so hard and why these attacks keep happening. I just told Niko about it, and he's going to help…" Her voice trailed off. Shaina looked at the two of them with unblinking eyes. After an uncomfortable silence, Niko spoke up.

"You want in?"

A slow smile spread onto Shaina's face. "Absolutely I do."

A knock sounded from outside the room, causing all three of the recruits to jump. The door opened and an earth spirit poked its head in from the entryway.

"I have been instructed to escort the three of you back to your rooms," it said. "All recruits have been ordered to stay in their lodgings until daybreak. So if you please, follow me." Niko, Kaeli, and Shaina stood. Kaeli offered Shaia an arm for support but Shaina shook her head.

"We can talk more about this later," Kaeli said under her breath. They met the spirit in the hallway. It bowed, and with a flash of green light, teleported the recruits back to their rooms.

CHAPTER 26

Kaeli woke up to a quiet, persistent knock on her door the next morning. She let out a sigh and turned her head toward Shaina, hoping that her friend would be the one to get out of bed and answer it. No such luck. Shaina was buried deep in her comforter and breathing heavily. Not quite a snore, but enough to let Kaeli know she was knocked out cold. Kaeli groaned and threw the sheets off her body. Rubbing her eyes, she made her way to the door and opened it. The same earth spirit that had taken them back to the room stood in the entryway, hand poised to knock again and solid black eyes wide with what Kaeli assumed was surprise at seeing her disheveled appearance. The spirit quickly bowed.

"My apologies for waking you so early. The zodiacs wished for me to relay a message. Lady Aries wanted to do it, but Sir Leo suggested I come instead." The spirit paused as if waiting for Kaeli to respond. When she didn't, the spirit cleared its throat to say, "They wished me to let you know that training has been canceled for today. Given the events that transpired yesterday, they thought it best for the recruits to adjust to Earth for a couple more days before using your powers under strenuous conditions. You have the day free to yourself and may do with it as you wish, so long as you do not use your powers."

"Thanks for letting me know." Kaeli covered her mouth as she stifled a yawn. "Is there anything else?"

"No, miss," the spirit shook its head. "You may return to sleeping if you wish."

"Thanks," Kaeli said again. The spirit turned to leave, and Kaeli shut the door. Standing in the entryway, staring between her sleeping friend and her own bed, Kaeli let out a sigh. She was already up. Might as well stay up and get ready for the day.

About an hour later, Kaeli trudged her feet across the hallway to Lukka's room. Her insides twisted as she played his reaction to learning about what she'd told Niko over and over again in her head. It wasn't pretty, but she knew this conversation needed to happen. She took in a deep breath as she stood in front of his door. Letting out the exhale, she knocked.

Lukka opened it before the sound of the first tap finished.

"WHAT HAPPENED YESTERDAY?!" His hair was a disheveled mess and he only wore his boxers."We heard about—actually felt—the earthquake and then next thing I know, all the zodiacs started teleporting in and out of caves and locked us all up in our rooms. I couldn't get any info out of Aries. She was busy flipping out, saying stuff about how she had to fix shit with the Lunar Zodiacs. Seriously, Kaeli, it was crazy here yesterday. What happened?" He actually looked... worried. Kaeli definitely wasn't used to seeing that look on his face. She let out a sigh.

"My group was attacked in the cave by some… terrifying… creature. Shaina lost control of her powers, causing the earthquake. The ground in the cave split open, and a bunch of shadow snakes came out of it." A shiver ran down her spine as she recalled how they ripped the creature to pieces. "The zodiacs showed up and the snakes went back to the hole before Virgo shut them in, but Lukka… this whole thing with Ophiuchus… I think it's much bigger than we thought." She quickly shut her mouth and peaked through the doorway to see if Daniel was in the room. She shouldn't have mentioned Ophiuchus without checking first. "Is Daniel here?" she whispered.

"Nope," Lukka said as he opened the door just wide enough for Kaeli to walk through. "Come on in."

"Thanks." Kaeli stepped through the opening and shut the door behind her. She surveyed Lukka from the corner of her eye. She was used to seeing him half naked since sweatpants without a shirt was his preferred loungewear… but this felt more awkward.

"Like what you see?" Lukka grinned. Kaeli rolled her eyes and pushed her way past him, sitting herself down at the desk and looking at anything *but* him.

"Put some clothes on and I'll tell you the rest of the story."

"If that's what you want."

Kaeli just arched a brow and examined her nails as if they were profoundly more interesting than anything Lukka had to offer. He chuckled and disappeared into the bathroom. The minute he shut the door, Kaeli let out a sigh of relief, clenching her hands briefly before releasing. Looking at Lukka like that while trying to tell a story was impossible. His abs were way too distracting.

Lukka emerged from the bathroom a couple of seconds later wearing a plain red t-shirt and some baggy jeans.

"Alright, I'm dressed. Tell me the rest of the story!"

"Okay," Kaeli exhaled, mentally preparing herself for Lukka's reaction as she relayed yesterday's events. She paused before the end of her story. She needed to tell Lukka that Niko and Shaina knew about their plans to hunt the snakes, but she was not looking forward to the inevitable explosion. Lukka picked up on the reluctance.

"Please don't tell me you did what I think you did," he said as his voice darkened. Kaeli's gaze flickered to the floor as she pressed her lips together in a grimace. A heaviness dropped to the pit of her stomach. She shook her head and stared at Lukka straight in the eyes. Maybe it wasn't smart to face the bull head-on, but she was going to do it anyway.

"I told Shaina. She wants to help us... and I told Niko."

"WHAT?!" Steam curled off Lukka's skin as an orange glow pulsated around his hands. "We *saw* Scorpio talking about working with Ophiuchus. How could you be so stupid?!"

Kaeli arched her brow at the insult and clenched her fist as she fought to contain the fire roiling in her gut. As much as she despised insults to her intelligence, she'd expected this reaction, and setting the lodge on fire wouldn't do anyone any good.

"He's not working with Scorpio," she said, keeping her tone cool and even. "We talked about it."

Lukka narrowed his eyes and crossed his arms over his chest. "How do you know, Kaeli? Scorpios aren't exactly known for being trustworthy. Niko could have been lying to you."

"Just..." Kaeli pursed her lips and let out a sigh, "trust me. I've worked with him *a lot* more than you have. I won't just spill everything. Clearly, he spends a lot of time with Scorpio, and that's a safety consideration… but *he spends a lot of time with Scorpio.* We need someone like that who can get inside details."

"Fine," Lukka grumbled. "Have you told Joseph yet?"

Kaeli shook her head and opened her mouth to respond, but a knock cut her off. She closed her mouth. Lukka stood up to answer the door. Thank goodness he had put on clothes. The last thing Kaeli wanted was for someone to catch her in the room alone with a half-dressed Lukka.

"Is Kaeli in there?" It was Shaina. Kaeli popped up from her chair.

"Yes!" she answered as she made her way to the door. "What's up?" As she approached, Lukka stepped out of the way to make space for her.

"The twins apparently just got back to the hotel. Niko mentioned that it would be cool if we all did some exploring in the touristy area today—to decompress from what happened yesterday." Her gaze flickered to Lukka. "I'd invite you too… but it was going to be like a team bonding thing…"

"He'll be okay," Kaeli said as she reached up to pat Lukka on the shoulder. His mouth flattened to a straight line and his shoulders fell as he flashed her an unamused glance. Kaeli resisted the urge to pinch his cheek. A smirk crossed her face instead. "See you later, Lukka."

"Just try not to get yourself killed this time," he said.

"I'll see what I can do." Kaeli turned to Shaina. "If we're going out, I need a different outfit. Help me decide?" Shaina nodded and the two girls crossed the hall back to their room.

✶✶✶

About an hour later, Kaeli and Shaina met up with Niko, Ryan, and Alex in the lobby. Signs throughout the lobby pointed to a secluded area with the words *This Way to Town*. The group followed them in relative silence until they reached a teleportation pad. A large earth spirit, who rivalled Pyronius in stature, stood in front of it, arms crossed over his muscled chest. Kaeli slowed her pace, allowing Niko and the twins to approach the guardian spirit first. Shaina hung back with Kaeli. The spirit regarded them through half-lidded eyes, looking thoroughly unimpressed.

"Do you have your room keys?"

"Why do we need our room keys?" Ryan asked.

"Do you have them?" the spirit growled.

"Yes, we do." Alex shot his brother a pinched look. Ryan widened his eyes and shrugged his shoulders.

"Good." The spirit unfurled his arms and explained, "You'll need them to exit and enter back into the lodge. I could be wrong, but it doesn't look like you've stayed with us before?" Everyone in the group shook their heads. "Thought not," the spirit sighed. "This teleportation pad will take you to a secluded room with a single door. To exit that door, you will need to swipe your key card. It will then open to an alleyway that leads out to the main street. When you're ready to come back, you just follow the same alleyway. You'll need your keycard to get through the door again. Once you're in the teleportation circle, say *Celestial Lodge* and it will take you straight back here. Got it?" He arched an eyebrow. Everyone nodded. "Good." He motioned for them to step into the portal circle. With a mumbled word, they were off.

They reappeared in a completely white room reminiscent of an asylum. A single fluorescent bulb hanging from the center of the ceiling illuminated the cramped space with a bright light that made Kaeli squint and cup her hand over her eyes. The only color was the faint, green glow of the portal. Kaeli steadied herself again to regain her bearings. She'd spent months using the celestial teleportation system and she *still* wasn't used to it.

It'd gotten to the point where Niko had even stopped teasing her about it because there was nothing new to say.

"This room makes me uncomfortable." Ryan's gaze darted around as he shifted from side to side. "I gotta get out of here." He walked up to the door and swiped the key card. A muted beeping noise sounded and the door swung open. A gust of fresh air flowed through the room, instantly relieving some of Kaeli's nausea. She stood up and followed everyone else out the door.

The alleyway wasn't the dingy, trashed back street she imagined it would be. It was immaculately clean, with a paved cobblestone street and planters containing small white and blue flowers. The uneasy nausea faded away. They walked in relative silence until they exited the alleyway.

Kaeli caught her breath as they stepped out onto the main road. It was dotted with different shops and restaurants stacked on top of each other against a green mountain backdrop. The road itself curved around a crystal blue bay. Docks jutted out to a variety of boats sitting offshore, bobbing up and down in the water. A fresh sea breeze caressed her face and Kaeli smiled.

"This is *exactly* what I needed today," she said.

"Me too," Shaina agreed.

"Let's find food," Ryan said. "I'm starving." Niko stuffed his hands in his pockets as he turned in a slow circle, taking in the surroundings.

"There's a bakery café right there." He pointed at a blue building not too far off.

"That's perfect!" A smile worked its way onto Kaeli's face. Pastries and coffee. There really wasn't any better way to start the day.

The café itself was beautiful—wide-open space, floor-to-ceiling windows, shiny concrete floor, and twinkling lights dangling from the ceiling. A couple of long wooden tables sat at the center of the space, but the rest of the café was filled with plush chairs situated around coffee tables that each looked like an individualized piece of art. The smell of freshly baked pastries mixed with espresso filled the air. Kaeli had a huge grin on her face. *This* was paradise. Ryan flashed his celestial credit card.

"What does everybody want? Food and drinks are on me," he winked. Shaina actually laughed, and a wide smile to spread across Ryan's face. Once they'd ordered and gotten their food and drink, they settled into a secluded corner, far away from other customers that started to trickle into the establishment.

Conversation was pleasant, but superficial, as everyone talked about everything *besides* what happened during training the other day. Ryan tried to bring it up once, but Shaina's expression had darkened so quickly that he instantly shifted to a different topic. Kaeli was content to sink back into her chair and sip the mocha and munch on the croissant she'd ordered. She was just about to take another bite of the flaky bread when she looked at the entrance and instantly froze.

A chill ran down her spine, numbing her to her immediate surroundings as she spotted a large, hooded figure standing in the doorway. A pungent odor that reminded her of sewage rot wafted off of him. His hood was pulled down low, covering most of his face, but she recognized the clothing. It was the last thing she'd seen Trent wearing before she'd left on the day of the earthquake. She took in a slow, steady breath as her heart hammered in her chest. Just because this particular person was roughly the same build and wore the same clothes as her brother didn't mean that it was him. In all probability it wasn't him. What were the odds that he'd lived through the earthquake and then was somehow on this island the same exact time she was, anyway? Still... she slumped down in her chair as she sniffed at the air, tapping into her instincts. Even if he wasn't Trent, this guy was bad news. Niko seemed to notice her odd behavior.

"What's going on?" he asked.

"I think we should leave," she whispered. The other three in the group fell silent at her urgent tone. She nodded her head in the direction of the shady newcomer who meandered toward another secluded table and said, "This makes absolutely no sense... but I get the feeling that that guy is my brother." Shaina and Niko turned around in their seats to look. Kaeli hissed and they turned their attention back to the table. "If that is him and he sees me, it's going to be bad news," she squeaked and ducked behind her croissant as the newcomer turned to look in their general direction. Niko and Shaina sat up a bit straighter, positioning themselves to cover Kaeli a little more.

"Alright, well let's wrap this party up and take our stuff to go," Ryan said, standing up from his seat. He made his way to the counter. Kaeli dared a glance at the stranger. He stared intently at them.

"Crap, he's looking this way," she muttered.

"He doesn't look so great," Alex said. "There's something... dark... around him."

"Stop staring at him!" Shaina said. Ryan returned holding a large paper bag and started packing up the food.

"He looked away," Alex whispered. "He's kind of looking everywhere actually. Like he's sniffing the air or something."

"Again," Shaina hissed, "*stop* looking at him."

"Alright, he's distracted now. Let's get out of here," Ryan said as he stuffed the last pastry into the bag. They all stood up. Niko wrapped an arm around Kaeli, pulling her in close to his side. The hammering in her heart

Alyssa Markins

quieted just a little at his touch. She wasn't alone. If anything happened, she had her friends here with her.

They followed the curve of the bay until they happened upon a circular courtyard enclosed by tropical plants and dotted with cushioned benches. A babbling fountain stood at the center of the courtyard. Streams of water crossed in front of a statue of Aphrodite emerging from a clam shell. A few birds skipped between the legs of the benches, but other than their occasional chirping and the running water, it was fairly silent.

The five sat down and Ryan began passing out the food. Kaeli took the remainder of her croissant and nibbled at it. Her appetite had completely disappeared, but she didn't want the food to go to waste. Her mind kept combing over the details of the stranger, trying to figure out if he was indeed Trent. It made no sense, but she couldn't shake this sixth sense that he was. Maybe it was her instinctual abilities. And the darkness Alex had mentioned. Kaeli had noticed it too. Almost like a shadowy haze surrounded him, but none of the "normal" people at the cafe seemed like they saw anything out of the ordinary. Maybe they were just so uncomfortable they tried not to notice.

"So," Ryan spoke up between munches of food, "what's the deal with your brother?"

"Do you seriously have to talk with your mouth full?" Shaina protested. "It's gross." Ryan swallowed and stuck out his tongue, but otherwise waited for Kaeli's response. Kaeli paused, feeling like she owed her friends and explanation, but not wanting to relive details from her past. She pressed her lips together. Navigating this situation might be easier if they knew what was going on.

"When I was young, my father died… in a car crash I thought was an accident, but I found out in Scorpio's training session that I actually caused it when I first manifested my fire abilities." She glanced at Niko, remembering how he'd held her that night in the grove as she'd cried all over him. She quickly tore her gaze away and took a deep breath. "My brother, Trent, always blamed me for the death of our father and never forgave me for it. He took out his aggression in… unhealthy ways. My mother was too much of an emotional wreck to ever do anything about it. I learned how to fight back, but…" Her throat closed up as the words seemed to leave her. She didn't want to say anything else. Shaina rubbed her arm. A tight-lipped smile crossed Kaeli's face. No one spoke. Even Ryan didn't try to say anything. They continued eating their food in silence.

Shaina offered to throw away the trash when everyone was done. When she returned, she plopped back down on the bench next to Kaeli.

"Why don't we do a little shopping?" she suggested. "We've got these unlimited credit cards we'll never have to pay off. It would be tragic if we didn't put them to good use. Plus buying stuff is supposed to release happy endorphins… or something like that."

Kaeli smiled, for real this time. "That sounds perfect."

They ventured deep into the custom boutique stores. Each building was painted a different, vibrant color, but they all had a similar architectural style: pointed roofs supported by crossing wooden beams and rounded doorways with stained glass windows that reflected the midday light in colorful patterns. All of the restaurants were officially open and smells of cooked fish and fried foods wafted into the street. More people walked around now, and Kaeli's muscles noticeably relaxed.

After Shaina and Kaeli had spent several minutes obsessing over a fashion boutique that specialized in custom clothes for women, the boys decided to split off, leaving the girls to fend for themselves amongst the endless clothing options. They stayed for about an hour, piecing together different outfits. Kaeli decided to get a long, flowing skirt that swished perfectly around her figure as she walked and paired it with a matching lace halter top.

As they left the store, they checked the immediate area for the boys. It would have been nice if the zodiacs had given them a celestial cell phone to use while they were on Earth in addition to the credit cards, but unfortunately, that wasn't the case. After checking all the store windows within a half mile, however, they decided to head back to the lodge with their purchases.

They found their way back to the cobblestone alleyway and were just about to enter through the door when a dense fog settled over them. Kaeli brought her hand to her nose and started coughing as a familiar pungent odor filled the air.

"Oh my gosh, what's that smell?" Shaina coughed as she tucked her head into her arm. The odor infiltrated Kaeli's sinuses, making her eyes water. It smelled like a rotting corpse.

"Let's get out of here." Kaeli took out her card and swiped it. The door's sensor beeped and Kaeli put her hand on the handle to open it.

"Hey…" a deep voice sounded from behind them. Kaeli froze. Every muscle tensed in her body so tight that she couldn't even move to face him. Trent. Using all her willpower, she pried her fingers off the door handle and turned to face her brother, dropping her shopping bags to the floor. Shaina pressed herself as far into the wall as she possibly could, still coughing at the stench. Kaeli's eyes widened as she took in the full view of her brother. He removed the hood from his face and flashed a serpentine grin as a forked tongue flickered in and out of his mouth. He had been horribly disfigured into some reptilian monster. Kaeli could only spot traces of the human he'd once been. The dark fog that had settled over the alleyway emanated from his body. Twisting shadows decorated the exposed part of his neck and face like a living tattoo.

"Kaeli, we need to get out of here," Shaina squeaked.

"It's been a long time, sis."

Kaeli instantly turned to swipe her key card again, but a rock-solid shadow pushed its way between her and the door, blocking access. Kaeli let out a shaky breath as she turned to face her brother again. The zodiacs had instructed them not to use their powers, but she had a feeling she would need to. Her mouth went dry as she struggled to speak. "What... what are you doing here?" A tremor she desperately wished would go away traced her voice. If there was one thing she knew about Trent, it was that he fed off fear. Every time she fought back, the outcome was better than if she didn't. Shaina cast furtive looks between Kaeli and her brother. Kaeli clenched her fist, allowing the faintest bit of her fire's warmth to gather in the palm of her hand.

"I've been sent on a mission. One that's been driving me *crazy* since for some reason you haven't been on Earth for the last several months." The serpentine smile on his face grew wider, almost splitting his face in two. "But as soon as you returned, I felt it. I could *smell* you. So I came here. And I found you."

"What... kind of mission..." Kaeli's voice cracked. Trent laughed. Shadows rolled off his body in waves, as if they laughed too.

"You're finally going to die today," he let out a satisfied sigh, "and then I'll get to go back and see *her* again."

"Like hell," Kaeli growled. She didn't fight to stop her fire anymore. It sprang to life around her fingers and her eyes glowed. She would show no mercy, whether they were on Earth or not. She had to end this before she or Shaina got hurt. Trent laughed again.

"I've been waiting for this for a *long* time." He held both of his hands out to the side. Inky black shadows gathered around them. Kaeli looked at Shaina.

"If you want to freak out with your powers again and swallow him in an earthquake, you have my full permission."

"Two against one isn't exactly a fair fight." Trent's voice started to morph. Something deep and ominous doubled over it. He stretched out a hand and a shadow shot out toward Shaina, completely entombing her in solidified darkness. Kaeli snarled and was only briefly aware of the warmth crawling up her arms and the slight prick in her lip as her canines sharpened.

"What did you do to her?!"

"Just leveling the playing field." Trent cocked his head to the side. "I just trapped her in a dark abyss. She'll be fine. I can't say the same for you." His nonchalant behavior only fueled Kaeli's rage. Her fire boiled in her gut until it exploded as she charged toward him. A scream ripped from her throat as fire shot down the entire alleyway, surrounding them with a raging inferno mixed with shadow. Her fingers extended into fiery claws and she swiped at Trent, but he dodged her attacks every time, slithering in and out of the shadows as if he were a part of them.

They danced, a tornado of shadow and fiery light. Kaeli lost all sense of herself as she completely succumbed to the fire. She only saw Trent and his serpentine smile as he drew her farther and farther away from the door leading back to the lodge.

Kaeli lunged again, but the fire became too much for her to hold. Her lungs burned, and then her foot tripped over a loose cobblestone. She pivoted to steady herself, but Trent landed a blow to her gut. Kaeli doubled over and a shadow came from behind, clubbing her in the back of the head. Falling to her knees, she flailed her arms for balance, heaving for breath. She caught sight of Trent's foot seconds before it connected to her temple. Pain blasted through her head as starbursts speckled her vision. She flattened to the ground.

"I thought this would be a little more challenging," Trent scoffed. "Maybe I didn't need to even the playing field after all."

He nudged Kaeli's bruised body with his foot. She grunted as she struggled to push herself away. For the first time, she registered the panicked screams. Sirens blared in every direction. Fire raged in front of the alleyway, blocking any view of the street. Terror dropped to the pit of her stomach. She'd done that. She'd destroyed this town.

Trent sighed. "Unfortunately, I've still got a lot of pent up energy. I don't think your friend will be much of a fight either, but..." He flashed a wicked grin at Kaeli. Shadows swirled around him, batting away the licks of flame that tried to consume him. "It'd be fun to see you watch her die before I kill you." He stepped over Kaeli and started walking toward the dark abyss holding Shaina. Panicked adrenaline ripped through Kaeli's mind, giving her just enough energy to push herself to her feet.

"Don't." Her lungs fought for air. The word was barely louder than a whisper, but Trent stopped and turned to face Kaeli. He looked her up and down.

"And what exactly are you going to do about it? Look at this." He motioned to the alleyway burning up with fire and said, "You've destroyed *everything* here besides me." He tipped his head back. A mock pout crossed his face. "I *almost* feel sorry for you. But if it makes you feel any better, you won't be alive much longer to witness the aftermath."

Something shifted in the fire and shadow as Niko came charging through the flame and fog. But it didn't look like Niko. His eyes glowed a deep, intense blue, and his skin had turned into black exoskeleton armor. His fingers extended into sharpened spikes and a huge scorpion tail extended from the lower base of his back. His celestial form would have terrified her if she didn't struggle for breath and consciousness.

Trent shifted closer to the shadow entombing Shaina. Close behind Niko, the twins appeared. They weren't in their celestial forms, but the air currents swirling angrily around them sucked the oxygen and lowered some of the fire. Kaeli sank against the wall, the flame parting to make space for her. Trent's gaze darted between Niko and the twins before returning his attention to Kaeli.

"Looks like we'll have to finish this up another time." With lightning speed, he rushed to where he held Shaina captive and in a swirl of shadow, they both disappeared. Kaeli's heart dropped as a scream tore from her throat. The fire raged around her. Red clouded her vision. Voices shouting her name sounded like a faraway memory before the heat and smoke consumed her senses, deadening her to the world.

CHAPTER 27

Kaeli snapped awake in her room at the lodge. Her fists instinctually ignited on fire before a slosh of freezing water dumped over her head. She blinked as the icy cold seeped into her senses, cutting through the disorientation and bringing back, in vivid detail, everything that had happened. She looked around the room and spotted Niko sitting in a chair opposite her bed. He studied his hand intently as a small stream of water danced between his fingers. He looked up and made eye contact with her, a grim smile crossing his face as he leaned back in the chair.

"You can't use fire like that on Earth. Stuff actually burns."

Water dripped from the ends of Kaeli's hair as she tried to sort through her thoughts. The memory of Niko charging through the flames in his scorpion form. The twins. The heavy smoke and fog. Trent had disappeared with…

"Shaina!" Kaeli shot a glance at the bed next to her. It was empty. Quick, shallow breaths escaped as she forced herself to breathe. The room spun around her. "What happened?" The words came out in a raspy stutter that she barely recognized. Her throat burned. Niko shifted in the chair.

"Trent disappeared with the shadow cocoon right before you passed out. The twins and I did what we could to contain the fire in the alley. We made a path to the door and took you straight back here. The lobby was in complete pandemonium. Leo saw me holding you and told me to bring you back here. I'm not supposed to let you out under any circumstances." Kaeli stared at Shaina's empty bed. Niko followed her gaze.

"Was Shaina in that cocoon?"

Kaeli's lower lip quivered as she nodded. She squeezed her eyes shut and leaned against the headboard. Her whole head throbbed, and pain radiated from the swelling pressure around her eyes.

"How long have I been out?" Her voice sounded weak and distant in her ears, as if it belonged to someone else entirely. If it didn't hurt so bad to talk, Kaeli would've thought it did.

"A couple of hours," Niko replied. The door creaked as someone slowly opened it. Kaeli's eyes shot open just as Niko darted up from the chair. Leo entered, followed closely by Pisces. Leo walked straight to Niko and started muttering incoherent words under his breath. Pisces, her hands already illuminated with a soft blue glow, headed right to Kaeli. She placed the tips of her fingers delicately on either side of Kaeli's temples, and Kaeli let her eyes flutter closed as the warm tingling sensation buzzed through her head. She was only briefly aware of Leo as he hovered over her, asking Pisces if she would be alright, blinking her eyes open just before he left the room. Niko watched Pisces intently as she worked her hands over Kaeli's face and the various bruises that had formed during the fight. Kaeli's muscles noticeably relaxed as the tension gave in to Pisces's healing abilities. Pisces only worked for a couple minutes before deeming her work done and briskly exiting the room. Kaeli pushed herself to an upright position and turned to Niko.

"What did Leo say?"

"Apparently, we're all evacuating back to the Celestial Realm within the next hour."

Kaeli's mouth went dry as her heartbeat raced. She gripped the bed sheets so tight her knuckles turned white as her eyes darted to Shaina's empty bed.

"But—"

"I know," Niko said.

"I'm *not* leaving without her."

Niko sat back in the chair letting out a heavy sigh. He leaned forward, elbows on his knees and hands forming a triangle as he stared intently at Kaeli.

"Leo adamantly told me that I can't let you leave this room."

Kaeli opened her mouth to protest, but Niko held up a hand to cut her off. "But we're definitely not leaving until we find out what happened to Shaina."

Kaeli allowed herself to sink into the pillows and the weight of Niko's words sank into her mind. A small smile tugged at the corner of her lips. They would rescue Shaina and then they would all go back to the Celestial Realm safe and together.

"Trent has an extremely pungent scent now. If we can find even just his general location, I should be able to track him." Kaeli twisted the ends of her hair around her fingers as she looked up in the general direction of the ceiling. "But where should we start looking?"

Niko rubbed his chin as he looked off into the distance at nothing in particular.

"We could try the caves. We know there's some sort of connection to the snakes. It's not much, but that's about the only lead we have at this point."

Kaeli nodded as her brain searched for pitfalls or alternatives. The zodiacs were already evacuating the building. If there was enough of a crowd, they might be able to blend in with the masses and sneak out a door. Her eyes widened as an idea lit up her face. She smacked the palm of her hand on the down comforter. Niko's head whipped toward her.

"I know you said *I'm* not allowed to leave this room," she grinned, "but are you?"

Niko tilted his head and raised his eyebrows. "Potentially. Why?"

"You need to go get the twins and bring them back here!"

A slow smile crept onto Niko's face. "Their illusion ability. I'm really not supposed to leave you alone... but if you had a serious health concern, I could be trying to find Pisces or a water spirit. Can you manipulate your internal temperature to fever levels without causing an actual fire? Just in case someone pops in while I'm gone."

"I'll figure it out."

"Good." Niko pushed himself out of the chair. "Then I guess I better find a healer. Since you're so clearly sick right now and my healing abilities can't handle it." He winked and made for the door. Kaeli let out a couple of deep breaths as she allowed herself to relax back into the bed. This would work. They would find Shaina and then they could all go home.

Niko returned minutes later, the twins in tow. After catching them up on the rough logistics of their plan, Ryan and Alex transformed themselves to look like the earth spirits working at the lodge. With Ryan leading the way out front and Alex following up in the back, they exited the room and made the trek down to the lobby.

The lobby was a cacophony of bodies and spirits scrambling back and forth, opening different portals, and screaming at each other. Libra, Aries, and Capricorn did their best to herd people to their correct destinations, but their efforts did little to calm the chaos. Disguised as the earth spirits, Ryan and Alex pretended to usher Kaeli and Nico to one of the evacuation points while the group steadily wove their way to the front entrance.

Kaeli let her gaze erratically flicker across the room, doing everything in her power to avoid eye contact with anyone while still seeming like a confused, distraught recruit. A glimmer of gold caught her attention on the upper levels of the lodge and despite her attempts to keep a roaming gaze, she found herself locked into direct eye contact with the same man she'd caught watching them before. Looking at him now, she was sure that he had to be Gold Dragon. He had the body of a man, but his face was elongated into that of a sleek dragon. Shimmering scales covered his skin and reflected light as he leaned forward on the railing and cracked what looked like a toothy grin. Kaeli wasn't entirely sure. His snout made it difficult to interpret the facial expression. He winked. Kaeli's eyes widened as she quickly tore her gaze away and retrained her focus on the back of Ryan's head as they exited the building.

The sun had almost dipped below the horizon by the time they reached the caves. A hazy mist rose from the ground as a crisp wind whistled through the trees, sending a shiver down Kaeli's spine. She inhaled deeply, hoping to catch even a hint of Trent's putrid scent, but all she got was a whiff of pine. The four stood in front of the caves motionless.

"Should we try going back inside the original cave?" Ryan asked. Niko turned to Kaeli.

"You smell anything?"

Kaeli furrowed her brows and closed her eyes as she took a series of deep breaths. At first she couldn't sense anything, but then… the faint scent of a rotting corpse materialized out of nowhere from deep within the cave.

"In there," she said, pointing. "It's faint, but definitely smells like him."

"I'm not so sure this is a good idea" Alex shuffled back and forth as he looked around at the group. "Maybe we should let one of the zodiacs know and they can come handle it."

"Trent is here *now*," Kaeli said. "You don't understand what he's capable of. If there's a chance to rescue Shaina, we need to take it."

The hair at the back of her neck stood on end seconds before an ominous laughter echoed from inside the cave. The mist thickened to a murky shadow as Trent emerged from the cave. Kaeli's heart pounded in her chest as heat flushed through her body. Niko took a step closer to her. The twins widened their stance, summoning small whirlwinds of air around their hands. Trent's reptilian form blended in with the looming darkness, hiding everything but the glint of his white fangs in the moonlight.

"I'll admit, it didn't take you as long to find me as I thought it would."

"Where's Shaina?!" Kaeli would've lunged straight for her brother if Niko hadn't placed a hand on her shoulder.

"Tell you what," Trent's gaze narrowed in on Kaeli as a malicious smile widened across his face, "I'll let you know where she is if you survive this fight."

Kaeli screamed as she tore away from Niko and pounced at Trent. He disappeared into the shadows, only to reappear several paces away.

"Too slow." He laughed. His eyes glazed over with a cloudy darkness. The shadows shifted around him, hugging his form. He spread his arms wide and a stream of shadow shot out, encircling the recruits. Kaeli took a step closer to Niko and twins but kept her gaze trained on the shadows. They danced and morphed until the ring had transformed into shadowed copies of Trent with hazy gray eyes.

"Think there might be a better way to resolve your family issues?" Ryan whispered. The shadow forms charged, and Kaeli lost sight of Trent as flames instantly leapt to her fingertips. She'd have to do this close combat style. Fighting with fire in the real world was extremely inconvenient. One of the shadow forms came at her with a punch. She spun to dodge and sent a backfist flying to its face. The shadow burst into a murky vapor that lingered in the air. So these things weren't very durable, but the more they got hit, the more difficult it would become to see. Kaeli's attention snapped back as another fist jabbed at her through the darkening fog. She ducked and slammed an uppercut punch into where she assumed the figure's jaw would be. Her fire hit the mark, but the resulting darkness completely obscured any view of her friends.

An unseen force smashed into her gut, hurling her backward.

Kaeli doubled over trying to gasp for breath. Her fire flickered out as she fell to her knees. A wind swirled through the shadows forcing the haze outward. Kaeli pushed herself up as her breath started to return. Alex had surrounded them in a vortex of wind, creating a pocket of clear air. Kaeli's eyes darted back and forth. Still no sign of Trent.

"Where's that bastard hiding?" Ryan growled.

Without warning, spears of shadow shot out from the darkness. Niko tackled Kaeli out of the way, but not before one of them nicked her skin. Pain shot through her head and she was vaguely aware of the warm liquid trickling down her temple. She looked up at Niko. His chest heaved and his pulse hammered against her skin. He stared into her eyes and raised a glowing blue hand to the side of her head. The throbbing pain instantly eased and he offered a grim smile.

"Alright, that's enough with the games." Trent appeared from the haze near the trees. His face twisted into a purely feral expression. He knelt and placed his hand on the ground. A ripple of shadow flew out, knocking their group backward. Before Kaeli could fully regain her balance, four shadow snakes shot out from the trees. Three of them went straight for Niko and the twins, plunging headfirst into their backs. Kaeli's breath hitched in her throat as their eyes glazed to black. Shadows swirled around them in a terrifying dance as all three let out a hissing laugh that echoed throughout the forest. The fourth snake stared at Kaeli but didn't make a move toward her.

"Now it's just you and me, sis."

"I'm going to kill you," Kaeli said through gritted teeth as she pushed herself back up to a standing position.

"The same way you killed Dad? That means you'll have killed *half* your family."

Red spotted Kaeli's vision as she formed her fire into a whip. She lashed out as Trent moved back. The tip wrapped around his leg just before he leapt out of reach. He let out a yelp as Kaeli pulled back on her fire, toppling him to the ground. With lightning fast speed she closed the distance between the two of them. The fire turned into a bolt of light in her hand. A feral roar ripped from her throat as she stabbed the bolt through Trent's chest. His eyes widened and he gasped for breath as he struggled to fling

Kaeli off of him. She summoned all her strength to keep him pinned, digging the bolt deeper into his flesh. The shadows around him flickered as his arms fell limp to the ground. Kaeli let out a few raspy breaths as her grip on the bolt of light loosened.

"She is... at the... door..."

Kaeli barely caught Trent's last words before the life left his eyes and his body stilled. Every muscle in her body shook uncontrollably as she pushed herself off her brother's corpse and tumbled to the ground.

The remaining snake circled around Kaeli as she sat next to Trent's limp body. The bolt of light stuck straight through his chest as black blood oozed to the ground, his eyes staring distantly off into nothing. Bile rose in Kaeli's throat. She tucked her knees into her chest, curling into a tight ball. Time slowed. The snake let out a hissing laugh and drew closer toward her.

"Poor little lion." Its tongue flickered in and out, brushing against the tip of Kaeli's nose. Kaeli squeezed her eyes shut and turned her face away. The shadows pressed in around her, supporting her, almost as if trying to comfort her. "You've been through sssoo much. But not to worry. Sssoon you will belong to massster."

Kaeli let out a shaky breath and forced herself to meet the snake's crackling electric stare. She couldn't give in. Not now. Not after everything she'd already done. "Not if I can help it," she growled.

"Many have tried to ressssissst. None have sssucceeded." The snake opened its huge maw. Silver fangs glinted in the pale light. The snake gave her no time to react before it plunged through her chest. Kaeli opened her mouth, gasping for air that refused to fill her lungs. Shadows clouded her vision and the world swirled with darkness. The snake's hissing laughter rang through her mind.

Resssissstanccce isss futile. The words echoed through her, commanding her to give up total control. Kaeli felt herself stand and watched her feet move her toward Niko and the twins. *You baby ssspiritsss are ssso eassy to manipulate. Like puppetsss.*

"N-no." Her voice sounded weak and distant echo. Step after painful step, the snakes forced Kaeli, Niko, and the twins toward the center cave. As they approached the opening, shadowy tendrils extended toward them. Kaeli watched in horror as they wrapped around Niko and Ryan's wrists and began writhing up their arms toward their necks. The sound of her pulse pounding in her ears thrummed louder as she noticed a small, familiar snake marking at the base of their necks.

"Sssoo helplesss," the snake whispered in her mind. The tendrils reached toward Kaeli and she squeezed her eyes shut, trying to focus every ounce of energy she could into regaining control of her body. She had to fight this.

"I. Am. Not. Helpless!" She forced the words out. Sparks of light flickered around her fingers. Light. Not fire. She could feel the uncertainty of the snake inside of her as a comforting warmth spread through her chest. It wasn't the same warmth of her fire. This one felt more like a caress. The type of warmth when the sun hit her skin. The tendrils paused in their advance. Kaeli held onto that warmth, focused on expanding it until it filled every part of her being.

"I AM NOT HELPLESS!' she screamed. The small flickers flittering around her fingers grew to beams of blinding white. Kaeli screamed again as she exploded into a burst of light. Became light. The warmth intensified, burning away the darkness of the shadow. The snake shrieked in pain as Kaeli allowed the light to consume her. The tendrils of darkness strangling Niko and Ryan began to sizzle, until they sputtered out completely. Kaeli opened her eyes and gasped as her lungs filled with fresh, undiluted air. Everything was wrapped in her light. Her light. She turned toward the entrance of the cave. She didn't know why the snakes wanted to take her and her companions to this cave in particular, but she knew it must've had something to do with Ophiuchus and the door.

"I am not helpless," she whispered to whatever shadowy force was inside the cave. "I am strong. Never forget that."

The sky returned to its starlit glow. Kaeli inhaled deeply, the scent of fresh pine once more wafting through the air. She heard a groan and turned to see Alex clutching the back of his neck.

"What the heck just happened?"

"I don't know, bro, but I can't stop seeing spots." Ryan winced as he rubbed at his eyes.

Kaeli's gaze flickered toward Niko. He stared back at her, head tilted to the side, as if seeing her for the first time. He opened his mouth to speak, but before he could utter a word, a crack of lightning split the sky. When it faded, Leo and Gemini stood at the entrance of the cave. A muscle in Leo's neck twitched as he pinned the recruits with a cold stare. Gemini, on the other hand, smiled at them with a lazy grin. Kaeli's eyes darted between the two zodiacs. His demeanor seemed wildly out of place next to Leo.

"We're leaving. Now." Leo said through gritted teeth. He nodded to Gemini. The smile on Gemini's face grew wider as he clapped his hands. A powerful shock of wind blew from the trees, pushing the four recruits to the zodiacs. Leo started to glow as the air swirled violently around them. A tornado of light encircled them, and then, they were gone.

They reappeared back in the Celestial Realm. Kaeli stumbled and nearly fell, but Leo grabbed her by the arm and pulled her upright.

"We're going to the library," he said. His grip tightened around her arm and Kaeli bit her lip to keep from yelping. She looked up at Leo, confusion swimming in her eyes, but she didn't dare ask any questions. She'd tested Leo's patience plenty during the last several months, and she feared that this time, maybe she'd gone too far... even if it was to save Shaina. She looked back toward the platform as she and Leo crossed the bridge. Zodiacs started to materialize, dragging recruits with them. Kaeli turned back to Leo.

"Shaina..."

"We'll talk about it later," Leo cut her off. "Nothing is safe right now. We never should have brought you back to Earth."

CHAPTER 28

The library was in absolute chaos. Fire spirits had invaded the lobby, rushing in different directions, yelling things at each other. Kaeli's eyes darted around as she tried to pick up pieces of information. *Invasion.* The one repeated word she was able to distinguish amongst the cacophony of voices. Kaeli bit her lip as she caught glimpses of a few of the zodiacs dashing between groups of fire spirits. Aries. Scorpio. Virgo. A few of the air spirit librarians hovered near the aisles. Pyronius stood at the center of the lobby with Liani and Aurae. It looked like Liani had managed to change the information desk into arsenal storage. Fire spirits formed an organized line to pick up weapons before receiving directives. Kaeli stumbled forward as Leo gripped her wrist and dragged her toward the trio of spirits. Kaeli looked back at Niko and the twins. Gemini remained near them but had his attention otherwise occupied with a new group of fire spirits entering the library.

"What's the status report?" Leo asked Pyronius as they approached the desk. Pyronius crossed his arms over his chest.

"There's been a breach. Shadow forces have been attacking. We've been sending spirits out to portal spots across the Celestial Island. There are casualties, but we don't know numbers." He paused. "I think it would be wise if the zodiacs started implementing some evacuation measures."

Leo's jaw tightened. A vein started to pop out of his neck.

"Not trying to question anybody's authority here," Liani's high pitched voice cut in, "but wouldn't Pyronius and some of the other higher-ranking spirits be better utilized in battle? Seriously! We're just sitting here directing traffic at this point."

"The primary portal to the dream world is located in the library catacombs." Leo shook his head and said, "We need you here... just in case." Liani let out a heavy sigh but didn't argue any further.

"There's just been a breach at the Yantari mountains," Aurae interrupted. Her fingers traced over a map of the Celestial Realm that lay spread out on the desk counter. Figures, shadows, and words in a language Kaeli didn't understand swirled over the ancient parchment in real time. Aurae looked up, her eyes locking onto Leo. "We sent a small group of spirits there, because the Yantari are so territorial... But the size of this... We may need to send some of the zodiacs to make sure nothing gets through the mountain pass."

"Shit." Leo turned to Kaeli. "I need to find Aries. Stay with Gemini and your recruit team until I can find you again." Kaeli nodded, but Leo didn't even stick around long enough to see her response. She glanced at the three spirits behind the desk, but they were caught in conversation, pointing at different locations on the map and talking strategy. A prickling sensation shot down the back of her neck as she made her way back to Niko and the twins.

"*What* is going on here?" Ryan asked as she approached. Kaeli gnawed at the inside of her cheek.

"As far as I can tell… there's been a breach at the portals and there's a shadow invasion." Her voice quivered and her chest caved in. This. Everything. It was *too much* right now. She'd just killed her brother. Intentionally. And Shaina was still missing. Her ears started ringing and a wave of dizziness came over her.

"Whoa." Niko's voice sounded like it was far away, but Kaeli was vaguely aware of his cool touch on her arm as he caught her before she could fall. Slowly, the ringing started to fade and her vision returned to normal. She let out a heavy breath.

"Before I—before Trent died…" Kaeli swallowed. She needed to focus. Shaina was still in danger. "He told me where to find Shaina. There's this door that I think is the source of the shadow snakes and… he said Shaina was being kept there." The guys looked at her with wide eyes. Alex stuffed his hands in his pockets and shifted.

"How do you know we can trust him?" he asked quietly. Ryan shot his brother a glare.

"We get a lead on where to find Shaina and you just want to *ignore* that?!"

Alex kept his gaze trained on the floor, kicking the toe of his foot into the ground.

"Do you know where this door is?" Niko asked.

Kaeli shivered as the prickling sensation returned. "It's here… underneath the library. If we can somehow manage to sneak away from this…" she motioned to the pandemonium swirling around them, "I have a feeling we'll be able to find it… or it might find us."

Gemini moved away from the group of fire spirits as they trotted off in unison down one of the aisles. His eyes methodically searched each of their faces as he approached. When they landed on Kaeli she found herself glancing down at the floor to avoid his piercing gaze. He propped one hand under his chin crossing his other arm over his chest. Kaeli ventured a look up as silence fell over the group. Gemini's mouth was set to a neutral expression, but a type of mischievous smile danced in his eyes.

"So, the four of you thought it a good idea to take your chances against dark forces of unknown power to save your friend?"

Kaeli pursed her lips to a thin line as an uncomfortable pause settled over them once more. Ryan shifted slightly behind Alex. Gemini dropped his hands to his sides and let out a half-hearted chuckle.

"Well, I can't say I blame you. Your intentions were heroic, however stupid your methods may have been."

Kaeli opened her mouth to protest, but Gemini held up a hand, silencing her.

"I know Shaina is in danger, and unfortunately, we're kind of dealing with an invasion at the moment." His eyes seemed to lock on all of the recruits at once as his voice dropped. "The zodiacs may not be able to expand extra resources to find her at the moment, but it wouldn't be unreasonable to think that a small group of recruits with a tendency to disobey instructions might get lost in all of this." He smirked and said, "I need to go brief another incoming group of fire spirits. My attention will be otherwise occupied for the next five minutes." As if summoned by his words, a new squad of fire spirits entered through the library doors. Gemini winked before turning his back and walking over to greet them.

Kaeli stayed rooted to the ground, rapidly blinking as Gemini moved farther and farther away.

"Did he really just imply—"

"Yes!" Ryan popped up behind her, making her jump. "Now what direction do we go to find this door?" Kaeli's eyes flickered over the many aisles of books.

"It's in this general direction." She pointed to the rows of books on the west wing of the library. "It's a maze once you start walking through it, but we haven't had a problem finding suspicious shadows so far…"

"Alright then, let's go." Ryan took a step, but Niko grabbed onto his shirt collar, jerking him backward.

"We need to be *a little* more strategic about this." Niko cleared his throat and motioned with his head toward the front desk. Aurae passed a cursory glance their way before turning back to Pyronius and Liani.

"Right," Ryan frowned. "Okay, we wait for the right moment. Alex and I will illusion ourselves into some giant fire spirits, then you and Kaeli can hide behind us. It'll look like we're just running around with all these other guys."

"I'm starting to sense a pattern with our escape plans," Kaeli said, "but it's better than anything I can think of."

"I don't know, guys." Alex let out a long breath. He locked eyes with Kaeli and swallowed.."I don't feel right about this."

"Dude." Ryan placed a hand on Alex's shoulder and spun his brother to face him. "You know what's at stake. We *have* to do this." Alex grimaced, but didn't argue.

They waited for a passing group of fire spirits to step between them and the front desk before Alex and Ryan transformed into two spirits rivaling the size of Pyronius. Shielding Niko and Kaeli from view, the four made their way as inconspicuous as possible to the aisles of the west wing.

They did their best to hide behind corners and bookshelves whenever a group of fire spirits passed by. Alex and Ryan obscured them from view when confrontation was absolutely unavoidable, but no one stopped or even questioned what they were doing. Deeper and deeper, they ventured into the labyrinth of books. Kaeli led, relying mostly on her gut instinct to take them through different twists and turns. The guys followed in silence.

It wasn't until they were hopelessly lost in the depths of the library that Kaeli felt it. A shiver snaked down her spine as the familiar caress of darkness brushed against her mind. Unintelligible whispers floated through the air and she came to a full stop. Ryan nearly bowled her over.

"Everything okay?" Niko asked.

"I think we're close…" Kaeli let her voice trail off as she closed her eyes and tried to focus on the whispers. One called to her over the others—a soft, dangerous lull beckoning her to… Kaeli's eyes shot open as she zeroed in on the tiniest tendril of shadow peering around the corner of a nearby bookcase. Kaeli took one step forward. The shadow retreated slightly, but the whispers echoed louder.

"Found it." A determined fire settled into Kaeli's gut as her gaze locked onto where the shadow disappeared. She turned to the boys and said, "This way." She chased after the shadow, not even caring to check if Niko and the twins kept up with her.

It wasn't long before she rounded a corner and saw the gaping entrance to the catacombs tucked away at the dead end of the aisle. Shadow tendrils whipped wildly like an angry octopus from the stairs leading to the depths of who knew where. Kaeli paused, her heart hammering in her chest. Something was different this time. The shadows didn't try to pull at her like they normally did. Instead, they waited. As if they knew she was coming. As if they expected her to follow where they beckoned. The sound of her pulse flooded her ears. Something was very, *very* wrong. What if Trent had been lying? It's not like she had any reason to believe he would try to help her save Shaina. A gentle touch on her shoulder snapped her out of her thoughts and she turned to see Niko. He looked deeply into her eyes, cutting straight through the fear and doubt.

"Is this it?"

Kaeli swallowed and nodded. Niko offered a small smile. His eyes flashed with a determined fierceness that brought Kaeli a modicum of confidence.

"Then let's go save Shaina."

Kaeli nodded again, but this time with resolute purpose. Shaina needed them. And whether she was down there or not, Kaeli couldn't risk it. The twins shifted back to their regular appearance. Niko and Ryan walked past her, entering the shadows first. They took two steps down the stairs before the darkness completely enveloped them. Kaeli moved to follow them, but Alex grabbed her hand. She tilted her head as she turned to look up at him.

"Kaeli... I..."

But he couldn't finish his sentence before an ear-splitting scream pierced the darkness below. Kaeli tore away from Alex and bolted down the stairs, straight to the arms of the abyss, only vaguely aware of Alex trailing close behind her.

Kaeli found herself at the bottom in no time, the descent deceptively short. She squinted as her eyes struggled to adapt to the darkness. The library entrance at the top of the stairs emitted the only light, and although she'd only taken a few steps down, it was a small pinprick, like the shadows attempted to swallow it. As her sight adjusted, she roughly made out the shapes of Niko, Ryan, and....

She froze, every muscle in her body tensing. There were more people down here. More than there should have been. A silhouette blocked the dim light at the top of the stairs. Kaeli spun around, but before she could get a look, they were plunged into complete darkness. The scream sounded again, and this time Kaeli's voice tore from her throat as she joined it. By the time it faded, her throat burned. Instinctually, her hands ignited with fire in a desperate attempt to escape the all-encompassing darkness.

As the light from her flames bounced around the catacombs, Kaeli's heart dropped to the pit of her stomach. Her breath caught in her throat. Shaina was here, her eyes completely glazed over with murky darkness. Shadows wafted off of her, and Kaeli had no doubt she'd been possessed by a snake. What she didn't expect to see was Virgo standing behind Shaina, gripping her arms. Or Scorpio standing next to Niko. Or Gemini, his arms looped over the twins.

Kaeli took a step back, her eyes darting between Niko, Ryan, and Alex. Nausea fluttered in her stomach as she raked a hand through her hair. Behind all of them loomed Ophiuchus's door.

"What... what is..." The chains on the door rattled as if someone pounded on it from the opposite side. Kaeli flinched. Her fire flickered.

"Oh, this is rough." Scorpio took a step toward her. Kaeli retreated back another step. He held up a hand and paused looking over his shoulder at Niko. "There's always that awkward moment when you first betray someone where they're trying to figure out what's going on. Hate that."

Kaeli's gaze locked on Niko, but he refused to meet her stare.

"You..." Hot tears threatened to stain her cheeks. She couldn't look at him. She whirled on the twins instead. "You all *knew* about this?!"

Ryan shrugged, looking almost bored. Alex blinked rapidly. His shoulders sagged as he turned his focus toward the floor.

"I wanted to tell you... tried to tell you..."

Gemini placed a hand on top of his head and ruffled his hair.

"You did what you had to do."

Kaeli looked back at Shaina, her stomach twisting in knots. If she didn't pass out first, she might throw up.

"I don't... why?"

"Sweetheart, there is *so* much more going on here than you could possibly understand at this point." Scorpio moved toward her again. This time, she didn't retreat. "Long story short, Ophiuchus has chosen the five of you to open the door and bridge the gap between the Celestial and Dream Realms." He stood directly in front of her now. Reaching out a hand, he gently brushed his fingers over the snake mark on the back of her neck. Kaeli winced but didn't give him the satisfaction of recoiling. Scorpio smiled and said, "Niko, Ryan, and Alex have made the decision to do this willingly. Shaina... not so much."

Kaeli furrowed her brows and brought her fire closer to her chest, trying to create some space between her and Scorpio.

"Why didn't I—"

"Know about any of this?" Scorpio let out a bitter scoff. "That would be Leo's fault. He's very adamantly against this whole thing and as such, did everything he could to shield you from it. But this moment," he spread his arms wide, "was inevitable." He let out a sigh. "Now, we've got two options here. You can either help us the easy way or the hard way."

"Like I would ever willingly help you." Kaeli tried to lash out at Scorpio with her fire, but shadows shot out from the door and restrained her wrists before she could even move a muscle. She thrashed against them. Their vice grip held fast. Kaeli gritted her teeth and growled as Scorpio smiled.

"I had a feeling that would be your answer."

Kaeli shivered as his inky darkness caressed the outskirts of her mind. The shadows tightened around her wrists, trying to choke out her fire. Kaeli closed her eyes and tried to delve into the source of her light. But she couldn't. Her eyes shot open. The shadows weren't choking out her power. They were trapping it. Keeping it just out of her reach. She cringed as Scorpio's presence rippled with amused laughter against her mind.

You said you wanted to do this the hard way.

The words echoed through her mind.

That makes it all the more fun for me.

"Wait…" Kaeli forced the words out.

She had to buy time, even if it was a pathetic, last-ditch attempt. If there was any chance someone would find them in the most remote area of the library during this chaotic shadow snake invasion, she needed to take it. Pathetic attempts were all she had at this point.

"Why us? Why couldn't you unlock the door yourselves?" Kaeli tried to pull against the shadows restraining her wrists, but they wouldn't loosen. Scorpio tilted his head back. His face twisted into an expression of jealousy mixed with… pity? Kaeli furrowed her brows together, trying to get a read on him.

"Only mortals can unlock dreams," he said, pausing for a moment. His voice sounded far off, as if remembering a distant memory. But the moment of introspection lasted mere seconds before he shook his head and let out a sigh. "But that's enough time wasting. We need to open this door."

Scorpio's presence stayed at the back of her mind, almost like a sedative force that kept her from resisting too much. The shadows pulled her into line with the other recruits. Kaeli struggled to breathe as the shadows forced her hand closer toward the door. The chains continued to clang and rattle, the noise crescendoing as the recruits came closer. Niko and the twins pressed their elements to the door. Shaina followed suit. As soon as she made contact, she gasped and started coughing. The shadows cleared from her eyes but continued to press around her. Her body trembled uncontrollably, held up only by the darkness swirling around her. Her terrified eyes locked on Kaeli.

Your turn, Princess.

The shadows pulled Kaeli's hand to the door. As soon as her skin made contact, a searing pain shot through her neck. Scorpio's presence instantly withdrew from her mind, but the shadows held strong. A dark glow blasted through the crevices of the door. The Ophiuchus constellation lit up with purple light. A high-pitched, manic screech sounded from the other side and the chains burst apart.

The shock wave sent the recruits reeling backwards. Niko caught Kaeli before she stumbled to the ground. She didn't have the strength to jerk away from him as her stomach roiled. The doors had burst clean open. Shards of the ancient barrier scattered all across the room.

"Aaah."

Kaeli's blood froze in her veins, all warmth instantly draining from her body. She knew that voice.

Elethia emerged from the door, shadows twirling around her in a terrifying dance. Kaeli collapsed to her knees, arms hanging limp at her sides, energy completely spent. Snakes shot through the gaping entryway at lightning speed up the passageway and into the library. One stayed behind, curling its way around Elethia. It slithered to the center of the room and raised itself up, towering over the recruits and zodiacs.

"The door hasss been opened. Ophiuchusss hasss returned."

A malicious smile curled on Elethia's lips as she stretched her arms and looked upward. She let out a melodic laugh that echoed off the walls of the hidden room.

"It's *so* good to be free."

EPILOGUE

Lukka paced back and forth, his hands clenched into tight fists. Before the shadows had completely overtaken the library, hell maybe they had overtaken the entire Celestial Realm, Aries had snatched him up and created a fiery portal to *this* place. Some sort of celestial safe island. She'd barely explained that the portal would only allow the people she permitted in and out, but that he would be stuck here until she returned before stepping back through it. The portal remained, a taunting vortex of fire that just *stayed* there. Lukka wanted to follow her back through, but the searing pain that shot through his body the instant he tried was enough to keep him put.

Which had led him to his current state. Here. In front of a three-bedroom bungalow. With nothing to fucking do. The island looked like a tropical paradise in the most surreal way possible. Groves of palm trees surrounded the bungalow and vibrant flowers dotted the landscape with patches of pink, orange, and purple. It was the endless waterfalls falling from the surrounding asteroids, however, that really should've taken his breath away. That and the literal sea of stars that crashed in waves on the shoreline of the island. But he couldn't bring himself to appreciate any of it. Instead, he paced in front of the portal, occasionally picking up a stray rock and throwing it at the vortex, watching as it incinerated to ash before making it all the way through.

He bent down to pick up another rock when a rushing wind hit his face. A sound like crashing waves flooded his senses. When it faded, Ryu stood in front of him, her ears completely flat and her body hunched almost in half. Her tail whipped back and forth as she stared at Lukka with fully dilated pupils. Lukka opened his mouth, but no words came out. He kept his gaze trained on Ryu as he slowly took a couple of steps backward. Had Aries sent Ryu here for some reason?

"Heeeey there." He held his hands out, palms facing downward in what he hoped looked like an extremely nonthreatening position. Ryu seemed to get her bearings as she stretched out to her normal length and straightened her ears. Her tail still swished wildly around her body, but she didn't look like she would try to kill him if he made a wrong move.

"What… are you doing here?" Lukka asked, keeping his voice soft. Ryu shook her head, the scales on her body rippling, but she took a step toward Lukka. Then another. Then another. Until she stood right in front of him. Lukka froze as Ryu shoved her head under his hand and his vision went completely white.

A murky image of Kaeli appeared, along with the chained door they'd found in the hallway. Lukka could hear his pulse pounding in his ears as shadows raged around her, dragging her by her wrists toward the door. His throat went dry as Kaeli screamed, trying to break free from the shadows but failing. Red dotted his vision, completely blocking out the scene with Kaeli. He squeezed his eyes shut, forcing the rage back. When he opened his eyes,

Ryu was shaking uncontrollably. His muscles twitched and his fire roiled under his skin, begging to get out. To consume. To destroy.

"She opened the door." He tried to form the words as a question, but his voice darkened. His berserker state threatened to break through his last shreds of control. A surge of strength coursed through his body as his chest heaved up and down. Kaeli was in *danger*. And he was trapped here. On this stupid island. Unable to do *anything*. His fire screamed at him now. If he couldn't calm down, he would go berserk. Ryu took a step back, but bobbed her head up and down in response to his question. The pressure built until he couldn't take it anymore. Releasing a guttural roar, Lukka rushed toward the shoreline and exploded in an inferno.

He burned. Screamed. Released every ounce of fire until there was nothing left within him to burn. Completely drained, he fell on the sand, tears trailing down his cheeks. The sand shifted behind him as Ryu approached. Letting out a soothing coo, she kneeled down and rested her head on top of Lukka's neck. Lukka let out a shaky breath as his limbs rested limp and useless next to him. Tendrils of steam curled off his skin.

"I'll find you, Kaeli," he whispered. "I'll find you and *I'll kill* whoever did this to you."

Alyssa Markins

Thank you for reading!

Please add a review on Amazon and let me know what you thought!

Amazon reviews are extremely helpful for authors. So are social media posts
;)
I'm so grateful you took the time to support me and my story.

ACKNOWLEDGEMENTS

Over the five years it's taken me to write and publish this book, I've always wondered what it would be like to write the acknowledgements section. Now that it's actually happening, it feels kind of weird, almost bittersweet. This book has taken up half a decade of my life, and I'm happy to release it, but also sad to let it go. *So much* has gone into this novel creation process, and I 100% would not have been able to do it on my own. I'm incredibly grateful to everyone who's helped me.

To Alyx, you were there from the *very* beginning of this story, and it absolutely would not exist without you. Thank you so much for the late nights talking with me to work through plot holes, giving me the brutal honest truth when entire characters needed to be eliminated from the story, and for always cheering me on, even if it was from a distance. I would not be the creative person and storyteller I am today if we hadn't spent years writing stories together in middle school, high school, and college.

To Chi, my amazing friend and business partner! The ONLY reason I'm now a published author is because you are in my life! This seriously could have taken me another five years if I didn't have you in my corner, making sure I stuck to deadlines and then helping me readjust and come up with a plan of action when I didn't meet them all. Words could never describe how grateful I am to be working with you and building our publishing empire together. I'm so excited to see the things we create in the future.

To my editors Camilla and Laurel, who helped me turn this book into something I'm actually excited to share with other people.

To my cover designer Maja! The first time I saw Perilous Star as a book cover, I was squealing for probably five minutes straight. Seeing the cover helped the book become real to me and gave me the push I needed to get serious about releasing Perilous Star.

To Lizz, Nadine, Rhea, Veronica, and Kat for beta reading the early version of my manuscript and volunteering feedback. You not only helped shaped the story and make it better, but also helped me realize I could have confidence in myself as a writer

To my family, for encouraging me throughout this process. A lot of creatives don't necessarily have the support of their family members, and I'm so grateful I do.

To Nana, you may not remember this, but in my first year of college you read part of a rough draft from a book that I will never release to the public. Although you didn't get a chance to finish it, you wrote me a letter telling me about how much you enjoyed my writing style and that you hoped I would keep on writing. I've kept that letter on every desk I've had since then, and at times when I felt like giving up, I would read it and keep going. You have no idea how much your support has meant to me.

To the Pathfinder community at Awaken Church San Diego (with special shoutouts to Ernie, Fiona, Blyss, Halle, and Colin & Melissa Higginbottom). I would not be pursuing my purpose if I had not met you. Thank you for helping me realize that it's not only ok for me to be my full creative self, but that in doing so, I'm able to make a positive impact in people's lives.

And last but *definitely* not least, to God. Thank you for blessing me with the ability to create. It is such a gift, and I never want to take it for granted. When I write, I feel Your pleasure.

Alyssa Markins is an author based in San Diego, California. She graduated from Vanguard University in 2013 with a Bachelor of Arts degree in English, and then again in 2018 with an MA in Education. After teaching English as a Second Language in South Korea from 2015-2016, she made the decision to seriously pursue a writing career. In addition to writing, she is passionate about God, reading, dancing, helping other creatives realize how epic they are, and her cat, Oreo.

CONNECT WITH ALYSSA ON:
>Website: www.alyssamarkins.com
>Instagram: @alyssa.markins
>YouTube: www.youtube.com/alyssamarkins

Made in the USA
Las Vegas, NV
04 May 2021